A MATTER OF TRUST

POWER AND PRIVILEGE IN CANADA'S TRUST COMPANIES

PATRICIA BEST & ANN SHORTELL

VIKING

VIKING

Penguin Books Canada Ltd., 2801 John Street, Markham, Ontario, Canada L3R 1B4
Penguin Books Ltd., Harmondsworth, Middlesex, England
Viking Penguin Inc., 40 West 23rd Street, New York, New York 10010 U.S.A.
Penguin Books Australia Ltd., Ringwood, Victoria, Australia
Penguin Books (N.Z.) Ltd., Private Bag, Takapuna, Auckland 9, New Zealand

First published by Penguin Books Canada Ltd., 1985

Printed and bound in the United States of America

Canadian Cataloguing in Publication Data

Shortell, Ann.
  A matter of trust

ISBN 0-670-80208-5

1. Trust companies - Canada. 2. Trusts and
trustees - Canada. I. Best, Patricia. II. Title.

HG4358.S55   1985   332.2'6'0971   C85-098660-5

Acknowledgements

The idea for this book grew as we covered the shocking trust company collapses of 1982 and 1983. There was, we decided, a larger story to be told. Over the course of the following two years as we researched and wrote, the pattern we had initially discerned became clearer to everyone as more trust companies failed. But despite a continuing series of events that is changing the face of the industry, our final product bears a startling resemblance to our original proposition.

Thanks to the people who were there along the road:

Former co-workers for their partnership when working on some aspects of the business at *The Financial Post* and particularly *Post* editor, Neville Nankivell, for his early support; our agents Nancy, Stan and David Colbert for their belief in us and their unflagging encouragement; our publisher Morty Mint for an initial enthusiasm that has only increased with time; Theresa Butcher for her open library door and kindly humour; Jamie Fleming for his bread-and-butter help; Peter Foster, for pushing us in the right direction; the Ontario Securities Commission and Charles Salter for their invaluable assistance; Wallis King for agreeing to read the book and waiting until it arrived; Jennifer Hietala for her indexing assistance; the special sources who vetted certain rather delicate portions of the manuscript, and the many sources who will *not* be named, and thus, must have told the best stories; the friends who put us up and put up with us, with particular thanks from Ann to Marianne Tefft. We would also like to thank our editor, David Kilgour. It is difficult to quantify the support and understanding he has given us. And of course, special thanks to our husbands, Carlo Liconti and Michael Judge, for their patience and faith.

For Margaret and Norman Best
                                P.B.

For Iris and Vincent Shortell
                                A.S.

Contents

Introduction

After lying dormant for decades, Canada's $60 billion trust industry is shuddering with change. The institutions founded in the last century as safe homes for the fortunes of the wealthy live on today, and now, as then, a select group of wealthy Canadian family names — Bronfman, Jackman, Desmarais, McCutcheon, Roman and Eaton — have control of many of the country's trusts. But whereas the trusts used to shelter existing wealth, today they create it by providing excellent returns on investments. These rewards have also attracted a new breed of owner — the non-Establishment entrepreneur — and the resulting clash of cultures has sparked dramatic showdowns for control of the massive pools of money held in the vaults of our trust companies. Government, like the smallest boy playing tag, struggles to catch up. Both federal and provincial regulators and their political bosses have spent the past two years scrambling to get a grip on the changes not only in trust companies, but in all financial institutions.

The four pillars of Canadian finance — the trusts, the insurance companies, the investment dealers and the banks — are competing for the $675 billion business represented by the Canadian borrower and saver. But even with this money kingdom neatly divided into four species, there remains a menagerie of hybrid companies and services. There are mortgage loan companies — some standing alone, some owned by banks, many owned by trusts. There are life insurance companies with billions in pension funds, and there are the smaller property and casualty insurance companies. There are the local and central credit unions and *caisses populaires,* which are dominant forces in the West and in Quebec. And then there are the banks: the Big Five towering, with their $345 billion in assets, over the financial landscape and the smaller Canadian-owned regional banks and the foreign-owned business-oriented banks.

Few Canadians clearly understand what a trust company is, even though this institution touches almost everyone who saves money, mortgages a house or has a maiden aunt who leaves Bell Canada stock in trust. Trust and loan companies have under their control 15% of all of Canada's financial market assets; by contrast, Canadian-owned banks control 54.5%. And in the public's mind there is a great difference between these two deposit-taking and lending institutions. That emerged recently in a poll done by Decima Research Ltd. of Toronto for the Ontario government's Task Force on Financial Institutions. While 60% of those questioned felt "very confident" about leaving money in a bank, only 30% felt the same way about a trust company. And while 6% felt "not too confident" about banks, 20% felt the same way about trust companies.

That unease is in great part the legacy of the highly publicized confiscation of three trust companies by the Ontario government in 1983. But for all its blood and guts, the Greymac Affair as it became known was only one of a string of fascinating tales in the trust business.

Power is no longer conferred in the sprawling trust industry, it is grasped. Once a trust licence is gained, the rest is simple. Trust companies, which, unlike banks, can be wholly owned, are malleable, board directors suggestable, government regulators like as not agreeable to the owner's wielding the mace of authority. A new, renegade owner can use the old gentlemen's rules of the business to further his own plans, the ragamuffin can play the gentleman. The old guard's influence is on the wane and the entrepreneur's star is in the ascendent.

This was the theory we held when we set out to write a book about trust companies. We are not detailing the perils of a widow leaving her money in an uncaring trust officer's hands.* We are not chronicling the history of each large com-

---

* Alix Granger has already covered that ground in a slim but excellent book, *Trusts & Trust Companies in Canada: What You Need to Know to Avoid Getting Taken.*

pany, nor sketching the office of each chief executive. The trust business is too varied, the companies involved too numerous to make that either a worthwhile or an interesting exercise. We talk about the original foundation of the business — the trusteeship of estates — but we concentrate on the newer yet increasingly dominant business of mortgage lending and its potentially treacherous link to real estate. There were more than 130 trust and loan companies in Canada at the end of 1984; we deal extensively with 20 and peripherally with another two dozen. A surprising number of those about which we have written no longer exist.

While we could not deal with every nook and cranny, we hope we have succeeded in extracting the essence of the Canadian trust industry. We have attempted to distill the motivations of the various companies' founders, managers and purchasers and to collect droplets of that potent, combustible intoxicant, the influence that holds sway over billions of dollars. We have had to take the industry apart to examine how it fits together. We have approached this book with the journalist's critical eye in examining a sector of Canadian business that such diverse voices as Hal Jackman and George Mann contend needs strong, thoughtful analysis by the press.

In dissecting the factors that have stretched the industry into its present form, we have gained an understanding of the bases for the present systems of outmoded and inept regulation. Regulators have been using flyswatters and prayers to control a business that just isn't the same as it used to be. They are only now equipping themselves to deal with a business that has evolved from an oligarchy formed a century ago to an industry largely based on money and chutzpah. We can only hope regulators find the strength of will to hound these businessmen in a manner not exhibited in the past.

This book chronicles the shift in mores that has seen an Establishment business dedicated to passing on the wealth of the grandfather to the grandson itself pass into the hands of men whose heritage is a blank page, whose connections are built with skill rather than based on family. That is, we think, a healthy change, since ability surely provides a better basis for business than nepotism ever could. The newcomers do not want their companies to administer estates; they wish to mould them into replicas of desired but as yet unattainable individually owned banks. Unfortunately, some of those squeezing through the door have been motivated by lust for companies they can fashion into their very own cashboxes; this short-term outlook has led to unconscionable abuses of the business and revealed systemic problems in regulation.

The regulatory breakdown has only been compounded by an erratic political response to financial institution failures. The motivations for depositor bail-outs have been short-sighted, and the defences given for them boil down to a "throw money at it and it will go away" approach to the business. There has never been an adequate explanation, for example, of why some depositors in failed trust companies have been automatically paid back all their money, others only up to the $60,000 deposit insurance limit. The public is very interested in that question, as a recent letter to *The Globe and Mail* demonstrates. "By what convoluted logic do governments decide which group of depositors deserves to be rescued and which are unworthy of the authorities' largesse?" the writer asked. He remembered that six years earlier Astra Trust depositors had received only the deposit insurance limit, and he resented payoffs for Crown Trust and Pioneer depositors that exceeded the limit. "But what upsets me even more is the obvious preferential treatment accorded one group of 'victims' over another. The inevitable conclusion is that in the governments' view some depositors are more equal than others."

The question that has obsessed us concerns the vast chasm that has grown between trust companies' original purpose and their more venal uses. How could companies originally dedicated to caring for the investments of others, to the safe, sure maintenance of the *status quo,* have become the most scandal-ridden financial institutions in Canada during this century?

The business is a reflection of those who have worked in it. There have been two kinds of people in trust companies since their inception 113 years ago, and they are best illustrated by two characters who are no longer in the business, but will always be of it.

At Royal Trust in Montreal 50 years ago the chief general accountant was disparagingly referred to as Whispering Willy. He wore the green eyeshade and straw armbands of the day to keep clean the cuffs of his white shirt as he laboured away at the company's books. Willy had a peculiar affection for the financial statements of this then-private company; he would allow no one else to peek and wore the key to the general ledger around his neck. When an assistant was assigned to him to learn the ropes, he waited in vain for three months for instruction.

But every man's hold on his company weakens someday. Willy had a heart attack and was rushed to the hospital. He lay in his bed, unable to speak, clutching with a trembling hand the key that still hung from his neck. The assistant, who had to prepare the directors' quarterly report, was forced to pry it from him with Willy's doctor hovering in the background and his wife weeping in the corner. Willy was effectively retired.

George Marks left the trust business no more dramatically but rather more publicly. A Hamilton, Ontario native who moved to the U.S. as a child and became involved in California real estate after World War Two, Marks bought control of a dormant Alberta company, Farmers & Merchant Trust, in 1957. With his wife on the board and his father-in-law as mortgage manager, the firm became most aggressive in mortgage lending and branch openings, offering incredibly high interest rates and dividend payments on mutual funds that far exceeded their earnings. He expanded eastward to Montreal, and even more interestingly, opened branches in Nassau, the Bahamas and Jamaica. The company also purchased a Bahamian insurance subsidiary, using a payout from that company to offset Farmers' operating loss in 1961. Farmers was fined a paltry $150 in 1962 after pleading guilty to operating a loan and trust company in Saskatchewan without a licence.

But the best story was never told. Marks spearheaded a loan for a gambling casino and hotel in Jamaica at a time when the Jamaican government outlawed gambling. The loan, which broke a long list of trust company regulations, is now long since paid off.

Marks moved to Nassau and sold most of his Farmers & Merchant holding in late 1962.* After a series of losing investments, including one in a Prince Edward Island company called Major Trust, he turned up in Britain in the mid-seventies, complete with the added surname "de Chabris," the titles Duke, Baron and Serene Highness, and a noble French father on his family tree. News reports described him as a Canadian millionaire and mysterious patron of the British Liberal Party after he bought into the Liberals' foundering National Liberal Club with a $216,000 cash infusion and transformed it into a nine-dollar-a-night stopover for "uninhibited Scandinavians," according to one news report. But Marks's politics didn't gell with the old guard; he was much more rigid in his beliefs about what a Liberal should support than even the old-timers. In the end he packed his wife and two children into their powder blue Rolls Royce and motored home to their Canterbury mansion. He had learned quite literally that no one buys his way into a gentleman's club.

Whispering Willy reinforces, George Marks explodes the myth that since trust companies are regulated they only attract a certain kind of operator. The public, buffeted by 14 trust and loan company failures in five years, has learned the hard way to be wary of that comforting thought. People want to know whether they can have faith in trust companies. The answer must be, based on events, that we can't trust government regulators to know what is going on or to do anything about it when they do know. We can't trust every entrepreneur to distinguish between his own and his company's funds. We can't trust old-line managers caught in a garrison mentality to protect all their shareholders when fighting for their own positions. Whispering Willy's industry will never be the same; George Marks's will never change.

Patricia Best and Ann Shortell
Toronto, July 1985

* The company has changed hands and names a couple of times since then and is now Toronto-based Eaton-Bay Trust, run as part of a financial subsidiary by the Eaton family with Conrad Black and Toronto's Bassett family holding chunks.

1

The Family Compact

It was January of 1963, and the seven royal commissioners probing the black hole of banking and finance in Canada had spent a hard ten months hearing endless submissions from staunchly vested interests in a dozen locations across the country. Their leader, the Honourable Dana Harris Porter, chief justice of Ontario, would soon sit down to write a report for Mitchell Sharp, the Liberal minister of finance, whose Conservative predecessor had felt there was room for a review of the banking system, even though one had been done in 1933.

The chief justice, the farmer, the banker, the investment dealer, the academic and the two corporation executives on the commission were in Ottawa delving into the last corner opened up by their broad mandate: the incestuous relationship between the nation's two types of lenders — the chartered banks and the trust companies.

A small circle of financial men ran the country's banking, trust and insurance operations, sitting on one another's boards and sending one another business. The links between the trust companies and the banks constituted an intricate maze of interlocking directorships that maintained the façade of independent institutions while permitting the banks to exercise over the trust companies a level of influence usually associated with ownership. In 1963, the nature of these links was not widely known — a credit to the secrecy and smug insularity of the system.

By the end of the 1950s, the trust industry was dominated by Royal Trust, with assets under administration of $2.1 billion, and by Montreal Trust, whose assets remained a sacred mystery. Number three was National Trust, with almost $700 million under its administration, followed by Toronto General Trusts at $550 million and Canada Trust with almost $400 million.

At times, the banks proceeded by quiet, persuasive shareholding. The Commerce Bank had been in at the founding of National Trust and, in an informal partnership with Canada Life Assurance, continued to control that trust company, each partner holding 17% of National's common stock.

The usual route, however, was control by directorships. The Royal Bank and Montreal Trust had 15 common directors in 1958, and Royal Bank directors occupied the posts of chairman and vice-president. Board meetings were virtually seamless. Four other banks — the Bank of Montreal, the Commerce, the Toronto Dominion and Banque Canadienne Nationale — each had a director or two on Montreal Trust's board as well. The other great link-up was between Royal Trust and the Bank of Montreal, which shared 14 directors. Once again bank directors held the offices of chairman and vice-president at the trust company. The bank had started the trust for its customers and made certain it retained its control. In effect, a handful of men controlled combined assets of more than $4 billion in the two institutions.

The overlap didn't end there. A total of 21 Royal Bank directors sat on six trust company boards, and 14 Royal men sat on the boards of seven life insurance companies. Similarly, 20 Bank of Montreal directors also sat at the board tables of eight trust companies, and 16 of them sat on life insurance boards.

The Commerce Bank, even before its 1961 merger with the Imperial Bank, was a phenomenon, with 25 directors sitting on the boards of eight trust companies. One pre-eminent Commerce director, the legendary Canadian capitalist J.A. (Bud) McDougald, controlled Crown Trust. Commerce directors held the posts of chairman, president and vice-president at Crown. McDougald's long-time associate Maxwell Meighen was an Imperial director and held 17% of Canada Trust's parent, Huron & Erie Mortgage Corp. Two other prominent shareholders in Canada Trust were London Life Insurance and Mutual Life. Nine Commerce directors also sat on National's board.

"We couldn't break in on a piece of business that the Royal Bank controlled, because it went to the Montreal Trust. And we couldn't break in on a piece of business the Bank of Nova Scotia controlled, because it went to Canada Permanent," says J. Allyn Taylor, president and then chairman of Huron & Erie Mortgage/Canada Trust from 1958 until 1970. "These interlocking directorships between trust companies and banks were a very, very effective barrier to us when it came to developing corporate business. The banks naturally fed it to their associates."

The trust companies had their own hidden weapons. The estates they managed proved fertile turf for intercompany holdings: for example, the M. Ross Gooderham estate, managed by Toronto General Trusts, held half of the shares of the Manufacturers Life Insurance Co.

It was against this backdrop that the royal commissioners conducted their delicate probe that January.

John C. MacKeen, a Halifax "corporation executive" with an acute awareness of the power of the banks, broached the subject. "Mr Mulholland," he said, addressing his question to Robert D. (Pete) Mulholland, vice-chairman of the Bank of Montreal (no relation to William Mulholland, current chairman of the same bank), "there has been a good deal of discussion on the interlocking directorships. In your opinion, does it not very frequently happen that a man slated to join one board of directors of a bank, may be a director of a trust company or vice versa and it is simply because he may have such qualities and experiences and contacts that he is a desirable person to serve on the boards of both the trust company and the bank, rather than the fact that being a director of a bank he's invited to be a director of a trust company for that reason?''

"Very importantly so," Mulholland, a past president of the Canadian Bankers' Association, astutely concurred.

MacKeen continued his helpful line of questioning. "Do you see any advantage in precluding a trust company director for instance from joining a bank, or vice versa?''

"Definitely not, Mr MacKeen."

The pair could have been reading from a script annotated with dollar signs.

Away from the artificial light of the hearing rooms, in the market-place, banks and trust companies were becoming almost indistinguishable to the average consumer. Banks were experimenting with the mortgage market, and trust companies had awakened to the fact that they had to embark on enormous branch expansion to compete for new deposit business.

The trust industry's block-buster merger was engineered by Toronto Dominion Bank in 1961. Two major Toronto-based companies were merged — the venerable Toronto General Trusts and Canada Permanent Trust, a "classy" mortgage lender with less than $200 million in assets under administration. TD had control of Canada Permanent and bought Toronto General Trusts stock to force the merger. Public attention focused on concentration of power in the financial industry.

The mergers, the greedier bank shareholdings and the invasion of turf had done what years of interlocking directorships had not: they had raised the question of basic conflicts of interest entrenched in the invisible links of historical patronage.

The solidarity of the system was a spectacle to behold. Only one trust company came out publicly with the stand that ownership by banks not be allowed. Montreal-based Trust General du Canada's president Marcel Faribault felt so strongly that ownership somehow made a difference that he submitted a separate brief to the commission, recommending that banks not be allowed to own any shares of a trust company. It was a question of principle.

"I had the opportunity of submitting a separate brief to my board of directors. It so happens 11 of those directors are also directors of banks. They were unanimous in expressing the opinion that it was not proper for a bank to control a trust company, and, generally speaking, for any company to control a trust company." The interlocking directorships, Faribault felt, meant nothing to the company's structure or operations.

But commissioner Dr W.A. Mackintosh, an economic historian and principal of Queen's University, was worried about such close ties: it was enough that they were there between trust companies and banks, but what if the trust companies graduated to banking status! With the traditional Canadian myopia that causes observers of the financial system to see only the banks, he suggested that links between banks would be much more serious.

Neil McKinnon, Commerce's president and a man of strong opinions, protested that the customary affiliations hadn't stopped the trust companies from expanding their banking business: "I think the evidence we have found of their own expansion in the last dozen years demonstrates the fact that managements have acted independently, serving their own interest, and not referring to the interests of any particular director."

McKinnon was also pushing an open-door policy for future bank expansion — including freedom of banks to move into the trustee business. "My view is that the wider the area of competition among financial institutions, the more beneficial it will be for the country and for all the companies engaged in this particular field." He trotted out the familiar circular argument based on the banks' omnipresence: since they had branches across the country, they could better serve the consumer in all fields within the financial spectrum. Besides, "strangely enough," there was nothing like effective competition to spur on management. *

* Bud McDougald, McKinnon's close friend and double on both the bank board and the board of Crown Trust, didn't have the same view. He believed Crown should stay out of the banking business; that was the Commerce's territory.

Commerce vice-president Page Wadsworth described the situation as he saw it: with directors on several boards, "we have no influence, direct or indirect, on the management or policies or flow of funds of any trust companies." How Commerce-groomed directors could be that ineffective was not explained.

The trust companies were more defensive about the relationship. They had always been less comfortable dealing with Ottawa than the banks were; their timidity was legendary. Their brief to the commission all but ignored the ties. Walter Bean, vice-president and general manager of the Waterloo Trust & Savings Co., squirmed under questioning about this very sensitive area. When asked about its effect on competition and the consumer's best interest, Bean replied, "It has not been something which is causing us great concern, let us put it that way."

Dr Mackintosh had by this point distilled the essence of the bank-trust relationship: when the trust companies were the banks' creatures, it was not ownership that was important, but influence. "I infer from some of this that effective control is not too important; that you have a great variety of these arrangements. In some cases there are some of these relationships — the next thing to an agreement between the companies to take in each other's washing, if you are in the laundry business. There is a developing interrelationship which is not covered at all by any prohibition of, say, a bank holding more than fifty per cent of a trust company stock."

The corporate boundaries were well demarcated; the trust executives didn't have to hustle business, because they knew which banks would be sending them what business and because, as Royal Trust's president Jack Pembroke admitted, efforts to convert customers did not succeed very often. "We see, certainly, nothing sinister in it."

When it was all over, the commissioners concluded that although there was nothing sinister, there was something not right. They recommended that the interlocking directorships — arrangements that had allowed the banks to smother their customers in services that the banks themselves were not, strictly speaking, allowed to provide and to bar a good many unaffiliated trust companies from the lucrative inner sanctum of corporate business — be dismantled.

The practical effects of bank influence on trust companies' lending operations and branch expansion had, they decided, been benign. The banks had helped out with branch locations and thrown some business scraps to the trust companies. "There is no evidence that banks have tried to inhibit trust company growth by limiting their branch expansion or controlling this source of competition in other ways."*

In the end, the Porter commission's report did very little to upset the equilibrium of the chartered banks. Interlocking directorships with the trust companies were barred in the 1967 Bank Act revision, but a bone was thrown to appease the banks: mortgage lending was opened to them, no holds barred. Seventeen years later they passed the trusts as the country's largest mortgage lenders.†

"We were always the poor relation," Canada Trust's J. Allyn Taylor says of the trust industry's lobbying power. "The lending powers of the banks were so much broader — and still are — as a result of the Porter commission's decision to let everybody get into everybody else's business. Of course, if you're going to do that, then you have to give them the same ground rules and that's what we haven't got today."

---

* One former Royal Trust employee recalls pressure in the early 1960s when Ken White, Royal's president a decade later, was manager of the Toronto branch. The overly enthusiastic employee had managed to move $3 million in deposits in one month to the trust company — which, unlike a bank, had no interest rate ceiling on deposits — from the Bank of Montreal. He was basking in his accomplishment when White called him in. There had been a complaint from someone at the bank that some young trust officer had taken deposit accounts, and White had been told to inform that junior employee to "lay off."

"I told him, 'I hear what you're saying, Sir,'" the trust officer reminisces. "As I walked out the door he sort of winked and said, 'Keep up the good work.' But he could report at lunch that he had done it."

† Trusts weren't the only mice trampled. The Porter commission also recommended that banks be permitted into the consumer loan business, with the result that consumer loan, or finance, companies are virtually extinct today.

Trust companies have had their own peculiar ground rules since their inception in Canada more than a century ago. The business has two roots: a few companies sprang from nineteenth century mortgage loan companies with acquired trust powers, but most started as trustees of estates with mortgage investments.

British common law always viewed a trust as a confidence reposed in an objective but benevolent individual who had a duty to act with fidelity and diligence in all dealings for the client. Trustees of estates were expected to act as personal financial advisors, taking care of the heirs' money, investing it profitably in supposedly safe investments such as mortgages and bonds so that when the trusts lapsed — usually after a specific period of time — the heirs would inherit their property intact. The concept of trusteeship took on a sacred aura. Lawyers, accountants and others of supposed expertise and respectability traditionally have acted as trustees for their clients, and still do. Often, they weren't paid for the service, but presumably they received other business from the same clients. These days they receive a fee, usually based on the size of the estate and the time involved in administration.

With the tremendous growth of the financial system in the nineteenth century, and the growing wealth of Canadians, the management of estates became a much more complicated affair. It required an ever-widening variety of specialized skills, perhaps better supplied by a team of financial advisors in a corporate structure than by a friendly old family lawyer. There was also a need for a trustee able to watch over business shareholding and lending arrangements. But the traditional financial institutions, the banks, were uneasy about taking over the handling of these estates and trustee duties, a kind of business their corporate laws and minds didn't encompass. They made most of their money in business, or commercial, loans. At the same time, however, they didn't want to lose all control of their wealthy clients' assets. The solution was to set up separate corporate entities — the first trust companies — and keep a close eye on them.

In large measure, then, trust companies were bankers' creations, established to do the jobs commercial money-lenders didn't do: act as trustees tending estates, look after the safekeeping and transfer of stocks and bonds and make mortgage loans. But their original role as pawns of the banks has changed dramatically.

The Porter commission provides a freeze-frame perspective on the evolution of banks and trust companies. In 1964 the banks were still ensconced in their traditional role as corporate lenders, although they had entered the personal loan business in a big way after a loosening of their lending laws in the 1954 Bank Act (they had long lent to a select clientele who could back their loans with stocks and bonds, part of the mercantile creed) and had fledgling, non-competitive versions of chequing and savings accounts. With the lifting of their 6% ceiling on lending rates in 1967, they were commercial banks on their way to becoming full-service, retail banks.

Trust companies 20 years ago were also expanding their banking activities. They had always been trustees, but one aspect of their business also made them bankers — their mortgage loans. Graham Towers, when governor of the Bank of Canada in 1953, had pushed them into actively expanding their deposit-taking business in an attempt to foster competition for the banks. The decision nicely matched their powers, and they invested their expanded deposits in the burgeoning postwar mortgage lending business. When the Porter commission was examining the trusts' ties to the banks, the trajectories of the two types of financial institutions were beginning to overlap.

Anyone who walks into a trust company branch today will find personal loans and mortgage loans available, although he or she is more likely to borrow for a house here than for a car. The consumer will find savings and chequing accounts aggressively marketed, tax-geared investments such as Registered Retirement Savings Plans being pushed, the full range of savings packages available at a bank, and credit cards and automated banking machines. Banks and trust companies use the same hype to attract savings dollars and promote their interest rates. The big difference is that for the corporate customer, banks still rule the market and trust companies are new, small and restricted players. Banks also have the clout that size and market saturation bring to the personal banking business, and they naturally dominate. But for the individual, trust companies can offer more than banks. Their trustee powers are translated into a complete set of investment products that banks can't yet provide. Although banks have talked in recent times about gaining trust powers, this has not yet been high on their endless list of lobbying priorities.

The changes that have occurred since 1964 have been built on competition but spurred by ownership changes in the trust business. When Dana Porter and his clutch of commissioners pondered the system, the banks and the old boys manipulated trust companies through ownership positions and board seats. Not many of the Porter commission's recommendations made it into law; the ever-successful lobbyist bankers saw to that. But the death of interwoven directorships and the limitation of cross-investment between banks and trust companies to 10% altered the balance between the two. More important, a new kind of trust company chief began to worm his way into the business, silently accumulating the stock of an established company or applying for a licence for a small company with big plans. These renegade entrepreneurs set about to mould their companies in the image of banks at the same time as the old-time companies were awakening to the potential of their banking role. The next step was predictable: trustee business, the foundation of the trusts' respectability, became just another product line to be marketed like hamburgers along with other services and products.

There was an inevitable clash between the new trust companies and the old-line chieftains. The new companies were run by owners, or by managers with a strict understanding of what the owners expected. The old companies were often run by the banks' hand-picked managers, who treated the companies as their own, not their shareholders'. The old companies felt they knew best because they followed the unwritten rules of corporate etiquette; they understood that the age-old underpinning for the system was co-operation with the banks, and while expanding their reach, they never lost sight of the traditional concept of a trust company as fashioned by the bankers.

It was in the newcomers' best interest that the old-fashioned image of a trust company hang on; that was the image they were buying. They understood how valuable the traditional appearance of a stolid, safe institution would be when it came to marketing trusts as banks. The sanctity of trusteeship would cast a halo over the trusts' other business.

In 1872 the Toronto General Trusts Co., the first in Canada, was incorporated by a special act of the Ontario legislature. Royal Trust, Montreal Trust and National Trust were all operating by the turn of the century.* It is these same, old-line companies, buoyed by mergers and competition from a few additions, that today offer the gamut of trust services.

---

* National's formation reflected the interdependent nature of the business plutocracy: its first president was Joseph Flavelle, head of the Grand Trunk railway and a Commerce director, and its board reeked credentials. But one prominent contact refused an invitation from Commerce and Canada Life president Senator George Cox to join. Cox penned a note to the most prominent man in the country on July 18, 1898, offering him a special deal on shares before they were sold to the public. Would Sir Wilfred Laurier, prime minister of Canada, serve as a National director? "We understand of course that we could not expect your attendance at the meetings, except on rare occasions when it might happen to be convenient, but Mr Flavelle . . . and others who will be more immediately associated with him in management, are all gentlemen upon whose integrity and ability you can implicitly rely." Not only was Laurier to be excused from meetings; Cox would pay for the shares, and Laurier could later pay for them or transfer them back to Cox. Laurier answered from his home base at Arthabaskaville, Quebec, two days later. It was thanks but no thanks. "I have made it a rule, however, since I have taken the responsible office which I now hold, not to be connected with any kind of business, and I have come to this conclusion for reasons, which it would be too long to set down here, but which, I think, would be approved." A casual observer might assume that the senator either misunderstood or disapproved of Laurier's motivations. The prime minister's reasoning wasn't followed by many. Good men were good men, after all, and there was no need for artificial barriers where personal integrity could be relied upon. During the next century, almost every financial institution of any stature would secure a modicum of political clout.

By the early 1930s the trust industry had grown to one-tenth the size of the banks, but the outlook of the trustees had been indelibly warped by the stock market crash of 1929. All investments, no matter how safe, were affected by the crash. Trust officers who prided themselves on prudency and good judgment watched the net worth of prize accounts melt away and clients turn from wealthy beneficiaries into paupers. For decades to come, the business would have a Depression mentality.

In the post-World War II boom, the moribund trust industry lagged behind other financial institutions. In the early 1950s, trust fees didn't make for exciting business. The industry showed an average annual asset growth of little better than 6%. But in 1956 a change in pension fund legislation cut trust companies into a lucrative piece of business that had been the private domain of insurance companies. This new market for pension fund investment management pushed average annual asset growth in trust companies to almost 11% during the late fifties — better than all the competition. By the early sixties, trusts had climbed back to their position of three decades earlier — one-tenth the size of the banks.

They built their savings-lending branch systems through the sixties, often by acquisitions. The large, national trust companies of today grew as the "corporate" companies swallowed the grass-roots competition. New, regional companies opened their doors in the sixties, but many foundered or were swallowed. In 1984 there were 133 trust and loan companies, but 75% of the industry's business was in the hands of the 6 largest.

Fiduciary is one of the ugliest words in the English language. It is no wonder that most people shun the Latin term for its Old Norse counterpart, *trust*. Trust officers, however, take joy in speaking of a company's "fiduciary relationship" with a client. Trust officers are slow to change.

They enjoy the traditions of their role. They have always seen their job as a service, not a business. The heritage of common law — that companies can't "profit" from management of properties in personal trusts — means that companies, like individual trustees, make their money on fees for the service. They do, however, profit directly when they act as agents rather than as trustees.

Today the powers of the trust companies are the same as they were a century ago: estate management, corporate trusteeships, mortgage lending, a limited amount of personal loan business. The last two "intermediary" operations — taking in money as deposits and sending it out as loans — are treated in the books as taking in deposit money in trust for the depositor, to fit the old trustee mould.

Trust companies are kept in line by limitations on the amount of money they can borrow from the public. They must have a minimum amount of capital in their coffers; the amount varies with the provincial or federal incorporation regulations. A company is assigned a number, be it 6, 12, or 25, and that number is multiplied by the company's own value in capital to reach the amount of funds the company may collect in deposits. For example, a company with a borrowing ratio of 10 times its capital could borrow $10 for each $1 it owned in cash or assets. This is how trust companies lever their holdings in order to pull money in from the public and send it back out in loans. (Banks, in contrast, have no "leverage" limit but must set aside a portion of their assets as reserves, to guard against default.) The number, or multiple, is supposed to be set by government regulators on the basis of stability and track record. Every company, of course, wants to lever its assets by as much as possible.

Their diverse powers make trust companies, of necessity, subject to diverse regulations. The two types of business they conduct straddle a constitutional crack in regulatory powers. The duty of trust between a trustee and a beneficiary is a matter of property and civil rights, a provincial responsibility. The ability to take deposits from the public and lend the money back out is banking, a prize of federal jurisdiction. The overlap in regulatory reach has traditionally been settled Canadian-style: with a bit of power for each level. Federally incorporated companies, supervised by the loan and trust division of the federal Department of Insurance, part of the Ministry of Finance, must register in each province in which they operate. Provincially incorporated companies, supervised by their own trust officials in the provincial Consumer ministries, must register out-of-province branches with other provincial ministries. And in those provinces with stock exchanges, securities commissions oversee publicly traded trust companies and securities transactions, with the Ontario Securities Commission (OSC) taking a particularly prominent role.

Like much of Canada's trust legislation, however, these provisions have been warped by inconsistent enforcement, entrepreneurial drive and the shocking neglect that has left the federal Trust Companies Act 53 years without major revisions. Banks update their mandate and successfully lobby for new powers during decennial revisions. These revisions may stretch for years before the updated legislation is introduced; the last "decennial" revision of the Bank Act actually stretched 13 years before its 1980 completion, and the 1990 version has already begun. But the revisions often allow banks the opportunity to enter new businesses, as when, in 1967, they were given entry into unrestricted mortgage lending. Despite federal reviews of the financial system in the thirties and the Porter commission in the early sixties, banks are the only financial institutions with this ten-year automatic review, an inequity the present federal government has promised to redress.

Bank executives have always had favoured status with politicians; they forced the federal government to institute a 10% ownership limit on their shares in the early sixties, in the name of nationalism, when Toronto Dominion Bank was threatened with a take-over by a U.S. bank. Trust company managers have long hungered for the same safety from take-over, but it has never been granted. That open-door policy on ownership of a trust company has allowed the essential changes in the companies — and the bitter, harmful take-over battles that have seen one company after another bought up by entrepreneurial

interests despite the (usually underhanded) defensive tactics of
the old guard.

There have been minor changes to the Trust Companies Act
and other regulations, but they haven't solved the basic regulatory conundrum: owners of new trust companies must obtain
a licence to do business, a basic barrier to entry; yet ownership is so easily transferable that existing trust companies can
change their stripes with chameleon ease. These days there are
provincial companies incorporated in the East that operate
mainly in the West; companies with offices in one province
but investing mainly in another; companies shifting their head
office with ownership changes. In fact, companies completely
change character — location, company name, even the type of
business they do — without regard for regulatory predilections.
The politicians have decided a barrier is needed and then have
refused to patrol it.

Ottawa is the dominant partner in the system of dual federal-
provincial licensing. Besides regulating federal companies, it
has agreements with Nova Scotia, Manitoba and P.E.I. to
regulate their provincially chartered companies. With the introduction of federal deposit insurance for banks and trust and
loan companies in 1967, it assumed another duty: ensuring for
the Canada Deposit Insurance Corp. (CDIC) that any insured
company in the country is properly run and regulated. CDIC
was a typical government solution to the same old market
problem: the stability of the system. Banks aren't allowed to
fail in Canada, because lawmakers and bankers still believe
they are operating in a small, closed system where the fragility
of one company could blow over the granite edifices built by
the largest. Trust companies can fail, however; shortly before
the CDIC was founded, one company did; while the merits
of the CDIC were being debated, another threatened to; and
there have been more than a dozen in trouble since. The solution to depositor protection was this skeleton organization,
created as a Crown corporation, run by a board of civil servants and funded by banks and trust and loan companies, with

fees on a sliding scale based on size. The smallest are the most likely to falter, but they pay the least.

"It's very much a truism," says a former trust officer: "The first generation makes it, the second lives off it, the third blows it. The effect of the trust company is to slow down the blowing in the third generation. It is handed out piecemeal."

The estate and trust business, the original business of trust companies, is based on the old-fashioned notion of preserving wealth for future generations. Trust officers sort through an estate, value the assets, pay funeral expenses and taxes and parcel out lump-sum payments to beneficiaries. That's phase one — and it can easily take a year or more. Then, if a trust is established, the estate's investments are planned. When not specified in a will, they fall under the guidelines of the court; these restrict estates to very conservative investments, such as government bonds. But trust companies often urge clients to leave the investments up to their judgment — and that can lead to disagreements over whether funds should be invested for short-term capital gains or long-term security.

Clients really began complaining about trust company investment practices when inflation hit. With trust funds often tied up by restrictive instructions to invest in low-yielding bonds, income just didn't pay the bills of many beneficiaries. They were embarrassed when requests to dip into capital were turned down. It became increasingly ludicrous for a company factotum to be inquiring about the need for an expensive model of car, for example. And the problem could be more serious. Admits the trust officer with the "blow-out" theory: "On the few occasions when there was a grandson with entrepreneurial spirit it probably held him back."

Another perpetual complaint about trust companies is the puttering and paper shuffling done before any money is available. "We always loved being appointed the sole executor," says one ex-employee. "We could take our own sweet time in administering the estate. The longer the administration, the longer the fees last."

In every province but Quebec, a trust company must "pass" its accounts through a special branch of the provincial court system, surrogate court, after the "executor's year" — usually a year and a day — when assets have been collected, debts have been paid and the estate is ready for distribution. That's when the beneficiaries may formally protest if unhappy with the service or the fees. In Quebec — which operates under a system of civil law rather than British common law — unhappy heirs have to sue through the regular court system.

Sometimes co-trustees can disagree violently. Observers have criticized National Trust for "abandoning" the Billes family when its family company, Canadian Tire, was basically put up for auction by the court in 1984 at the request of a group of charities led by the Toronto Humane Society. Co-founder John William Billes had left one-third of his company in trust for two dozen charities, with his wife, one son and National Trust as co-trustees. His family received annuities and shared the income with the charities; on their deaths the shares would be sold and the funds divided up. Dividends, however, were low, and eventually the charities decided they wanted more diversification in the portfolio and a higher return for their money. The Toronto Humane Society, which wanted to pay for its new headquarters, contacted the trust company. National decided that the charities had a legal right to demand more diversification in the portfolio; the Billes family disagreed. The co-trustees landed in court, and the ruling was that the Canadian Tire shares should be sold. The three children of a very irate octagenarian Alfred Billes, co-founder with his brother John, made the highest bid and ended up owning 60% of the company. The cash was handed out in mid-November 1984: the family heirs received a $3.3 million payment in lieu of their annuities, and the charities reaped an $83.3 million reward.*

* The largest recipient, University of Toronto, received $13 million. The others were an interesting mix, including the United Way, the Salvation Army, the Boy Scouts of Canada, the Canadian National Institute for the Blind, the John Howard Society, the Canadian Bible Society and the instigator of unrest, the Toronto Humane Society, a relatively minor beneficiary at almost $2 million.

"Isn't that amazing," Martha Billes, one of the cousins who bought the shares, commented to a reporter. "You can die and leave a will and they can change it and change it until they get their way."

Companies in recent years haven't pursued estates as they used to. Beginning in the sixties, as the intermediary operations grew, the personal trust business with its court-set fees lagged. By the end of the decade trust companies realized they had to appeal to a wider group, offer packaged products and make volume pay.

Readers of self-help magazines have become the prime targets for these new financial packages. The Registered Retirement Savings Plan is the Big Mac of the financial planning market, the best-known, the most comfortable, the option innocuous enough to fit all tastes.

RRSPs allow an investor to build up money for retirement, watching it build through tax-free reinvestment each year and collecting the large pool of funds down the road — hopefully still at a tax saving if he or she is in a lower tax bracket after retirement.

The money can be deposited in a "banking" account. It can be placed in a mutual fund RRSP, which may in turn invest in stocks ranging from blue-chip to speculative; in bonds; in preferred shares; in mortgages; in short-term "money market" debt; in a fund that itself invests in commodities such as gold or silver; or in real estate. Or the investor can decide not to opt for a package and can dabble in both types with a "self-directed" RRSP.

At first RRSPs were available only at trust companies, as part of their trustee business. But Revenue Canada opened the doors to banks, brokers and others, although some of these newcomers must have a trust company as a passive trustee for the funds. The trust companies do earn a fee for this business — say, $100 annually — but definitely prefer to capture the customers themselves. Competition for the public's contributions is stiffer every year.

Mutual funds, which provide a portfolio investment without the worry of making the decisions, are not available just at tax time. This has never been a "trustee" business. Instead, the trust company is acting as an agent for the investor, placing his or her money in a fund developed at and run by the company's investment department. The trust company doesn't guarantee the investment, although the company does pitch its own investment prowess, as do insurance companies and mutual fund marketing companies.

These personal savings and tax-oriented investments are around for the same reason as the traditional trust arrangement — to keep money from the tax collector and make it magically multiply. But none of the new investment plans with imposing initials or the tidy acronyms favoured by bureaucrats is the personal preserve of trust officers. Trust companies must slug it out with other financial institutions for a share of this market. To improve their odds, trust companies have begun using the skills of the once-sniffed-at banking types in their branches.

Tending corporate accounts, like so much trust business, is a matter of watchful waiting. When a trust company takes on a bond trusteeship for a corporation, for example, it is representing the interests of the buyers of the corporation's bonds. Its role is completely passive — until something goes wrong. It is acting as the bond- or debt-holder's representative, the one who checks to make sure the corporate borrower lives up to its end of the bargain. Ordinarily, this responsibility involves straight accounting, registering bond ownership, exchanging and redeeming bonds, collecting and distributing interest payments. But the responsibility shifts from factotums to executives when payments aren't made or the corporation begins to crumble.

Bond trusteeship and stock transfer business are usually lumped together, but there is a basic difference: while transferring and keeping track of companies' stock, a trust company is not responsible as a trustee. It is merely acting as the company's agent, moving the paper around. Its most important contribution is the computerized list of shareholders it has, and trust companies compete for business on the basis of their ability to break down the list for a corporate treasurer's immediate consumption, and do the paperwork for dividend reinvestment and new share purchases or rights issues. But acting as transfer agent and registrar for stock doesn't mean the trust company feels it owes the customer any loyalty. During real estate developer Robert Campeau's 1980 attempt to take over Royal Trust, National Trust was the company that collected the stock tendered to him. But that didn't stop National from buying a slice of Royal shares and holding on to them rather than tendering to Campeau.

Before retiring as National's chief executive, J.L. (Les) Colhoun, a sprightly fellow with a barrister's eye, took on his final nursemaiding of a bond trusteeship gone wrong when, in August 1982, Vancouver-based Daon Development Corp. stopped paying its debts. National was trustee for the holders of $80 million in Daon debentures. Colhoun decided that the best way to recover the debenture holders' money was not to place Daon in receivership. Had anything gone wrong during the two years of negotiating with North American and European lenders' committees that took place before a successful debt restructuring was accepted, the debenture holders would have had a good case for taking National to court. This is the trust company in its traditional role, representing the debtholders at negotiating tables stacked with bankers.

Pension fund business, like bond trusteeship, originally landed where the corporate connections were strongest. When trust companies entered the field in 1957 they wangled a slew of corporate pension accounts away from insurance companies. To attract clients, they offered a higher rate of return with their trusteed plans — about 8% annually — than the insurance companies had been providing, by guaranteeing a ceiling — an average of 4% annually. They didn't guarantee that return, as the insurers did, but clients knew they would receive whatever return there was, whereas the insurers pocketed anything above the guaranteed ceiling.

Trust companies weren't swift or sophisticated in investment strategies for their captive clientele.* But by the mid-sixties companies were demanding profitable performance. Pension funds today hold huge blocks of stock and swing the weight of billions of dollars in assets. Trusteed funds — which must have a trust company as trustee but these days not usually as manager — totalled $8 billion in 1967; they were more than ten times that amount in 1984, almost 15% of the assets in the financial system, and larger than the intermediary operations of the trust industry. The numbers are so big that performance is critical. If well managed, a $1 million investment made in 1979 would have become $2.1 million by 1984, according to one firm that does nothing but act as a watchful eye for funds. If bumbled, it could have risen as little as $280,000 in the same period. Payment for management of these assets is now based on performance, and pension funds demand some aggressive risk-taking. Successful in-house experts are high priests for the followers of lucre. In a bid to win back clients lost to independent managers and consultants, trust companies are setting up independently managed subsidiaries, which they hope will generate an entrepreneurial spark.

Trust companies have inched as close as they can to being banks, but their banking is still done by sleight of hand. They are not creditors, but institutions receiving funds from the public in trust and guaranteeing their safekeeping. The banking side of the business, however, has come to dominate the strategies of trust managers and the preoccupations of regulators.

A trust company uses the deposits it collects to make investments, basically by lending out the money at a higher rate. The

* The 40 stock "recommended" list at one large trust company showed the pace of those days. "Montreal drew up the list," says the old-timer. "It filtered up to Toronto the next week. We responded. By the time it got out to Vancouver, it'd be another month or so. On several occasions we were actually selling the stocks and our branch office in Vancouver was buying them."

difference between the deposit and the lending interest rates is the spread, or gross profit. Trust companies specialize in mortgage lending, and their deposit base reflects this. Traditionally, they were interested in only longer-term funds to match their mortgage terms — although they used to be careless about this matching of terms, at times with horrific results.*

As mortgage terms became more flexible, trust companies were able to compete for shorter-term funds as well. That statement can be turned around: when depositors decide they want to place their money in a financial institution for only a short time because they think interest rates are rising, a trust company can offer only short-term mortgages.

Mortgages have always been a part of estate portfolios. But they did not become a predominant business for most mainline trust companies until the late fifties and early sixties. Trust companies have always been an important factor in the mortgage market. But they've never been the single dominant force, having been pre-empted first by insurance companies and more recently by the banks.

The two large, old-line exceptions to the landed-gentry roots of trusts are Canada Permanent, whose trust arm is still a subsidiary of its mortgage company, and Canada Trust, the country's largest trust company. Both began as mortgage lenders, growing from the roots of British-style "building societies," which developed in the late eighteenth century. Members placed money in the pot, and the societies auctioned the funds to the member willing to pay the highest bonus on top of a fixed

---

* Twenty-five-year government-insured mortgages, seemingly the safest possible investment until the early '70s, created problems for a number of trust companies that used short-term deposits to fund these long-term loans, particularly Guaranty Trust. Guaranty was run for years by a maverick named Wilson J. Berry, who had founded the company in 1925 in Windsor, Ontario. His management style was a blend of chaos and autocracy: there were no operations manuals in the branches, and Berry insisted on approving every mortgage. If he was on holiday, there were no loans. He was haunted by the memory of farm loans he had made that had almost bankrupted Guaranty in the thirties, and he vowed that he would never again place the company in jeopardy. He built a portfolio of safe, long-term, low-rate mortgages that nearly did the company in when interest rates rose.

interest rate. The sole purpose of the building societies was to accumulate capital so that their financially inexperienced members could build homes. When every member had received a loan, the intention was to wind up the society. But human nature being what it is, original members were replaced with new ones by society managers set on entrenching themselves. By 1875 the building societies were no longer restricted to lending to members and could invest funds in mortgages and government securities. Building societies had become loan companies.

The loan companies, which grew so rapidly that they controlled 24% of financial intermediary assets in the late nineteenth century, thrived by marketing low-rate debentures to British, most often Scottish, investors, then lending money at higher rates in Canada. But during the 1890s, interest rates for Canadian loans dipped below those in Britain, wiping out that advantage. The loan companies didn't build their Canadian investor base, and by 1944 their share of deposits had dwindled to only 2% of Canadian financial assets.

Loan and trust lenders dealt with real estate boom, bust and boom in the first half of the century, and each fall in the market demonstrated the risks of offering property loans in inflationary times. After the Second World War institutional mortgage portfolios ballooned: in 1949 insurance, trust and loan companies passed the $1 billion mark in outstanding mortgages, half of that chalked up in three years on more than a million new homes.

In the late fifties, insurance companies decided commercial mortgages were a better match than residential ones for their long-term policy liabilities, and they left trust companies to take up the slack. Ottawa didn't think the trusts could handle the load alone and, instead of testing their ability to cope, forced the banks into the mortgage market by means of the federal National Housing Act.

For once the game wasn't played with the rules of the banking oligopoly. Prime Minister Louis St Laurent decided at an October 1, 1953, cabinet meeting that the banks had to be brought in. He knew the bankers — commercial lenders with

an abhorrence for government interference other than that
which kept up the barriers to entry in the banking business
— wouldn't like it. The prime minister simply issued a press
release announcing that the banks would now be able to
provide higher-risk mortgage loans insured by the federal government under the National Housing Act. "Lesse majesté,"
laughs Dave Mansur, who was then president of Central Mortgage and Housing Corp. (CMHC), which administered the National Housing Act. "Oh, the protests were just unbelievable. . . . The financial community abhors change."

Mansur hurried the bankers up with a nifty little bit of
mutual backscratching with the Bank of Montreal (BMO),
CMHC's bank. Within three days BMO announced it had
financed 317 loans for a new subdivision in Pointe Claire,
Quebec. The jaws clamped shut and the bankers took out their
pens to write loans.

Once the banks were in the mortgage business, they liked it.
By the early sixties, they were pushing for the power granted
with the 1967 Bank Act to lend mortgage money without restrictions or government insurance. Banks could turn their
money on and off like a tap; they didn't depend on the
business, and when they cut margins it would mean only a loss
that could be offset by other business. But for trust companies,
forced to follow the rates set by the banks or lose customers,
it was "life or death," says Richard (Dick) Humphrys. For
more than 30 years until his 1982 retirement, ramrod-stiff
Humphrys was the federal superintendent of insurance, the
Grand Pooh-Bah of trust regulation. He puts one in mind of a
corporate undertaker: he has the same ever-watchful, cautious
approach and the same limitations on his vision, which extends
only as far as the government wants to see. Humphrys says the
trust companies' case was known to politicians before Ottawa
gave banks the key to the mortgage market in the 1967 Bank
Act revisions. "Any arguments put forward were not convincing publicly versus the argument that this would be better for
the borrower."

Since 1980 the banks have written the most new mortgage commitments; in 1984 they surpassed trust companies in size of their total mortgage portfolios. The trust companies, of course, have met the banks on their own turf, going after personal and corporate loan business as much as they can.

Whenever new rules are finally introduced for the trust industry, basic changes will be made that will confirm the dominance of the banking side of the trust business. This confirmation will occur whether or not the new rules include the controversial formal corporate split of today's trust company into two parallel, co-operative businesses, a bank and a trust firm — a proposal being studied by the federal government. There will no longer be a trust relationship between a federal company and a customer placing money on deposit. It will be replaced by the debtor-creditor relationship of banking. And there will no longer be a need to slip business loans onto the books in a circuitous manner, expressing them as stock purchases rather than as loans because trusts' corporate lending powers are limited. Corporate lending will be allowed on a broader basis. If they're not allowed to hive off their banking business in a separate company, trust companies will still have come so close to being banks that the new function will have overtaken their original purpose — trust.

For decades trust companies lived on fees. For years they have lived for spreads. Now, the promise for future profits lies principally in fees from personal trust business; trust companies hope to use that as a basis to increase their deposit clientele base. As one trust employee said simply, "We know they have the money."

The major companies have divided their operations, not into banking and trust businesses, but into operations for personal and corporate customers; they have reassigned branch managers and restructured their executive tiers to target the two markets separately. The old-line strategy of thinking trust clients are special people, quite separate from mortgage borrowers, has been replaced by a desire to draw the householder into the world of investment planning. The shift is in the outlook of the trust company owner: instead of looking at the types of business involved, he is looking at the types of market. Since the purposes of the regulators and the new trust entrepreneurs are so at odds, chances are they will both succeed: the trust company will revert to being the sage investment counsellor, the lending operation will move its corporate body to a new office on the other side of a very thin wall — and the owners of both will work to ensure that the two remain inextricably linked in the public mind.

However the companies are viewed, the connections between trust companies and other segments of the business community are as powerful as ever. The new owners, like the old, have their unwritten rules, and they have become a united club. In 1984 Canada Trust, the last "widely held" trust company — though a misnomer for rule by management, it does permit a measure of independence — was about to join the club.

2

The Last Stand

A chain-smoking Mervyn Lahn stands tall at the fort gate, rifle in hand, facing an attacking horde. He is the last of a breed, a formidable opponent to the spreading financial conglomerates owned by secretive, wealthy individuals. And he wears his white hat righteously. He is protecting the independence of management, the integrity of the financial system and the rights of small shareholders who, like himself, have benefited during the past two years from the doubling in value of the shares of Canada Trustco, the last independently owned and run trust company in the land, and phenomenally successful.

As president and chief executive officer of Canada Trustco — with assets of more than $12 billion it is the largest trust company in the land — Lahn would perhaps be more accurately portrayed with a grenade; he is not afraid of sharing his views, and the more public the forum, the better. His speeches, delivered in a rich southwestern Ontario voice that easily acquires a harder, sarcastic edge, are studies in outrage and audacity. During a lively company annual meeting in 1984 in the wake of the trust companies scandal that had rocked Ontario, in the space of 20 minutes Lahn took aim at cowardly industry advisory committees, a court system that rewards white-collar crime and preposterous legislative proposals, finally zeroing in on officialdom, which he clearly found lacking: "Almost unbelievably, the Ontario government, acting in undue haste in response to its self-acknowledged supervisory inadequacies, proposes to add further injury and insult to the industry operating environment. Over-reacting to the failure of small, individually owned loan and trust companies which were grossly mismanaged and inadequately supervised, Ontario advocates ill-advised and unduly stringent legislation and regulations."

He was the only executive in the loan and trust business to openly criticize the government's handling of the Greymac Affair and its political consequences. But he saves his most ruthless indignation for the evils of closely held financial institutions, cloaking his opposition to them in the serviceable fabric of the public good. Only when individuals or groups of associates own trust companies do scandals like those at Greymac, Astra and Fidelity happen. And Lahn sees no difference between the dangers of any single owner, be he a Leonard Rosenberg or a Peter Bronfman.

"They say, hell, it won't happen with a major company. But have any of the owners had their back absolutely up against the wall in a very difficult period of time? That in the hope of saving the whole damn empire, if I do just this one thing with somebody else's money, I may save the whole pot? Have they ever been tested? The answer is no. But if you go back in the history of the world and people are put to that test, not many of them make the grade."

This is a cherished line of reasoning often used by the country's big chartered banks in their drive to create a playing field in their own image. The cause, however, was lost even as Lahn spoke in his modest Toronto office, where he tends to spend two of every five working days, away from the company's London, Ontario, headquarters. Giant Manufacturers Life Insurance Co. had moved inexorably into a position of power within Canada Trust. To forestall a fate that has befallen every other trust company, Canada Trust's board of directors voted in 1969 to limit the amount of shares in the company that any one shareholder could vote to a maximum of 10%, no matter how many shares he actually owned — a practice that worked reasonably well until ManuLife, as it is universally known, and its chief executive, the aristocratic Sydney Jackson, turned up in December 1982 with $53 million to raise ManuLife's stake in the trust company's common stock to 27% from 10%, with clear designs on the rest of it.*

Syd Jackson likes to tell people the company decided to buy a stake in Canada Trust because it's such a good investment. "So far it's turned out in my view to be the best trust company in Canada by quite a bit," the tall, navy blue Jackson will say from a taupe couch in his arena of an office overlooking Toronto's Rosedale ravine. And he's right. In the days following the release in April 1985 of Ottawa's proposals to unleash the forces of trust and insurance companies, ManuLife made $17 million on paper with its investment.

But ManuLife's investment was also in its own future. Under current legislation mutual life insurance companies are barred from owning more than 30% of another company. "The second reason we bought was as a defensive measure. All the other trust companies had been bought and we didn't want the government to say, 'Okay, now you can own a trust company' and [then find] there was no trust company available."

"If you have a strong shareholder," argues Jackson, whose company, as a mutual rather than a share company, is owned by its 950,000 worldwide policyholders, "he will take the interests of the company to heart far more than management."

These words have the effect of galvanizing Lahn into hyperbolic overdrive. "I don't want to get into all that crap about when one person owns a financial company and loots it, but that's the sort of thing that happens."

Repellents, such as constrained share provisions, have proved nuisances rather than deterrents to determined suitors in past

* ManuLife bought the stock from two long-time shareholders of Canada Trust who had mixed motives: Maxwell Meighen, who had been thwarted by management in an attempt to take control in the early 1960s, and London Life Insurance Co., whose parent company had begun acquiring control of rival Royal Trust.

cases such as Canada Permanent and Royal Trust. Thus, modern-day manager Lahn devised a typically unorthodox strategy for repelling the sharks that circle his company: he decided to make Canada Trust so good, the return so attractive to shareholders, the share price so lofty that any interested acquisitor would have to pay through the nose. And he was able to do it because his equally independent predecessors in the executive suite had laid the groundwork in the '60s, when they decided that Canada Trust should become a bank in all but name.

Canada Trust has been a renegade all of its corporate life. Of the big trust companies, it is the most prominent to have started out in business as a mortgage company rather than a trust for the elite. Canada Trust is a product of its country roots. Established in 1864 as The Huron & Erie Savings and Loan Society, it brought debenture money from Scotland and lent it out to people homesteading in the fertile farmland of southwestern Ontario. By the turn of the century, its increasingly prosperous customers were demanding trust services, and so the company acquired a federally incorporated Calgary institution known as General Trust Corp., moving it to London and changing the name to Canada Trust Co.*

The mortgage and trust parts of the company existed side by side under the incredibly cumbersome name of "The Huron & Erie Mortgage Corp. and The Canada Trust Co." until the 1960s when, in typically cautious trust industry style, the "Huron & Erie" part was dropped over the course of five years. By this time, the company had swallowed more than a dozen loan and trust companies in Ontario and the West; eventually it adopted Canada Trustco as an umbrella name for the trust and ancillary companies.

Since the 1960s it has led the trust and banking industries

---

* This dual nature of the company, which is actually a loan company with a trust subsidiary, is important even today. When a depositor buys an investment certificate at a Canada Trust branch, the money may, as a result of inner company requirements, actually go into a debenture in the loan company. To the customer it is all the same.

with its innovative marketing and operating style. It is obsessively systematized, and it is the only company where management has remained king, its planned succession smoothly unfolding, undisturbed by any proprietor's hand.

Although Merv Lahn dominates the present by force of his personality, a more lasting impression on the company was left by the remarkable J. Allyn Taylor.

A true gentleman, as rare as a smiling teller, Taylor in his quiet way was a giant of the country's financial world during his tenure at the top of Canada Trust during the 1950s and 1960s. He was a Westerner, from Winnipeg, who began his career in the trust operations of Royal Trust during the 1930s. Lured over to Canada Trust with the mission of developing trust business for the largely mortgages-oriented company, Taylor moved to London and began climbing rapidly up the corporate ladder.

Taking over as president in 1958, Taylor perceived that Canada Trust's real competition lay with the banks — not with fellow trust companies, as many of his colleagues believed. That meant improving Canada Trust's branch system.

Two years after assuming the presidency, Taylor and a handful of his managers began a selling job on the board — a collection of conservatives with an appreciation for the status quo. The seemingly benign Taylor was selling a new direction for a company that, as the older directors were quick to remind him, had been in the business for almost 100 years. But the company had spent most of the 1950s asleep. In large part the problem was lack of a retirement policy for management and the board of directors, then chaired by V.P. Cronyn, a descendant of one of the founders.

Taylor's scheme triggered explosive growth, opening 30 branches in a few years, building when it was cheap to do so and changing the complexion of the company dramatically. Querulous board members asked why he was opening a branch here and a branch there, and a running difference of opinion between the board and management persisted like a troublesome cough. But what caused hearts to stop in the Canada

Trust boardroom in 1962 was a decision by Taylor, on the insistent advice of his accounting department, to invest in new-fangled computers.

"I guess I've been a people person. What I've tried to do is take the skills of others — which were far greater than my own, and I mean that," he will say in typically self-deprecating fashion, "and use them." (His people skills, in fact, enhanced his public image. "He's a very wily fellow under that tremendous air of bonhomie," comments Conrad Harrington, president of Royal Trust during the 1960s and a great, albeit clearsighted, admirer of Taylor's.)

Taylor ventured into an executive committee meeting one day with a recommendation that the company rent some IBM equipment that was going to cost nearly $200,000 for one year — an expensive and risky venture. When questioned by several blustering directors, Taylor admitted that he wasn't sure the investment would lead to better service for customers or savings for the company. Finally one of the directors broke: "Then why in hell are you recommending this kind of an expenditure?"

"I said — and I think my answer was prophetic," recalled Taylor, " 'Because I think we're going to be up to our hips in paperwork if we don't do it.' "

It is a moment remembered with satisfaction, because it gave tiny Canada Trust — in 1963 it had only $270 million in assets compared to National Trust's $1.2 billion — a running start on computerization. A London branch was the first one on-line, and by 1972 the company was promoting its "Unibranches," which offered customers any-branch banking, made possible by tellers' access to the on-line computer system. Other institutions followed several years later.

Equally crucial to the company's later success was another early venture by Taylor and his young protégé, Arthur Mingay, into an area of business that would prove to be one of the largest and most profitable: pensions.

Mingay, who began with the company in 1938 in his home town of Windsor, would assume the presidency of the company 35 years later when Taylor moved up to chairman. But he was spotted by Taylor in 1954 while labouring in the Chatham, Ontario, office as a trust officer. Taylor, then assistant general manager, was looking for someone to spearhead the company's entry into the pension business. Timing was crucial: Ottawa was about to change the legislation, allowing trust companies into what had previously been the insurance companies' domain, and Taylor knew his competitors would soon be planning to get in on the action. One or two other candidates in the company had been tried, but they had proved more interested in the glamour of a big-city Toronto posting than the scintillations of pensions.

One month after the federal government passed the legislation in 1957, Canada Trust had a program ready for marketing. The young Mingay moved to Toronto and began selling large companies on pensions managed by Canada Trust — a company with no previous corporate business to speak of — eventually winning, on the strength of sheer determination, accounts far out of proportion to the size of the company. By 1967, when personal retirement savings began to take off, Canada Trust had already been aggressively marketing its retirement savings plan for ten years.

Taylor laid the foundations for the mammoth structure that followed with a series of acquisitions of smaller companies — Waterloo Trust and Halton & Peel Trust in 1968 — building on strength in the southern Ontario triangle running from Toronto to Windsor to Niagara Falls. That year Canada Trust had the largest number of branches of any trust company, growing to 77 from 19 branches 10 years earlier. Taylor had anticipated that the loosening of the Bank Act in 1967, which allowed the banks into the consumer and mortgage lending fields, would make it almost impossible for go-go expansion of trust company offices. "It is very fortunate that this policy was pursued," he told a luncheon gathering of the Toronto Society of Financial Analysts in October 1968, "because virtually all these new offices are successfully established and their business will continue to grow notwithstanding the greater competition. It won't be easy in the foreseeable future for trust companies to establish new offices."

All the same, growth was spectacular. The assets of the company increased by 754% from $153 million at the start of the 1960s to $1.3 billion at the end of the decade. One former employee in head office savings operations remembers the branch in the Shoppers World plaza in east Toronto as a roaring success from the first day it opened. "We would work in the savings operation till 5:00 on Friday evening, then go straight to the branch and work all weekend hand-posting the week's business, stopping only for a shower and a few hours' sleep." That went on for several months, and when it was over the company rewarded them with a word of thanks.

It was Arthur Mingay's role to weather the stormy seventies, when trust earnings rose and fell as the banks muscled in on the mortgage market and seemed headed for the trusts' fiduciary business. Interest rates began to gyrate. Peter Maurice, now executive vice-president of investments at Canada Trust, attended the Trust Companies Association annual meeting in 1975, a few years after he had left manufacturing to join the trust company. He sat in quiet horror as the association president that year, a clearly defeated Donald Neelands, who was also president of Canada Permanent, made a vivid speech about the impending doom of the industry, declaiming that the trust companies could in no way compete with the banks and that there was no light at the end of the tunnel for any of them.

But Mingay had other worries. Not very long after assuming the presidency in early 1973, he declared that he was concerned about the image of his company. Few Canadians, he lamented, realized the size of Canada Trust, which was the most profitable trust company in the industry at the time. "We're still encumbered by the old Huron & Erie image."

Mingay's tenure as president would be remarkably short, given the previous long run under Taylor and Lahn's subsequent ascendancy in 1978, and there were those who had misgivings from the outset. At the time, Taylor fans concluded that he was selflessly stepping aside as president and taking the office of chairman in order to make room for Mingay and that the shoes would be tough to fill.

Mingay is a man of two sides. Like many of his generation in the industry, he is imbued with the quiet patience of the "trust" side of the business. When he left his pension job in 1960, he promised himself he would stay abreast of what to many is the somewhat tedious subject *as a hobby* and was truly disappointed to discover that things were changing too fast in pensions for this to be possible.

However, his mild-mannered, even bland, demeanour hides a certain ruthlessness. In the typically tight-fisted style of Canada Trust, Mingay could prevent promising employees from jumping ship without upping the ante. As a young manager making $3,000 a year, Peter Dennett, now a retirement savings plan consultant, was approached by free-spending York Trust and offered double the money, an expense account and a car. Several Canada Trust people had already gone over. Mingay had been expecting something like this, and he sent a message to Dennett to come up and see him — if he had the time. Dennett indeed had the time, and soon enough Mingay was telling him the story of when he was just out of school in Windsor and Ford Motor Co. had offered him twice the money of Canada Trust. He was always glad, he said from behind his general manager's desk, that he had taken Canada Trust. "He didn't offer anything or make any promises, but he led me to believe he respected me and there was a future for me. I stayed," recalls Dennett.

Melvin Hawkrigg, president of Edward and Peter Bronfman's Trilon Financial Corp., which controls Royal Trust, regards Canada Trust's "super management team" as a legacy of Taylor, with Mingay executing Taylor's grand plan.

"They know where they're going and they've got their game plan well laid out," says Hawkrigg, who once worked for Taylor at Canada Trust. "Who's responsible? You have to look back over the management situation. First, J. Allyn Taylor, who's just a superb individual and one of Canada's outstanding citizens. Then, he made sure Arthur Mingay came along and followed his steps."

Canada Trust's phenomenal success in meeting the banks

head-on in the savings and lending business stems from a corporate structure set up in about 1970 when Taylor and Mingay decided the company needed product managers — unheard-of in the staid financial world. Staff in the branches, they reasoned, could not be expected to stay on top of product developments, legislative changes and market shifts, so they designated product managers and marketing managers for all the products Canada Trust offered. Out of that decision came the most consistently innovative marketing in the financial industry.*

The innovation, aggressiveness and leadership continued. By 1975 the industry was offering mortgages of less than a five-year term; Canada Trust went in for this in a big way, and soon 30% of its mortgage customers were opting for one- and two-year terms. The Permanent and Royal stood back, reluctant to accept the change.

At the end of 1975, when trusts and banks were battling for consumer loans, Canada Trust had $30 million of that type of business. One year later the amount had increased 250%, to $112 million.† The company had done it by cutting its interest rate below that of its competitors. But to balance the demand, it offered a free set of luggage or a stereo to anyone borrowing more than $2,500 if the borrower also opened a savings or chequing account.

"We've outlawed give-aways because we feel that might persuade the wrong type of person to take a loan," sniffed Canada Permanent sales promotion manager Bernie Kerwin at the time. "Of course, if it induces a good borrower to switch from another lending company, then that's good business."

By 1978, Taylor was 70 years old. Memories of aging, recalcitrant chairmen of the past persuaded him that it was time to

---

* In J. Allyn Taylor's time, the company had jolted the banking world when, in 1960, Huron & Erie-Canada Trust offered a choice of a Kodak camera or a Cory coffee percolator for every savings account of $10 or more opened. The company was also giving money away: 10¢ to each visitor to a new branch. It was a gimmick to illustrate the interest earned on $2.50 left for a year.

† In 1976, trust companies had 2%, or $350 million, of personal loans while banks had 59%, or $17 billion.

move over. That meant that after only five years as president Mingay had to move up, and the resulting vacancy was filled by the 45-year-old Merv Lahn, a "hidden asset" of Waterloo Trust, which had been taken over by Canada Trust in 1968.

"In Canada Trustco, over the years we've been very hepped on planning," Mingay recalls now from his chairman's office, an uncluttered place bathed in yellow and sunlight, "planning what you're going to do business-wise and executive-wise." In a way, Mingay became a victim of that planning process, his tenure a diversion as much as a bridge between two sure-footed men.

Merv Lahn was brought to London head office in 1972 to be chief operating officer from his post running the Kitchener-Waterloo region. He had been assistant general manager of Waterloo Trust until 1968 when Canada Trust took over the small regional company. It had a fine reputation in the industry — many felt it was the best small trust company in the country — and Lahn had enjoyed broad responsibilities for the entire operation.

Lahn's first contribution to the London office was a number of electric management meetings where his hard-driving personality made it clear who was the new operational boss. Major decisions were rapidly made on the direction of the company, the relationships and autonomy of senior managers and what Lahn expected from them. In return Lahn asked them what they wanted, and one of the answers was a stock-option plan, which they got.

One of the first things Lahn did was reverse Mingay's emphasis on head office experts; he courted the regional managers and branches, in the belief that they were the bulwark of the system. And he made it clear he expected performance.

Head office executives came out of a momentous meeting one day with the future of the company as a bank clearly mapped out. "Then we got down to business," says one manager who was there. "There was some turnover, some left because the kitchen got awfully hot." But the rest focused on the company's intermediary operations, leaving much of the traditional trust side to limp along.

"Our direction and style grew up from the inside, but it has been single-minded," says Peter Maurice, a corporate planning man who had come to Canada Trust in 1972 with an engineering education from Reed Paper and Maple Leaf Mills.* "I think we've had the tightest strategy of anyone. We've been on the same course for a long time."

The branches took on a different look. They were identified by striking graphics, and the newer ones were American-style free-standing branches in the suburbs with ample parking and branch hours that stretched from 8 A.M. to 8 P.M.

The marketing was turned up a notch, the fruits of that strategy evident in full-page newspaper ads and counter-top brochures. "Win a Home in Florida!!" screamed one such newspaper ad intended to lure depositors in fall 1984 with the prospect of winning a house in "The Moorings of Manatee"; every $200 deposited with Canada Trust entitled the customer to an entry form. Then there was the trade-in allowance. "Trade In Your Account. Get $25 Cash!!!"

From the 1977 promotion, "WAM — Win a Mustang," to 1984's "WIN one of 15 Buicks!!!" in which every $200 deposited in a Canada Trust account entitled the intrepid consumer to an entry form for a chance at a Buick Century, the company stirred things up.

Promotions offered a $25 cash bonus for every account of more than $3,000 transferred from another bank or trust company to a Canada Trust SuperRate Account, which pays 2% more than regular daily interest account!!!! Plus people hours, not bankers' hours!!!!

As for mortgages, the minds at Canada Trust devised "sales" of them with "discounted" interest rates. In 1981 the company was the first to introduce a six-month floating-rate

* The 47-year-old Maurice will likely be the next chief executive officer of Canada Trust, although he is now one of a potent triumvirate of executive vice-presidents under Lahn. The signal that he is on the road to the very top will be an appointment as senior vice-president. That will place him above Jack H. Speake, who heads up client and corporate services but who, at 56, has his age working against him, and above 46-year-old John D. Richardson, in charge of regional branch operations.

mortgage for residential properties. Three years later, as the big banks rumbled into the mortgage market again following the collapse of corporate loan demand, Canada Trust introduced weekly payments on mortgages — the first institution outside the credit union movement to do so. It then pushed the stakes higher by allowing free-of-charge lump-sum payments amounting to 15% of the value of the mortgage at any time in the year.

"Trying to sell money is not different from selling merchandise in Sears," Mingay offers as the company's philosophy, "because if you aren't selling all your merchandise, what do you do? You have a sale. And the only reason we've got a sale at a certain time is because we can't get the various mortgages we want because of competition on rates and everything else. We try to plan a series of marketing events throughout the whole year. And the staff, they love it! There's action, mortgage applications are just flowing in." As early as 1979, the company offered periodic 10% and 20% "discounts" on loan rates.

A June 1980 article in *Financial Times of Canada* devoted to the company's sharp management drew the link between marketing innovation and controlling the company's assets and liabilities through the choppy seas of interest rates and bank competition. "Canada Trustco seems to have lost none of its marketing vinegar. As mortgage demand collapsed in March because of high interest rates, the company scooped the competition with a six-month mortgage. Then, as rates peaked and the big banks scrambled for floating rate deposits, it introduced no-charge chequing on daily interest savings accounts."

The company never loses sight of its main target, the banks. "8 to 8 Monday to Saturday. Some banks offer almost as many services as we do. But not at these hours." And "Your bank account is obsolete. Canada Trust revolutionizes savings accounts," a brochure contended.

The SuperRate account introduced in 1984 offered a higher rate of interest on chequing-savings accounts, with stepped-up rates for higher balances. Its immediate effect: in less than a year the company's portfolio of that kind of account reached more than $1.5 billion, more than any other savings or chequing product in the company's history. Canada Trust was the first, although almost everyone else eventually brought out a version.

"I suppose we do a lot of things others don't wish to take the risk of doing, mainly because there's usually significant costs associated with the introduction of a new account," says Lahn. In the case of SuperRate, with its higher interest rate, the company was increasing the cost of the funds it was borrowing in the form of deposits from the public. They expected a massive switch-over from other accounts and calculated a minimum level of new business from other institutions to cover the expense. There was also a break-even point that the company had to reach before the inevitable imitations sprang up at competing institutions.

Two months into the promotion, Toronto Dominion Bank hit the market with a copy. Lahn was surpised by the speed. He called TD's president Robin Korthals with congratulations. "Good for you, Robin," he said. "I didn't think you could react that quickly." This in fact was a compliment, given that systems drive the business and that new-product introductions usually take months of programming and systems work. Korthals reportedly responded with a chuckle and something about ruining a good industry.

Certainly, many of Canada Trust's firsts were crafted to fit the company's immediate needs, then marketed in the context of the consumer's needs. The "Cash & Carry" investment certificate, launched in 1981, was an ingenious bit of work: marketed as a convenience to holders of one-year investment certificates, the certificate was an "improvement" in that at the end of the term it was automatically rolled over into another one-year certificate at the current rate. What a step saver. And what a way for the trust company, in the midst of high interest rates, to avoid locking itself into long, five-year terms.

Canada Trust was also the first institution, back in early 1983, to levy a fee for use of its MasterCard credit card — a move the banks enthusiastically followed.

More recently, a scheme promised to pay up to $300 to anyone switching an existing mortgage to Canada Trust. (The fine print showed the rebate to be .5% of the mortgage value, up to $300, but the company charged a fee of $150 to process the new mortgage.)

Then there was the mortgage-burning contest. Amid much fanfare, in March of 1984 Canada Trust came up with the ultimate gimmick. Anyone taking out a new mortgage with them or renewing an existing one would automatically have a chance in a monthly draw. The prize: the right to wipe out up to $100,000 of a mortgage. It was generally accepted as the first mortgage lottery in all of North America, and Canada Trust was counting on doing six months' business — or $250 million — in three months.

The odds were estimated at one in 6,000. "That's much better than Lottario," Victor Harkness, administrative co-ordinator of residential mortgages, brightly told consumer columnist Ellen Roseman. But one week after the contest began, Edmonton police, acting on several telephone complaints, charged the company with running an illegal lottery. Guilty of lack of dignity, maybe, felt some of its competitors, but by May an Alberta provincial judge had cleared the trust company, and its officials were promising another go at it.

The unrepentant mortgage-burning was part of what the experts like to call the corporate culture. The phrase punctuates every conversation about Canada Trustco. It has provided a mould in which each member of the management team is shaped; it has provided consistency and, ironically, conformity in an organization that prides itself on non-conformity.

Reflecting on his outspoken criticism of the Greymac Affair, Lahn says: "You've got to get things up under the sunlight. I don't see it as unusual. It's part of the corporate culture of the company."

And although it is easy to focus on Lahn as the creator of that aggressive, irascible culture, he is in fact a creation of it, a good fit. Stock analyst Terry Shaunessey of Gardiner Watson sees the unusually able management of the company as organic. "Lahn has perpetuated the corporate culture, but Canada Trust is good because of all the people, not just Lahn. And this goes right back to J. Allyn Taylor. Peter Maurice could take over right now, if he had to.''

One manifestation of the corporate culture is the unique goals gimmick. Since the mid-1970s the company has published profit objectives and has asked shareholders to judge its performance against them. This has evolved into a formal set of nine objectives prominently displayed in annual reports, along with an evaluation of last year's performance. Much is made of this device by Canada Trust's senior managers, and the public laps it up. Soon after it was introduced, analysts of the financial industry began applauding the company's openness and frankness. It was great PR.

Frequently the company falls short of its objectives, but its failures somehow endear it to shareholders all the more.

In 1979 recently installed president Lahn told shareholders that net earnings for the first quarter of the year were down 41%. "I'm not very proud of the results. Most of it was due to the savings interest rate being up 2¾ percentage points over a year ago.''* All the same, the "candid" Lahn won over *Financial Times of Canada*'s Susan Goldenberg, who took a look at the company and its management for readers and noted, "Most rate its management in the top three of Canada's eight major trust firms and some go so far as to call it the best." She went on to document the emphasis on detailed planning, manifested in twice-yearly sessions with vice-presidents of assorted stripes and the heavy use of charts and loose-leaf binders. In such a way the folklore was nurtured.

In 1982 the company failed to meet five of its nine objectives, but a rapid drop in interest rates saved the bottom line. "I have no excuses," said Lahn to shareholders in February 1983. "If this would have been a report card, we would have failed." Nevertheless the extraordinary 44-page annual report

---

* In 1980, as interest rates climbed and stayed high to everyone's disbelief, Lahn explained the company's unaccustomed profit drop of 30%: "Grim consolation comes from being anything but alone in such a misforecast, which bespeaks that one should be aware of consensus prognostications." It was classic Lahn.

with management's nine key objectives displayed in four-colour charts won over the critics. For the sixth consecutive year, the publication was chosen by *The Financial Post* panel of experts as the best of the crop in the financial industry.

Julien Hutchinson, then financial institutions analyst at Wood Gundy Ltd., raved that Canada Trustco's managers are so "brilliant that the quality of its management excels that of Canada's top banks which are more than seven times its size."

The ambitious objectives the company sets have to do with return on equity, the spread between deposits and loans, growth in demand deposits, computerization of the branches, fee increases from trust business, reduction in loan arrears, improvement in real estate earnings, setting of the number of branch openings and the return on assets. Lahn likes to say of these difficult goals, which reflect his hard-driving philosophy: "If you achieve everything you have in the way of objectives, then people are going to sit down and say isn't that great, we did it all. No way do I ever want to see that happen." It is all part of the corporate creed: Canada Trust managers must embody ambition, independence and candour, and corporate goals are designed to challenge executives to achieve peak performance.

Despite setbacks, in the five years 1979-83 net earnings grew at a compound rate of 15% a year. During 1982 and 1983 Canada Trustco outperformed both the TSE 300 Industrial Index and the TSE Bank Index.

That accomplishment was the result of a two-pronged corporate strategy that included the aim of being the lowest-cost producer of deposits in Canada and the goal of diversification of its loan portfolio. Since 1980 the company has had the highest rate of growth of low-cost funds, which are primarily demand deposits (that is, personal savings and chequing accounts and corporate current accounts), of any major financial institution in Canada. That puts it in the best position to reduce interest rate spreads in order to gain market share with more competitive rates. Canada Trust's market share in demand deposits went from 4.34% in 1981 to 4.96% in 1983, while all the major banks except Toronto Dominion lost market share.

That's one reason why the banks don't like the trust company.

The reason for the rapid growth was the number of branches opened. In 1980 Canada Trust's demand deposits were $2.4 billion; by 1983 they had hit $4.1 billion. During the same time, the number of branches went from 173 to 197 while chartered banks closed almost 500 branches. By the end of 1985, the company will have opened 12 more, making the network, at 220 branches, the largest of any trust company.* Still, Lahn estimates that even apart from the gaping hole in Quebec, where there is only one branch, the company needs another 100 branches to generate the volume of business necessary to achieve the long-time goal of being the financial industry's lowest-cost producer. By bringing costs per unit down, the company will be able to afford to do what it must do in any case to stay competitive — spend enormous amounts of money on data processing and product development.

There is another reason for the banks' dislike of Canada Trust. In 1980 the company decided to tread on their turf by moving into corporate lending, thereby diversifying into much-needed variable interest rate assets. It quickly became the leading trust company in that area, with a portfolio of more than $2 billion.

The company concentrated on term loans to large corporations and Crown corporations, with the idea of absorbing a lot of lending dollars with a little staff and in that way being able to compete with the big banks on price.

Canada Trust does not have the attitude, said one company executive with a jab at the banks, that "prime is something set in heaven."

Unfortunately, the company made several large loans at the start of the recession, and they quickly fell apart, but the net

* The key to Canada Trust's branch expansion has been its cell approach: building on the strength it already had in some communities, determining the optimum number of branches in order to reach all segments of the market and then setting priorities to bring areas up to full strength. One such "cell" is southwestern Ontario, where in London and Kitchener Canada Trust has a market share of retail banking greater than any one of the chartered banks. The midwestern Ontario cell, which includes the Hamilton-Niagara region, is 90% completed, but the Toronto cell is seriously deficient, with fewer than half the right number of branches.

losses on the company's five-year adventure in corporate lending are actually a fraction of the additional income the new
area of business generated: about $7.5 million after tax com-
pared to almost $100 million in revenue, all of it earned at
floating rates when the prime went from 12% to 21%. That
blemish is, however, not the largest on the otherwise immacu-
late face of Canada Trust. The firm has labour troubles.

At King and Westminister streets in Cambridge, a small industrial city in southwestern Ontario, a straggle of three
strikers fought a losing battle outside a Canada Trust branch
for more than a year. Of the original 13 women who walked
out, a handful stayed to the end, the others having gone back
to work or quit. Financial institutions have not been hotbeds of
union organizing, one reason being the union strategy of organizing on a branch-by-branch basis, a slow and treacherous
method without remarkable success.

Two of Canada Trust's branches were unionized, however,
by the unlikely Canadian Union of United Brewery, Flour,
Cereal, Soft Drink and Distillery Workers. An August 1984
report in *The Globe and Mail* explained that the union was
invited into the Cambridge branch because "the strikers complained of arbitrary managers, an increase in work hours without more pay and petty work rules." But resentment among
employees had been festering since the year before, when the
company added a half-hour to the workday, with no corres-
ponding increase in pay. The move was one result of management's obsession with operating expenses.

After waiting until a month after they were legally entitled to
strike, the Cambridge workers had walked out in late March of
1984, focusing their discontent on the wage increases the company had offered. The increases averaged 4.1%, but, typically,
Canada Trust had given some of the workers higher raises and
others nothing at all.

Merv Lahn plays especially tough with pinko unions. He
hired hard-ball law firm Hickes Morley Hamilton Stewart
Storie to fight the union or, rather, to represent Canada Trust
at labour hearings.

Another union, the Union of Bank Employees, tried to organize Canada Trust workers in the London area, sending out 700 letters about an information session; the letters were addressed individually to workers but were delivered in bulk by courier rather than stamped and sent through the post office. Employees who turned out for the meeting said managers were taking the letters off their desks. Lahn replies, "We don't distribute junk mail of any kind."

But behind the newspaper reports was another story. Nelda Woods, who lived in Cambridge, had gone into her safety deposit box at the local Canada Trust branch to get some jewellery. A stick-pin was missing. To complicate matters, Woods just happened to be Lahn's sister.

Havoc ensued as accusations flew about the whereabouts of the pin. Tellers at the branch became angry at the cloud of suspicion hanging over them, while the manager of the branch grew increasingly unreasonable. Workers were asked by the manager to take lie detector tests.

Some time later the brooch was found, lying in a corner nearby. Whether it had been abandoned by a would-be thief or simply unearthed from where it had accidentally fallen, the air in the branch was poisoned. Representatives from the union were approached.

But Lahn will not draw a connection between the incident and union organizing. The branch manager was fired not, Lahn will admit, just for his handling of this particular incident but for larger problems in the management-subordinate relationship. "But whether or not it was my sister really doesn't have much to do with it in my view." Lahn's view of the whole episode is a familiar one of chief executives: "As a footnote to Cambridge, we never missed an hour of activity in the branch, business has never been better, all but four of the employees came back to work, most of them shortly thereafter."

As for the lie detector tests, "I don't think we ever had anyone take one." Pausing, he taps his fingers impatiently. Lahn, of course, blames the union for spreading this story, although he doesn't deny the story now and didn't deny it to the many reporters who called him about it. "If there were [lie detector tests], they'd be taken by the police, not us." Lahn's brother-in-law was a local police staff sargeant in Cambridge.

For a long time, journeying between London and Toronto, Lahn made a habit once a week of dropping into the Cambridge branch — which ironically was a former Waterloo Trust branch and still employed many people from his Waterloo days — "simply to give whatever morale boost" he could.

By early 1985 both the bargaining unit in Cambridge and the first unionized branch in St Catharines had applied for decertification. Battling union incursions, however, is a cakewalk compared to Lahn's war on number-one enemy ManuLife.

After the insurance company bought its 27%, Syd Jackson naturally applied for voting rights and board representation. An inkling of his reception might have been found in statements to the press after the increased stockholding was announced. One ManuLife executive brightly told *The Financial Post* of the possibilities for complementary business between the two financial companies. Lahn's immediate reaction: "There's no intention of joint dealings in the near, medium or long term."

The warmth of that statement soon found substance in action. The independent board members at Canada Trustco, that is, everyone except Mingay and Lahn, decided that the voting restriction to 10% of the company's total stock, regardless of the voter's actual shareholding, would stay. But they then threw up a more imaginative road-block. ManuLife, they contended, was a foreign-owned company, because the majority of its voting policyholders were outside Canada. The Loan Companies Act, under which Trustco operates, prevents non-resident shareholders who own more than 10% of a loan company from voting the shares. It would be up to the federal Department of Insurance to decide.

In the meantime the company invited one director representing ManuLife to be nominated for a board seat. Syd Jackson came aboard in 1983.

That year new road-blocks were tried. In May the company issued new shares, usually a signal of a need for more capital.

The investment community, however, suspected it had more to do with major shareholdings since the share and warrant issue diluted ManuLife's stake to 20%, forcing that company to build up again — which it did.

Jackson's first-hand encounters with Canada Trustco's management came as a surprise. He went into the boardroom curious to see whether such a strong personality as Lahn was surrounded by yes-men. To Jackson's astonishment he discovered the company's management had depth and quality extending through the ranks below Lahn.

This discovery does not make Jackson a charter member of the Merv Lahn fan club. "Merv is convinced he's right about the path he's taking the company," says Jackson, perhaps foreshadowing changes a ManuLife controlling shareholder would make. "It remains to be seen if he's not right, whether he listens to people telling him that."

Certainly, Jackson does not agree with popular opinion that the Canada Trustco board is both independently minded and active in monitoring management. "They run the show," he says of Lahn and Mingay.

But other directors, perhaps with less vested interests, disagree. "There's more involvement, more information and more detail given to the board than I expected," maintains Bernard Ghert, new to the Trustco board but a veteran chief executive of a single-shareholder-dominated company, Cadillac Fairview Corp. "It's not a question of entrenching management."

It can appear that way, however. For two and a half years Canada Trustco prevented ManuLife from voting even 10% of its shares. The life insurance company sent in proxies at the trust company's annual meeting held in February 1984, but they were disallowed. "We feel like orphans," said Thomas Di Giacomo, ManuLife's executive vice-president, at the time. "The whole thing is silly." Finally, in June 1984, the Liberal federal minister of state for finance, Roy MacLaren, confirmed ManuLife's status as a resident Canadian company.

The decision signalled the start of a frenzy of buying on the stock market. On the morning of August 15, six minutes after

the Toronto stock exchange opened, a 500,000-share block of
Canada Trustco stock changed hands at $26.75 a share. It was
a record, and much higher than the 1984 low of $19.25. The
block was crossed by McCarthy Securities, home of analyst
Robin Cornwell, who regularly and enthusiastically had talked
up Canada Trustco as an investment. The purchaser remained
a mystery, but the $13 million block amounted to 2.3% of the
company, and the rumour mill's scenario had the Belzbergs'
First City Financial Corp. making the purchase. It emerged several weeks later that the mystery buyer was ManuLife, lining
its lair, and the seller was long-time Trustco shareholder and
southwestern Ontario soul mate Waterloo-based Mutual Life
Insurance Co.

The unprecedented trading in Canada Trustco stock continued through the fall, and a new player appeared with a 6%
holding: George Mann's Unicorp Canada Corp. "We think it's
a good investment," pronounced Unicorp president James
Leech, echoing Jackson's words.

Then, in early December, several large blocks of shares and
warrants changed hands at the record price of $29.38 a share.
More significant, the shares were crossed by Gordon Capital
Corp., trusty advance troops for the Brascan acquisitors in
take-over wars, and new employer of Robin Cornwell.*

It seemed allies were falling into position in anticipation of
changes in federal government legislation concerning financial
companies.

Merv Lahn opened up his annual-meeting speech in late
February by telling a joke on himself. There was plenty of good
news for shareholders again. Profit was up 50% for 1984.

Then he let them have it. From his podium in London's
Holiday Inn City Centre ballroom, Lahn once again addressed
the subject of ownership restriction for trust companies, with
regard to upcoming legislative changes.

"The issue has become almost a purely political one due to
the sad fact that all major Canadian trust and loan companies,

---

* Robin Cornwell was a player in the fight to take over Canada Permanent in
1981. His engineering enabled ManuLife's 11% shareholding in the trust company
to turn a handsome profit, which it ploughed back into Canada Trustco shares.

apart from Canada Trustco, are now controlled directly, or indirectly, by dominant shareholders," he said, his voice hardening for the blow.

"With an election years away, a political decision might be swayed by the views of influential party backers and fund raisers rather than by sheer logic, common sense and widespread opinion. Several of the 'trust company owners' fall into the category of influential Conservative party backers and fund raisers. It would be naïve to expect an ownership restriction to be forthcoming." *

Lahn then told a discomfitted audience the obvious, that the company was clearly a "sitting duck," and went on to advertise for a white knight. In "Companions Wanted" style, Lahn outlined his corporate version of tall, dark and handsome. "The second best position to independence for shareholders, customers and employees would be control by a large, responsible Canadian-owned and -controlled company, itself with widespread ownership and no dominant shareholder," he said.

"Fewer and fewer acceptable suitors exist, but there are two or three which would be eminently suitable. Hopefully, if an unwanted and undesirable suitor makes a proposal, an integrous, independent, compatible and most of all wealthy white knight will immediately appear on the horizon."

The first company sidled up five months later. Genstar Corp. had been a friendly acquisitor of Canada Permanent Mortgage Corp. four years earlier, but it was not satisfied with the profits or the potential of that company and was anxious to spread its reach in financial services. In late April it began silently stockpiling shares of Canada Trustco. George Mann sold his 6% holding — half going to ManuLife, half to New York brokerage firm Morgan Stanley, which was acting on behalf of Genstar. Three days later, other Canada Trustco shareholders, including Mutual Life, sold a total of 1.1 million

---

* Lahn's pointed references were to H.N.R. (Hal) Jackman, controlling shareholder in National Victoria and Grey and Joe Clark's perpetual bankroll, and Edward and Peter Bronfman, emerging as tremendous Tory backroom manipulators with their minions' fingers on the Mulroney government's pulse.

shares through Gordon Capital. Gordon had begun its mission to acquire for Genstar a foothold in advance of an assault on Canada Trustco. Then in early August Genstar made its move. The Toronto Stock Exchange had become alarmed at the rapid rise in Canada Trustco's share price and slapped a halt on their trading. A day later, Genstar announced a $434 million cash bid that would increase its holding to 50.1%. Genstar was not in the habit of making hostile takeover bids, but a tight-lipped Lahn made it clear that he "was not the author of it."

A long hot summer battle loomed. No one expected Lahn to surrender easily, although it was not clear who would materialize as his publicly sought white knight.

Merv Lahn would go down with six-shooters blazing.

3

The Old Guard

Conrad Fetherstonhaugh Harrington stares at the 8-by-11-inch black-and-white photographs ranged along the boardroom wall. Here are the presidents of the past, the men who built the Royal Trust that he joined in 1945 and that pensioned him off 33 years later. He still has an office in the company's Montreal tower; he's still a director. But this tall, portly gent with kindly eyes and a colonel's moustache follows his own strict code of conduct. "I'm not trying to be one of those old guys in the flanks who all of a sudden comes alive and makes a nuisance of himself every now and again," he declares with spirit. "I tell people who come here and say 'Well, we've known you for 30 years Con' — I just say, 'Look, you've got to consider me as dead. I can tell you who to talk to, but I'm not picking sides and trying to throw my weight around with the younger men.' They're bearing the heat of the battle of the day and it's their time."

Over his left shoulder, on the far wall of the boardroom that used to house directors' meetings but now is a rarely used appendage of a regional office, are paintings of all the company chairmen, including Harrington, larger than life and in vivid colour.

The final image in the row of snapshots is of Mike Cornelissen, Royal's current president and a man who tailors his work to a pattern cut by the company's major shareholder. That is the company's style these days. To Harrington's mind, it's simply a different company from the one he ran. The strength of *his* Royal, the Royal that stood in Montreal's Place D'Armes for decades as a symbol of stolidity, the Royal of men who handed down the mantle of management from generation to generation, lay in the very fact that there was no one, strong owner. The managers could tend to clients' estates, first in Montreal and then across the country, the clients secure in the knowledge that the men running the show were thinking of what was best for all. Their Royal was founded with the idea of honourable patronage; the best families patronized them, and they, in turn, graciously bestowed good management and sound advice.

Lord Strathcona is the first man pictured, with the white beard and cold eyes common to turn-of-the-century photographic subjects. One of a string of CP Rail men among the founders, he was Bank of Montreal president and high commissioner to London at the same time; the trust company was a sideline. He is followed by a string of Bank of Montreal types, guarding over the company the bank founded in 1899 to coddle the estates of its valued clientele. (Until the twenties, it was a company bylaw that a majority of the directors be bank people.) But it isn't until 1943, with the appointment of Robert Jellett as president, that the real story of the Royal Trust men begins.

Jellett was "assigned by the Bank of Montreal to Royal Trust in 1902 as 'an unredeemable loan'" according to corporate legend and was actively involved with it until the early sixties. The innocuous notion of "nice" never arises when talking about Robert Jellett. He was strong, he was strict, he had his own views and ran a tight operation, introducing innovative adding machines and automatic addressing machines and expanding the company's public relations and advertising during the Depression while taking care always to scrutinize employee salaries.

Jellett prided himself on visiting the accounting department each Christmas Eve, with its bookkeepers perched on their high stools, green eye-shades to protect the vision and straw cuffs surrounding their white shirt-sleeves. He would sit there and personally write out Royal's final accounting statement of the year. It was a sign of character to be able to write a clear hand.

He also spent years collecting names as others collect stamps, a hobby with business benefits. Jellett's yellow filing cards were covered with details about the lives of prospective customers; the number of cards grew to the thousands.*

Montreal Trust, backed by the Royal Bank, and Royal, backed by Bank of Montreal, stood across the square from each other and represented the two sides of the business street. No one ever crossed from one to the other. But in the thirties, Montreal did something unthinkable in the trust business: it raided Royal's estate department for personnel. Montreal had decided its group wasn't up to scratch, and with the aid of a little extra cash it persuaded Royal employees to make the walk across the square. Jellett said for years that the company was well rid of *all* those people.

Jack Close, a scion of British country squiredom who spent decades at Royal despite left-wing leanings he flaunted in his younger years, tells how Jellett didn't like taking the word of reporters on what was building in Europe in the late thirties. He purchased a powerful radio receiver and called his executives together to listen to one of Adolf Hitler's famous worldwide broadcasts. They gathered in the boardroom, the cream of the Montreal business establishment, in anticipation of a revealing speech. They were stupefied when the broadcast began — in German! It had never occurred to this group of Anglophiles that Hitler would speak in his own mother tongue. The task of translating fell to Close, who sweated through the broadcast of Hitler's plans for a master race and his hatred of Jews. The capsulized radio translation at the end of the speech painted matters in much more restrained colours. Jellett was stunned by the difference.

* Robert Service "poet of the Yukon," was one prospect; tracked down in Monte Carlo, he gave Royal his Canadian assets to administer.

The war years brought operations to a standstill; there wasn't enough staff. Older members went off to work for government operations; younger ones enlisted. The year 1945 was restocking time. That's when Ross Clarkson hired Harrington, no callow youth and no ordinary choice. His parents played bridge with Jellett, and he had practised law before enlisting. He came back a major and determined not to return to a law practice he found dull. Clarkson hired him when Jellett was on the annual grand tour of the British office. Jellett blustered when he returned. Clarkson later told Harrington of Jellett's reaction. "He said 'What the hell are you doing, Clarkson, we can't afford people like that. Been to college, *TWO* degrees, I'm not going to pay for that sort of thing around here. That's not how we built this company.'" Harrington finds the recollection typical Jellett. "Long years later, when I was beginning to get my nose up through the crust, Mr Jellett then used to say, 'Oh, Harrington here is a very good young man, I had a lot to do with hiring him myself.'"

It was no wonder that the more sophisticated Clarkson, with 52 years at Royal, lived in Jellett's shadow for decades. But he assumed the presidency for five years starting in 1950, and his witty, winning ways earned him his employees' admiration and the fond moniker "Mr Trust Company." Clarkson presided over the company during a period of growth, including Royal's lobbying for entry into the pension fund business. He enjoyed heralding the company's national stature.

Royal was a national company, but each branch was quite autonomous. Out in Victoria, for example, the branch used to be called "Winslow's Trust," after a long-time branch manager. In Quebec City, first Rene de Lery in the twenties and then his son Charles in the fifties ran the branch, dealing with many of the same customers. In the Toronto branch of the 1950s there was a very old-time, formal tenor to affairs. The branch secretary sat at a desk at the entrance, and each employee received his keen scrutiny upon signing in. If his or her dress was not suitable, the employee was told so in no uncertain terms. There were retired Bank of Montreal managers who would arrive daily, dressed to the hilt, to sit in the vault and carefully clip dividend coupons with Exacto knives. At lunch they were off to their clubs; there was no hurry in this backwater of the business.

Harrington started off in Montreal at a desk in the estates department, a clerk with two other beginners and a benign trainer with the handle Cuthbert Pashley. There was one telephone, and the newcomers were given files to read. Each file contained one estate. Pashley said, "You read the files, then someday you may run your own file if you make out well." Harrington felt he was inhabiting a Dickens novel as he watched the porters set out the blotting paper and fill the ink-wells nightly; he retreated to the wash-room when he had need of a smoke. For a while he thought of leaving, but eventually he decided he did have all the right credentials to rise to the top. He was, after all, a product of the Westmount Gang, "the warp and the woof of Montreal as it then was." Grandfather Fetherstonhaugh — on his mother's side — was one of the largest dry-goods wholesalers in Canada, his warehouse at the bottom of the hill. He was a very stout member of the strict protestant sect the Plymouth Brethren.* Great-grandfather Dawson — on his father's side — had been principal of McGill. He also led a revolt in the local Presbyterian church when there was a push to allow organ music at services. These connections made Harrington a perfect recruit for Royal, which had always split with Montreal Trust the business of the Anglo business class. Royal's own stock had a special place in the mind of the investment community. It was "book stock," stock provided by the company rather than openly traded. It was a classy addition to any portfolio, says one old-timer. Potential buyers wrote Royal a letter saying they had done or planned to do business there and would like to own stock. The request — and the one doing the requesting — would be carefully checked.

A former employee describes three lists: A, B and C. If

* A fellow Plymouth brother was A.J. Nesbitt, founder of stockbroker Nesbitt Thomson. A.J. conducted Fetherstonhaugh's funeral. But when Harrington arrived at Royal, he found the brokerage firm's issues weren't all thought up to snuff. "The first thing that was done when any estate was brought in . . . was to see if there were any issues underwritten by Nesbitt Thomson."

Royal liked you, the writer, as much as you liked the company, "you probably would get stock," which was carefully apportioned to those who could bring business back to Royal. "If you were perhaps up and coming and you didn't rate getting stock because of your lack of maturity, you'd be on the B list — which meant that perhaps in time you'd get on the A list. And of course, the C list means those that were undesirable, and they stayed on the C list."

Company employees could add a name to the list only if they were very senior themselves. If an employee actually received "five or 10 shares," says Harrington, "you were considered one of the most favoured people in the company." And stockholders didn't want to have it taken away from them — a right the company used, regularly scanning the ownership lists for holdings whose owners weren't sending business Royal's way. "Just suppose it was the widow of some wealthy old man, who was in an institution incapable, deaf and dumb," he explains. "But you had to use a little common sense and humanity because some people had been told by their husbands on their deathbed, 'Never sell your Royal Trust or your Bank of Montreal stock. Never sell.'"

The stock's value was decided by the company at each annual meeting, usually a three-minute affair followed by a posh luncheon at the St James Club in Montreal.

The working conditions were most unappetizing. In Toronto, Wallis King, a trust officer and head of the local staff association in the late fifties, lobbied to have the notice boards removed from the wash-rooms so that men and women could read one another's messages. The two sexes never mixed. The women were in the stock transfer and bond departments, their desks in neat rows with a martinet at the front supervising as they passed certificates down the line, one filling in a particular portion, the next checking her work, the third filling in, the fourth checking, until the certificate reached the end of the line, complete and accurate.

The staff's private lives were company business. For decades management trainees and clerks couldn't marry until they reached a certain salary. In one instance, when a Western branch employee earning less than $150 monthly broke the rule, his widowed mother had to sign an agreement to supplement his income.

Certain intangibles were definite plusses. A Toronto employee was asked on joining in the late fifties if he was a Mason. "I didn't know what it was, and I said, 'No, I'm an Anglican.'" That, of course, was most acceptable as well. It was no wonder that as years went by the company earned the fond nickname "The Rusty Trust."

Even under Clarkson and his successor Jack Pembroke, who moved up to chairman in 1963, the company was still moving in the old world of estate management. It was developing the pension fund business. In February 1956 Royal adapted U.S. ideas and burst on the Canadian investment community with a series of "classified investment funds" — one for investments in government bonds, one for corporate bonds and preferred shares and one for common stocks. Corporate pension funds with less than $300,000 in assets suddenly had a lot more to choose from with this new "pooling" approach. But it still served an exclusive clientele. It was president John (Jack) Wells who brought the company into the new world of asset management for the general public in 1963.

"Wells was the Pope John of Royal Trust," says former vice-president of finance Richard Thurston (Dick) La Prairie in his soft voice. "He's the one who opened the windows." La Prairie, who was 25 years at Royal before he quit in mid-1981, was a Wells protégé. He can wear a checked jacket, striped shirt and paisley tie with a dandy's sense of style and could be likened to a friendly, gentle eagle.

La Prairie's memory is sharp. Wells brought him in as a hatchet man of sorts to set up an internal audit system in Toronto and then shake up company organization with an efficiency study. He ended up as one of the men who made Royal move in the seventies.

Wells was a finance man who rose from the investment side of the company, and he made that route fashionable. Ken White, a broker at A.E. Ames Ltd., was brought in through that door and became one of Wells's inner circle. Wells liked to gather a few bright minds around him and brainstorm about the company's future. He didn't include by this time general manager Harrington.

The two men represented diverging views of how to run the company, what was important to a trust operation. Wells was a finance buff. But he liked his home and his family and headed out to Pointe Claire each evening, his business done. He didn't see any reason to socialize with the business community.

Harrington enjoyed making Royal a name by his presence in the right drawing rooms. It was a skill he was born to; it was a skill he used to build his end of company operations, both in Montreal and in Toronto. As head of the 1958 United Appeal campaign in Toronto, he combined forces with E.P. Taylor, Eric Phillips and the McCutcheons to raise more money than any other group in the country.

Royal needed this type of profile in a city in which its presence was only as a branch, with the branch manager competing against presidents and old-line Toronto directors and advisory boards. Harrington once counted 240 people associated with trust companies headquartered there; he had 8 or 10 on his local advisory board to help him out. But the Toronto companies, such as Toronto General Trusts and Canada Permanent Mortgage, were still sluggish. Harrington made his mark in Toronto, returning to head office after 11 years, in 1963, as a vice-president and board director.

It wasn't the type of skill Wells respected, but Harrington still had his own supporters. When Wells became president in 1963, after exerting his power as general manager during the fifties, he tried to oust Harrington, but he didn't succeed. There was bile between the two. But when Wells had his first heart attack, Harrington carried the company through the crisis. Wells died in 1966, a heart attack wiping out his recovery from a stroke in 1965. Harrington was elevated to the presidency, and for years he and Ken White ruled in tandem while Pembroke continued to occupy the chairman's seat.

Harrington had set up the business development department

after the war. It was basically the old-boy corporate network spinning off business. Some young trust officers hustled group business — one signed up 500 pilots in a year by telling tales of what happened when one died without a will — but this was not the usual style. Later, as an executive during the late fifties, Harrington would open doors for pension fund staff by calling on his contacts.

Because of the successes of independent pension fund and investment operations, the trust industry began losing people in the late fifties and early sixties. Salaries, while higher than the banks', were still low. In 1958 a trust officer starting off might make $4,200. In the early sixties there was an exodus to jobs in the U.S. for triple the cash. Others simply went into business for themselves — and tried to take their accounts with them. At Royal, dress codes crumbled and salaries climbed as the company competed to keep staff from leaving the industry or jumping to a fancier title at one of the new, "pseudo-trust companies," which hired people to skim the cream from the "guaranteed account" or intermediary business with a two-man money market desk.

Royal had to move into the deposit business, one it had been avoiding but could no longer ignore. In 1963 it opened its vaults to customers' deposits, with the Toronto King Street branch as the testing ground. But although it was in the new business, the old attitudes lingered. An employee of that era says, "We never saw our careers developing through the savings operation."

There were good reasons for Royal's clique to have resisted the move into deposit business; by becoming a bank, they were severing their umbilical cord with Bank of Montreal. Pete Mulholland at the bank sent around a message in the early sixties: Royal's information booklets couldn't be handed out at bank branches anymore; the bank had other trust clients to think about as well.* Life became more competitive with the slew of

---

* The cordial backscratching included $50 Christmas presents to bank branch managers for their referral business, up until the seventies.

new, small but aggressive intermediary companies with trust licences. But Royal — like the other big companies — was still self-centred. "The attitude at the Royal Trust," says Wallis King, "was that these companies existed at our pleasure. We could put them out of business if we wanted to."

Royal adapted the old rules in the new business. Harrington frequented the clubs — he belonged to eight, among them Montreal's Mount Royal and St James and Toronto's York — and he and chairman Jack Pembroke successfully fought a federal rule change outlawing clubs as a tax write-off. Of course, no one ever did any business there overtly, but a casual inquiry about interest rates could result in a $6 million deposit later that day.

Other trust companies fell prey to the increased competition. Toronto General and Canada Permanent merged in 1961. And Montreal Trust, Royal's decades-long competitor, was left in the dust, falling increasingly behind in asset growth and profitability. Pundits blame management incompetence, well-meaning but definitely not impressive men. In the late fifties a couple of senior officers who indulged in four-hour lunches made a few mistakes about real estate deals. "There was no question of there being theft or robbery or fraud, but there was bad judgment," says one observer. "You don't need many of those to have people running like you have the pestilence."

Paul Desmarais bought a controlling shareholding in Montreal Trust from Canadian Pacific in 1967. Harrington describes him as "a stick-with-it fellow. . . . He came to see me once, he just dropped in and he said, 'I don't understand how you can make money in this damn trust company business.' I said, 'Well, that's because you don't know how. If you really are getting desperate, Paul, go away and think about it and then come back, we'll sit down together and we might take you over.'" Desmarais, used to sitting on the other side of the table, didn't return.

Royal entered the real estate brokerage business in the sixties. Before this, real estate sales and property management had been a poor sister to estate operations. The company bought its first brokerage firm in 1961 and purchased seven more between 1964 and 1970, including Toronto's Chambers & Meredith, a $5 million purchase. That one didn't pay — and it seemed Royal learned a lesson about negotiating with real estate salesmen. One of the partners immediately took advantage of the fact that the purchase didn't bar him from setting up shop again, and opened an office across the street from the largest branch.

But a decade later Royal was again taken to the cleaners, this time on a much bigger deal and by a much bigger operator.

The seventies was a decade of big buys, big deals, big plans. The first play was the 1972 purchase of International Bank of Miami, which heralded a strategic move into Florida. The company had looked at possibilities in Texas, New York, Illinois and California but had chosen Florida. In Florida Canadian snowbirds would recognize the name, and from there Royal could expand its South American operations. The company could also get in on the ground floor of legislative changes allowing branch banking in the financially backward state. Royal squeezed in before the state outlawed out-of-state ownership of banking and was "grandfathered" in the legislation. In 1975 it spent another $16 million on six more banks purchased for twice their book value, and its total capital commitment there by 1978 was almost $40 million. The returns weren't high as the decade waned. The linchpin manager had died of a heart attack and wasn't adequately replaced when management tried to handle problems from Toronto. And for all the accountants' scrutiny before the fact, some of the purchases were in much worse shape than Royal had thought.

Royal's expansion from the fifties on was dependent on its computer capacity. In 1974 it secured its own system's needs and prepared to cash in on the demands of others by buying 94% of Toronto-based Computel Systems Ltd.

Bob Horwood, Computel's founder and president, approached the company. Ken White, then still Harrington's second, decided he liked the deal and wanted Horwood to remain as manager — on certain conditions. La Prairie says White "asked me two things — get Horwood's shares, and get his beard shaved off." The shares were no problem, but La Prairie wasn't prepared to ask anyone to shave off a beard. "I said, 'There's two people you'd never hire, George the Fifth and Jesus Christ.'"

The purchases surprised and excited the financial community. The next one was a shocker. In July 1976 Ed Daughney, now president of First City Trust, had convinced his then boss George Mann that he should sell his troubled United Trust. White saw the advantages of doubling Royal's savings branches to 92 and increasing its real estate brokerage branches by one-third, to 142. Deposits would pour in with the added clout a Royal Trust sign would have in those locations. He was right about that: deposits doubled in a year and a half, and Royal did gain offices in Toronto and 10 new Ontario centres that would have cost $200,000 each to set up from scratch.

But Royal ended up closing 20 of the real estate branches and 12 of the savings offices. Royal paid Mann $23.8 million in company shares, which meant it paid twice the value of United on its own books — and the company's value was a matter of dispute. Cynics say the price was about three times the company's worth. The next year Royal made only a 2% return on its investment. In the long term everyone agreed: George Mann got the better of that deal. Arthur Mingay at Canada Trust, who talked with United about a sale, let Ken White know exactly what he thought. He sent along a present with a little note: "Here's a package of marbles because I think you've lost yours."*

Mann had become the second largest shareholder of Royal, ranking behind only McGill University, which was a founding shareholder and had seen its holding swell through legacies from the Montreal elite. He was not, however, allowed on the board. The damage done by taking his company but refusing to acknowledge his right to representation would rebound on

* This is particularly amusing since Canada Trust paid almost two and a half times its book value for Lincoln Trust at about the same time. Of course, Lincoln was not on the ropes.

management when he decided to sell those shares four years later.

The same year it bought United, Royal management reorganized its corporate structure to fit the realities of the new, separatist Quebec. It formed both a federal holding company and a federal trust company. The change was complicated and required a continual shuffling of paper back and forth — four years later board meetings were still sorting out which company should hold certain assets. The flip-flop "took the steam out of the organization," says La Prairie.

The stock price almost halved between mid-1976 and early 1978, but trust company analyst Robin Cornwell believed in Ken White's team in those days. He wrote in an April 1978 report for since-merged securities broker Pitfield Mackay Ross Ltd. that although earnings had been below average in the two preceding years, Royal had good potential if it pulled in its horns and simply enjoyed the benefits of its expanded savings branches, brokerage operations and Florida banking network, used its existing capital to make 15% more mortgage loans each year and collected more deposits. That potential could sky-rocket if Royal further expanded its capital base by issuing preference shares as other trust companies had been doing.

Others thought management was living in a cloistered world. After the move to Toronto in the mid-seventies, Royal became just another branch on the street corner rather than an integral part of the small Montreal Anglo business establishment. It couldn't compete in the ordinary hustle of the market-place.

White was every bit as much a member of the old school as Harrington. But his personality led him to magnify incidents and, supersensitive, he also magnified the problems of being a manager in charge of a huge trust company. The company had always been the men who ran it. But now the man who ran it thought he was the company. White had been a good manager while rising through the ranks, and his aggressive approach had stood him well. Now, as chief executive, aggressive became domineering, and people were afraid to stand up to him — or even to bounce an idea off him, in case he didn't like it.

He thought Trudeau a communist, Ottawa run by the French — and once blustered that he would beat up a young CBC reporter who did two stories on the company's head office shift. "His idea of public relations," says his long-time aide, "was that when he said something it was right and should be reported."

Harrington stepped aside as chairman in 1978, at 65. "I wasn't going to block anybody." When White turned 65 in 1979, he arranged for the board to change the mandatory retirement provision in his case. He brought up his own people, tapping about half a dozen as worth considering for the succession. He liked, according to one observer, to see how people stood up to having to jockey for position. But he took four years to establish a successor.

The coterie dwindled as, one by one, its members were discarded, left or died. Finally, only one little Indian remained, and John Scholes assumed the duties of right-hand man. He wasn't actually appointed president until 1981, but as executive vice-president he was around whenever White initiated an idea or plotted a course of action. Others were in senior management roles, but Scholes had been annointed well before La Prairie left in December 1980 to start a business of his own. Scholes, like White and Wells, had risen through the investment side. He was a devoted family man; that was his favourite topic of conversation. But he was independently wealthy, and there was a feeling that he didn't want the top job badly enough.

By the end of the seventies, White, although still top dog and hanging on to power, liked to enjoy his Florida condominium and his summer home in rural Quebec. Scholes was a good aide de camp, and White was comfortable with his role in the company. White is said to have been obsessed with quarterly results, to make sure that he was staying on top of fast-growing Canada Trust, that Royal was still number one. Stories abound about the continual development of a five-year plan, known as the "five-minute plan"; drafts went promptly into the filing system, and the five-year strategy changed every five minutes.

Bay Street will now say the company, which was being managed by committee and had stopped being aggressive, was a sitting duck. But most were shocked when, in August 1980, Royal was threatened with a take-over. The bid failed, but it led to changes that would eventually sweep out the old guard and forever alter the company and the industry.

4

The
Outsiders

The attack on Royal Trust came from a man who was definitely on the C list. NQOS, as they would say at the clubs — Not Quite Our Sort.

Yet Robert Campeau is a man with flair, a builder around whom others build legends. His house-by-house beginnings in suburban Ottawa, his extremely profitable office-leasing contracts with the federal government, his early-1970s alliance with Power Corp.'s Paul Desmarais and sudden buy-back of his company with shekels borrowed from Switzerland, his sumptuous suite with a particularly lavish bathroom in the Harbour Castle Hilton Hotel on the Toronto waterfront — all the bits and pieces of the life he had constructed by mid-1980 took on a special glow when he was in the room. Campeau can say nothing and dominate a conversation. So it's no small wonder that the one story he chose to tell — repeatedly — to reporters and regulators during and immediately after his run at Royal Trust itself became a legend.

Campeau's version of the meeting between the smiling upstart Franco-Ontarian contractor and White, the thin-skinned trust company patriarch, runs this way: Campeau had been trying to arrange a meeting for four or five days. White put him off, saying they could meet when he arrived in Montreal the next Friday. But Campeau wasn't to be put off: he called from the Sherbrooke airport at 7 A.M. on Wednesday, August 27, to announce his imminent arrival at White's summer hideaway outside Bromont, Quebec. White grudgingly acquiesced. They sat on the lawn and parleyed about the weather in the rolling hills of the Eastern Townships for a quarter of an hour.

Then Campeau announced his plan for a take-over of Royal, the $413 million financing being provided by the Bank of Nova Scotia. He wasn't interested in the daily operations of the company, most definitely not in the fiduciary side and not even in mortgage operations. He would leave them be. But he wanted two or three board members. "And we wanted to make a contribution towards the development of the real estate arm of Royal Trust," Campeau said later. "I told Mr White, 'This is the contribution that we feel we can make. You are administering pension funds which have a desire to get themselves in real estate, and this would be a very good opportunity [for a developer].'"

Campeau knew White was old enough to want to retire when his time came, he told the chieftain in his pleasant, arrogant way. The purchase of George Mann's shares, held in his new company, Unicorp Canada Corp., he added, was already arranged.

By this point White's thin skin was rubbed raw. "I don't see why you don't go and take over something else," Campeau was told. "Really, this is my company." Campeau was quick to reply. "I said, 'Well, it may be your company, but we are making an offer to the shareholders. I don't see where this is going to disrupt your role in the corporation whatsoever.'" At that, White began to rave. According to Campeau, he declared it would certainly affect his role at Royal Trust. He would quit. "'And I really don't like you, Campeau, and I don't like Paul Desmarais and I don't like Conrad Black and I don't like Edgar Bronsman [sic]. I don't like all these guys making bids for public corporations and I wish to Hell you would stay where you are and don't bother us. This is really going to complicate

the Bank Act and it is really not helping the French Canadian
and English Canadian situation.'

"'What do you mean by that?' I said, 'Our money is money,
isn't it?'" White ended his tirade by saying Campeau should
"pull this bid. . . . I'm going to call my friends and I am going
to lock up 51% of this stock before you can turn around. . . .
You may think or you may tell me that money talks and really,
in the end, shareholders are going to make up their minds, but
I'm telling you that I have got ways to persuade these friends of
mine. I will lock up more than 51% of the stock before you
have the time to turn around.'" White then showed Campeau
off the property.

This was the first notice White had had of the bid. Interestingly, he had not received a pleasant warning phone call
from Bill Mulholland, chairman of the Bank of Montreal.
Campeau had let him know about the bid the night before, but
he had done nothing to protect what had once been a key for-
tification in the bank's financial fiefdom. He had not warned
management; he had not alerted the round table of friends to
whom White would reach out for aid in his jousting match with
the future. Mulholland obviously viewed the bank and the trust
company from a more independent stance than had traditionally been assumed.

The announcement of the bid was made at noon. An acquisitor like Campeau, an entrepreneur accustomed to running
his own shop, prefers to go for 100% or close to it — especially
if he intends to make drastic changes, such as forcing a merger
or wholesale shake-up. But not every take-over depends on the
winning of total ownership. Some strategists have adopted the
techniques of a Conrad Black or a Bud McDougald and need
as little as 20% on their own or with allies to exert sufficient
influence.

Shock that Campeau would attempt such a thing quickly
turned to righteous anger down the line as White gathered his
army to defeat the upstart. After visiting Mulholland he called
Royal's investment broker, Austin Taylor of McLeod Young
Weir (MYW). Taylor was perfect for the role of champion of

Royal; he was one of the loyal shareholders whom Harrington and his predecessors had cherished for so long. Later, appearing before the Ontario Securities Commission (OSC), the elephantine Taylor emitted a surprisingly personal rivulet of thought: "I speak with a degree of feeling. . . . My father was a very able man and he saw fit to give me very little advice in my life, much to my detriment. . . . But one of the pieces of advice he did give me, at one time he said, 'Firpo' — which happens to be my nickname — 'Firpo, never sell your Royal Trust shares.'" Taylor's misty eloquence prompted OSC chairman Henry Knowles to make the crafty reply: "I won't ask you to tender."

Taylor drew up a list of companies that might gang together to make a group counter-bid for Royal. It was a bizarre mix of Crown corporations, pension funds, management-controlled institutions and very individualistic entrepreneurs, both old money and new. Their common currency was the power to buy quickly.*

He was to be well paid for his efforts during the next month: $100,000 for his firm and the same for Dominion Securities and Nesbitt Thomson, the other two brokers drafted. As well, MYW earned $100,000 for an official opinion that Campeau's bid was "financially inadequate," and made money trading 70% of the shares that changed hands in the next few weeks.

When White arrived at head office the group therapy sessions began. White chaired 10 executive committee or full directors' meetings in the three weeks between his visit from Campeau and the failure of the initial bid for 100% of the stock; one the day after that bid was raised from $21 to $23 for common, $29.93 to $32.97 for preferred shares; and a final one October 3 to confirm that the vanquished Campeau was withdrawing from the field. There was always a phalanx of senior

---

* Taylor's "Plan A" list included every provincial pension fund, 15 insurance companies, three of the Big Five banks and three other trust companies — Canada Trust, Canada Permanent Trust and Crédit Foncier. There were 27 corporations and corporate pension funds. Thirteen individuals were listed, including First City Trust's Sam Belzberg and NorthWest Trust's Dr Charles Allard.

and middle management to provide answers, run errands, hear the board's thoughts on their troop movements. Scholes, La Prairie, vice-presidents John Matthews, Ewart Wickens, Roger Otley and others worked in concert, long-time internal divisions ignored. They collected names, they drew up lists, they set down reasonable explanations for their actions and poked holes in the reasonable explanations provided by the enemy.

At the August 28 executive committee meeting, chaired by White, a list was passed around of principal shareholders. It revealed that this "widely held" company, like most, was controlled by a small group of commercial stockholders. Matters had changed mightily since it first listed its stock. Twenty-five shareholders now held 41% of Royal's common shares. The Quebec government, in the form of its pension fund Caisse de dépôt et placement du Quebec, had 1.29 million, and it also headed the list of top 10 preferred shareholders, with 312,500 Series A shares. So much for White's worries about dividing the French and English communities of Montreal.

The Campeau press release was tabled, and a draft of Royal's proposed message to shareholders was approved. And White, ever nervous of the media, read aloud the press announcement he would be making later that day.

The committee agreed to recommend to the directors that Royal — under White's leadership — do everything it could to stop the take-over.

At times they didn't have to lift a finger. Robin Denman, the investment manager at Commercial Union Insurance — where White was chairman of the board and head of the investment committee — was "appalled" by the bid and after talking to Royal vice-president Roger Otley urged president Allan Saville to support a share purchase. Denman chewed over the problem all weekend. It sounded as if the bid could be a close call; if he doubled the company's holding to 1%, that could be the stopper. On Tuesday, September 2, he called White and told him of the plan. White immediately held up his hands. He couldn't comment. Denman should do what he thought best. Denman did just that, buying through MYW and making a space in the investment portfolio by selling Commercial Union's holding of Bank of Nova Scotia stock. After all, Scotiabank was funding Campeau.

Credit Foncier's Robert Gratton (to be Montreal Trust's Robert Gratton a few years later) called MYW's Montreal office August 28, and Gratton and White, flanked by executives, met in Toronto that evening to discuss a share purchase. But Credit Foncier didn't buy, because the financing wasn't available. It wasn't for lack of trying by Royal staff. Vice-president Ewart Wickens tried to arrange for TD to provide financing. He even said Royal would buy some of the bank's equity holdings, increasing its liquidity and enabling it to fund purchases of Royal stock. (He didn't say how this eager-beaver move, one step away from Royal financing stock purchases itself, would affect his own company's books.) Wickens also approached the Montreal Bronfmans' Cemp Investments Ltd. about providing financing for purchases. These were the very folks White had castigated in his diatribe to Campeau.

Taylor tried Cemp as well, calling Harold Borts, a company executive, at his Montreal home that first Sunday, August 31. Like Credit Foncier and the others, Borts and the Cemp group smelled market profits from an escalating take-over fight. Cemp was to closely follow the play.

Taylor also called Toronto Dominion president Dick Thomson at home and, in a Sunday evening meeting, explained Plan A. TD wasn't enthused about it, but Thomson decided to buy stock. White would come to feel thankful to Thomson, and this would make the banker uncomfortable. He wasn't buying as a favour but because he thought there was a good chance the stock — and the company — had potential. He also wasn't necessarily against developers entering the business. He called client Donald Love of Edmonton-based Oxford Group Ltd. and took a sounding of the industry: would they all be making bids on trust companies? It made sense, from the perspective of marketing properties to pension funds, a growing business in real estate. He thought Campeau's idea would make "a good marriage." Love agreed, worriedly. He didn't like to see potential financing sources cut off like that. But it "triggered my imagination," Love said later. He bought a block of 10% of Royal's shares as well and visited White later in the month to let him know that he was hoping a business relationship would flower.

The first full directors' meeting was called by telex the day Campeau visited White and was moved up twice — each time by telex. It was held the Tuesday after Labour Day at 2 P.M. Twenty directors and three honorary directors quickly quit the cottage and the sun for their corporate roles; they understood the urgency. It was brought home again with a request for any telephone numbers and addresses at which they could be reached during the next few, crucial weeks. Each director found a loose-leaf folder of papers and newspaper clippings at his seat.

This was Scholes's first meeting as a director; he had been appointed at the July 15 meeting, when there was not a hint that the next time the group gathered they would be defending the company's independence. But while it was Scholes's maiden voyage, White was clearly at the helm. He told *his* version of the Campeau meeting and the events that had followed. Then he outlined the action plan. Three law firms had been speedily retained: Faskens and Calvin in Toronto; Phillip Vineberg in Montreal; Fried, Frank, Harris, Shriver & Jacobson in New York.

The legal beagles thought they had a couple of good points for a court fight. Campeau had active developments in the U.S., which meant that the banking authorities wouldn't allow him to take over the Florida operations. And the arrangement with George Mann's Unicorp might be seen as a sweetheart deal that would be subject to a follow-up offer.

After a long debate, one worried director asked if they had to take action; yes, answered R.N. Robertson from Faskens, a directors' circular must be issued and it must point out deficiencies in the bid. That was the law. They could decide to make a recommendation and would be protected if they did that in good faith and after due diligence.

The directors, after this first hour of bandying about facts and fears, were in complete agreement. The actions that White had already been taking for six days were certainly the right ones. The company must be saved.

Once that inevitable conclusion was reached, White's gang could tell the directors what it had already been doing to meet the corporate goal officially set only minutes before. Scholes said MYW's preliminary work revealed, not surprisingly, that Campeau's offer was substantially lower than the company's real worth. Next, he reported that some shareholders were already apparently backing up Royal by buying shares in the market. And he told them that Royal and Bank of Montreal were hatching a plan — which would be presented to them later — that was "dependent on obtaining prior clearances from certain Canadian and U.S. regulatory authorities with whom the bank is meeting today." (It was a complicated purchase of a bank subsidiary, which would have allowed Royal to issue more shares to the bank, thus making Campeau's work harder. But Mulholland decided against it; it was legal, but it violated "the spirit of the law.")

Scholes also mentioned Taylor's action plan for a counter-bid, but he didn't give any details. He didn't have a chance, with White interrupting him to announce that MYW and Dominion Securities had picked up 86% of a 1.9 million block of shares that had just crossed the Toronto Stock Exchange floor.

White and Scholes, immersed in the fray, were way ahead of the directors in their appreciation of the issues. The directors were still nonplussed by the very idea of a single-bidder take-over. They were still talking about Campeau's audacity and their fiduciary responsibilities and were even worried that there might be a run on Royal branches. They agreed that it would be desirable to warn the governor of the Bank of Canada of the possibility.

White boasted that he expected a number of clients to make public statements of support, "notably Stelco and Molson's." None was ever forthcoming. But some of the private comments made by depositors and other clients and passed on by the local branches for the directors' edification are incredible in retrospect. London, Kingston, Windsor, St Catharines, Hamilton all reported in: more "sophisticated" customers were worried about putting money in, others thought the whole thing a lark. There were scurrilous comments aplenty: from people who had lived in Ottawa and didn't like Campeau; from a couple of clients who had been associated with him in deals and who didn't have "much use for the man." One page of this material, labelled "Testimonial of Support," told of a Montreal lawyer named Frank Common who was not a shareholder and was in fact a friend of Campeau's — but didn't think he should be able to buy Royal. "He suggests that in addition to any consideration of money we should use the argument that Royal Trust is in a position of Trust [sic] in respect of confidential information regarding its personal and corporate clients and that it would be wrong for this private information to fall into the hands of a single shareholder." This flotsam was actually tabled for the consideration of the board.

White also distributed a list of the major shareholders who were onside. Stelco — whose president was a director — had assured him it would move its account if Campeau were successful. An executive at Canada Trust, not a shareholder, had called him to say (naturally enough) that he thought it terrible and ask what he could do to help. Guardian Insurance was unhappy with Campeau. Syd Jackson from ManuLife had frozen the company's shares and would let White know if any of the segregated accounts sold. The first thing Thomas Galt at Sun Life did when he heard of the bid was to call his friend Jackson for *his* reaction. Standard Life was horrified. Shell Canada called to say it would move its business if Campeau won. In company after company the investment manager would not be making any decisions about this sacred cow stock. More significantly, Sun Life was buying $10 million more to help. McGill University had frozen its holdings and wasn't tendering. Old families showed their stuff. Bank of Nova Scotia might be funding Campeau, but director Lord Ivey, when phoned by Harrington, was also appalled that the "finest trust company in the world," one used by his family for 50 years, could be so put upon.

It was after this that a second resolution was passed: senior management was authorized by the board to take any action necessary to fight the offer on legal grounds. Shortly afterward the meeting broke up, although it was never officially adjourned and was continued three days later, on Friday at 2 P.M.

By then other events were falling into place. Independent counsel had been retained to advise on what to do about trust account stock. The court battles were ready to be launched.

Roger Otley had the floor that Friday. He started his talk on the trust accounts by emphasizing that since 1967 the company had never recommended the purchase or sale of Royal stock. It was there because people had it there forever. About 14% of Royal's stock was in trust company accounts. Half of that was in safe custody accounts; in other words, Royal was only the caretaker, and the owner would be making his own decisions. Another 20% was in accounts where Royal was a co-trustee, and the other trustee would be asked to make the choice. Royal was sole executor of 12% of the shares within its corporate vaults. In those cases it might sell some of the stock.*

Taylor arrived, hot-shot securities law partners Howard Beck and Garfield Emerson in tow, to explain his firm's opinion that the bid was financially inadequate. He wasn't providing an exact estimate of what the company was really worth; it was perfectly acceptable and strategically smarter not to. Yes, he told one shareholder, Royal was on his firm's "buy" list for shareholders, with a value of well over $21. The trio departed.

The directors pored over the circular that would be mailed that weekend; La Prairie walked in to say that both it and Taylor's opinion looked fine to him. The circular had their

---

* It ended up selling 25% of the stock — and there were complaints about the sales from loyal clients who didn't want the bid to succeed. Very few who had the choice tendered.

stamp of approval — and once again the meeting was suspended, this time until Monday at 2 P.M. With each suspension the list of directors present dropped; by Monday there were nine, with two honorary directors hanging in as well. The directors' circulars had been mailed, the court writs were being scheduled and a hearing was set for Thursday.

When the executive committee met again the next Thursday, there would be more meaty matters to chew on. Campeau had been calling Mulholland at the Bank of Montreal to sound him out about the bid, and Mulholland willingly donned the robes of *éminence grise*. The bank president told the developer in one meeting that he agreed with others: Royal shouldn't be in one person's pocket. But, he said, it wasn't the Westmount Gang against French Canada. If he would modify his position a bit, he would find a lot of people backing off and letting him own part of the trust company. At another meeting, which Mulholland managed by slipping out of an afternoon meeting to talk to Campeau in an adjoining room, they knocked together a proposal. Mulholland later insisted on calling Campeau "the author" but agreed he deserved "at least a footnote." And he called White on Wednesday, September 10, to arrange an explanatory meeting. White hopped over to the bank, but his back went up when he heard what Mulholland had been up to.

White opened Royal's executive committee meeting the next morning with the Mulholland compromise, "which perhaps could terminate the 'war' and allow Mr Campeau to save face."

Campeau, White reported, wanted 25%, three directors and antidilution protection. White told them he had already personally "rejected out of hand" the offer — but promised he would tell them of it. There was a unanimous recommendation by the committee not to entertain a compromise, and the recommendation was passed on for presentation at the next board meeting.

With that back-up assured, White reported that it looked as if at least 41% of the shares — and an additional 10%, after a long-distance chat with Sun's Galt — wouldn't be tendering.

That brought it up to the magic number of 51%, and White was sure Campeau would be denied. Otley updated the report on shareholders: one-third had been canvassed, and 65% of those were planning to hold on to their shares.

It never seemed to occur to White that companies were picking up shares for reasons other than unalloyed friendship. Love at Oxford wanted to make sure Campeau didn't corner financing or pension fund clients, and to open a new channel for his own business. Royal Trust estate and trust accounts held 5% of Noranda Mines Ltd's shares. Canadian Imperial Bank of Commerce chief executive Russell Harrison and White were old friends, but Harrison had turned down his request to buy until he realized that if Campeau won he might lose Royal's business to Scotiabank.

White knew, however, that for all the present posturing the long-term future of Royal was up in the air. He was still hoping that with Campeau beaten back there would be time to wait for the government to bring in a 10% ownership restriction. But after musing about the future, he returned to the present problems, telling the others he was still looking at an issue of preferred shares to make Campeau's job harder.

The directors turned out in force again for the Tuesday, September 16, regularly scheduled meeting of the board. They heard a summary of White's meeting with Mulholland. Then White told them that the Supreme Court of Ontario had dismissed Royal's court action and the company would begin an appeal. He also recounted his and the others' phone and personal contacts with shareholders.

Otley again outlined the Royal holdings. The investment, portfolio and trust committees had all looked at those cases: first from a long-term-portfolio perspective, second from a short-term-gain view and third from the elevated position of one deciding on the most prudent decision. Of Otley's running count of other shareholders, he now had 73% not tendering. The OSC had been asking questions, directors were told, and Royal had given them a detailed report on clients' holdings and purchases and their own shareholder canvass. White chimed in to assure everyone that people had fallen in step and bought shares to help Royal out of this mess. With that intro, it's no wonder the board unanimously endorsed the rejection of the Mulholland compromise.

White also sketched the significant new face of the company: after the frantic buying and selling of the last few weeks, three institutions now owned slightly less than 10%, two 5% each, a number 1-3% each. He planned to talk to Finance Minister Allan McEachen later that day to discuss protective legislation so the company would never lose its independence. The meeting was suspended for two days.

Noranda chief Alf Powis called White on the 17th to check on progress and was assured Campeau would fail. TD, which had been making noises that it was "lonely" sitting with a 10% block that could end up as a nasty minority position, received a call from White, and a reluctant Thomson agreed to a meeting. White told him a number of choice, inside tidbits about others who had bought to allay TD's fears, and talked of Royal's earnings prospects. Thomson didn't promise, but he didn't tender. (He also held off when Campeau raised the stakes, although he was looking for a price that was not much higher than the offer of $23. "We were hoping, I guess, that there might be a third act.")

Taylor was still busy trying to create a more concrete form of insurance — a competing bid. While White was assuring a favoured few that victory was his, Taylor was meeting with still-interested Cemp Investments Ltd.'s Jim Raymond and his associates, and two other men with a keen interest in buying a national trust company: Leonard Ellen and Reuben Cohen. This duo, owners of Central Trust, had long coveted a national base and had lost Crown Trust a year earlier, after a seven-year pursuit. They would be satisfied with nothing less than control.

As it turned out, it was nothing more than talk, but Ellen and Cohen would surely have blanched had they known the identity of the other potential white knight being considered by Taylor: CanWest Capital Corp., majority owner of Crown Trust and their antagonists across the board table there. Can-

West's irrepressible Israel (Izzy) Asper had been interested when Taylor filled him in during a long-planned Winnipeg swing earlier that week to celebrate — read advertise — a switch in regional office location. Taylor hosted 400 of Winnipeg's business clan at a Fort Garry Hotel reception on the 14th. Asper reached out to touch flesh as he left, and said, "If there is anything we can do to be of assistance, just call us." It took Taylor only three days to think of just the thing.

Taylor stayed up late after meeting with Cemp and Cohen and Ellen. He went to bed at 2:30 A.M., his head spinning with half-formed ideas. He was up early on the 18th to call Asper, whose ever-fertile imagination instantly went into overdrive. The answer was yes, but there would be conditions. Anyone who knew anything about the hands-on CanWest style knew what that meant.

The board meeting on the 18th was a continuation of Tuesday's session, held over because Campeau's bid was to close the next day. It convened with 17 of 20 directors participating by phone, but no news to discuss. Then a special executive committee meeting was called only an hour and a half later, when there was big news. The CanWest offer was outlined by Scholes, and they bounced around ideas about how CanWest would fare with U.S. regulators, how it would regard the 10% voting restriction, and the state of CanWest's own relationship with its controlling shareholder, Canada Development Corp. Then White walked in, 40 minutes late, bristling with important information. Izzy Asper wanted a 100% deal, he said. He wanted to make an announcement before the markets opened the next morning — the day Campeau's offer closed — and would make sure his own board met very early the next morning in Winnipeg. He was willing to outbid Campeau. He envisaged CanWest's Crown and Monarch coming under the Royal umbrella. He was demanding three to five CanWest directors and an expectation "to exert substantial control over the affairs of Royal." The financing would come from Bank of Montreal. Ironically, this was a much more aggressive proposal than the one that would have saved face for Mr Campeau.

Asper wouldn't move without board approval, so they had to decide fast. They set a board meeting for 5 P.M., and White went off to talk to CDC president Tony Hampson.

The decision was made late that afternoon by conference call. White reported that Tony Hampson was negative, and the board agreed.

The day after the Campeau bid expired, they met again; they had been contacted only the day before, a Sunday, and those who made it in person — 14 of the 19 participating — signed waiver forms agreeing to the lack of notice. Campeau had extended his offer; they didn't know how much he had collected. It appeared that at least 60% of the issued capital would not be tendered, but this could change, and in addition there was a substantial number of shares in the hands of smaller shareholders. MYW had handed in a letter earlier that day saying the offer was still inadequate. A draft of White's letter to shareholders was generally approved. This was the next to last in the series of meetings. The offer would run out this time on September 30, and when the next "special" board meeting was held, on October 3, it had one purpose only. White wanted to thank everyone and share his heartfelt relief now that he could breathe again.

It was White's moment for gloating. He wouldn't have much more than a moment. Events had taken place between the final two board meetings that cancelled out all the strategies formulated at all the pow-wows of this clan of panjandrums.

White and his advisor, Taylor, were operating on two different planes. Taylor just couldn't be as sure as White that hands locked in friendship would continue to bar Campeau's way. The jump in price could make the difference. Taylor had exhausted his supply of white knights, but his lawyer, Howard Beck, pulled out a contact of his own. He called long-time client Paul Reichmann, vice-president and powerhouse at family-owned development and financial firm Olympia & York Developments Ltd. Royal was also still trying to line up financing for share purchases — just in case — and O&Y's name had come up in a conversation between Wickens and stockbroker Bell Gouinlock as a potential buyer for preference shares. Beck made his pitch September 21, two days after Campeau extended his offer. The next day word came back: O&Y would be interested in 50% of the company. White balked. Reichmann had second thoughts as well — why 50% when 20% would be a solid enough position for someone interested in an investment rather than a take-over? Taylor and Beck told Paul and brother Albert of White's opposition to a majority shareholder, and they answered that if they were "welcome," they would be happy to buy just 10%, picking up another 10% down the road. They would want board seats.

This time White thought it over, calling a couple of members of the executive committee to test out the proposal. He still was clinging to the hope that this would keep Royal "widely held." White decided "there was no reason not to be reasonable," Taylor says. The unthinkable of a few weeks ago was to take place. An upstart real estate developer with a penchant for taking over other companies, and one White had tarred and feathered along with Campeau in his summer-home speech, would become a linchpin shareholder with White's blessing. White's principle of independent management was sacrificed even as his company was snatched from Campeau's grasp.

It wasn't simply the agreement with the Reichmanns that irretrievably altered Royal. The rest of the stock was now in very few hands. Toronto Dominion, Sun Life, Oxford each held 10%;* Sun board members Powis of Noranda and Ian Sinclair of Canadian Pacific had ordered their companies to buy. Commercial Union had followed through; CIBC, Hong Kong & Shanghai Bank and Deutschebank all responded to telephone calls by placing orders. Almost $164 million was spent by these "friends," and the total traded was more than $200 million. More Royal stock traded on the stock exchanges in one month than the company's volume during the preceding three years. It

---

* TD would be forced by banking regulators in the U.S., where it also operates, to reduce this to 5% — by selling at a loss to Cemp Investments — and would be publicly embarrassed by its ignorance of the rules.

could be — and would be — very easily bought and sold in the
months to come.

Campeau clutched his 25% — shares he had agreed to buy
from Unicorp and a chunk from the Caisse de dépôt et placement, the second-largest single stock owner in the country and
one not concerned about rifts between the English Canadian
and French Canadian communities. He didn't buy the shares
tendered by small shareholders, who were the real losers —
they didn't make a profit, saw the stock price fall again and
ended up owning a company different from the Royal they
knew and loved. Some observers felt Royal was irretrievably
tarnished. "Management didn't think of the shareholders'
position," commented one. "It was treating them as if it was
still 'book' stock and shareholders knew management's aims
when they bought it." Campeau would sell soon after. But in a
certain way he was a winner; he walked away from the field of
battle with his company and his future intact.*

The struggle put up by Royal, a spectacle of high drama, was
played out soon enough in another theatre. But by the time
Canada Permanent Mortgage Corp. entered the spotlight, the
supporting cast supplied by Bay Street had lost its loyalty to
the old guard. In a truly remarkable about-face, having read
the signs of the times, they came down on the side of Modern
Thinking. Once again the plotline pitted widely held ownership
against single shareholders; once again there was the subtext of
dynastic preservation and the exclusion of outsiders. But it was
a last hurrah for the trust industry of the past.

Late on the afternoon of Friday, May 15, 1981, Toronto
Dominion Bank chairman Dick Thomson, barely three months

---

* He also made sure federal and provincial authorities knew White was giving his
"friends" inside information ordinary shareholders didn't know. The OSC investigated information leaks or "tips" about whether or not companies were tendering their shares. White and Scholes had their personal trading privileges suspended
briefly in 1981 after a showy Ontario Securities Commission hearing, and in spring
1982 the federal government launched a suit against Royal's directors on behalf of
all the small shareholders who lost money by not having access to all the information
the favoured few large buyers did. That suit is still before the courts.

out of an Ontario Securities Commission hearing room where he had been forced to reveal his key role in "defending" Royal Trust from Robert Campeau, placed a telephone call to Eric Brown, chairman and chief executive of Canada Permanent. The banker asked for an 8:30 A.M. appointment the following Tuesday, after the Victoria Day weekend. When Brown said he couldn't meet because of a scheduled audit committee meeting, Thomson audaciously asked him to cancel it.

Brown naturally enough refused, forcing Thomson to finally reveal his mission: the announcement that Sam Belzberg, whose family owned 93% of First City Financial Corp. in Vancouver, intended to make a bid for the 126-year-old Toronto-based trust and mortgage company. Brown felt there was a second reason for the call, that Thomson was attempting to get him to cancel the meeting, where directors planned to deal with the prospectus for an upcoming common share issue. By the time the two hung up, a meeting in Toronto between Sam and Canada Permanent executives was scheduled as well.

The news of the take-over bid immediately sparked expectations of a Royal Trust Part 2, another entrepreneurial outsider groping an old-line financial dowager. The Belzberg reputation quickly became a matter of widespread speculation.

In a profile on the eve of what was to become a 12-week battle, *The Financial Post* described Belzberg as "regarded warily by many in the Vancouver business community as tough and demanding with both employees and business partners." It went on to quote one anonymous Vancouver executive who claimed to know Belzberg well: "He's just a guy who wants every business transaction to go 100% his way.'"

As the battle for control of the Permanent unfolded, much would be made not only of Sam's worth but, more important, of First City's worth, because the take-over was to be paid for in First City shares, rather than cash.

Cash was too expensive for an entrepreneur like Belzberg, too risky for an investment genius like Belzberg. Paper, on the other hand, would bring the world to him, opening up the little-known First City's public shares to a wider audience. As it turned out, cash was the only way to buy what was otherwise available only by accident of birth: control of a major, national, prestigious financial institution.

The Belzbergs had several strikes against them: they were Western, they were Jewish, they were nouveau. In all, they were *outré*.

The family climb out of immigrant poverty was classic stuff. Patriarch Abraham had emigrated to Canada in 1919 from Poland where he had been a fishmonger. Finding little in the way of opportunity for fishmongers in his adopted Calgary, Abraham began the slow ascent through various jobs until he found success in trading second-hand furniture and used that as a springboard into small-scale real estate dealing.

His three sons, Hyman, Sam and Bill, and two daughters, Fanny and Lil, grew up in a household imbued with the virtues of religion, hard work and, above all, family. Out of this has grown a private, clannish corporate culture. One profile of the Belzbergs in the heady spring of 1981 described them as "Semitic Waltons, the products of a loving but stringent family and hard-time economics."

During the fifties and sixties, the family's adventures in real estate escalated. The tenement holdings and warehouses gave way to serviced housing lots, then shopping centres, apartments and commercial developments.

Shrewd property trading and prescient investment in oil and gas leases — by the end of the sixties the Belzbergs controlled 35 million acres of federal land, which they sold for a handsome profit — allowed the family to prosper, with Sam, as always, providing the leadership and the focus. He was the brightest, the most educated and the most aggressive.

In 1962 the Belzbergs had incorporated City Savings & Trust. It was the forbear of First City Trust, which by the end of 1980 had reached assets of $1.5 billion as a result of an explosion of growth in the preceding five years. But with only two dozen branches, it was not the big time. Sam Belzberg dreamt of a financial empire. In August 1978 he tried to take over Winnipeg-based Monarch Life Insurance but was beaten by a competing bid. In July 1979 he took a look at acquiring Metro Trust but ran into a road-block in the person of Metro's controlling shareholder, H.N.R. (Hal) Jackman. A year later he launched negotiations to acquire finance company Canadian Acceptance Corp. but couldn't agree on a price with the company's American parent. Finally Belzberg settled on the Permanent. With $9.5 billion in assets, it was a Goliath; with its palatial marble and brass headquarters in Toronto and a roster of past presidents including Gooderhams and Oslers, it was a Siren. Belzberg planned to consolidate the company with his own and use the Permanent's extensive real estate offices for First City's development activities.

The Belzberg camp had the sponsorship of TD's Dick Thomson going in, and it is extremely unlikely that they would have attempted the take-over without it. But after the first contact between Thomson and the Permanent, the wagons circled and the Belzbergs were inside taking the shots.

"It's an interesting question, 'Is there an Establishment in the financial services industry in Eastern Canada?'" muses one senior First City lieutenant — off the record, of course, in case there is one. "If you're not a member of it, I don't think you're necessarily welcome into it. I don't think there's anything unique to the principles of this company. If you're not part of the old true blue, there's no way you're going to become a part of it in this century.

"Whether the so-called Establishment banded together, as a practical matter the sponsorship evaporated and that was an important fact. I don't know why; I don't know whose IOUs might have come into play."

Once again members of the country's business elite became entangled in a take-over battle, this time demonstrating their extraordinary flexibility in matters of principle. Thomson's TD bank was principal banker to both the Belzbergs and the Permanent. Toronto Dominion's relationship with the Permanent went back decades to the alliances of banks and trust companies, and it had engineered the merger of the Permanent with Toronto General Trusts. But now TD was bankrolling the Belzbergs' bid with a $175 million line of credit to underpin the cash option in the $300 million offer to shareholders.

The Belzberg offer, contingent on obtaining a minimum of 75% of the company's shares, contained two options. One, which would result in the family's retaining 41% of First City, traded Permanent common and convertible preferred shares for First City common. The second option was an exchange of the Permanent shares for a package of First City common, preferreds and convertible preferreds that could be cashed in at the end of the year. This would leave the Belzbergs with up to 75% control of First City, depending on how many common shares were taken up by Permanent shareholders. The deadline for Permanent shareholders to tender their shares to Belzberg was set for midnight on June 12, 1981.

Another war-horse from the Royal episode entered the fray — at Belzberg's side. "Firpo," known as Austin Taylor in the newspapers, somehow had lost religion. He seemed to no longer believe in the principle of safeguarding widely held trust companies from interloping single shareholders or in the sanctity of a company's ownership restrictions.* Taylor and his McLeod Young Weir brokerage house were acting as the Belzbergs' financial advisor and stood to gain a cool $1 million if Sam succeeded.

Once again the incumbent management, Permanent's chairman Eric Brown and president J. Harold Deason, rallied the board to work out a defence strategy. In large part they were defending the company's lacklustre track record. Growth had been slow, earnings had been dropping for several years and the stock price had meandered around the $18 mark for almost ten years.

Wednesday, May 28, the Permanent's board met to consider the offer it didn't want and told management to prepare a circular recommending that shareholders reject it.

---

* In 1974 Canada Permanent shareholders had moved to place a restriction in the company charter on the transfer and voting of shares amounting to more than 10% by any single shareholder or allied group.

In the weeks following the Belzbergs' announcement, while shareholders sorted through arguments in a raging debate on the value of the deal, the Permanent fought a delaying action in courts and securities commissions across the country. Brown sought protection from Ottawa, just as Royal's board had done with no success. In a letter to Finance Minister Allan Mac-Eachen, Brown pleaded for a public statement of government policy on restricted ownership of federal financial institutions. He did not receive any kind of reply.

But damaging the Belzberg bid was a controversy surrounding MYW's attempts to "help." With 93% of First City held by the Belzbergs, the company had a tiny 425,000-share "float" — the number of shares available for public trading. In the two weeks immediately following the announcement of the bid for the Permanent, MYW purchased 37% of the float — equal to all the trading in First City shares during 1980 — at prices above $24. They called it market stabilization, designed to prevent wild gyrations in the stock price that would confuse the Permanent's shareholders. Before MYW's action First City shares had been offered at anywhere from $18 to $25 in thin trading. In fact, the shares had enjoyed a remarkable and fortuitous rise in value from $8 in 1980 to $13 in January 1981 to $25 the day Thomson called Brown.

A good many saw it all as funny business. Investors and analysts began wondering about the true value of First City and began selling their Permanent shares into the open market in hordes, taking sure profits while they could. Although the Belzberg offer ostensibly put a worth of $36 on Permanent shares, based on a First City value of $24 a share, in the weeks following the take-over announcement 3 million of the 7.1 million Permanent shares outstanding were traded by nervous holders at $28 or less.

Finally, the Ontario Securities Commission, under the crusading leadership of Henry Knowles, stepped in. For the first time it questioned a dealer's "market support" activities and found MYW guilty of unlawful manipulation of the share price in an attempt to artificially inflate the value of First City's offer. After a marathon hearing, ending at 1:30 in the morning on June 6, the commission unilaterally extended the Belzbergs' June 12 deadline by two weeks to give investors room to sort through the debris. The extension was the deciding factor in the Belzbergs' bid for control of the Permanent.

With the reprieve the Permanent camp, in an attempt to retain permanence, shook the bushes for a white knight. During the week of June 15th, they entertained proposals, all of them either legally impossible or corporately improbable. Chief among the unacceptable were inquiries from Vancouver businessman James Pattison and the exotic Ghermezian brothers of Edmonton. More palatable but just as unlikely were advances made by Michael Burns and Harold Livergant of the Crown Life/Extendicare organization, Merv Lahn of Canada Trustco and James Burns of Power Corp.

By June 29, after a week's negotiations, the Permanent board had settled on its white knight: giant, Vancouver-based but San Francisco-run Genstar Corp., a diversified real estate, financial services and construction conglomerate, which proposed to merge the Permanent with a federal loan company it would acquire. Genstar was offering $30 cash per common share and $35.70 cash for each preferred share. But it wanted the trust company to assign it an option at $25 a share for treasury shares amounting to 10% of outstanding stock.

Genstar had materialized as a white knight only one day before First City's offer was to close. "A lot of people thought we were through," snarled James Pitblado, then a Dominion vice-president. "Genstar's bid is a cash offer, not what I call Bel dollars."

Meanwhile, Belzberg had received tenders for 71% of the stock by the Friday, June 26, deadline, less than the 75% minimum in his offer, which he felt was necessary to change the 10% voting restriction and take firm control of the company. So he took a gamble. He extended the closing date on the offer to Monday, July 6, and waived the 75% condition, confident that those who had tendered would not withdraw in favour of Genstar's cash. It was an interesting move, given that most of those who had gone over to Belzberg intended to take First City's second option, with the delayed cash sweetener.

On Thursday, July 2, the Genstar counter-bid — which had been announced in the media but could not begin until Belzberg's offer expired — stumbled. That morning Genstar's financial advisor, Wood Gundy, had jumped the gun and solicited 13 of the Permanent's largest institutional shareholders who together held 40%. Gundy executives had suggested they withdraw their shares from the First City tender. In return Genstar would guarantee to buy their shares at $30 cash.

The OSC took an exceedingly dim view of this and, in a meeting that evening called at First City's request, decided Gundy's actions amounted to an illegal take-over bid. Nevertheless, Genstar took the opportunity at the hearing to up its offer to $31 cash for common and $36.90 for preferreds and, further, discarded the troublesome merger idea. The following day Pitblado of Dominion, who had been crossed by the Belzbergs in a real estate deal several years earlier, assessed the new bid as "fair and superior to the First City offer."

By the time Belzberg's new deadline of July 6 had expired, he was left with only 32% of the Permanent's stock, but he still had done better than many expected. The reason was his allies: the TD with 7%, Andrew Sarlos's HCI Holdings with 4%, Manufacturers Life Insurance with 11%. Others who were helping to scoop up Permanent shares in the open market and then tendering to Belzberg for shares, at the behest of Sarlos, included affiliates of Edward and Peter Bronfman, and the Reichmann family, owners of Olympia & York Developments Ltd.

In the following ten days, Belzberg forked out cash at $32.50 a share and garnered an additional 21.2% through purchases on the stock exchange and through private deals to put him in control of 53.2%. One was with Sarlos, who had built up another block of 9%, paying $31 a share; another lot came from his friends the Cemp Bronfmans, who bought on the market at $30 and sold for $32.50; and another was from Richard Roy Kennedy, who with 8.2% was the largest non-institutional shareholder, having begun buying Permanent stock in February, and the only board member to accept Belzberg. (Later an Ontario Supreme Court judge would find the private agreements a contravention of securities regulations and a conspiracy to injure Genstar.)

Genstar was furious. It was still barred by the July 2 OSC order from making market purchases until July 21, as a result of Wood Gundy's ham-handed effort. (The commission revoked the prohibition July 14.)

The OSC was furious with the Belzbergs, immediately launching a hearing into their plan to make a follow-up bid to minority shareholders with $32.50 in shares, not cash.

And market players were furious about the ensuing confusion. "It's like trying to follow a housefly that never seems to settle," sniped Ward Pitfield, president of dealer Pitfield, Mackay Ross Ltd., dripping with Establishment hauteur.

The warfare sparked yet another round of lawsuits and complaints to securities regulators. (By July 16 half a dozen hearings had already been held into different stock market manoeuvres of the two competitors, and the affair was becoming the most regulated take-over battle in memory.)

With Genstar's offer drawing to a close, Canada Permanent shareholders assembled in the ballroom of the Royal York Hotel in downtown Toronto on Thursday, July 23, for a vote on a resolution to apply to Ottawa for deletion of the company's 10% voting restriction. The meeting had originally been called at Genstar's request, but the company was now faced with someone else as a majority shareholder. Ironically, Genstar voted against the resolution; First City, for.

By the time the Genstar offer had expired at the end of July, the "white knight on a slow horse" had managed to acquire 39%; even with its 10% treasury option and the dilution of First City's position that would result, a loggerhead had clearly developed, and neither acquisitor would be able to make the changes it had planned for the Permanent. But Genstar suspected it had a deal in the bag.

The stalemate had been obvious to both parties for some time. In mid-July, when Genstar found out about First City's

53%, its two senior executives, Angus MacNaughton and Ross Turner (who, in an unusual arrangement, have rotated the post of chairman and president since 1976), decided that the game was over and that they wanted to "walk away" as soon as possible. They met Sam Belzberg in the Vancouver airport on July 16 for a 45-minute meeting and, after congratulating him, started to discuss a negotiated settlement with First City. Mac-Naughton was firm that any sale must involve the 10% treasury option and a cash price of $32.50. Any suggestion of a partner-ship was quickly nixed.

Sam began working on raising the money to pay Genstar, enlisting Austin Taylor in the consideration of a First City share issue. It's a matter of speculation how hard Belzberg tried, but by July 27 he had become "a little bit dejected" about the state of the stock market and the general economy and concluded that raising the funds would not be easy.

Saturday, August 1, long-time Belzberg legal retainer and right-hand man Daniel Pekarsky telephoned MacNaughton and was told Genstar indeed had 39%. Pekarsky and Belzberg would be in Los Angeles on other business, and a meeting was arranged for the following day at Turner's home near San Francisco. Later that day Pekarsky and Belzberg say they dis-cussed the possibility of selling to Genstar instead.

It was the Labour Day weekend; a summer had passed since Belzberg first took a run at the Permanent. At the Sunday meeting all agreed that the impasse had to be resolved with one's buying the other out. Because First City was on the scene first, it would have first chance; the Genstar executives agreed to give Belzberg more time to come up with the money. But by late afternoon, as Pekarsky and Belzberg were leaving, talk turned to the possibility of Genstar's doing the buying. Belz-berg mentioned a price of $36 to $36.50. MacNaughton said no.

Several days later, after speaking to Taylor, his brothers and others, Belzberg said, "We just said, 'This is not the deal we started out to do.'" He called Turner August 5 and asked him for an offer. He said he would consider selling but that $34 was too low. Turner promised to get back to him.

The following day, after a number of phone calls among the four negotiators, Genstar offered $35 a share. "I accepted over the phone," he recalled later. "I said, 'We will shake hands.'" Belzberg had made the decision instantly, without taking the trouble to poll his board directors as the Genstar executives had done.

Suddenly, twelve weeks after he had triggered the onslaught of hearings, lawsuits, press conferences and share tenders, Sam Belzberg had pulled out, settling for $158 million for his 53% control block.

Shareholders who had tendered at $31 lost no time in crying foul. Chief among the complainants was Unicorp Canada Corp., controlled by George Mann, who had started buying Permanent stock from panicky shareholders after he was certain the First City bid would be contested. He approached the OSC about taking action.* Regardless of Mann's entreaties, the OSC was concerned about possible violation of securities regulations that give all shareholders the right to the same price when a bid escalates in the latter stages of a take-over. Genstar was staring at the possibility of paying an additional $13 million to early-bird tenderers.

Many months later, despite the conviction of OSC director Charles Salter that the two tenders were "linked like sausages," two out of three OSC commissioners hearing the case found that Genstar had not made a deal with First City until after its general offer had died, and therefore did not owe other shareholders $4 a share more. Genstar had spent $260 million for the right to take up the reins of the trust company, and more people on Bay Street thought it was too much than thought it too little.

The Belzbergs, on the other hand, had netted $5.5 million, at best a consolation prize for losing what they wanted and needed most. Sam Belzberg had gone into the contest with the risks and rewards carefully calculated, as always. In the end the risks of leveraging his empire were too great.

* In one of business life's many ironies, four years later, in his bid for Union Gas, Mann had one deal for early tenderers and another for tardier shareholders when it appeared he would not otherwise gain control.

Under Genstar the old Canada Permanent management was swept out. MacNaughton and Turner quickly rolled a Genstar real estate subsidiary into the trust company and launched a search for a new chief executive, by November 1982 lighting on John Hilliker, vice-chairman and 30-year veteran of the Bank of Commerce. It was a coup, although Hilliker was rumoured to have gone over only when offered an enormous ($500,000) salary. Soon after, president Harold Deason, a 29-year employee of the Permanent, resigned over "differences in management style"; his ally in the take-over battle, chairman Eric Brown, had departed immediately after the change of ownership. As morale at the company plummeted in the turbulence, Hilliker, as chairman, president and CEO, embarked on a massive program of cost control and debt reduction and brought in other new executives from the Commerce.

At Royal Trust Ken White was equally unlucky. After the defeat of Campeau, the Reichmanns continued to buy — up to 23% of Royal. And they began to think that the company needed a shake-up, one they didn't want to deliver. Their joint-venture partners from Calgary developer Trizec Corp., Edward and Peter Bronfman, had just that sort of management team. They were accustomed to going in and shaking up companies. They used the piggy-bank approach: shake it long enough, perhaps dig a knife in and wiggle things around inside, and the money will start to come out. Trevor Eyton was the man at the Bronfmans' Brascan who usually worked on the piggy-bank.

The Brascan purchase of 17% between March and June of 1981 was "happenstance," almost a favour to the brothers Reichmann. As Eyton tells it, Paul Reichmann arrived at Eyton's office one day and began discussing the trust company. "He said, 'Trevor, I've got 18% of Royal Trustco and you and Jack [Cockwell, second-in-command at Brascan] are really better at public companies and those kinds of relationships.'" Eyton agreed to meet with them and discuss the company's problems and the potential investment blocks that were still scattered around. Brascan bought, Eyton now says, "for two reasons. One, because Albert and Paul asked us and we would tend to respond to their request. Two, we had London Life and we thought we needed some more meat there." The idea of the insurance company and the trust company adding to each others' meat-and-potatoes product lines was beginning to take shape.

After they bought, the Brascan boys arrived at Royal with their request for "proportional board representation." They never buy anything without taking a very close look first at how much work it needs. In this case they felt it needed some very basic planning, which management wasn't providing. Eyton says he admired White's strength but wished he were 20 years younger. The newcomers felt that, battling on his own, without the support of young, ambitious executives to help him fuel the engine, White had run out of steam.

Their claim that White wished to leave isn't borne out by the facts. He fought. The Reichmanns were quite happy with their end of the bargain; they sat back and let the Bronfman boys do the negotiating. Eyton and Cockwell tried to curb their natural ebullience, saying they were in no hurry, they could wait three or four years for board seats as long as they felt the company was moving in the "right direction." But when they found that it definitely wasn't, they moved fast. "We were increasingly firm," says Eyton. "We thought we had to be."

"It was [the] Campeau [bid] that brought to light all the places that Royal Trust wasn't going," says one former employee. "It exposed the soft underbelly."

The new directors were upset at the lack of information on basic corporate strategies. Staff recommendations for moves that would cost the company money were only two pages long and didn't have any numbers behind them, Eyton complains.

The new owners also didn't like the Florida banks. They didn't approve of the expansion that had occurred in the seventies: it just wasn't reaping a high enough return. The money could be used better elsewhere. Eyton and Cockwell began making weekly visits to John Scholes's office to see how plans had progressed. The door was always open, and Scholes was invariably polite. But the hired hands they wanted to send over to bring operations into their sphere of influence were blocked at the entrance. Scholes wanted to run the company, and he wanted to keep his own executive group. But he found it harder and harder to make decisions. Anyone would find it tough to hold out against the force exerted each Friday by the team of Trevor Eyton and Jack Cockwell. It was no surprise to anyone when Scholes walked out the door in late 1982.

White had arrived back from a long sojourn in Florida to give Scholes a hand, and he hung on after his second had retired from the field. He maintained a stiff upper lip about the Eyton group's moving up from 17% to more than 20%, and although Eyton had declared early that his group objected to the voting restriction, they didn't push it at first. Then they did: Eyton told White he wanted the board to proportionally represent the Bronfman/Reichmann 40% ownership. Brascan by this time had nominees on the board, but Eyton hadn't joined because he enjoyed his directorship at Bank of Montreal. He requested a chance to speak to the board. White offered him a shot at the executive committee. Each said his piece; Eyton left without satisfaction. It wasn't long before he took another run at White's blockade. The next time he brought along an ally.

For Toronto Dominion president Dick Thomson, "the third act" had finally arrived. It wasn't the opposing take-over bid that he had expected would allow him to unload his shareholding at a handsome profit, but a shareholders' group that promised a higher rate of return. TD was already wrapped up with Brascan in London Life.

Eyton and Thomson walked into White's office together. Eyton chuckles when he remembers the scene. "I said, 'Ken, we've always talked about 40% of the stock. I really am here today, and Dick is testimony to it, we're here today representing more than half of the stock in the company. We want some changes.'" He had a list of four or five items at the ready.

"That was the only time Ken really got upset. He wasn't physically abusive or anything, but there was a great moment. . . . He leaped out of his chair and he said, 'I don't need to sit here like this and take this stuff from you. . . . I'm going to go.' And Dick Thomson and I with our great logic called him back and said, 'Ken, you can't go, this is your office.'" Eyton roars at the thought. "We were in his office!"

White turned back reluctantly, red with agitation. But he must have known that Thomson's third act was the curtain closer.* Machiel (Mike) Cornelissen, a South African-born accountant who had restructured Trizec Corp. after the Bronfman-Reichmann group moved in a few years earlier, made the jump from board member to president of Royal in early 1983. He always moves in high gear: in six weeks he had drafted a corporate strategy to replace the six-month effort of a group of outside consultants. He doesn't like consultants; they "borrow your watch to tell you the time" and, more important, "take away all that knowledge" when they're done.

Soon after, White announced he was stepping down as chairman. Board member Fraser Fell, whose legal partners at Faskens had been so active in Royal's fight to fend off outside control, headed the nominating committee that decided to replace him with Eyton. It was a temporary arrangement until the company was reorganized to Brascan's satisfaction and the perfect candidate was found to fill his shoes. After the change was official, Eyton again visited White's office. "I said, 'Ken, Mike wanted to tell you, but I thought I should tell you, I've been appointed chairman in your place.' And he turned and came around and shook my hand." A man who believes in lineage, in tradition, White was able to find a point of connection in Eyton's having shared his high school Alma Mater. "At least you went to Jarvis [Collegiate in Toronto]."

The board was beefed up with Brascan appointees, but few of the old guard chose to leave, although the stresses and strains of the take-over battle had taken a toll. "It was hard," says Harrington. "It's not like a soap factory — who gives a damn. These men took their duties as directors of a trust com-

* White refused an interview because of the federal court case but thought the timing was right for a trust company book. The industry "as it used to be," he said, was "a dodo bird" because of the ownership question.

pany very seriously. That's why a lot of them are still there, because they felt — a hackneyed phrase — responsible to the widows and the orphans. . . . For us it was very much a changing of the guard when we changed the owners."

The directors stayed, but the executives didn't. Of 39 vice-presidents in the corporate telephone book in 1985, 20 remained from pre-Brascan days.

One long-time industry employee sees the sad side of the changes: "The loyalty factor has been driven out of the trust industry by the new people. Now, they get five or six years out of a person and move you on." But for Conrad Harrington "the company has been very kind." An office, a part-time secretary, a limousine for as long as he was chancellor of McGill. It was simple: the new group wanted him, and he felt a duty to stay on. He has struck a bargain with fate.

"I said to them, 'I'll be perfectly frank with you. If you want me to stay, I'll stay, and I can't be certain that because you've taken this over that it's going to be a shambles, but — I have my own standards.'" The two sides agreed: if Harrington didn't like what he saw, he'd say so.

At a 1984 Royal yuletide party, Harrington was one of the most popular guests. New chairman of the board Hartland Molson McDougall, who like so many before him had joined the board from a position at the Bank of Montreal and whose family ties go back to the first Molson who placed funds at the Royal for safekeeping decades ago, was thrilled to point out "the old chairman's" presence. Then he made the mistake of saying that the chairman who had succeeded Harrington was not in attendance. It was a significant gaffe.

5

The
Ownership Game

"We never had an easy time with any of these things," sighs
Reuben Cohen, his country cadence rising and falling as he reflects on corporate battles from the quiet comfort of his Moncton law office.

It's true; doing business has not been easy for media-shy
partners Reuben Cohen and Leonard Ellen.* This may seem
incredible since the pair started in the mid-forties with modest
means and by the early seventies each was worth about $25
million. Today these two children of Jewish Russian immigrants own about 45% of Central Trust, a stockholding worth
about $25 million to each. They also have investments in
companies that manufacture aircraft components and home
heating equipment, provide lenders with insurance on their
mortgage loans, explore for and distribute natural gas, sell investment funds in Canada and invest in insurance companies in
the United States. Montreal-based Ellen has built a lumber
business from scratch. The companies they have stakes in control more than $5 billion in assets. But, like Robert Campeau

* Cohen and Ellen *never* give interviews; their one past exception was a
45-minute effort in an airport hangar. But when they do open up their office doors,
their down-home East Coast hospitality shines through.

and Sam Belzberg, they know what it's like to be shut out of the inner sanctums of the financial world. Their business finesse and their expanding personal wealth haven't helped them when their dreams have come into collision with the strictures of the denizens of finance.

The current fight, with court cases still pending, is for a small Halifax company, Nova Scotia Savings & Loan. Cohen and Ellen are pitted against Halifax Developments Ltd. and the Sobey and Jodrey families, two of Nova Scotia's finest.

There's the added edge of bad feelings among the members of the small Eastern business caste; Donald Sobey sat on Central's board at one time, and Cohen and Sobey still share a car on occasion when they travel from meetings of Dalhousie University's investment committee. There's also been talk about vitriol flowing between Cohen and the Jodrey clan; another Jodrey-related company, Toronto-based Crownx, dealt itself into the bidding fray in 1983.

Cohen isn't afraid to let his bile show. The loan company "found that the national institution was more acceptable than we were. Why? Well then, you'll have to investigate some of the Establishment mentalities, dear. I think that goes beyond the realm of my capacity."

It's only the most recent chapter in the saga of Cohen and Ellen's dream of a large, nationwide trust company fashioned out of little Central Trust, a Moncton company they moved to Halifax. "We had an aspiration and a goal," says Ellen. They've single-mindedly chased that goal for three decades, since travelling salesman Ellen met lawyer Cohen in the early 1950s, had him draw up some lumber contracts and asked about investment opportunities. Perhaps it is that single-mindedness that has prevented their seeing what have seemed to others to be obvious hitches to many of their attempts to build by acquisition. They haven't always understood the mix of motivations that has prompted otherwise sensible business people to refuse their offers.

The most painful example is their fruitless 12-year struggle for Crown Trust Company, which they had abandoned by the time they managed to scoop up the company's remnants from the Ontario government in early 1983. Incensed by their shoddy treatment by the Canadian Imperial Bank of Commerce, a Crown shareholder and one of their own bankers during their continual bids for Crown during the 1970s, they sued the bank for damages set at a maximum of $10.5 million. In a 4-year legal battle, what Ellen calls "our ultimate dream" was stymied, partly by malice aforethought, partly by fate.

Cohen and Ellen were not, however, entirely innocent victims in this corporate morality tale. They were experienced businessmen attempting to put into play for their own benefit the financial establishment's rules.

The duo decided that acquiring Crown would be the perfect way to make their jump to national stature. It had a strong Central Canadian presence and about a billion dollars in estate, trust and agency business; it didn't need capital; the company was bursting with undeveloped potential. They began buying shares through jointly owned Standard Investments Ltd. in June 1971 and had 7% of the stock by year-end

Crown had two corporate roots. Trusts & Guarantee Co. was formed in 1897 by a small group of Ontario businessmen. It swallowed a couple of small companies over the years, but its thrust remained tending to the estates of fine old Toronto families. The name Crown Trust was part of a late-forties buyout of a Quebec firm founded at the turn of the century by a group of mining entrepreneurs to handle their stock transfers. Some of Trusts & Guarantee's original clients were also mining company founders, including John McMartin of Hollinger Mines Ltd., who died in 1918 leaving an estate that owned a quarter of the trust company's shares.

By the 1940s Toronto tycoon J.A. (Bud) McDougald, McMartin's nephew, was using Crown to manage the affairs of his own estate and those of a few close associates, including the McMartin clan. Until dual directorships on bank and trust boards were barred in the 1967 Bank Act amendments, he sat on both the Crown board and the board of the Canadian Imperial Bank of Commerce. When forced to choose, he opted for the bank board seat, making use of the Toronto chapter of a gentlemen's club "advisory board" system to effectively control Crown without even gracing the board table. Perhaps because of his dual loyalties to the bank and the trust operation, McDougald didn't cotton to Crown's expanding its mortgage and savings operations. Banking was the preserve of the banks. Although he himself owned little Crown stock, "it was McDougald's company," says Ainslie St Clair Shuve, who retired as Crown president in 1979. "McDougald was a personality and a presence. Anything he was involved in, his personality and presence was felt."

Cohen and Ellen decided that to make their bid for Crown a friendly deal they would need the bank's blessing — and money. They had dealt with Toronto Dominion, Royal and Bank of Montreal through their different companies but didn't know the brass at Commerce. Their closest contact at CIBC was a Moncton branch manager, Ruth Caines, an old school chum of Cohen's. She ran a CIBC branch in the building that housed Cohen's law office, and when he dropped in to chat she often tried to talk Reuben into giving her some business. He did open an account in 1964 for his Moncton property development company, Brentwood Realty, and later a law firm trust account.

In late 1971, with Ellen's eager approval, Cohen met with John Seaborn, a Halifax-based vice-president at Commerce. He told Seaborn about the pair's interest in trust companies and their plans for further purchases. They were looking for an introduction to Bud McDougald as a step towards buying Crown. Seaborn agreed to arrange a meeting with Commerce president Page Wadsworth. In March 1972 Cohen and Ellen transferred Standard Investments' business to Mrs Caines's branch.

In April, Cohen and Ellen arrived in Toronto to speak with Wadsworth, a man each had already met on his home turf, Cohen at a branch opening and Ellen only the week before at an investment seminar at his own Montreal brokerage firm,

C.J. Hodgson.* The pair did not waste their hour with the keeper of the keys. They spoke their minds: they wanted to purchase Crown Trust and merge it with Central. They would need money, and they wanted an introduction to kingpin McDougald. Wadsworth agreed to give them the introduction. "That in itself was, for us, a great step forward," says Ellen. He and Cohen left the meeting with a warm feeling about their prospects.

As is common in high-level diplomacy, the meeting's outcome varied depending on how the nuances were understood. Wadsworth did speak to McDougald and provide a letter of introduction. McDougald, however, told Wadsworth he was not pleased with this interest in his personal trust company. Wadsworth did not pass on this confidential information to Cohen and Ellen.

Wadsworth did not know McDougald well. He couldn't turn to bank chairman Neil McKinnon, McDougald's close friend, for counselling; the bank's chairman and its president were barely speaking. McDougald certainly didn't confide in Wadsworth that McKinnon had arranged to increase the bank's own holdings of Crown Trust stock to just less than 10% in late 1971 — at the behest of McDougald and as a foil for Cohen and Ellen's bid for control of Crown Trust.† The limit was set to conform with Bank Act restrictions on cross-ownership by banks and trust companies. As few people as possible were to know of the purchases; the stock was to be acquired without pushing up the price of the thinly traded securities. By November the bank had spent almost $1.4 million increasing its

* When Ellen bought controlling interest in the company in 1970, the high school drop-out took an active role in running it. "In order to qualify," he says, "I had to go back to school and take the exams of the Ontario Securities Commission, the QSC . . . as well as the New York Stock Exchange and the Securities and Exchange Commission."

† Ellen thinks his and Cohen's early stock purchases of trust companies were the "best kept secret in the financial community," and this was true; for years almost nobody knew even about the Crown investment. But McDougald had been monitoring their purchases since they began stockpiling Crown shares.

Crown stockholding from 15,000 shares to 74,900, paying an average of $18.14 per share. An April 1973 internal memo made it clear to the bank's investment department that this stock had sacred-cow status. "The impression which I received from the chairman's comments," noted vice-president T.L. Avison, "was that we were holding this stock, quite apart from its intrinsic value as an investment, for reasons of policy and therefore no sales should be contemplated solely on a basis of market or price consideration."

The very opposition that Cohen and Ellen were taking such pains to avoid was a secret but definite reality. They had been prepared to hear a negative response, but they never dreamed that the bank was already actively opposing them. Had he known of the bank's position, Wadsworth would have told Cohen and Ellen he could provide no help. Had they heard this from Commerce, Cohen and Ellen would have cut their losses and put their money to work somewhere else. But it was only when he became chairman later that year that Wadsworth found out just how little help he could give Cohen and Ellen. Then he felt trussed with his own bonds of silence.

A memo about a meeting with McDougald illuminates Wadsworth's dilemma. "McDougald thinks Cohen and Ellen would quickly resell for a profit rather than treat Crown as a long-term investment," Wadsworth noted. "Mr McDougald apparently has had several frank discussions with Cohen and explained his position." Ever since their meeting with Wadsworth, the pair had been buying Crown stock. There was never much for sale, but they bought whatever small blocks were available. Cohen and Ellen first met with McDougald in early 1973, and they continued to see him from time to time for the next five years. McDougald liked Cohen and Ellen, but he didn't plan to sell his trust company to them. "There was the ethnic element involved there," says former Crown president Shuve with diplomatic finesse. Somehow McDougald kept this astute, prudent pair dangling for five years without encouraging a formal offer for the shares held in estate accounts and co-managed by Crown. Yet as far as Cohen and Ellen knew, their affairs were going swimmingly, both with McDougald and with Commerce.

They never tried to pressure their way into management decision making — read McDougald decision making — although their share block would have dictated an immediate management shake-up to a mind like Trevor Eyton's. Instead, they put Crown on the back burner and concentrated on amalgamating their Maritime-based holdings, first marrying Central with Eastern Canada Savings & Loan in 1974, then with Nova Scotia Trust in 1976, with their handyman Henry (Harry) Rhude, a former corporate lawyer par excellence and Nova Scotia Trust director, becoming president. The plan to amalgamate Crown and Central was always there, but Cohen and Ellen began playing with a number of other trust company stocks. The reputation that this earned them — as "greenmail" specialists who would buy for a quick resale — did not help their credibility as long-term trust company owners. In the 1970s they made bids for three other trust companies and explored others, including National Trust — like Crown, a fixture in the estate business. Out of all that speculation they gained only Federal Trust, a small Toronto company — and analysts questioned whether that purchase was worthwhile.

Their run at Montreal Trust began in 1971 and ended two years later when they sold their holdings to Montreal magnate Paul Desmarais, who already held 24%. Ellen strode into Desmarais's office in his customarily intense fashion and laid a cheque for $15 million on the table with a blunt, "Yours or mine?" The pair ended up with a $2 million profit. Most everyone ranked it as a smart investment play, but Cohen even today views it differently. "There was a neutral block. If we could have obtained it, I think we would have kept that stock."*

Cohen and Ellen increased their lines of credit with Commerce through the seventies, buying more Crown stock. And the bank was pleased to have the business; Standard Invest-

* The deal fit both of Ellen's avowed business aims: "All I want is to be recognized for the quality of what we're doing. That's the only legacy I'll ever leave," he says. "En route, I want to make as much money as I possibly can."

ments was allowed to borrow at prime, although it was not a
large account. "We consider this account to be an important
one to this branch," said a February 1974 memo to Halifax.
"Both men are influential in their fields of endeavour and Mr
Cohen carries considerable influence in New Brunswick and is
a strong force in the Conservative Party."

Back at head office the bank was juggling a number of considerations. Wadsworth's 1974 memo musings also outlined an
interesting scenario that would have merged Crown and National Trust, the two trust companies in which the bank had a
holding and an unofficial voice. "Some years ago there was
discussion as to the possible merger with National Trust, but it
was felt best to hold this off and that from this bank's point of
view our interests were best served with a 10% interest in
each." The memo even included a behind-hand justification
for the Crown share purchases, as well as a look forward to
future complications. "When the shares of the McMartin
estate are to be sold the situation will have to be faced, and
at that time a merger with National might be in the best interests of all concerned." Despite the bankers' constant plea that
one employee can't control what another does, Wadsworth did
add a note about future treatment of Cohen and Ellen: "In the
light of the above we should in no way encourage Cohen and
Ellen that a deal with Crown Trust is possible." Wadsworth
also says he tried, when visiting with Cohen and Ellen, to
discourage them subtly.

Cohen and Ellen never got the message. They believed
McDougald was about to arrange the sale of the 25% McMartin estate shareholding in Crown when he died. The Standard
pair moved fast on the news of what they thought an untimely
end to their negotiations, sending a $33 offer on April 12, 1978,
to the two McMartin estate executrix-heirs, Mrs Jean Mulford
and Mrs Rita Floyd-Jones, and to Crown itself, also a co-
executor. When there was no reply, Harry Rhude sent a May 4
telex saying they would better any offer in cash for the shares
(trading at $25 on the open market) at any time in the next
month. They also continued to court the bank. On April 25

Cohen invited Commerce president Donald Fullerton, who was winging through the Atlantic provinces, to dinner at his home along with a contingent of Commerce employees. He drove them back to their hotel, making sure Fullerton lingered in the car for a chat. Fullerton doesn't remember exactly what was said that night; he had no knowledge of the Crown machinations, although he knew about the bank's holding. An eager Cohen recalls the talk much more clearly. He asked about buying the Crown shares and was given a "No — not for sale" in reply.

Crown Trust management was also busy sorting out the future of the trust company. Shuve says he didn't, as president, think about what was best for the company. Instead, he thought about what would benefit the McMartin estate. Crown was a co-trustee and had to advise what would best serve the beneficiaries. The entire board, he says, discussed the matter — from the viewpoint of trustees of an estate rather than that of a board of directors protecting the interests of shareholders. As a result, Shuve and chairman Harold Kerrigan travelled to Europe and the United States, talking to all the ultimate heirs about selling the shares. Once that decision was made, there was no doubt to whom they would go. Conrad Black, who was gathering the reins at McDougald's Ravelston Corp., needed control of Crown — which housed a chunk of Ravelston shares in estate accounts — to consolidate the empire under his own insignia; he bid $34 a share. "The two co-executors," says Shuve, "were very definite in their wishes." Commerce was also comfortable with the arrangement. Black joined the bank's board and became a member of its executive board in December; the bank supplied part of Black's funding for his purchase of 44% of Crown. Black's only interest in Crown was its holdings of Ravelston empire stock. His agreement with the McMartin estate was that if he resold within a year the estate would receive any profit he made.

Shuve called Cohen to tell him that the shares had sold to Black. "We didn't give up," says Ellen. Black began talking to Cohen and Ellen almost immediately about a sale a year down the road, when he was sure of the profit for himself. They first met in Toronto on July 18, 1978, lunching at Black's Bridle Path house. Black told him they should not look upon his move on Crown as being "unfriendly"; he would decide his position during the coming year but would probably eventually sell. In January 1979 they met at Black's winter home in Palm Beach. Rhude drafted the substance of the "conversations" into a letter outlining their "understanding." It couldn't be a formal agreement, or Black would have to hand over the profit to the McMartin estate. It didn't seem to arise that there might be a conflict of interest in a trust company's two major shareholding groups' essentially planning to circumnavigate an agreement that was made to protect one of the estates the company was counselling.

But whatever it was called for the purposes of financial sophistry, the draft document set out clearly the terms hammered out from the half-year of negotiation. A quarter of Black's shares he would sell at $38, so he wouldn't be making a profit on shares sold to him by McDougald's widow. The rest — some shares picked up in the market, the rest bought from the McMartin estate — he would sell at $41, after the July 5, 1979 deadline imposed by his no-profit agreement.

During the seventies the personnel at Commerce's executive level kept moving in and out the revolving door. By 1978 Russell Harrison, who was as close to Black as McKinnon had been to McDougald, was the bank's chief executive. Harrison watched the play surrounding Crown shares and became worried that the bank might be caught if Black sold his block. He didn't know the irony of the bank's being potentially caught with a block of shares that they had purchased to forestall the possibility of the trust company's changing hands.

In late 1978 or early 1979 Black broached the matter of the Crown shares. He told Harrison that CanWest Capital Corp. of Winnipeg would be the likely buyer. The pair decided it would suit both their interests if neither sold without the other; together they held 54% of the company. Harrison knew the bank's block of 10% was pivotal, but he didn't want to see the bank left behind, a minority shareholder with devalued stock.

The bank was in the midst of selling stock for tax benefits. He left all negotiating for the highest possible price in Black's hands. "I was wearing my director's hat that he not be left, if you will, holding the bag," says Black.

Black's technique with Cohen and Ellen seemed to be to run hot and cold. Igor Kaplan, his lawyer, never replied to Rhude's January 3 letter outlining the "understanding."

While Black's people were exploring whether CanWest would better Standard's offer, Cohen and Ellen had just had another deal slip through their fingers. Central's December bid for Crédit Foncier Franco-Canadien ranks among the best examples of bad timing in Canadian business history. Cohen, Ellen and Rhude were so astute about almost everything. They fingered the company — the country's fourth largest trust company and slightly larger than Central — when no one else did. Crédit Foncier had branches across the country, a solid commercial mortgage lending operation and, best of all, under-valued real estate assets still on the books at their 1930s repossession values. This real estate was worth much more in the booming West of the seventies and, whether sold or converted to market value on the books, would mean a big boost to the company's potential to take in deposits from the public. It was like buying a company and being given the money to expand it as part of the deal. And it was available. They made a $138-per-share offer to 20% shareholder Cie Financière de Paris et des Pays-Bas and announced that the offer hinged on picking up an additional 35% in the open market. But, says Ellen, "all the bases were covered — there was no question of the acquisition." They went public with the news December 5. The next day the Parti Quebecois launched a counter-attack: Consumer and Corporate Affairs Minister Lise Payette announced retroactive legislation controlling who could take over a Quebec-based trust company, "in the interests of Quebec." The deal was blocked.

At a late-night meeting held with then-Finance Minister Jacques Parizeau, an icon in Quebec's church of economic nationalism, the Central forces found, as Ellen now says, that the government's action "had nothing to do with business." A former Trudeau supporter, whose office still sports a photo of his wife with the former prime minister although he now castigates Trudeau for his socialist policies, Ellen reserves a special brand of smouldering resentment for Lise Payette. "I don't think they even knew I was a Quebecker."

Cohen, in contrast, hugs his feelings to himself. Talking with Parizeau about the subject was, Cohen says with his customary understatement, "a new experience for me." Quebec participation in the company was offered; it wasn't accepted. Central withdrew two weeks later, and Montreal City & District Savings Bank filled its shoes. Now Cohen shrugs off what might have been the best deal he ever encountered. "When you hit something like that you sort of lose your appetite for it anyway."

But they didn't lose their appetite for Crown. Ellen called Kaplan in March 1979, but his instincts told him there was no point in pushing matters until the year was up in July. On June 27 Ellen dialled Black; the next day Black returned the call. "The year is just about out," said Ellen. "Have we still got a deal?" Black answered that he had another offer, an oral one of sorts; he was still a little sceptical about the possibility of someone else being ready to offer $44 a share. Ellen was quoting $41.50; would he raise his price? Ellen, believing this was the latest round of horse-trading, answered, "No!"* Their limit would be $41.50 a share. It was a fateful answer, although Ellen couldn't guess that. He knew others, including National Trust, had looked at Crown, but he thought no one would pay that kind of money for the minority block. Ellen hadn't an inkling about the bank-Black sell agreement; as far as he was concerned, the bank shares weren't for sale. He didn't know that CanWest Capital Corp., headed by partners Israel (Izzy) Asper and Gerald (Gerry) Schwartz, had been kicking around the idea with some of Black's associates for months.

* Cohen would never be accused of enjoying horse-trading. His father, a grocer, made his money after arriving from Russia by importing draft horses for the post-World War I immigration wave to Western Canada. "My father loved horses," says Cohen. "He would sleep in the stable with horses." Reuben didn't inherit the interest; it was enough for him to witness his father giving the animals enemas, his arm covered with axle grease.

It was a canny plan, concocted by Asper, a tax expert and former Manitoba Liberal leader, designed to place CanWest in control with 54% a scant month before the Ontario Securities Commission implemented plans to force follow-up offers to minority shareholders at the same price as that paid for block control purchases. CanWest would gain control with the bank and Black's shares; that made them worth the $44 to Asper and Schwartz but would push down the price of the remaining Crown shares, held basically by Cohen and Ellen, who by now had 32%.

The Commerce's Harrison knew that in selling the Crown shares he was going against the expressed wishes of a bank client, Standard. He didn't know the rest of the case history or the bank's sordid reason for buying its Crown stake. But Harrison never contacted Cohen and Ellen to find out if they wanted to bid on the bank's shares. Harrison relied on another bank customer, Black, and he personally gave the order for the bank's sale of its 10% holding in partnership with bank director Black's sale of his 44%. Black's people drafted the documentation and handled the sale, with Peter Cole, then Commerce's vice-president of investments, attending the closing. CanWest Capital gained Crown, and Cohen and Ellen again lost their hopes of a national trust company.

Black called Ellen late in the morning on July 17 with the news that he and the bank had both been bought out at $44. Ellen was aghast — particularly that he hadn't known that the pivotal control block held by the bank was for sale. When Black told him the bank had sold its shares, Ellen said, "Well, in that case, sell mine at $44 as well." The partners sent off a telex to Harrison, blasting him for irresponsibly selling the shares without arranging an offer at the same price for all shareholders. It was a harbinger of the four-year-long court suit and public airing to come.

CanWest wasn't interested in playing footsie with the minority shareholders. Black claims to have urged CanWest to contact Cohen and Ellen and "treat them in a considerate way." When CanWest contacted Ellen July 18, Gerry Schwartz told him they weren't interested in buying at the moment, but maybe later — at a lower price.

By 1982 the share price for Crown stock had plummeted to almost one-third of what CanWest had paid. Cohen and Ellen honestly thought $44 a share was too high a price to pay for the Crown stock, but they would have paid that for the bank's portion, had they been given the chance to stop the shift in control. They would have thought longer about buying the whole piece at that price.* At $41.50 they were already offering a premium for control. As it stood, Cohen and Ellen had devalued stock backing loans from the bank, which were secured with their personal guarantees. They had to pay $1.5 million to Commerce to make up the difference. In July 1982 the unhappy duo paid off their loan and moved their accounts. "I don't think we had any alternative," says Cohen today. "I had the feeling [our business] wasn't welcomed."

The Crown Trust that CanWest won was a company sadly in need of a shake-up. "We knew that it was a company that was yet to enter the 20th, much less prepared for the 21st century," says Asper. CanWest moved in its own management talent. Some of the estate business, which liked Shuve's conservative style, followed him out the door. "They were concerned about the quality of ownership," Shuve says, emphasizing that he never counselled anyone to leave. Part of that concern, he says, was again "the ethnic element." Jews owned trust companies, but not companies like Crown. "That was really the first move by that ethnic group into the Establishment section of the financial community," says Shuve.†

CanWest had shopped around. One of its unstated goals, Schwartz says, was to make the jump from being a private

---

* Cohen learned to be careful at an early age. He still has his old red passbook from an account opened in November 1933 with a $15 bankroll, and he enjoys running his finger down the page, pointing to each deposit. It was four years before the first withdrawal, when he left for Dalhousie. Opening the account was "the proudest moment of my life," he says.

† For Asper it was just part of the breakdown of the traditional Canadian "ethnic pecking order." He remembers losing a few trust accounts but didn't attribute it to race or religion. "I would be the last to know because I'm not a paranoid." On the other hand, he did notice the reaction to CanWest's introduction of a senior female investment manager at Crown. "It is an industry which has its traditions and prejudices, no question about that."

Winnipeg company to being "a recognized face in Toronto." Asper was particularly happy about buying Crown because it had the reputation on the estate, trusts and agency side of the business — where CanWest intended to concentrate. It had new ideas about how to use trust powers. Before buying the company, Asper gave the CanWest board "a list of 19 current, desirable products that didn't exist." He wanted Crown to sell tax shelters, packaging deals to take advantage of foreign investment, oil and gas, film and real estate taxation loopholes. Crown would give credibility and clout to this oft-times hairy business.

But CanWest had major management problems. In three years Crown was headed by four different chief executives; there was a turnover of middle management as well.

An offer in October 1982 for the company's stock at $62 a share was too tempting for CanWest's board of directors, many of them stockholders weighed down with their own debt problems and hoping for fat dividends after the sale. Cohen and Ellen had just sold their third of Crown to Toronto real estate and produce magnate Joe Burnett for $32, and Burnett was handily flipping those shares through family companies to his old associate, Leonard Rosenberg of Greymac Trust, at $62. Schwartz struck the deal in Rosenberg's Toronto office. "I did a little mental calculation, sitting there," he says. Rosenberg was offering to pay what Schwartz figured the company would be worth in five years, if Crown president Neil Tait's best projections came true. CanWest sold that week.

Whether the CanWest years were good for Crown is a matter of hotly disputed opinion. But the big dispute in April 1981 centred on CanWest's decision to stop paying dividends on common stock. Cohen and Ellen were furious. "I don't know where the money was going," Cohen says. "It wasn't reflected in the profits available to shareholders."

Dividends are a very important commodity to investors of Cohen and Ellen's stripe. With 32% of Crown, they received about a quarter of a million dollars annually from the dividend payments, money that could be used to purchase other investments or to help defray the nagging bank loans at the

Commerce. Cohen and Ellen didn't enjoy seeing the money ploughed back into Crown by a majority shareholder making changes in which they had no say.

Central came under criticism at the same time for keeping up its dividends. Beginning in 1981, without enough profits to pay them, it dipped into the company's retained earnings. This wasn't done for Standard's benefit ($2.8 million annually in common share dividends), Cohen says, but for the thousands of small, Maritime shareholders. "To every one of them dividends are very important."

Not every shareholder agrees. George Hawkins, a former Canada Permanent Mortgage executive who was a year ahead of Rhude at Dalhousie law school, was already worried about Central's position at the 1980 annual meeting. He met with Rhude before the meeting and used the answers to his pointed questions to frame his public queries later that day. Hawkins says flatly that the dividends continued to be paid because Cohen and Ellen needed the money. That's debatable. But Central had made some unfortunate investments — one, in the Mortgage Insurance Company of Canada, resulted in a loss for Central of $10 million by 1983 and another $5 million in 1984 — and many analysts claim the company paid too much ($9.5 million) for Toronto-based Federal Trust in 1980.

Cohen and Ellen have also suffered the loss of two valuable executives. Orville Ericksen, a former president of Maritime Life, sold the pair on investing in an insurance holding company in Atlanta. Ericksen began changing the board and setting the wheels in motion — then dropped dead of a heart attack. Now there's "a good caretaker administration," says Cohen, but the investment potential is lost.

In mid-1984 Harry Rhude's office wall sported a birthday card signed by staff: "Remember," it said, "you're not old until people start treating you with unaccustomed respect." He may have found them more respectful when he returned from a hospital stint after a heart attack in late 1983. "Handsome Harry" Rhude, who Cohen and Ellen often relied on to handle negotiations for Crown and others, died in March 1985.

Ironically, it was the sale of Cohen and Ellen's shares to the Burnett family companies that started Crown on the twisting road that led, four months later, to Central's finally gaining ascendency over Crown. Joe Burnett swears he was buying Crown for his younger brother Teddy and that he dropped out of the race only because Teddy didn't feel it was worth being dragged over the coals by the Ontario Securities Commission — which was using an outstanding income tax evasion charge as a method to block the sale to Burnett. In any case, the Burnetts made a $6.5 million profit by reselling to Rosenberg, a former employee with whom Joe Burnett had made half a dozen commercial real estate business deals earlier that year.

Rosenberg's three-month ownership of Crown Trust is perhaps the best-documented debacle in the history of Canadian finance. A six-volume government commission, two books and thousands of court documents outline detailed versions of the events that made financial history between October 1982 and January 1983. In the first month in which he had control of the company, Rosenberg racked up almost $120 million in loans on two large real estate transactions; when the Ontario government found out Crown had approved $63 million in third mortgage loans as part of a three-company package of $152 million in loans — for apartment buildings that had instantaneously risen in value from $270 million to $500 million — the politicians realized how lax their regulation had been and rushed in to belatedly unscramble Rosenberg's omelette. They seized Crown and two other companies in January 1983, with hired guns deciding the fate of companies the bureaucrats hadn't been able to handle.* Crown was first: a plan was devised to remove any suspect loans and sell off the rest of the company.

Enter Cohen and Ellen, once again. Ontario didn't do the predictable and give Crown to trusty Victoria and Grey or musty National Trust, both controlled by Ontario political power Hal Jackman. Still, it didn't change its thinking enough to finally welcome Vancouver's Belzberg family, owners of First

* For more detail on this case see Chapter 9.

City Trust, into the Ontario end of the industry. It chose, in typical governmental fashion, the middle course. The Central folks had learned the value of political neutrality in Quebec City four years earlier, and they bent over backwards to do exactly what Ontario wanted. Central finally won Crown, at a price-tag of $20 million.

Crown's name was tarnished, but Central didn't inherit the deals that pulled it under. Instead, it ended up with the branches it had always wanted, good locations in provincial capitals and a solid presence in Quebec. It also finally had the nutmeat of the trust business, the estate trust and agency accounts. Before the Crown agreement it had about $2.9 million in estate and agency business; after 1983 that side of the business was at $10 million and growing.

Ellen and Cohen still were bitter. When they considered sale of their Crown shares in August 1982 to Joe Burnett, one of the considerations was whether a sale would affect their lawsuit against Commerce. They pressed on with the suit, gaining sympathy but not a legal victory. In mid-1985 the case was still under appeal. (They claimed in court that when they sold, at $34.50 a share, they lost $2.18 million from share devaluations and bank loan interest costs.)

The long-sought goal was finally achieved. Cohen and Ellen are now the respected controlling owners of a national trust company, having proven themselves an acceptable alternative to a different kind of outsider: the entrepreneur who wanted to use a trust company as a mechanism to boost his personal fortune.

6

The Lust
for Trust

*"Why does anybody want a trust company? It's pretty simple. You put
in $5 worth of capital and you can borrow $125 of somebody else's money
and invest it. You can invest it improperly, you can do all sorts of weird and
wonderful things.*

*. . . And if you look at the people in Canada who have been interested,
they've all been in the real estate business. It's a great way to finance a real
estate business."*

Arthur Mingay — Canada Trust

When developers talk about the "synergy" between real estate
and trust companies, they mean money. Money raised by the
trust company that needs to be invested; money that will
build office towers, apartment buildings and shopping centres;
money that can be lent for mortgages on tracts of residential
land. This synergy is what Robert Campeau had in mind when
he made his 1980 run at Royal Trust; it's what the Belzbergs
have done successfully at First City; it's what Peter Pocklington failed at miserably with Fidelity. To them real estate and
finance are simply natural allies.

This alliance has, however, been viewed by the more traditional elements of the trust company business as a sin punish-
able in the lower reaches of Dante's hell. As soon as a real

estate entrepreneur makes sheep's eyes at a trust company, the buzz of titillating if not downright salacious gossip begins; he's planning to rape the company, the upright members of the financial community will say. He's planning to take depositors' money and use it to finance his own schemes.

These defenders of the traditional trust company refuse to acknowledge that the link between real estate and trust companies is real and that it doesn't have to be sinister. When Campeau announced his bid for Royal, he declared he wouldn't use the company's money for his own ends. But he believed he understood better than management did how the company's money should be used. Royal under Campeau would have been a different company — maybe even a better one. The problem comes down to a difference in judgment. Real estate developers think differently from managers trained in the cautious handling of estate money. They have what is called by economists a "high time preference"; in other words, they are willing to risk more for immediate returns.

One of the first ways developers are seen to have taken advantage of trust companies in the 1970s and 1980s is in the method they have used to raise the money to buy them. George Mann perfected the "roll-in" method of boosting a trust company's capital base, and thus its deposit-taking ability, by selling it real estate from another, related company. He made the first-ever sale of real estate to his United Trust in the early 1970s. Peter Pocklington later used the same basic method at Fidelity Trust. In each case, the company's capital, the book value of the company's own assets, was increased by the purchase of real estate that the entrepreneur running the company already owned. Real estate can be valued at either its historical cost or its present resale value. In both of the cases just mentioned, real estate was revalued and the company's value increased with the new, higher valuations. This was the same method later used by the famous Leonard Rosenberg and Andrew Markle to boost the value of the capital bases at their Greymac Trust and Seaway Trust. Since the ability of a trust company to collect money from the public is based on the amount of capital it has, revalued real estate means a company can grow quickly.

But it doesn't have to be the wrong way to grow. If real estate really is worth more than its historical cost, revaluation is a legitimate way of valuing a company's assets. In fact, revaluation was something that the federal Department of Insurance was encouraging in the 1970s. Alan Marchment, president of McCutcheon family-controlled Guaranty Trust, was merging some of Guaranty's assets with those of parent Traders Group in 1981. The deal included some land, purchased by a subsidiary years before at a book value of $12 million. Dick Page at the federal Department of Insurance urged Marchment to revalue the land at its present market value, but Marchment didn't do it. He didn't like the feel; interest rates were too jumpy. He decided it was better to be safe than sorry. Peter Pocklington, on the other hand, marked up the real estate on Fidelity Trust's books with the Department of Insurance's blessing. For years this "roll in" of real estate was pointed to as an example of real estate entrepreneurs' taking advantage of the regulatory system. But nobody seemed to question the methods of the regulatory system itself — how it judges the accuracy of an appraisal.

There are three basic ways of appraising the value of property. The first is to figure out how much it would cost to replace the property. The second is to compare it to similar properties that have recently sold and to set a "market value" or tentative resale price. The third, more sophisticated approach, the discounted cash flow method, is to look at how much income the property is pulling in and figure out the potential return available to an investor either now or in the future.

There is an argument even within the appraisal industry over how far valuation methodology can be stretched. Academics argue that value is value. If they can prove that a property will be worth a particular price in ten years, using a complicated formula that stretches the potential benefits out to infinity and back again and calculating a discount in case something goes wrong, then that's the value. But financial institutions aren't usually willing to lend on those numbers. They want to allow for a drop in prices by lending on only a certain percentage of the allowed-for value. And they prefer present-day numbers to any estimate of what the property's worth could or should be over time. The law allows companies to lend up to 75% of a property's value; but the word *value* has never been clearly defined.

The bottom line is that attaching a value to a property is subjective, and so the motivation of the person assigning that value is all-important. This is where the mud-slinging against real estate developers' involvement in trust companies begins. It makes sense, the line of reasoning proceeds, that real estate people who buy into a trust company are going to bend the rules as much as possible, try for the most favourable valuation, the most mortgage money. But the reasoning is faulty because it is based on the premise that all real estate entrepreneurs are out to bilk the system. Also untrue is the assumption that companies are ravaged only for the sake of real estate deals: Wilfrid Gregory, president of the long-ago-looted British Mortgage & Trust, played fast and loose with his Stratford, Ontario, company in the mid-sixties in order to make stock investments as much as to buy real estate.

The important question of right and wrong in valuation is really the larger danger of treating a company that takes deposits from the public as if those deposits were one's own. The key to closely held ownership lies in the motives of the owner.

It is always the new, small companies that are suspect. The old school looks askance at the reasons boot-strap builders have for entering the lending business. It's snobbery; it's territoriality. But it is true that new companies have more trouble managing their growth, and they traditionally haven't had the best managers. The sixties saw the rise of Metropolitan Trust, York Trust, Northland Trust and a host of others; some of these had very troubled histories, and almost all are gone, folded into other companies. The new companies that opened their doors in the seventies included a number of small companies still struggling along today; they also included Astra Trust, which operated with complete disregard for any rules and collapsed in 1979.

Old-line trust types didn't move around much, but the people who ran the small companies did. When Metro, founded in 1964 by German-Canadian Rudolf Frastacky to funnel West German money into Canadian real estate, and run with an eye to aggressive deal-making, was finally forced by controlling shareholder Hal Jackman into an unhappy 1979 merger with Victoria and Grey, its executives moved on to Fidelity Trust, Crown Trust, Continental Trust and more recently Counsel Trust and Standard Trust. Perhaps the ex-Metro employee with his ear closest to the regulatory grapevine, however, is former senior vice-president Jack Russell. He and Victoria and Grey had sharp disagreements, and Russell was out of a job. He left the trust business and now owns a pub around the corner from the office building housing the Ontario trust bureaucrats, who often retire there to hoist a few.

The problem the regulators might be mulling over at Jack Russell's is that things are more likely to go wrong when an owner or a manager has a company levered to the hilt, or has his own reasons for promoting high-risk mortgage loans. Murray Thompson, the Ontario trust registrar who couldn't figure out what to do about Leonard Rosenberg's aggressive activities at Greymac Trust and Crown Trust in 1982, still throws up his hands: "Once you've got a deposit taking institution, it's pretty hard to shut if off. Rules are great. It's nice to say, you have a 12.5 times borrowing level. But how are you going to tell the depositor that you can't take any more deposits?" It is exactly the same dilemma enunciated 20 years earlier by a registrar agonizing over British Mortgage.

The public would have been pleased if Thompson had shut off the flow of funds at Crown, Greymac and Rosenberg associate Andrew Markle's Seaway Trust in 1982 — particularly when they found out the risks being taken with their money. The fact that he hadn't was to cost both Ontario and the Canada Deposit Insurance Corp. a lot of money in the two years after Ontario finally did step in and seize Crown, Greymac and Seaway on January 7, 1983. Ottawa also seized the operations of two related federally licensed loan companies, Greymac Mortgage and Seaway Mortgage, but its biggest involvement came after CDIC paid off all the companies' depositors and set about trying to recover its money by nursing the companies' poor deals.

The Crown-Greymac-Seaway scandal was the turning point in public perception of the management of trust companies. It loomed large first with the autumn 1982 financing by the three trusts of the purchase of a huge group of Toronto apartments at twice their market value and then with the revelation that the same technique — handing out depositors' money for doubtful loans on properties owned by associated companies — had been used by the characters involved for years, and the government had allowed it. The resulting furor forced hasty, arbitrary government action.

Rosenberg and his cohorts weren't the only ones breaking rules; nor were they the first. But the size of their scheme and the personalities of the participants, particularly Rosenberg's, prompted a showdown between hapless regulators and Rosenberg, Bill Player and Andy Markle that would bring to light some heretofore well-cloaked truths about the business. (The deal and its ramifications are detailed in Chapter 9.)

Thirty months after the seizures of companies on the brink of disaster, no one had been charged with any criminal wrongdoing. One minor figure was charged with fraud in July 1985, but there was no sign of any other movement after a two-and-a-half year police investigation. Still, everyone knows that the trio did *something* wrong. So much has been written — two books and hundreds of newspaper articles — about the apartment sale, the January 1983 Ontario government take-over of the three trust companies and the way they had been making end-runs around the rules for some time that these activities have been woven into the fabric of our folklore, transformed into an urban myth.

These men are archetypes of the self-absorbed, high-stakes

gambler who should never be in control of a financial institution. The Crown Trust story *is* the story of lust, the same ingredient that prompts businessmen like Sam Belzberg and George Mann to buy trust companies and the same intoxicant that drives ne'er-do-wells like Steve Axton and Wilfrid Gregory to pillage them.

The most telling interpretation of their ambitions and achievements and those of all who lust for trust is a meandering tale with a twisted endline: a friend of a friend has seen Rosenberg, Markle and Player somewhere unlikely, say, in the Vancouver airport. They are huddled, the three of them (unbelievable since they haven't been together for years now), surrounded by well-suited yes-men with QCs. One is, perhaps, in a telephone booth; they are running back and forth juggling numbers, big numbers. The acquaintance's acquaintance is glued to the spot, entranced by the action. Then the big decision is made — and the yes-men walk with brisk, important strides over to the 649 lottery booth.

W.P. Gregory and British Mortgage & Trust

The same day Red Kelly told Prime Minister Lester Pearson he was quitting politics to concentrate on his career with the Toronto Maple Leafs, British Mortgage & Trust Ltd. shocked Canadians with front-page revelations of million-dollar bad loans and management greed. Long before Leonard Rosenberg's Greymac and Peter Pocklington's Fidelity, there was Wilfrid P. Gregory's British Mortgage — the first collapse of a financial institution in Canada since the Home Bank in 1923.

It is a story of the exploitation of the blind trust of the times. Shareholders, depositors and board directors trusted in those who ran financial institutions and believed those institutions embodied security and propriety, although, particularly in the days before deposit insurance, there was really nothing more solid there than a concept of fidelity. Gregory used that trust to his own advantage; he had discerned the opportunities for personal profit presented by millions of dollars invested in mortgages and securities investments virtually unmonitored except by Those In Charge within the trust company.

At the final shareholders' meeting of British Mortgage on Tuesday, September 14, 1965, an aged, broken W.H. Gregory, chairman of the Stratford-based trust company that had been run by his family since 1914, rose before the 300 shareholders present and in a barely audible voice said, "With a breaking heart I call this meeting to order."

The meeting had been called to reveal some of the details behind the crumbling of British Mortgage in mid-July and to vote on a proposed salvage merger with Victoria and Grey Trust Co. of Lindsay, Ontario.

BMT's president, and the man found ultimately responsible for the failure, was not there. Wilfrid Palmer Gregory, son of the chairman, had been forced to resign as president July 27 as a condition of the merger with Victoria and Grey. The British Mortgage board had been trying to get him to leave office for weeks after the true state of the company had become known to insiders. His family was the company's largest shareholder, but in his pursuit of power and position he personally had borrowed heavily to buy shares. He was ruined.

Harold Lawson, long-time president of National Life Assurance Co. but a BMT director for less than a year, had stepped in as caretaker president, and he ran the meeting. It was to have been held in the trust company's glorious granite head office, which sat on a promontory overlooking the Thames River and the main street of Stratford. But so many people showed up that the meeting was moved to the Avon Theatre, where the drama began to unfold.

It was the first time shareholders and the public at large were told of the desperate situation of the 88-year-old trust company with $120 million in assets, a stalwart of Stratford society and, as the biggest operator in the Stratford real estate market, of the local economy.

During the four-hour meeting, Lawson revealed the extent of the trust company's investment in Toronto-based Atlantic Acceptance Corp., a finance company that was at the centre of a web of international fraud. It had been set up in 1953 to finance the sale of television sets, but with its ability as a finance company to borrow large amounts of money by issuing notes to "wholesale" investors such as pension funds, it soon was lending on a much larger scale. By mid-June 1965, when it defaulted on a $5 million bank loan, it was the sixth largest finance company in Canada, with $154 million in assets and 130 offices across the country (in the 1967 Bank Act, finance companies were basically wiped out when chartered banks were permitted to do personal lending). It had become enmeshed in scores of at best crazy and at worst illegal business schemes, and Atlantic's president, C. Powell Morgan, had covered up Atlantic's maze of bad loans to about 30 interrelated companies. Later the collapse would be called Canada's worst financial disaster and would leave investors and creditors who lost $77.4 million stunned at the magnitude of the incompetence and dishonesty.

Lawson broke the news that auditors' estimates put the losses for BMT as a result of the Atlantic debacle at a minimum of $10 million. (As determined later, they were actually $7 million.) The problems of BMT were threefold: investments in common stock of Atlantic and associated companies; collateral loans to little-known companies and people associated with Atlantic; and a mortgage portfolio with 12% of the loans in arrears.

All the problems were the direct result of business deals made by Wilfrid Gregory over the course of his previous eight years as president. There were gasps from the shareholders when Lawson told them that the trust company had loaned just under $3 million, all of it supposedly secured with collateral, to four individuals and three companies associated with Atlantic Acceptance. But in one case they already knew that part of the security against a $650,000 loan had been sold.

Aside from loans, BMT had invested $7.4 million in securities — common and preferred stock, warrants, bonds, secured and unsecured notes of the Atlantic complex, as it came to be known; only $2 million was thought to be recoverable.

As if that were not enough, the trust company's mortgage portfolio of $85 million was struggling with $10 million in arrears, almost all of it loans on commercial and industrial properties developed by associates of Gregory and two of his mortgage managers. Then the meeting turned to the devastation wrought on the deposit side: demand deposits had dropped by a third in the three weeks following Atlantic's default.

It emerged later that Gregory, in his drive to enlarge and glorify the trust company he ran, had fallen in with the "notorious swindler" Morgan. Gregory was obsessed with making British Mortgage look bigger, better and more valuable in every way, and he became infatuated with the fast money and easy ethics of those in the Atlantic crowd. Even after the failure of British Mortgage, Gregory would acknowledge only that he had been unwise, not that he had acted improperly.

Throughout July and August, after news that BMT had some investments in Atlantic, shareholders and depositors were kept in the dark about the true state of the trust company. The price of BMT stock had slipped only a few dollars from its level of $32 in the three weeks following the Atlantic default. But a hint of the trouble to come appeared on July 5 when no one bid on the stock by the close of trading. Investors grew increasingly nervous until the evening of July 8 when mining magnate Stephen Roman, himself fulfilling a brooding desire for a trust company, announced after a meeting with Gregory in Toronto that his company, Denison Mines Ltd., was negotiating to acquire the trust company for $6 million. (When Denison's auditors took a look at the books, he let the offer lapse.) The following day, for the first time, it was revealed that British Mortgage held some of Atlantic's notes. A shocked Bay Street reacted by sending down the price of BMT shares from $25 to $8 in one day. Almost all of BMT's capital was wiped out.

Rampant suspicions persisted, and five weeks after Atlantic's collapse BMT was worth $2.75 a share in the merger with Victoria and Grey.

A year before, the shares of BMT had traded at $40 apiece. But the shares were so coveted that they were almost impossible to acquire, and those released in the settlement of an estate were quickly snapped up, frequently by directors of the company. Many shareholders had held BMT stock in the family for years and believed the shares were "as safe as money in the bank." More than half of the company's 1,000 shareholders lived in the thriving Stratford community of 22,000, and most of them, *The Globe and Mail* reported at the time, were "spinsters, widows, widowers, pensioners, retired couples and employees [of the company]." Now the shareholders faced a loss of $7.6 million — on paper because by early August few had sold.

They were uneasy about the lack of information on the company's difficulties, but that lack explains in part the sympathy extended to Wilfrid P. Gregory. For the most part, shareholders who could ill afford the loss were philosophical. "It's heartbreaking. . . . Most of my income depended on British Mortgage shares. It came as such a shock because we had absolute faith in the company all these years," an 80-year-old "spinster" commented. Up and down the streets of Stratford, neighbours were affected by the financial crisis, but they all felt sorry for the Gregorys — "such fine people." And they clung to their perception of Wilf Gregory as a highly respected lawyer and someone who had "done more for Stratford than anyone else." It was only 20 years ago, but times *were* different.

Behind the scenes, Harold Lawson and others had worked to save the trust company. At the time of the Atlantic collapse in mid-June many of the directors did not even know British Mortgage had invested in Atlantic and didn't suspect its troubles would affect the trust company. They received a letter describing Wilfrid Gregory's connection with Atlantic as purely personal, but it quickly became clear there was more to it when an apparently unconcerned Gregory began talking about possible mergers. His suspicions aroused, Lawson forced Gregory out into the open at a July 13 board meeting. The directors were appalled by the extent and nature of the involvement with Atlantic — astounding considering it totalled roughly $12 million. The habit of years — brief, formal board meetings — gave way to a week of almost continuous sittings as a rescue team led by Lawson took over the management of the company.

They weighed the value of informing shareholders against the certain panic that would erupt among depositors and the inevitable run on the bank. "No trust company in the country is liquid enough to stand a full-scale run by its depositors. We had to protect the depositors before we told the shareholders," Lawson said a few months later.

There were fears of other trust companies being swept under if BMT were to fail, and Lawson envisaged a domino effect of catastrophic proportions. In 1965 there was no deposit insurance. Although the Porter commission had discussed setting up a scheme, industry and government had hesitated. The near-collapse of BMT is cited as the reason deposit insurance finally was brought in. Very few other lessons, particularly on the regulatory supervision of trust companies, were learned.

During his scramble to rescue the trust company that July, Lawson first approached a major chartered bank about guaranteeing British Mortgage's deposits but was turned down. He then went to the Trust Companies Association with the same proposition. Again the answer was no, although some members thought it was a good idea. Lawson was surprised at the refusal, given his experience in the life insurance business, where failing companies were bailed out by the rest of the industry with the result that no policyholder had lost money in Canada for 100 years.

"It was at that meeting of trust companies," Lawson said later, "that I first heard the suggestion that the government should pick up the losses. The argument was that the government supervises the trust companies, and government supervision was inadequate, so the government should pick up the losses."

This was the opposite of the Porter commission's view that competent supervision could provide a measure of protection for the public but should not provide a warranty of protection. The Trust Companies Association had set a watermark for its industry's handling of collapses that reflected not only its weak-willed nature vis à vis the banks but also the growing feeling that business in general was not liable for its failures.

Lawson said later that the "greatest mistake in all this sorry record was to suggest that the government should be responsible for the company's losses and an equally great mistake was for the Ontario government to actually agree that it would make money available." None of the money promised by Ontario was ever used, but the promise itself served as support, as did a well-publicized show in which the Ontario Hydro-Electric Power Commission left investment certificates worth $100,000 in BMT. These gestures were enough to prevent a liquidity crisis.

The reason for British Mortgage's collapse was, as it turned out, much more than just bad investments: it was flagrant abuse of management power, bribery of trust company managers, collusion, abundant violation of Loan and Trust Act rules — all of it adding up to the destructive legacy of Wilfrid P. Gregory.

In an era of gentlemanly behaviour, Gregory was an anomaly. A lawyer by training, he had seen his father run the company until he was forced to retire for health reasons. (For a lifetime of service the company gave him a pension, and leave on full salary until his retirement date six months away.) Wilfrid was courted to succeed him, but he had already made a name for himself in local politics and the provincial Liberal party, in the Bar Association and in the founding of the Stratford Festival. He demanded an unprecedented reward for heading British Mortgage: a lucrative stock-option plan, a $20,000 annual salary with $2,000 annual increases, the right to other directorships and their accompanying fees, and the "princely" fees as corporate solicitor. The board, supremely confident that Wilfrid would carry on the conservative, capable traditions of his highly respected father (who would remain as chairman) and grandfather, acceded.

From the day Wilfrid assumed the manager's post in 1957, hitherto sleepy British Mortgage more than kept pace with the trust industry's growth; in fact, it changed "almost beyond recognition both in size and character under his sole and untrammelled direction." In 1957 assets were $30 million; by 1964 they were almost $107 million. The company de-emphasized estate trust and agency business and got into short-term notes and collateral loans, investing in real estate for its own corporate account, loaning on land for development and achieving 20% annual growth in its mortgage lending. The individual mortgage amounts grew bigger, and the investment portfolio all but abandoned bonds for stocks.

Under W.H. Gregory the company had been "moderately profitable and a byword of stability." Under his son W.P., riskier, more profitable lending began to compensate for narrowing spreads. By 1964, in addition to the 300% increase in assets, the company had gone from no branch offices to 15, had twice as many shareholders and had a $1.4 million new head office that the trust industry called the Taj Mahal behind Gregory's back.

His invitation to join the board of Atlantic Acceptance in 1959 — and the nomination of C.P. Morgan, president of Atlantic Acceptance, to British Mortgage's Toronto advisory board — marked the beginning of the trust company's investment in the Atlantic complex. By 1965 Atlantic accounted for a third of the trust's investment portfolio, but for several years before that Gregory had played an interesting game with regulators concerning these investments, most of which were in violation of the Loan and Trust Companies Act because of their risky nature or sheer volume. Large, numerous and varied, Atlantic-related loans and stock holdings rose and fell like the sea around the time of the provincial registrar's annual audit. In September 1962 Atlantic shares and notes held by British Mortgage totalled $10 million — three times the limit under

the regulations. But by October 31, when the annual financial
snapshot of the company was taken, they amounted to only
$3.2 million. By November they were back up to almost $6
million.

Wilfrid Gregory the lawyer continually fought the registrar
on almost every interpretation he made of the act. The registrar
for many years had been in the habit of making rules, with the
approval of the Trust Companies Association, "as a gloss
upon the act in those cases where it was silent." While other
trust companies deferred to the opinion of the registrar, Gregory, hostile to the principles of regulation anyway, viewed the
registrar's interpretations as irrelevant and applied the letter
of the law.

British Mortgage's auditors knew about actual violations of
the act and pointed them out to Gregory but never reported
them to the government. Their leniency went beyond that,
however. In 1964 Gregory changed the company's accounting
methods to effect an illusion of profitability and referred to
this action with a single sentence in his report to directors and
shareholders that year. It was a major concealment of the true
situation of the company, but the auditors — one of whom was
the grandson of a founder of the company — did only the
minimum.

Gregory's actions, as a government inquiry decided later,
were "not errors of judgment but morally obtuse." He was in
part abetted by the lack of disclosure requirements for all companies of the day, but especially for trust companies, which
were not required to reveal much more than the bottom line on
their earnings statement.

The theory was that trust companies were already highly regulated and monitored by the registrar. In practice they were
lucky to see him once a year. In 1964 the registrar, who doubled
as superintendent of insurance until 1984, had a staff of six
responsible for 34 trust companies, 19 loan companies, 108
insurance companies, 75 mutual benefit societies, 40 prepaid
hospital plans, 3 investment contract companies, 10 frater-
nal societies and 65 farm mutual insurance companies. He

enforced a hybrid Loan and Trust Companies Act slapped together in 1912 that contained a labyrinth of investment restrictions with holes big enough to allow a legal sharpie like Gregory to drive a truck through.

"As a general observation," commented the royal commission, "the regulatory authorities in both federal and provincial jurisdictions relied upon the good sense and prudence of financial institutions which prided themselves on their stability, the conservative nature of their operations and the important part they played in the economy."

This reliance on gentlemen's rules would come as a shock to the public in the aftermath of the scandal involving Leonard Rosenberg's Greymac Trust 20 years later.

And as with Greymac, the registrar dealing with British Mortgage was loath to use his one big power — to shut down errant trust companies — because of the harm to depositors and innocent shareholders. In the aftermath of British Mortgage, amendments to the trust legislation spelled out the quality test for investments and enshrined conflict-of-interest rules to guard against directors and officers with divided loyalties. But again, 20 years later the transgressions occurred regardless of the rules.

By the time the Ontario regulators had received British Mortgage's year-end returns for 1964, they were well aware of the company's peril. Twenty-eight mortgages totalling $7 million showed no principal paid in more than a year. A new chief examiner urged the registrar to do something and offered the services of two examiners, who would spend April of 1965 investigating the company. The registrar did nothing but send a strongly worded letter to Gregory, who in typical fashion replied with an effective blend of conciliation and intransigence. "Every borrower is a millionaire," he contended and then offered the lie that things had been cleaned up since the year-end.

Gregory's true nature is best revealed in his actions towards the end. Just after the collapse of Atlantic, when he was well aware of the effect it would have on British Mortgage, he persuaded a lifelong family friend to buy $20,000 worth of British Mortgage stock from Jack Tramiel, a principal player in the Atlantic complex of companies.* In early July Gregory had the trust company surreptitiously begin selling its own shares in Atlantic Acceptance, and two weeks later, when the price had plummeted to half value, he had the Atlantic stock held in estate trust and agency accounts sold. Finally, there are Gregory's last days in his Stratford office. After resisting his inevitable resignation for weeks, he began to move out, taking several days to destroy almost every file connected to his involvement in the Atlantic complex and corrupt mortgage deals.

For Victoria and Grey, which had been eyeing BMT for two years, appreciating the compatibility of the two rural-based, mortgage-oriented trust companies, the merger with British Mortgage was a boon. It doubled Victoria and Grey's size to 25 branches, the largest in the province, and BMT's huge losses provided handy tax benefits. Victoria and Grey also gained in other ways from the merger: as the Atlantic-related assets were liquidated many proved quite valuable, and over the course of several years the terms of the merger turned out to be generous to Victoria and Grey. And the manager of British Mortgage's St Mary's branch, William Somerville, went on to become Victoria and Grey's president for life.†

---

* After the collapse of Atlantic, Auschwitz survivor Tramiel, who headed one of the Atlantic subsidiaries eventually investigated, found backing to buy control of Commodore. Under his direction the company enjoyed great success with the Commodore 64 home computer. Tramiel went on to take over rival Atari in the U.S.

† No shrinking violet, Somerville tells the story of his ascendancy this way: as a successful businessman in drug wholesaling, he went to British Mortgage for a will in 1963. While hesitating over the final details of the unpleasant business, he received a call from Gregory, who persuaded him to open a branch in Somerville's home town, nearby St Mary's. "I knew nothing about the trust business, but took it anyway. Within a year it was a roaring success." At the time of the collapse, Somerville gained the distinction of running the only branch with no withdrawals — he was mayor of St Mary's then. After Victoria and Grey took over, its president, Walter Harris, called Somerville in: "They gave me five minutes with him; we talked politics for two hours. Then he said, 'Our only hope is you. Otherwise we'll go broke.'" Somerville wheeled and dealed on the problem loans and after three years was appointed assistant general manager.

In March 1967 a royal commission appointed by Ontario Premier John Robarts to inquire into the failure of Atlantic Acceptance and conducted by Hon. Samuel H.S. Hughes had finally turned its attention to the last phase of investigation — into how British Mortgage fitted into the Atlantic Acceptance puzzle. The entire complex, four-year inquiry was eventually boiled down to four large volumes of detailed descriptions and testimony and released in the fall of 1969. Even today the report is an outstanding example of accomplished, entertaining writing and includes section headings such as "New Wine for an Old Bottle," "Good Money after Bad: The Turf King's Solution" and "Disquiet in Berlin."

As a result of Hughes's investigation, twelve persons involved in the Atlantic affair were charged, including British Mortgage's mortgage manager, who was jailed on fraud and bribery charges. Lawyers and accountants involved were disciplined by their professional bodies, although Atlantic's principal auditor died in a mysterious plane crash before testifying. C. Powell Morgan died of leukemia before Hughes's investigation was completed. Gregory, who was never convicted, went on to rebuild his legal practice in Stratford.

The royal commission report, however, portrays the collapse of BMT as the fault of Wilfrid Gregory alone. "Gifted, affable, sought-after and acclaimed, Wilfrid Palmer Gregory was the respected head of a financial institution which was a familiar symbol of stability and strength, and which he did much to aggrandize and everything to destroy. The fact that his most destructive activities were concealed — and the evidence shows consciously concealed — from his fellow directors, most of whom were old friends of himself and his family, must be conclusive in tipping the scales of judgment against him, and the final attempt to destroy the evidence in his files was as consistent with his previous conduct as it was futile in result. It fell far short of what is expected of the head of a public corporation or, indeed, of any honorable man." Custom, and the traditional rules of conduct that had governed the trust industry since its beginnings, had failed.

Steve Axton and Dominion Trust

"Go phone Wonderboy." Lawyer Sheldon Kirsh wanted his recalcitrant client Nigel Stephen (Steve) Axton to arrive so the unsavoury business could finally be settled. Kirsh was standing in a courtroom at Toronto's Osgoode Hall on a Thursday morning in late October 1983 amid a clutch of anxious lawyers representing half a dozen interests. There was a tangible aura of suppressed relief: this court hearing would decide the fate of Dominion Trust.

Many of these lawyers had been working behind closed doors for weeks. The hearing was open to the public only because those involved assumed no one would sniff it out; it was originally to be held in a court official's office, but the crowd had grown too large.

The silence surrounding Dominion's sale to new interests was by common consent. It seemed everyone — the owners, the directors, the joint-venture partners, the Ontario government — had something to keep secret. Lawyers for the various parties went as far as obtaining a judge's order to seal the public court files on five separate but interrelated lawsuits against the company; the reason for this draconian measure was conveniently sealed inside those same files.

Steve Axton, whose background and credentials were as respectable as those of W.P. Gregory, had the most reason of all to keep mum. Wonderboy might have seemed like an appropriate handle for this dapper lawyer-financier-salesman already running to flesh when, in June 1982, at age 29, he was registered as Dominion's official buyer. The regulators didn't hear about the sale of the Sudbury-based trust company by long-time owner Peter Silverman until a routine report was filed a month later, and Axton didn't have a speck of trust company management expertise. But he had other "qualifications," according to Ontario trust registrar Murray Thompson. His father was a diplomat; he had graduated from Upper Canada College; he was a member of the bar. The regulators had nothing against him.

By the time he was forced to sell Dominion to real estate and brewing magnate Murray Goldman in November 1983, Axton had been forced out of his law practice, had been disbarred and had lost his fancy Rosedale home. Even his lawyer was making fun of him. But Axton must have managed to salt away a bit of cash. He abandoned Canada the week after the court hearing, under the cloud of an Ontario Provincial Police investigation — and the police traced him to a yacht in the Caribbean. They couldn't touch him there, where he quickly bought and sold a restaurant called Hemingway's in San Martine, but in February 1985 they laid the first of 50 criminal fraud and theft charges in Ontario for his plundering of Dominion's books. A routine check by the U.S. Internal Revenue Service that April on a real estate deal he was hatching uncovered Axton's name in the FBI files, and he was arrested while in Austin, Texas.*

This entrepreneur's rise and fall in the Ontario trust community of 1982 was overshadowed by Lenny Rosenberg's but was no less incredible. As he was leaving the courtroom that October afternoon, after hearing his lawyer explain for the better part of an hour exactly what did happen to Dominion Trust, Axton turned to a companion and commented with a smile that Kirsh's presentation to the judge was "not the real story, but some of it."

The real story may reside only in the mind of Steve Axton, but his methods of operation are quite familiar to anyone who has watched a huckster work the real estate market. Take, for instance, a townhouse development in downtown Toronto. In a wry twist to the old "Take my wife — please" joke, there were a number of investors who wished anyone would take those townhouses away. They had bought them as tax shelters under the federal Multiple Unit Residential Building (MURB) tax write-off program in 1981. Axton thought up the project before he bought Dominion, arranging the financing through

* Axton was held without bail pending extradition; he returned to Ontario voluntarily and spent his days in a Toronto detention centre while de rigeur lawyer Edward Greenspan — who had represented Astra Trust's Carlo Montemurro at a fraud trial a year earlier — negotiated with the Crown. No plea was entered to the charges as of August 1985.

two other trust companies, Standard Trust and Continental Trust. The townhouses were sold at $145,000 each. Two years later they were worth $110,000. The Toronto market had fallen, and mortgage rates had risen at renegotiation time. Worse, when some of the investors began to take an active role in renting these properties, which were plagued by a high rate of tenant turn-over, they discovered a big drawback to the $800-plus per month "luxury Cabbagetown" townhouses. Prospective tenants who arrived to look at the units after work were faced with a long queue of derelicts lining up across the street in anticipation of supper-time at the Mission.

Standard Trust president Brian O'Malley says the company originally felt comfortable with the deal: the buyers were there, the appraisals were there. Standard, a small, steady trust that believes in real estate development, bought an option on a piece of the development and picked it up after the units were presold.

The drop in value is a market risk for sophisticated, well-heeled buyers, O'Malley says. Although its value dropped, this project was a fairly standard MURB. But even here Axton showed his creative knack for making money. He and his partners bought a half-dozen of the units. Axton did all the legal work, including making sure the trust companies had the personal covenants of the investors to back the loans — for all except those half-dozen units. "Somehow Mr Axton had neglected to put his own personal covenants and the ones of his partners on [the registry certificate]," O'Malley says.

Axton approached Standard with another idea in 1982 before it found out about the lack of paperwork on his MURB investment. The scheme looked too good to turn down. He promised one-third of the profits on a Colborne Street building just for Standard's signature on the dotted line of an agreement to be a joint-venture partner — no money in, no covenant, no commitment. But the deal was too weird, so Standard did say no.

O'Malley felt Axton had changed since he began dealing with him at Standard back around 1978. Then, Axton had brought in a decent real estate proposal, acting as agent in return for the legal business. He was dealing with more than half a dozen trust companies in the late seventies and early eighties. He was one of a string of agents who walked in the door, but he caught their attention. "He was a very bright lawyer, very articulate, quite an impressive guy, good credentials," says O'Malley.

Colborne Street was a signal that Axton had changed. "After that . . . we noticed that Axton was starting to act erratic and we stopped dealing with him," says O'Malley. "He didn't make sense."

Continental Trust didn't seem to notice. It became a partner in the Colborne Street property — but on far different terms. It put up the money for a second mortgage, and lost it. Continental continued to do business with Axton right through his Dominion Trust period. Its senior management didn't have the kind of experience necessary to realize these weren't "normal" real estate deals. An employee was fired after Axton's practices were discovered; he was too close to his joint-venture partner. One source says he was living in a rent-free townhouse provided by Axton. A mortgage broker tells of dealing with Continental during this period: he had shopped a deal all over town and found it wasn't worth anyone's while. Finally, he took it to Continental, where his mortgage contact told him it was the best deal he'd seen in a year.

The federally chartered Continental had been an inactive company when Reuben Cohen and Leonard Ellen bought it as part of parent United Financial Management. They were interested only in United's mutual fund operations. But United Financial president Jim Clarke — a graduate of Metro Trust's Canadian Realty Investment Trust — wanted to activate it, and they gave him the chance. Clarke never knew how bad the Axton deals were until it was too late; he trusted his staff. He was frustrated that a "peanut" like Dominion could bring Continental such pain. It was painful for Cohen and Ellen; they had to channel about $2 million into the company to wipe out the shortfall on loans made in association with Axton; or for deals that Wonderboy had engineered. It was painful for Clarke; he lost his job.

Axton's deals turned Cohen and Ellen away from any idea of combining Continental with their Central Trust. They placed it on the invisible sale block in 1984, asking too high a price for most potential buyers, but finally closing a deal with two Westerners for $10.1 million in early 1985. Lenny Wong, the Calgary real estate salesman who sold Brittania Agencies to George Mann in the early seventies and who had millions of dollars of outstanding judgments against him in Alberta courts for real estate deals gone wrong, was brought to them by stock brokerage McLeod Young Weir, always so active in the trust business. Wong turned to Vancouver marble wholesaler, oil and gas drilling and high-tech entrepreneur Ronald Johnson for much of the cash.

The pair laid plans for expansion but were tripped up when the bankers' blanket bond, a regulatory requirement for operation, was cancelled by the bonding company. Johnson says the cancellation was caused by a lawsuit against the bonding company launched by Continental, but Ellen denies this; others say it was doubts about management capability that prompted the move. In either case, it shows the private sector making its own judgments about whether a financial institution should be allowed to stay in business. Shortly afterward, the Toronto Dominion Bank dropped the other shoe by refusing to clear Continental's cheques any longer.

Wong and Johnson fought over exactly who owned how much of the company — the land Wong was to contribute to boost the trust's capital base was no longer his. "He fell flat on his face and had to back out, leaving me with my cash in there and no partner," says Johnson. They both began almost immediately to tangle with federal regulators over the value of Continental's assets. Johnson was planning to sell Continental's poor mortgages, and says Minister of State for Finance Barbara McDougall initially approved the deal. But Ottawa had doubts about the change in ownership from the start. It placed Continental on a monthly licence and insisted the borrowing multiple be reduced from 23 to 15 times its capital base. Auditor Laventhol & Horwath, sent in by Ottawa to analyse Continental's books, was appalled by what it valued as $4 million in management contracts for Wong, Johnson and a few associates. Johnson dismisses this assessment: it wasn't a $4 million liability, he says, it was a "$50,000-a-month liability." As well, Wong attempted to buy a $485,000 house using a newly-issued $50,000 Continental Guaranteed Investment Certificate as the downpayment.

At the end of June 1985 Ottawa announced it was applying to wind up Continental. But Johnson refused to believe he was beaten — or to entertain offers of a discounted sale to such companies as Brendan Calder's Counsel Trust or Izzy Asper's CanWest. He says Continental could have earned a profit of $2.3 million in 1985, including cash paid to the company by developers as "inducements" for locating branches in particular office buildings. He continued to try and re-interest investors in buying preferred shares and to arrange with the Royal Bank of Canada for cheque clearing. Continental was still fighting the court application in August.

Whatever its eventual fate, Axton milked Continental. At one point about $20 million, or one-sixth of its mortgage loan portfolio, was tied up in Axton deals that included one mortgage that ranked behind *four* others on the priority list of who was to be paid back by the borrower. In one case, money for a mortgage financing being done by Continental was deposited in a trust account at Axton's law firm — and somehow $875,000 of it ended up in Dominion's vault. Continental sued to get the money back and was paid out of Murray Goldman's purchase purse.

In the end, it comes down to who should be allowed to own a trust company. Axton's June 1982 purchase of Dominion was a step observers in the mortgage community just couldn't believe. The circumstances of the purchase have never been publicly revealed, but the $2.4 million used by Axton to buy Dominion came from building contractor Joe Lanzino, an Italian immigrant with a large, wired fence around his Toronto home. Like so many, Lanzino had always wanted to own a lending institution. He thought he was finally going to see one in the family when he arranged with Axton for his 20-year-old novitiate son Vincent to take charge of Dominion in December 1982.

Dominion was used as a whipping boy by Ontario six months after Axton bought it, when he was about to turn it over to the Lanzinos. The government wanted to freeze Leonard Rosenberg in his tracks, so it introduced legislation that would allow its January 7, 1983, take-over of Crown, Greymac and Seaway. But Bill Davis pushed it through the house by telling Opposition leaders David Peterson and Bob Rae that he needed to stop the ownership switch at Dominion.

Not that the government officials were thrilled about leaving the company in Axton's hands after the crazy antics of his proposed sale. But they had their days and nights full overseeing the take-over of the three Rosenberg-related trust companies, so they didn't begin to deal with Dominion until spring. When they did, since they made only the routine spot checks of documents rather than a full review of the loans by this company about which they had serious reservations, it was luck that they uncovered Axton's special brand of paperwork.

A sharp-eyed regulator spotted a doctored document. Pages had been lifted from an appraisal report, but there had been a slip-up on the part of whoever did the refiguring. "They didn't change the rents, and he knew the rental income wouldn't support the development," says Murray Thompson. "By God, he should get kudos for that."

Next they found more doctored documents: an appraisal attributed to an appraiser who hadn't done the work although a facsimile of his signature was on the document; appraisals by someone who wasn't an appraiser and was using a clutch of false identities when signing the documents. (Stanley Lichtenstein pleaded guilty to falsifying documents in mid-1983 and received a jail term of less than a year.)

Something needed to be done. Axton's law partners quit the board that month, leaving only a single board member aside from Wonderboy. In May a team led by the head of Ontario's trust and insurance investigation unit, Don Reid, tried a new tactic in tune with the smooth style of the former Scotland Yard investigator and rising figure in the bureaucratic pantheon. Rather than again invoking the draconian measures used with Greymac in January, the Ontario government simply shut

Dominion down. It couldn't make morgage loans, it couldn't take deposits. And it was given a new, hand-picked and ministry-stamped, board of directors.

Then came the negotiations. When Axton was forced to unload it, Dominion was destitute. To buy the company, Goldman had to agree to pump $2 million in immediately to restock its empty coffers and had to manage a slew of bad mortgages besides. One lawyer compared the complicated sale negotiations to heart surgery. Certainly there were as many loose ends to be tied.

Dominion wasn't the only firm whose books had been tampered with, according to Axton's former law partners Harry Cravit and Rubin Dexter. They filed a suit stating he had misappropriated $390,000 in trust account funds from the law firm, forging signatures and depositing cheques in his own companies. He told them in May 1983, as he pulled large bundles of U.S. dollars from a satchel and waved them in the air, that he had sold his house to his mother and given his Mercedes Benz to his father.

Kirsh said at the court hearing at which the main outstanding civil lawsuits were legally dismissed that he and a few others had settled matters at an early hour that morning. There had been a number of late nights stretching to early mornings of tense negotiating; it's hard for lawyers to agree to lose their clients' money. One kicked a filing cabinet in frustration during an all-nighter in Goldman lawyer Barry Rotenberg's office.* The final suit to be settled was that of Lanzino, who had been a partner of Axton in a number of transactions at Dominion. Both he and Continental laid claim to Dominion shares. He kept stalling, hoping for some money, but there was none for him.

With Axton now facing 50 fraud and theft charges, it's possible that more of "the real story" will emerge in criminal

* Rotenberg, a real estate lawyer with a varied clientele that includes Toronto Dominion Bank and Leonard Rosenberg, was the one who thought up the idea that CanWest might sell its Crown Trust shares and approached Joe Burnett for an introduction to Ellen and Cohen.

court. But there will never be an explanation of why a young lawyer minting money hustling legitimate real estate deals would cross the line into the nether world of forged documents and disappearing funds. Suggested one observer who knew him when: "Greed overpowers you."

George Mann and United Trust

"We were so complacent and so smug in those days we didn't even pay any attention to a guy like George Mann. People pay a lot of attention to him now because he has a lot of clout. But we didn't even consider people like that as part of the industry."
—an old-guard member in good standing

George Mann feels he is letting a veil lift ever so slightly to show the fast-buck beginnings behind the polished coating acquired in the international league. Stories trip off his tongue even as he calculates their best angle of refraction.

Mann fancies himself a master manipulator, a comedic Machiavelli; he lets juicy tidbits from his phone conversation drop before his guests. His office is by Robert Dirstein of Yorkville, his suits are a bankerly hue and his friends are the most powerful of the business caste. But the veil is as transparent as the emperor's clothes. The pool-hall sharpie who swaggered in the streets of midtown Toronto 30 years ago is never far from the surface. "George was a naughty boy, very street wise," says Monty Beber, a mortgage broker who once worked for Mann's father, David, and now sits on the board of Calgary-based Northland Bank. The tough guy is still the hustler who designed his own advertising campaigns for Toronto-based United Trust during the first half of the 1970s — commercials featuring Dracula and mock bank hold-ups on radio so Quebeckers would know United was a "bank." He still proudly displays his scrapbooks from the seventies, pointing out with glee a photograph of himself flanked by two mini-skirted cuties modelling see-through umbrellas offered free to new account customers.

Mann has made a large impression on corporate Canada. His Unicorp Canada Corp., a real estate, energy, financial services and stock investment holding company, had $480 million in assets at the end of 1984. That figure was way out of date four months later, when Unicorp acquired 60% of the $1.5 billion Union Gas of Chatham, Ontario.

Mann has been an inevitable success in Canadian business because for two decades he has been playing by U.S. rules. The boys are tougher south of the border; they understand the value of push. Promoting the company promotes the owner. Mann was operating on that principle back in 1968 when he volunteered staff from the company that predated United, puny Ottawa-based Rideau Trust, to register members of the Trust Companies Association of Canada at their annual meeting, and grandstanded by providing the penny-pinchers with a surprise coffee and Danish treat at their morning break. The newcomer garnered heartfelt praise for the gesture, to his open amusement; it was a classic example of the gulf between administrator and promoter. Unlike other newcomers, who have used their blueblood backgrounds to blend into the trust business, Mann flourishes on the strength of his own brashness and colourful profile.

He began copying the brash tactics of U.S. savings and loan companies after buying into the money lending business with a piece of a small Ottawa loan company in 1964. And nobody has ever really pushed back. His Union Gas bid marks the first time he has faced U.S.-style take-over defence tactics in Canada. But while Union chairman Darcy McKeough, for all his political pull and business support, flailed about like a fish on a dock, Unicorp won with enough strength in reserve to simultaneously defend against another very hostile executive group. It is boosting its shareholding in New Jersey's City Federal Savings & Loan, whose $7.6 billion in assets rank it with the largest Canadian trust companies, to 24.9% from 8.2% over strenuous efforts by management to stop it.

Mann takes joy in the hostility, he revels in the heat, he confidently seeks out this "fun." There's always potential for the companies he seeks, there's always a quick killing from a turnover or a good trading position. He's constantly portraying himself publicly as a financial wizard who enjoys nothing so much as reading detailed financial statements on obscure companies in U.S. corporate snapshot publications like *Standard & Poor's*.

One of the most lucrative of his recent arbitrage plays — moving in and out of a company for a quick kill — was his 1984 purchase of 6% of Canada Trust. Mann says he knew when he bought it that he had a buyer and that earnings couldn't help but improve as interest rates fell. With ManuLife in at almost 30% and large blocks of stock crossing the trading floor every day, there was obviously a market being made by friends of the insurer and other speculators. Despite a bevy of rumours that Mann must be part of a behind-the-curtain plan to "warehouse" the stock for ManuLife or perhaps Edward and Peter Brontman, Unicorp sold eight months later for a profit of about $7 million.

Canada Trust, the last widely held trust company in the country, is the eighth Canadian financial institution in which Mann has had a significant investment. There have been four trust companies — United, Financial, Royal Trust (through the shareholding he gained by selling United to the industry giant in 1976) and Canada — a loan company, a mortgage company, a brief and very profitable fling with a small insurance company, and a chunk of the ill-fated Unity Bank of Canada.* There have also been two U.S. savings and loan companies — Trans Ohio, a money-loser sold to Metro Trust in the mid-seventies, and now City Federal — as well as a clutch of U.S. real estate investment trusts picked up for their property rather

* Mann bought 15% of Unity's stock in 1973 at a discount and joined the board, eventually becoming chairman. He was a linchpin in Unity's 1977 merger with Provincial Bank. In 1980 Provincial merged with National Bank, and Mann maintains a shareholding in National, his main banker and one of a number of companies that helped out with the Union Gas take-over. For a fascinating account of Unity's chequered history, see Walter Stewart's *Towers of Gold, Feet of Clay*.

than their operating potential. And Mann almost had 17% of major Canadian stockbroker Midland Doherty through a proposed 1980 merger that was the brokerage firm's first attempt to gain a public listing.

There's no reason to think he'll stop there. He enjoys toying with the possibilities presented by the federal government's open-door stance to new domestic banks and trust companies. In the first months of 1985 Mann called the boys at Genstar to inquire how serious they were about keeping Canada Permanent. It was no go there, but Mann floats the trial balloon that Union Gas's western Ontario outlets would make dandy drop-off points for consumer savings and investment centres. Mann likes the financial services business. He likes the profits that have come from selling if not running his own ventures; he likes the profile; he likes the feel of the money game. He always calls it banking.

Two decades ago a younger man without the lucite coating of convention traded the streets of midtown Toronto and the real estate brokerage business he had learned at the knee of his father, David, for the one-branch Ottawa money shop called Commonwealth Savings & Loan. The real estate salesman joined forces with developer Mark Tanz; the family firm, Mann & Martel, with 20%, ranked second to Tanz in ownership, and his official title of vice-president sat below that of president Tanz on the letterhead. Commonwealth's head office was soon shifted to Toronto, and Mann was happy to spend time on weekly strategy sessions for the company, one morning a mortgage approval session, the next a promotions and branch opening think-tank. This was much more fun than building or selling houses. He was in charge of the branch expansion, and his imported ideas about advertising and promotions to attract accounts drew crowds. The all-time favourite — one he would repeat at United — was the give-away of a blanket with each $50 deposited in a new account, a success story that speaks volumes about the Canadian psyche. The hours at the new branches were revolutionary: 9 A.M. to 5:30 P.M. Monday to Friday, 9 to 4 Saturdays. Commonwealth opened enough accounts in the next two years to somehow convince the Ontario regulators it was a sure bet for stardom, and its assets ballooned from as little as 6 times its capital base to 17.5 times its capital. It also took an unsuccessful run at Metro Trust — a bold move for a small company.

Mann bowed out of Commonwealth as a manager in 1968 and as a shareholder soon after.* He had enjoyed the game, but his roving eye had landed on the investment potential of his own family firm, Mann & Martel. That year, he bought out both his father and his father's partner, Paul Martel, and as always he had big plans. His father stayed on the company's board and is still a director of Unicorp, but the late Paul Martel moved on. His son, Toronto real estate broker Terry Martel, recently told *The Globe and Mail* that Martel Sr. "knew George was a rocket that was going to reach the moon or explode on takeoff." The firm was already the largest real estate broker in Toronto with 30% of the shared-listing business and blanket advertising that made it *The Toronto Star*'s largest classified advertiser. Mann saw a wad of investment potential if he could market that hype machine by listing his company on the stock market and selling the stock to the public.

He was forced to pull back by the gentlemen's rules of the Toronto Real Estate Board. The board's members also saw the potential of public brokerage companies, and these free-enterprisers turned white as sheets at the thought of Mann & Martel's dominating the market even further with all that additional capital. They flatly refused to let the firm remain a member of the board — which it needed to do to use the multiple listing system by which it garnered so much of its business — if it went public.

Trust companies were the only members of the real estate board that were allowed to be publicly listed. The next step

* In 1969 Commonwealth merged with Central Ontario Trust & Savings, which in turn merged with Ontario Trust in 1972. Control of Ontario Trust was sold to British interests the next year, but its directors had good political links, and the province said nothing about the out-of-country sale. Ontario was later purchased by Canada Trust.

was, in a favourite phrase from Mann's lexicon, a no-brainer. "The only way to take the [real estate] company public was to bend it into a trust company." Mann purchased Rideau Trust, Commonwealth's major Ottawa competition, from Jarvis Friedman, a lawyer whose relatives owned a local family retail chain. Friedman needed more capital — the small guy's swan song. Mann bought 51% with a $700,000 cash infusion. The company issued him new shares, and presto! its capital problems were solved. Mann erased the name Rideau — too regional. He opted for United, saying the name was chosen because it could be easily understood by ethnic home-buyers and depositors.

It would take a lot of rule bending to plunk Mann & Martel into United Trust. It would have taken a Yogi to bend it into any semblance of the traditional trust company. But Mann wouldn't need a Yogi, because he planned to bend the industry to fit his company. At the time, the old guard wasn't worried in the least by his big talk. They figured they could put upstarts like Mann out of business if they wanted to — they just didn't think it worth the bother.

The regulators, however, who did venture down from Olympus on occasion to see what "people like that" were planning for the business, paid attention. Gordon Grundy, trust registrar until 1974 (his previous job was running Hamilton-based Studebaker) was determined that Mann wouldn't be able to run a real estate operation from a trust company.

Before dealing with Grundy, Mann decided to "make a statement" to the realtors who had dared to stymie him. It could have easily been made with a thumb and a nose. He rented an empty space directly across the street from the Real Estate Board's headquarters, hung the Rideau Trust sign — the name was changed to United when the brokerage firm was finally merged — and staffed it with a former board president. "They went a little berserk when they saw what we had done to them," he smiles in relish at the memory. "We stewed them in their own juices." The board was even more upset when Ontario stalled on the merger of the brokerage firm and the trust company; the borrowing public wouldn't know about potential conflicts of interests, it raged, when a Mann & Martel salesman arranged a mortgage with the trust company.

Mann is in business for the fun, for the game, for the tricks. He despised Gordon Grundy for his rigid rule-maker pomposity, and although he smiled all the while they negotiated, he would teach this jerk a lesson after he had his way with him. It took two years before Mann could wear Grundy down. "We kept buggin' them and buggin' them and buggin' them," he says. But with wheedling and whiz-bang projections, "we were able to show them that this was probably the best thing that could ever happen to this little company." In September 1970 permission for the merger was granted. Then Mann had his chance at Grundy.

It was the Dracula radio jingle that really did Grundy in. Mann savours a verbal sketch of Grundy driving in to work from his Hamilton home, listening to the radio while on the expressway and palpitating in horror as he heard the Transylvanian count going in search for Mann & Martel and finding United Trust. Blood lust in the trust business! Added to that were the bold ads in newspapers in both Ottawa and Toronto announcing the amalgamation and name change. Grundy demanded the right to approve every ad that was to be run. This strong-arm tactic wasn't in the rule-book, but he wasn't going to allow these shenanigans. Mann obliged — but Grundy found the co-operation too much to handle. "We figure, OK, we'll fix these guys. So we start plowing ads down there for Gordon Grundy's approval, the likes of which you've never seen in your life. That lasts for three days, and they give up. They say don't do anything disrespectful, just get out of here, goodbye." The department never tried to sit on Mann again.

United started out with savings offices in the front of its branches, real estate offices in the back. Its mercury level shot up with Mann's fevered growth targets: 30 branches in the first two years. The money pouring in from deposits needed more and more capital from United to support its leverage. United boosted its capital base in mid-1973 with the first-ever sale of a property company to a trust company. The purchase of Douglas Leaseholds Ltd., which owned gas stations and commercial developments, added property assets to United's books. Mann was quickly taking advantage of a change in Ontario law; before this, trust companies couldn't own real estate aside from their own branch premises. When that rule had been in force, Mann had found a way around the technicality by purchasing real estate on his own account and leasing part of it to the trust company. In 1972 he had bought a cash-rich mining company and folded much of this real estate into it, and Unicorp was born as a holding company for his United shares. Mann also used a dozen or so companies he owned to fulfil divergent needs of United such as interior decoration — United branches came complete with chandeliers — and auto leases for branch managers.

Like Commonwealth, United was promotion crazy, hosting rock concerts and introducing the American Express gold card to Canada. Mann affected a moustache in those years as he greeted the Queen in his role as fund-raiser for Toronto's Mount Sinai Hospital. He had 82 branches by 1974 when they were rechristened Moneyshops, and he was oblivious to the fact that this was exactly what trust types were calling them behind his back — "jerkwater money shops," not real trust branches at all. Money shops suited Mann just fine. That was what he wanted, quick cashboxes that made money on savvy in the real estate market and the willingness to take risks.

The risks included a speedy one-day turnaround on mortgages, and loans to ethnic groups that had never before been targeted for special attention. Mann's real estate people had specialized in exploiting the house buying and upscaling of immigrants in Toronto, and he felt he knew them better than any other company could. United was constantly touting the fact that it advertised and served customers in two dozen languages. They would pay off their mortgages, they would work harder and save more than the white-bread middle class. The orientation of the real estate operation was sell; the instruction to the mortgage operation was service.

Mann, who had thought Grundy in outer space when the regulator talked of the inevitable conflicts of interest in housing a real estate broker and a mortgage lender under the same roof, claims he suffered under pressure from employees (he emphasizes that at least half the 2,300 sales force felt they could call him George). Every day his phone would ring with a very frustrated voice from one of the branches. "I used to have a phone call from the real estate manager saying, 'That S.O.B. in the mortgage department is killing my deal, he will not give me the mortgage, you've got to intercede. OK?' And I'd no sooner hang up the phone than the guy from the mortgage department calls me and tells me, 'That real estate manager is so highhanded and so impossible he's ridiculous.' And I'm listening to the two of them and I'm in the middle."

Despite this monkey-in-the-middle complaint, at first United, as promised to Ontario regulators, prospered. In February 1972 ManuLife was one of the investors through a private placement of shares, and when United finally was publicly listed after a share issue later that year, the ubiquitous Cemp Investments, owned by Charles, Edgar, Minda and Phyllis, children of Samuel Bronfman, bought a chunk and had a paid manager join United's board. Mann was sensitive to the endorsement; he was even more interested in capitalizing on the relationship to secure prime branches in Cemp-controlled Cadillac Fairview Corp. shopping centres, particularly in Quebec. United expanded into both Quebec and Alberta by buying up real estate operations. In Alberta that meant Brittania Agencies, the largest brokerage firm in Calgary, run by Lenny Wong, who a decade later bought Continental Trust from Reuben Cohen and Leonard Ellen. It was from this Calgary branch system that a series of fraud-related problems would surface — houses being bought, flipped (immediately sold again at artificially hiked prices to associates) and mortgaged by a friendly trust company manager at the second sale price, which was more than its real value. The conspirators would use the mortgage money to pay the original owner of the house its lower, real market price and have enough cash left over to pay

the mortgage lenders, real estate salesmen, lawyers and themselves a little bonus. If and when they stopped making mortgage payments the trust company would have to worry about
reselling the overmortgaged house, but the fraud artists would
all be a little richer. It was a classic scam, but it would throw
back in Mann's face the boast that he knew about everything
that went on in United. "There was very little happening out
there that I wasn't aware of on a daily basis." That, former
employees would testify in court, was part of the problem.

"It was a very unusual situation, it seemed that every function of the mortgage operation was influenced or there was
[*sic*] attempts to influence it by the real estate operation. The
continuous interference by real estate managers and the owner
of the company was very unusual and continuous to the effect
that if deals were not put together then I was not considered
doing my job. And there was no question if the deal was bad or
good, it was just a matter of you putting the deal together, and
that was the only priority."

These are the words of Marvin Michael Chochli, former Edmonton mortgage manager for United Trust. He was testifying
in a Calgary courtroom at the May 19, 1977, trial of Keith
Allister Walters, formerly the mortgage manager of United's
Calgary branch. Walters was being tried for defrauding United
Trust of $410,098 — for taking $2,626 in bribes from a developer and lending to him in 13 cases more money than properties were worth.

Walters, one of a group charged with similar offences,
pleaded guilty and was sentenced to six months' imprisonment
to be served on weekends, so he could support his family. The
money involved was a paltry sum, and in the end United didn't
lose a cent. The serious aspect of the trial from the perspective
of the health of the trust industry was Chochli's charge that
head office — the owner of United — had pushed people hard
to write mortgages without proper analysis.

Chochli's evidence damned United's organizational techniques. Employed as a provincial land acquisitions negotiator at
the time he testified, Chochli had been appalled at what he

found when he joined Mann's aggressive operation. There was no training for managers; he went to Toronto for a week to meet the folks at head office but wasn't briefed on United's policies or requirements. "The situation was that I was told to formulate my own policies and use my own judgments."

His own judgment was harsh. "I did have fairly extensive knowledge of mortgage procedures and appraisal and lending policies and government requirements and I found the operation just totally unprecedented." The mortgage manager should accept the sale price as the value of the property, he was told. He refused, and his immediate supervisor accepted his stance, but head office didn't. "Drive-by" appraisals were the norm for these deals. "It was one of the most unusual things that I have ever seen, the deals seem to be put together by phone," Chochli added. A photo or description submitted by the borrower sufficed. He said he was told to conform to this system or he would be out on the street.

He wasn't alone. John Sylvester Neilson had worked for United for two years and been promoted to general manager for Alberta. He testified that he resigned because he didn't like the structure of operations and the "moral fibre" of a new Alberta sales manager sent out by head office. Walters, he said, had real estate managers "lined up outside of his office with their deals to be processed."

Walters's lawyer used this evidence to argue that his client's acceptance of the bribe was tied to his harassed mental state — overworked, underpaid, not equipped for his job — and to pressure to do what head office wanted. Mann wasn't the only one being upset by telephone calls. Said Chochli: "I knew [Walters] was under pressure and I was aware of the continuous — perhaps threats would be a strong word but pressure by the owner of the company to satisfy the real estate needs. Otherwise there was no use in having that particular man around."

There was no training course for mortgage managers, there was no manual with lending rules. As far as Chochli was concerned, the mortgage departments were a sham. "The intent there was only to have a man in each location in order to prove to the Department of Insurance that they were complying with the government regulations in respect to mortgage lending. I believe it was only a fronting situation for the department. I was convinced of that.''

Mann the imperturbable is visibly disturbed by mention of the frauds, but he shrugs off the accusation that head office was at fault. "They of course traced everything back to me. Well, that would have been a great theory if I was just a manager, but I owned two-thirds of the company. Why would I cause anybody to lend money that could be put at risk if I owned two-thirds of the company? The logic wasn't there.''

His employees' charges against him are the sort of silly defence that must be resorted to when someone is "caught stealing," he says. Then, in an extraordinary admission of some kind of mismanagement, he backs over the claims of pressure-cooker lending in search of a justification. "Notwithstanding any kind of pressure head office might bring to bear to lend out more money, that doesn't allow you the right to be dishonest.''

He dismisses dishonesty as a hazard of a business where the inventory is cash. "We sent lawyers to jail and our mortgage guys went to jail and I think one of our real estate guys went to jail. That's all, nothing serious," he says light-heartedly. It wasn't serious to Mann's mind because United found the fraudulent Calgary loans 90 days after they were made, and the company recovered its money. Other companies with similar problems didn't pursue either the perpetrators or the cash, he says. United quietly searched the sale documents for the false legal affidavits and the skewed mortgage application form. "See, don't forget, it's a paper trail with this stuff.''

If there ever was, as Chochli suggested, a front for the regulators, it was convincing. Murray Thompson, who was appointed Ontario's registrar of loan and trust companies in 1974 after Grundy's death, respects George Mann. He says he never listened to the gossip. "Boy, if you want to know what's going on and not going on you go to the National Club for lunch. Eight people will tell you things. You come back and out of the eight, nine are wrong.''

But there was reason to listen. No matter the motivations of individual salesmen, the wily Mann had not proven himself a capable manager. He was good at blowing up the balloon, but he couldn't sustain the growth with anything more tangible than hot air. United began losing money in 1974, and suddenly there were no institutional investors or mainstream money interested in the company's potential. The rapid expansion had left United scrambling for cash flow and again and again hitting the ceiling of its capital base.

Ontario had investigator Bob Brewerton (now president of Sterling Trust) in the company on an almost full-time basis during the months before Mann sold to Royal Trust in 1976, and regulators met with United officials every Friday to discuss the company's eroded capital base. But as far as Thompson and his people were concerned, the problems were those of any organization that was growing too quickly. They were individual problems, not systemic delinquencies. Thompson wasn't worried by any fraud charges. He chuckles at the inherent conflict of interest. "It's always pressure. Every trust company that got into a real estate operation had that problem, because the real estate operation wanted to make a deal." People picked on Mann, Thompson maintains, because he was a real estate broker himself.

Thompson doesn't like to call the company undercapitalized and poorly managed; he labels the problem overexpansion. From that viewpoint, the regulator isn't forced to do anything. "The problems were manageable because the system found other people to take them over by way of amalgamation and merger."

For United it was an outright sale. Mann tried first to sell to Canada Trust, whose executive Arthur Mingay (Mann is possibly the only business associate who refers to Mingay as Art) had called on Mann a year before he sold. But by the time

Mann was ready to unload the sinking United, Mingay wasn't interested.*

He knew he had to sell or raise capital — and he couldn't raise capital with United's recent earnings record. But he didn't accept Royal's initial offer, holding out against the advice of United's latest president, Ed Daughney, and sure enough, wringing more from Ken White's negotiating team.

Royal found an operation that had worked partly on instinct but always pursued anyone else delinquent about written rules. "If some guy screwed us around we'd sue him, just like that," Mann says, snapping his fingers, "to teach him a lesson, to teach everybody a lesson, because that was our game. Royal Trust would walk away." There were about 15 lawsuits in the works when Royal bought United.

Royal had to work in tandem with another Mann company, Great Northern Financial. This mortgage brokerage operation reflected Mann's faith in the integrity of high-risk customers. He had a circuitous system of mortgaging and remortgaging worked out, but it amounted to United's standing first in line and Great Northern second in riskier loans.

For good credit risks it was always worth bending the rules. As former Great Northern associate Monty Beber explains: "Any jackass can look at a book and say you can only lend this much, [a borrower] must have income of X amount. Terms of reference are a lot of crap."

When Mann sold in 1976, he was ready to move on. United had become a "cat chasing its tail." Still, it's popular wisdom that he would have liked to be asked onto the Royal board as

---

* Canada Trust had its hands full with its acquisition in May 1976 of St Catharines-based Lincoln Trust, for which it paid a handsome price of $13 million. Lincoln's largest single shareholder was Lady Oakes, wife of Sir Harry Oakes of the Bahamas; but Lincoln directors controlled almost 10% through a holding company, Broburn. Lincoln Trust provided a sharp illustration of abuse of power in 1970 when a group of dissident shareholders tried to stop Lincoln's directors from issuing a rights offering to bring in more capital when a call could have been made on Broburn to pay in full the amount it owed on partly-paid-for shares. The dissidents also failed to stop the annual meeting at which 92% of votes cast supported the astonishing motion to "ratify, sanction and confirm all acts of the directors of the company since its incorporation."

the second largest single shareholder. He didn't have a hope. They might give him their shares to buy his company, but they still didn't approve of his style. He was glad to sell to Robert Campeau in 1980.

Mann didn't stay in neutral. He had Unity Bank — until it was merged. He and Ed Daughney, the man he brought in during United's final months, after president Eric Minns left, called on Murray Thompson and walked away with another trust company charter only a year after selling United.

For three years Financial operated as a subsidiary of Great Northern, with Beber on the board. Once again the company was doing riskier, high-ratio loans; in some cases, says Beber, the trust company would lend up to 75% on a property and Great Northern would take up to 20% more on a second mortgage. Daughney had been cleaning up problems for Mann at Great Northern, which had ended up with a spate of bad loans, the victim of another fraud perpetrated by inside mortgage managers. He then began running the trust company, but he and Mann fought over control of Financial, and finally Mann bought Daughney out in 1980, shortly before selling Financial in early 1981. (Daughney moved on to run an oil and gas company in Calgary for a year, then to the presidency of the Belzberg family's First City Trust in June of 1983.)

Mann's usually crystal-clear vision of exactly what he wants to gain from any company he touches clouds when he talks about Financial. The big company, big plans, big future he saw for United had dissipated, and that was really what he desired, not a scratch operation that would sit on the shelf. Great Northern's share price jumped on the stock-market when he sold Financial to Gerald Pencer.

Shortly after the Financial sale, Great Northern almost provided Mann's entrée to Bay Street. Mann had recently been given a seat on the board of broker Midland Doherty and proferred one on the publicly listed Unicorp to Midland president Philip Holtby; talk of a merger of Midland and Great Northern came soon after. The proposed Midland merger, cut from the same cloth as Mann's move to take his real estate brokerage firm public a decade earlier, was scotched by the OSC's intransigence and killed by a bad stock-market. But it showed how time can wash away details; Great Northern was resuscitated, and Mann and his Unicorp were about to become rising stars in analysts' reports and a scad of business articles.*

Mann had already begun using Unicorp, his holding company, to move into real estate and financial institutions investments in the U.S. as well as expanding his Canadian property fortfolio. Unicorp also began to take more and more interest in stock-market arbitrage, buying stakes in companies such as U.S. paint manufacturer Pratt & Whitney and selling for multi-million dollar profits. The addition of Lawrence Brenzel, a stockbroker who specializes in arbitrage, to the Unicorp board has helped this business grow.

Now Unicorp wins awards for the clarity of its annual reports, decorated by coloured graphs that show numbers going up and up and up. Mann's president at Unicorp, Jim Leech, exudes the essence of bright, hard and winning. It was the connections of this Ultra-Brite smiling executive from his days with Commerce Capital Corp. — former owners of Eaton Bay Trust — that triggered the Midland friendship. Now he and Mann hobnob with the nabobs. Unicorp has more than once purchased pieces of companies in concert with the "Edper" Bronfmans, Edward and Peter. Its successful run at Union Enterprises was aided by Paul and Albert Reichmann, among others. And Mann has purchased a home down the street from Quebec magnate Paul Dcsmarais. But people in powerful positions have learned what Beber says Daughney found out when he tried a power play at Financial: "You don't try George on for size unless you're willing to have a knock-down battle."

George Mann is still talked about in trust circles as a barracuda in business waters. Thompson, the regulator, thinks it's at least

---

* Mann claims to have only disdain for the Canadian business press, seeing its practitioners as uninformed, easy marks for puff pieces. He says he preferred the rougher treatment he received during his take-over of Union Gas as the type of U.S.-style probing that is good for the business community. But while his outer office boasted reprints of every puff piece in early 1984, a year later there was nary a reprint of the Union Gas stories.

partly envy. "Maybe he was too smart and maybe he was too quick, too bright. He's a very articulate bright guy." He doesn't believe it was Mann's methods that really prompted the trust industry's everlasting displeasure. "They're all doing it. He was ahead of his time."

Certainly others have since gone faster and further. Mann stiffens when he is compared to Peter Pocklington and is among the most righteous when talking of the harm caused by Lenny Rosenberg.

For others, there is a natural lineage between the first entrepreneur to roll real estate into a trust company, the first to shake the industry with his moxy, and descendants who have played fast and loose with the same material. Mann can't understand it — but he has heard it. One usually circumspect regulator spoke his mind during a chance encounter two years ago.

Mann was in the Ontario Ministry of Consumer and Commercial Relations' office building, a nine-storey coral brick edifice at Yonge and Wellesley Streets in Toronto, paying a visit shortly after Ontario seized Crown and Greymac in January of 1983. He ran into Harry Terhune, then Murray Thompson's second and one of the men who had inspected United's books and worried about its fate.

"I said, 'Boy, Harry, you've really had a tough time down there, eh?'"

Terhune responded that no one would ever know how tough. Mann was nonplussed by what came next. "'You know, we thought you were bad,'" Terhune said, "'but you weren't really so bad compared to what we've just gone through.'"

Mann, dumbfounded, held his tongue, and Terhune moved on. "When I got on the elevator, I said, 'You S.O.B.'"

The Belzbergs and First City Trust

First City Trust Co. is today, with $2.5 billion under its control, Western Canada's largest financial institution, but it represents less than half of the Belzberg family's total assets.

The 99%-owned trust company was once the wellspring of the Belzbergs' nascent empire and indeed provided much of the leverage for the family's rise to prominence. But the confines of the Canadian economy have proved too close for the three brothers, Hyman, Sam and Bill, and thus the trust has become merely a tributary of funds feeding the wealth that now flows to them.

The Belzberg name is a metaphor for success in the West. A Western lawyer managing investment funds for a now-wealthy Indian tribe tells the story of another fabulously rich tribe with $500 million to invest. The tribe's chief was searching for a good investment adviser, and the lawyer told him: "If I managed it, I'd write a cheque for $500 million to Sam Belzberg and say, 'Here's the money, I don't want to know what you're doing with it, but in five years I want the $500 million back plus 50% of the profits,' and I would know I'm in good hands."

The brothers, led by the middle one, 56-year-old Sam, have had the advantage of building a trust company in the West, free from some of the regulatory restraints of the East.

In the years from 1975 to 1980, the trust company's assets grew from $275 million to $1.5 billion. The growth came by unconventional means: the Belzberg institution dealt in leasing (forbidden in the East), mortgage lending, real estate development, mortgage banking and more recently high-roller stock plays. From its earliest years, First City liked to extract equity positions from the developments it was lending on, especially if they were buildings with no preconstruction lease commitments. If a builder wanted his project funded, he had to cut the Belzbergs in on it. First City operated more as a merchant bank than as a traditional trust company.*

First City Financial, 67%-owned through a complex series of family holding companies, is the publicly traded holding company into which the Belzbergs rolled most of their Canadian real estate and financial assets. In 1981, the year the Belzbergs

---

* By early 1981, First City Financial faced a battery of lawsuits over several deals that amounted to $60 million in plaintiffs' claims.

took unsuccessful runs at two Canadian trust companies and an American stock brokerage house, the holding company had more than $2 billion of assets running from 10% of the Bank of British Columbia to a wide range of classy hotels, shopping centres, housing developments and offices strewn across the lucrative American sun belt. Shareholders' equity, much of it the Belzbergs', had grown to $71 million.

The Belzbergs got their first taste of trust companies as silent partners in Dr Charles Allard's Edmonton-based North West Trust in the late 1950s. Their lust for trust ignited, the family moved on to found their very own City Savings & Trust in 1962, with a head office in Edmonton and $1 million in capital. City Savings, later renamed First City Trust, was set up principally to take advantage of the vacuum that existed in Western Canada for interim construction loans. The Eastern banks were loath to lend to entrepreneurial builders in "foreign" territory, but both land development and the West were home turf for the Belzbergs. They were known, says one Calgary real estate wheeler-dealer, as "tough lenders."

The trust company was always an innovative lender, explains a First City executive. "It has never operated with a manager's handbook, saying you can lend if the house is on the west side of the street, with an even number and has so many square feet."

It was the style of the Belzbergs: pioneering and unorthodox, but ruthless. Sam, like so many others who have come after him, wanted the trust company to fund his big ideas with money he didn't have. "He always considered the benefit of having other people's money," says Andrew Sarlos. "And he saw the benefit of combining the real estate experience and knowledge with the ability to commit funds — to bring ideas and concepts into fruition and that's what makes great real estate deals."

In the mid-seventies the 45-year-old Sam Belzberg had his ambitions pinned on the trust company, seeing it, as he confessed to one reporter, as a way of doing "anything I want in the financial and development field in Canada." Indeed, just before uttering these words he had unsuccessfully attempted to take over Western Canada's largest real estate broker, Block Bros. Industries Ltd., with the intention of using it to expand his trust company's capacity for growth.

Andy Sarlos has known the Belzbergs for a long time. He first went to work for Sam to help reinvest the bounty from the sale of Western Realty Projects Ltd., the family's major real estate holding, in 1973. The Hungarian ran the investment portfolio from a Toronto office but lasted only a year, finally leaving out of frustration because Sam was constantly second-guessing his decisions. Unlike 99% of those who offer opinions and theories on the Belzbergs, Sarlos does it on the record. He is old-world charm and new-world success. His prowess in the stock-market is such that his private limited partnership investment funds attract the astute likes of both branches of the Bronfman clan, Reuben Cohen and Leonard Ellen, the Reichmanns and a host of institutional investors including trust and insurance companies — and the Belzbergs.

"They were particularly interested in having money, to give them the security, the safety and the power that money can buy," Sarlos says of the Belzbergs. "They weren't too concerned about their image, or even what they were going to do with their money. The only thing they really cared about was the family — both family in the small sense and in the bigger sense."*

The Belzbergs hit paydirt with the sale of Western Realty, which had been formed to house 16 of their private real estate companies. This, and the earlier sales of millions of acres of oil and gas leases, was the foundation of their future wealth. They sold their 62% control for $48 million in cash, or $12 a share, to an English group. In the process they made many minority

---

* Sam Belzberg remembers his friends, too, and can be generous. When Sarlos and his partners took a nosedive with the stock-market in the early 1980s, Sam was one of the financier's network of allies who bankrolled a comeback. After receiving millions in financial help, Sarlos was felled by a heart attack. "I was very lucky and was able to repay him but when he gave it to me he had no assurance whatsoever that I would do it. If I had died, he might never have received it."

shareholders unhappy by leaving them to sell their lame-duck shares for $7.50 a share or be swallowed up in a subsequent merger. The deal had also left lifelong Belzberg family friends and business partners, the Singer family of Calgary, in the lurch, forcing the private Singers out into the open to share a public company with strangers, their new partners.

Part of the Western Realty windfall secured a base for the family in the U.S., where in 1974 they bought control of Los Angeles-based Far West Savings and Loan, with assets of $500 million; today it is almost as big as the Canadian trust company. They were way ahead of their time — along with George Mann, the first Canadians to see the advantages of an American savings and loan, but unlike Mann smart enough to buy a healthy one.* In typical style, the acquisition of the savings and loan was an extension of a business they already knew.

By the mid-seventies the brothers had scattered. The youngest, Bill, had gone down to Los Angeles to run Far West; Sam had woken up one morning despising the Alberta winter and had moved his family to balmier Vancouver; Hyman, the oldest, stayed behind with his own family, the Belzberg sisters and the parents in Calgary.

Hymie is a gentle man with a razor core. Despite his wealth he continues to run the family's original enterprise, a furniture store called Cristy's Arcade, from a brick warehouse in a decidedly unfashionable part of Calgary. He sits on the Belzberg company boards with his brothers and now his son and nephew. But he is more likely to find himself trapped behind his desk by a distraught home-owner pleading for leniency on a First City mortgage default. His office in the furniture store is

---

* They reap the benefits today. In 1982 Washington deregulated "thrifts,' as they are also known, freeing them from the confines of home mortgages and springing them into personal and commercial lending, direct real estate investment and the backing of stock-market plays. *Forbes* in its December 31, 1981, issue saw fit to single out the Belzberg's 72%-owned Far West as an abuser of the new powers, because of its profitable participation in T. Boone Pickens's stock raid on Gulf Oil and Saul Steinberg's raid on Disney Corp. In the Gulf deal, Far West made $8.5 million and First City Trust and Financial made $32.5 million — or 85% of the trust company's earnings for the previous five years.

a picture: a sweltering 90 degrees in March because his secretary feels the cold, it is furnished in vintage fifties with the cast-offs of brother Bill's early stint running Red Top Dog Food. Hymie has made the news twice: once in early 1981, when the Belzbergs were engaged in a hostile take-over bid for New York's Bache Securities Ltd., and it was reported that the FBI had spotted Hymie chatting to notorious mobster Meyer Lansky on an Acapulco beach in 1970; and then in December 1982 when Hymie was kidnapped and held for ransom by three armed men who were eventually caught.

Bill, the youngest, who spent some time struggling for a role in the family, is a good-time guy. "I'd much rather spend time with Bill than Sam," says Sarlos of the Belzberg who is well versed in art and good dining. Bill now basks in Beverly Hills luxury: a beautiful house filled with beautiful art, and outside a swimming pool and tennis courts. Not only does he know how to live; he has also built Far West into a major lending and real estate corporation with assets of $2 billion.*

"But if I have to do business," continues Sarlos, "I'd rather do it with Sam. He makes decisions." One of the legends surrounding Sam concerns his fast decisions. He once committed $15 million inside half an hour to help finance an oil and gas take-over. But he is not so much a fast decision-maker as a prepared one. And he does not feel obligated to consult his board or his management. Often before he makes a major decision he consults an inner circle of friends, one of whom is Sarlos.

A boot-strap mentality dogs Sam Belzberg to this day. Despite his protestations and the paraphernalia of a major corporation, First City is still very much a one-dimensional company, and that dimension is the chairman and chief executive officer, Sam. In a 1971 profile Sam boasted that board meetings of Belzberg-run companies never take a vote. "As chair-

---

* Far West's board boasts the presence of Monty Hall of "Let's Make a Deal" television fame, one of several quirky choices for directorship on Belzberg boards. Another is former Canadian ambassador to Iran Ken Taylor, who sits on First City Financial's board. The Belzbergs also have a weakness for Canadian senators.

man, I can recognize the mood of a meeting — if we're not all for it, forget it.''

From his own experience, Sarlos, who has been on his own since working for Belzberg, concludes that "once you work for Sam, your usefulness ends. He probably respects a few people on his staff, but he respects people who are on their own more because he figures once you decide to work for him you feel some limit to your ability.''

In the years since, the seed money of Western Realty has multiplied, producing corporate and personal wealth, and the Belzberg fortune has in one generation taken on Great Family trappings.

"Now," observes a sardonic Sarlos, "many things are much more important than money. Today what's important is to perpetuate the dynasty and to build it into a permanent lasting unit which is well regarded, which has social responsibility.''

Indeed, Hymie's and Sam's two sons Brent and Marc are positioned at First City offices in Vancouver and New York, learning the business, and all of the Belzberg men get together once a quarter to look over the family books. The Belzbergs are also well-known philanthropists. Two favourite recipients are the Simon Wiesenthal Centre for Holocaust Studies and the Dystonia Medical Research Foundation, both in Los Angeles. It is a remarkable change in only a dozen years. Other families, such as the Bronfmans, took generations to achieve it.

The genius of Sam Belzberg is that he was one of the great beneficiaries of the inflationary period and was probably one of the first to recognize the possibility of deflation — thereby switching from being an acquisitor of inflation hedges to being an acquirer of industries that would benefit in a stable, low-growth, non-inflationary economy. His acquisition in early 1985 of Scovill Inc., a Connecticut-based home-products conglomerate with assets of $500 million, proves the point, offering as it does a prospering manufacturing base more dependent on profit margins and efficiency than volume and growth. Ripe for rationalization, Scovill likely will be used by Belzberg as a building block, either to build around or to trade up.

A theory of those who know the Belzbergs, and one given much currency generally, is that the Belzbergs soured on Canada as a business playground after their defeat in the Canada Permanent take-over battle. "It limited their horizons and the Belzbergs are people with unlimited horizons. They are not prepared to be stymied," says Izzy Asper's former CanWest Capital partner Gerry Schwartz.

But the Belzbergs deny this, pointing out they were well into the U.S. by that time. Indeed the abortive attempt to buy Bache Securities, scant weeks before the move on Canada Permanent, had netted them $33.3 million in American funds and their first widespread attention in the U.S. To the American business community they presented the irresistible combination of success and trouble.

The Bache adventure had followed a successful purchase of a sun-belt home-builder and a Massachusetts-based troubled REIT, a real estate investment trust, with tremendous turn-around potential. As with the California savings and loan, they were among the first Canadians to think of it.

The Belzbergs, as Sam would declare when he used to talk to the press, have for some time been building towards a diversified financial empire. Aside from acquiring a small Hamilton trust company, they have been blocked from achieving that goal in Canada. But in the U.S., First City during the last several years has invested in insurance companies, Wall Street investment firms, a venture capital company and a pension fund management company.

Still, Belzberg financial companies, both American and Canadian, have made much of their money by *not* completing acquisitions. With the appearance of the Belzberg name on a securities filing, target-company managers go running for lawyers and white knights. But the Belzbergs' talent for turning a profit on unsuccessful take-over bids has given them a reputation as corporate raiders and greenmailers. First City, a 1981 *Wall Street Journal* report concluded, "risks being perceived as a trader rather than a builder of assets."

Today Sam Belzberg spends more time in New York than in his art-filled Vancouver office. Gone are the days of holding court in the Bayshore Inn lobby. With his "right arm" Danny Pekarsky operating the Belzberg holding companies from Vancouver, he is free to prowl Wall Street, building his half-billion-dollar securities portfolio. Operating from a Park Avenue West address — all the Belzberg companies have the right address no matter the city — he has a group labouring away, picking off underpriced investments with solid track records. Value and price are Belzberg tenets. Sam makes all the final choices himself, and once he has determined his buying and selling prices he sticks to his carefully plotted strategy, never succumbing to the hot-headed irrationality of bidding wars. It is the secret of his success. He directs the purchases for First City Financial and always offers subsidiary First City Trust an equal cut of the action. Depending on internal company needs, often for earnings or tax reasons, sometimes because of risk, the trust will buy alongside the parent.

As early as 1981, those taking a close look at First City had detected the reason for the company's above-average returns: "The profits on securities trading in the income statement real ly masks what is going on in the intermediary side," Terry Shaunessey, then an analyst with Gardiner Watson, observed. Of the $135 million that First City earned in the years 1979-83, 70% of it was from securities trading; 15%, from trust operations.

First City types are not only sensitive to charges that their bids for companies are designed not to succeed; they also take pains to demonstrate prudence in managing the trust company's profit taking in the stock-market since risk taking continues to be the essential element of the Belzberg style.

"A careful analysis, even a careless analysis, of our figures over the last several years will show that we have placed a lot of earnings gains into the trust company at the expense of the parent," says a senior but obligatorily anonymous Belzberg executive. As an example, after building up a 10% stake in a California life insurance company — as one of the fastest growing in all of the U.S. it was a typical Belzberg choice — in 1985 First City sold its stake for a U.S. $6.5 million profit — but not before Financial had sold at cost its two-thirds portion of the holding to the trust company so that the latter could take the entire gain. First City is the only major trust company to do this, although Stanley Taube's small Monarch Trust, which shares an address with Unicorp, is universally regarded as a prudent, careful master of the same art.

"It's a fabulous way to raise capital," says Ed Daughney, the trust company's president, who, unbeknown to most people, owns a small Toronto-based trust company of his own called Executive Trust. "It accounts for the exceptional performance of First City over the last three or four years." In fact, without the stock-market profit taking, the trust company would have lost money or merely scraped by during the last few years. Last year alone, First City Financial's $48 million profit was achieved solely on the strength of securities gains. The foundation of the Belzberg empire, Western real estate, was dragging the company down badly: mortgage loans had to be written down by $39 million, and properties held in the trust company were devalued by more than $17 million.

In this respect, First City had shared the fate of all the Western trust companies in the last few years as the rocketing land prices, debt-happy developers and energy boom of the seventies gave way to the plunging real estate values and worthless mortgages of the eighties.

First City's move into the stock-market has proved more successful than diversification attempts by other Western trust owners. But Sam Belzberg's spectacular stock plays have their risks. What goes up can come down.

7

Stopping
the Puck

"You use other people's money and other people's labour to build your dreams."

"You work on people's greed."

— Peter Pocklington

Peter Hugh Pocklington's utter lack of self-censorship is not the most amazing thing about him. That accolade belongs to his spectacular three-year performance as Canada's most cavalier trust company owner.

This short, slight blond man with the maharishi eyes, the hypnotist's voice and the evangelist's smile came into the spring of 1983 a legendary, self-made millionaire dabbling in the heady world of national politics. Wearing a conservative blue suit with a large gold elephant-hair bracelet, he cruised the nation in his seven-passenger Learjet 35, campaigning for the leadership of the federal Progressive Conservative party. On stage at the microphone or circulating through a crowd, he preached the same message: let's all stand on our own feet, let's get back to the basics of good business and free enterprise that made this country great. Behind the curtains of his campaign, however, the greatness was crumbling. Pocklington was scrambling to pay the expenses of his aircraft, negotiating the receiverships of his car dealerships and quietly meeting with federal government regulators about his trust company's desperate need for $20.6 million in new capital.

As the owner of a sober financial institution, Pocklington was able to inspire wild newspaper headlines with his hiring of a psychic as a business consultant, his dramatic SWAT-team rescue from kidnappers and his ownership of hockey great Wayne Gretzky. The apocryphal story about Peter Puck, as he became known in the instant mythology of Canadian business, is that he once confided that he stood in front of a mirror each day reciting "I am a god."

The fact that this charismatic, volatile risk addict could own and influence Western Canada's largest trust company — at its peak it held more than $1 billion in assets — is testimony to the difference between banks and trust companies.

In the fall of 1979 Peter Pocklington was riding high in Edmonton on the riches of Western Canadian real estate. He was doing the kinds of deals and making the kind of money that his soul mate, Nelson Skalbania, was celebrated for in Vancouver. Flipping apartment buildings, shopping centres and raw land the way a juggler tosses balls, Pocklington had amassed a personal worth estimated at between $20 million and $30 million. After arriving in Edmonton from southwestern Ontario in 1971, he spent the rest of the decade spinning the cash from his dollar-churning Ford dealership into vast real estate holdings in Alberta, Ontario and Arizona. Land prices during the late 1970s, fuelled by inflation and lubricated by oil and gas, were good to Pocklington, whose operating principle, recalled one business associate, depended on the greater-fool theory: he bought because he figured he could sell it tomorrow, unimproved, to somebody else.

Inflation's largesse supported Pocklington's increasingly diverse business investments: the Edmonton Oilers hockey club; the Edmonton Drillers, an NASL soccer team; a baseball team in the Triple A Pacific League; and Gainers Ltd., a major Western meat-packing company with $100 million in annual sales and attractive Edmonton real estate ripe for condominiums. Meanwhile, the underpinnings, his real estate company Patrician Land Corp., had swollen to an estimated $150-$200 million in assets, including a $50 million parcel of Toronto-area apartment buildings, huge tracts of undeveloped land southeast of Canmore, Alberta, and blocks of downtown Edmonton.

The sun did not always shine for Pocklington, whose ambitions were sometimes rained out in Toronto, where reputation can be as important as a Learjet. In late 1977 Pocklington's attempt to take-over troubled Pop Shoppes International for part cash and part debt was blocked by obstreperous minority shareholder Imasco Ltd. Five months later a 28-year-old Toronto psychic named Rita Burns announced she was suing Pocklington for $7 million because he had not paid as promised for her advice on his business deals, including the ill-fated Pop Shoppes bid. (After a sensational trial laced with sexual innuendo, the jury decided that she didn't have a case.) And in early 1979 Pocklington tried to acquire Toronto-based Commerce Capital Corp. for $10 a share but was beaten back by Eaton-Bay Financial Services Ltd. (owned 60% by T. Eaton Co. and 40% by Hudson's Bay Co.), which had offered $9 a share. The latter bid was significant because it marked Pocklington's first step towards acquiring a financial institution.

With Pocklington's purchase in late 1979 of Toronto's largest Ford dealership, Elgin Motors Ltd., located on several acres of prime Bay Street real estate, his financial clout became a source of wonder. In a feature on Pocklington in the September 1979 *Canadian Business,* writer Wayne Lilley posed the question "How secure are the foundations of this remarkable financial edifice? Pocklington maintains they're granite-like. As development companies go, he says, Patrician is not leveraged especially highly. 'It's a real estate firm and naturally we mortgage out what we can. But there are $50 million in net assets backing it up, so there's no danger of collapse.'"

But the stability proved an illusion. As events unfolded, it became clear that much of Pocklington's "empire" was highly leveraged and entirely dependent on inflation to feed its voracious interest expenses.

In late 1979 a struggling Winnipeg-based trust company, Fidelity Trust, was on the block. Under government surveillance because its capital base was rapidly eroding, the 70-year-old company at the end of that year had $515 million in assets and had lost $2 million after a number of profitable years. During the 1970s Fidelity had pioneered National Housing Act-approved mortgage banking; it originated, underwrote and then sold residential mortgages to Canadian and foreign investors, retaining the management of them for a fee. Fidelity had also invested heavily on its own account in these often rural-based loans, which were designed for situations where the mortgage was higher than 75% of the value of the property, or where the collateral behind the mortgage was weak.

By 1979, Fidelity, led by chairman Neil C.W. Wood, who didn't cotton to the rapid changes taking place in the trust industry, found itself awash in higher-than-average mortgage defaults. It also faced horrendously mismatched assets and liabilities and a sore need for equity. Not the least of its problems was its $8 million acquisition that summer of its chief Winnipeg competitor, Fort Garry Trust Co., from a numbered company partly owned by officers and directors of the Calgary-based developer Abacus Cities Ltd. The Fort Garry operation, with branches strung out from Montreal to Vancouver, was burdened with loans of "dubious value," $7 million of them to Abacus.

Fidelity appealed to Pocklington's sense of exploitation. He and his corporate lieutenant and backgammon partner, Harry Knutson, set in motion a highly complex plan to acquire Fidelity and merge it with Pocklington's real estate company, Patrician Land Corp. If Pocklington listened at all, he listened to the balding, bearded Knutson, who favoured fast cars, European tailoring and $40 bottles of wine. Knutson, an alumnus of Metro Trust, had been president of CanReit Advisory Corp. and its real estate investment trust subsidiary. CanReit had been speedily spun off to Izzy Asper's CanWest Financial

Corp. following Metro's take-over by Victoria and Grey. Described variously as the brains behind Pocklington and a hotshot, Knutson joined Pocklington in the late summer of 1979 as president of Patrician Land Corp. and Pocklington Financial Corp. (PFC), Peter's personal holding company. In a departure for Pocklington, who preferred to operate out of the glare of public scrutiny, without partners and through private companies, Knutson was given 10% of PFC.

The Fidelity purchase was fancy footwork indeed. In November 1979 Pocklington set up a holding company called Fidelity Trustco Ltd. and soon after bought 66% of the common shares of Fidelity Trust Co., announcing the acquisition in typical style on television between periods of an Edmonton Oilers-Toronto Maple Leafs hockey game. He paid for the Fidelity shares with $4.6 million in cash and $5.5 million in preferred shares of Fidelity Trustco, announcing that he would make the same offer to minority shareholders by the spring. But in the meantime, Fidelity Trust purchased from Pocklington's real estate company, Patrician Land, for $7.5 million in cash a parcel of downtown Edmonton properties. (Pocklington undertook to buy back the land, now the subject of a lawsuit, for $10 million in February 1983 but never did.) Shortly after, in February, the trust company acquired Patrician itself from Pocklington for $10.7 million, paid in Fidelity common shares newly minted from the treasury.*

That did two things. It brought Pocklington's stake in the trust company up to more than 80%, thereby cutting his cash costs in the follow-up bid to the remaining shareholders. And it sent $23 million, Patrician's book value, to Fidelity's capital base, thereby increasing the trust company's potential to take deposits from the public by $460 million. (Under federal regulations that allow a trust company to borrow on a multiple of its capital base, Fidelity's multiplier was 20 times its capital.) In

---

* Just before Patrician was sold, its real estate was written up "to approximate market value." Patrician's assets — composed of property Pocklington intended to flip for a profit, raw land and income-producing properties — amounted to $99 million after the write-up, with mortgages against them set at $72.5 million.

the end, Pocklington had paid almost $7 million in cash but had received $7.5 million back in cash from the trust company. He had acquired a major Western Canadian financial institution. And he had retained control of his real estate company in the bargain.

This sleight of hand, largely the work of Knutson, in effect injected a property company starved of cash flow but, on paper at least, asset rich into a cash machine, the trust company, that had the right to invest 10% of its depositors' money in Patrician's real estate. The federal Department of Insurance, acutely aware of the struggling Fidelity, approved the purchase on the understanding that Pocklington would not run the company himself. The concern was that he would bring to the trust business, with its treacherously fragile dependence on appearance and propriety, the operating principles of his real estate wheeling and dealing.

In January 1980 Knutson brought in CanReit colleague, Brendan Calder, as president of the trust company. Calder was familiar with Fidelity: he had completed a month's analysis of it for CanWest just two months earlier. Having judged it a poor buy, he was now going over, the lure of heading a billion-dollar trust company too much for a 33-year-old to resist.

Calder insisted on restrictions: that Pocklington stay out of the company's day-to-day operations and that the federal regulation that a trust company cannot invest more than 10% of its assets in real estate owned by a related company be obeyed. Both constraints were soon forgotten.

Calder, who quickly brought in yet another CanReit old boy, Ivan Wahl, as well as other new managers, began cleaning up the trust company.

"In the first three months, I had a run on the bank, I found out a fraud and the guy subsequently committed suicide on a Saturday morning. I had one branch manager go crazy on me in the elevator. I had one mobster that Abacus had been dealing with get 17 stab wounds in him between meetings — he didn't show up for the second meeting. This all happened in eight weeks [mid-February to mid-April]. It was crazy; it was unbelievable that there was so much going on. We kept on going and we got the thing running,'' Calder would recall later.

Fidelity picked up the pace, going from $487 million worth of public deposits in 1979 to $753 million by the end of 1981. Assets under administration hit $1.5 million that year. The synergy between Fidelity and Patrician was like magic: in 1981, when Patrician's retained earnings increased by $15 million after some large property sales, Fidelity's borrowing capability expanded by $300 million, even though the trust operation itself was losing money. Assets in Patrician hit $267 million. The annual report that year assured shareholders that Patrician had adjusted to the changed Alberta real estate market with great success, transforming itself from a property flipper to a long-range-thinking development company. Within the trust company, Calder and his managers trimmed staff, closed branches, slashed the number of non-productive loans and began matching the term and rate of incoming funds with outgoing loans. But the Pocklington touch was ever evident: the trust company board made room for a special consultant, former U.S. president Gerald Ford, whose chief contribution was lining up possible U.S. take-over deals and making a let's-free-enterprise speech in Edmonton at Pocklington's request. That year Pocklington — who was neither an officer nor a board member and who had been specifically excluded from running the company — charged Fidelity $3.56 million in "management fees and bonus" for his work as president (later chairman) of Patrician.

By the spring of 1982, however, Fidelity insiders were well aware of how drastically the situation had changed for Patrician. Big real estate deals so confidently predicted six months before had fallen apart; its revenues sank to $458,000 in 1982 from $40 million the year before. The source of trouble lay in the kind of real estate Patrician held: too few properties that generated income, and too much raw land chewing up interest expense. The company needed to unload its assets in the depths of a real estate bottom.

Like a junkie, Patrician needed an ever-increasing fix of cash to make mortgage payments. More and more, it turned to the now-profitable trust company, but there was always the snag that Fidelity could legally invest only 10% of its assets in a subsidiary. Pocklington was forced to seek other sources of financing. In April 1982, as interest rates peaked, his holding company, Pocklington Financial, borrowed $1.2 million from the Northland Bank, and his sports company, Pocklington Amalgamated Sports Corp., borrowed $10 million from the Royal Bank.

"The first time we went over that 10% rule, that was the beginning of the end," Calder recalls. "You've got the classic banker's dilemma: do you write it off now or put another $100,000 in? You've got a huge machine there. You've got almost $250 million worth of assets with negative cash flow. As soon as you write it off, you're dead anyway. That's where it gets crazy. That's the lesson you learn, and when you think of it for two minutes, it makes sense."

With Fidelity facing the prospect of taking a huge $17.6 million write-down on its real estate company as Alberta property values plummeted, Pocklington and Knutson came up with another of their brilliant ideas: buy a U.S. savings and loan company, plumb it for cash and sell Patrician into it. Conceptually, acquiring such a company was a smart move at the time. Interest rates had hit the roof and were heading back down, so interest-sensitive businesses were becoming more valuable. More important, Washington was heading towards deregulation of savings and loan institutions, allowing them to move out of the strict confines of home mortgage lending and into more lucrative corporate financing.

On the Friday before the July long weekend, Calder, who was at Harvard University on a management course, received a telephone call from Knutson asking for $2 million. He intended to buy First American of Texas, an attractive savings and loan company with a good branch network centred in Houston.

"Harry, why would you want two million bucks?" Calder asked.

"Well, because we're going to buy this company, and we need a $2 million deposit, U.S." was the reply.

"I can't give you $2 million."

But Knutson persisted: "We need it."

Calder insisted, "I'm not going to give it to you; you'd better take it to the board."

Calder spent the weekend telephoning the board members to rally support for his opposition. (The members included Douglas Fullerton, former chairman of the National Capital Commission; Simon Reisman, former deputy minister of finance; Byron J. Seaman, vice-chairman of family-controlled Bow Valley Industries Ltd.; Robert Wisener, a former governor of the Toronto Stock Exchange and chairman of MerBanco Group. There were a number of Pocklington-company representatives as well as Fidelity Trust chairman Allan C. Rose, a Toronto lawyer and Pocklington's own counsel. Rose had been involved in the early 1960s with the Commonwealth Savings and Loan Corp. in Ontario, along with George Mann.) The following week the board met via conference call, with Calder at Harvard and Knutson and Pocklington in Houston. The latter pair worked to convince the board to write a cheque for $2 million, arguing that they had all the appropriate legal and accounting opinions. The board members capitulated.

Knutson needed a certified cheque, and Calder saw a chance to thwart what he considered to be theft from the company. With co-operation from the tight management group at Fidelity's Bay Street head office, Calder had a $2 million cheque readied. Knutson had asked for it to be certified — something ordinarily done by the trust company's bank, Canadian Imperial Bank of Commerce. But, reasoned Calder, what do they know down in Texas. We'll use our "certified" stamp and do it ourselves.

After doing just that, Calder sent the cheque off, taking care to remove the $2 million from the trust company's account at the CIBC. "If they had tried to cash that cheque it would have bounced from here to Mars and back," Calder recalled later. But it bought him time to try to stop the deal. "I knew the money would never go, but the placebo was there. These guys had a certified cheque. It turned out, by luck, the other side couldn't cash it because they would have had to declare that they had a bid for the company, so they just kept the money. It looked like gold to them."

Calder spent the rest of the week building a case against Knutson's and Pocklington's claim to legal and accounting approval. The following Tuesday, July 13, the Fidelity board met, live and in person, to hear presentations by the company's lawyers, Davies, Ward and Beck, and accountants, Price Waterhouse, who explained that the deal wouldn't work. After hearing them out, the board decided as a first order of business to rescind the cheque. Then Calder told them there was no money behind it anyway and promised to do it again if he had to. The board told him to tell them the whole story next time.

His determination undiminished, Knutson continued to peruse savings and loans. Fidelity's management reluctantly made an analysis of the idea, knowing the regulators in Ottawa would never approve. By fall Knutson had found another. State Savings & Loan, with 29 branches in Hawaii and Utah and the slight defect that it was under government supervision, had been introduced to Knutson by Elmo (Bud) Zumwalt, a retired U.S. admiral and former head of the joint chiefs of staff.

Pocklington and Knutson devised a scheme to bolster Fidelity: Pocklington would buy 25% of the savings and loan from its parent, a Tennessee life insurance company. Shortly after, Fidelity would acquire the rest of the American institution by swapping 2,600 Toronto and Hamilton apartment units, held in its subsidiary, Patrician, that were valued at $80 million.

"We did all the analysis; this one was even worse, it was a horrible company," recalls Calder. "They went to the board and said, 'We want to spend a million dollars chasing this one' — because it costs money to chase companies: you've got jet rides, you've got accountants."

At this point Calder discussed, over dinner with some members of the board, the possibility of his resigning. The reaction: "Stay, this idea's not going to last."

Despite Calder's opposition, and affidavits supporting him signed by top management, at a meeting on December 8 all but three directors voted for the acquisition of State Savings & Loan. The majority agreed mainly because Knutson and Pocklington appeared to be doing it the right way this time, with plenty of analysis. Board members Fullerton and Reisman, however, had sided with Calder, and the following day Fullerton resigned. Reisman indicated he wanted to go as well, but the argument that two such resignations would imperil the public's trust in Fidelity persuaded Reisman to hang on for five months more.

At the end of the board meeting, Calder stood up and with a smile on his face went over to Pocklington as if to shake his hand. Instead, Calder said: "I always thought you were an asshole. Now I know you are."

From that point on, the owner and the manager were enemies, barely speaking to each other. The State deal never was completed. It became entangled in an underbrush of regulatory bodies and jurisdictions. By that time, however, more pressing problems were determining the course the company would take in coming months.*

The federal government had become very interested in what was going on in Fidelity. Since the summer, Dick Page, the man in charge of trust companies in Ottawa at the Department of Insurance, had watched Fidelity grow weaker. It had never enjoyed the complete faith of the regulators, even before Pocklington's time. But at the end of 1982 the government began renewing Fidelity's licence on a monthly basis. Trust companies are usually licensed annually.

The preliminary numbers for Fidelity looked extremely bad. It had lost $19.1 million, Patrician owed it some $130 million in intercompany loans with little hope of repaying them, the trust company had been borrowing from the public well above its authorized multiple of 20 times its capital base and federal regulators had slapped a ceiling on how much Fidelity could take in deposits — effectively tying its hands. None of this was

---

* For Calder, Pocklington's victory at the board meeting signalled the end of Fidelity. Two days later, with only Reisman's knowledge, he went to see federal regulators about a soft landing for the trust company.

known to the people with $840 million on deposit at the trust company until May when, six weeks late, the 1982 annual report was released.

The delay was the result of some twisted bookkeeping that the company's accountants, Price, Waterhouse, had not liked. Two deals, born of cash-poor Pocklington's desperate attempts to keep Fidelity afloat, provide fine examples of the fragile nature of the underlying support for the public's money. A portion of the $11 million profit Fidelity reported in 1981 resulted from the sale by Patrician of the valuable Elgin Ford property Pocklington had bought on Bay Street in downtown Toronto. The buyer was Tridel Construction Ltd., owned by the Del Zotto family; the Northland Bank based in Calgary lent the Del Zottos $2.5-$3 million for the deal. As is typical in the real estate business, Patrician was able to record a profit on a sale when 15% of the $17.5 million purchase price had been received and the conditions of the agreement fulfilled.

This done, Patrician entered into a joint venture with Tridel to develop the property, and work began on demolition of existing buildings and final land assembly. However, market conditions in Toronto were rapidly changing, and the partnership soon broke down. Tridel returned the land to Patrician in April 1982, taking back the 15% down payment. But by this time, Patrician, and therefore Fidelity, had recorded the sale, at a profit, on its 1981 books, which had the effect of adding a significant amount to the trust company's borrowing base and, therefore, expanding its deposit-taking ability.

In another attempt by Pocklington to extricate Patrician from its burgeoning debt to Fidelity, he came up with a scheme to buy Patrician's 2,600 Toronto and Hamilton apartments for a small amount of cash and a mortgage from Patrician. The aging, low-rise buildings, known as the Peel-Elder apartments, after the firm from which Pocklington had acquired them for about $27 million, had been reappraised at $70 million. With about $37 million in debt against them, Patrician would be able to record a profit of $40 million. Believing the Department of Insurance would approve the deal, Fidelity management bit the bullet and began discussions with auditors to take a $17.7

million write-down on other real estate held by Patrician. But by late February federal authorities, already nervous over another Toronto apartment flip involving a trust company owner — Leonard Rosenberg — had quashed the sale.* "Auditors don't allow you to go back and forth on these things," lamented then-Patrician president Richard Melchin. "But we wouldn't have taken so many write-downs if the apartment deal was not looking good."

Distressing though the snowballing deterioration at Fidelity was, Pocklington was distracted by a larger concern: his headstart run at Joe Clark's job as leader of the federal Progressive Conservative party.

In July of 1982 Pocklington took steps towards fulfilling a lifelong ambition: to become prime minister of Canada. He announced a grand, 20-stop (later expanded to 32-stop) speaking tour to prepare Canadians for his solution to the nation's economic ills. "I guess, in times of peril, people with the skills should be prepared to step forward and help out the society that they are a part of," he said at the time. Pocklington had another, typically unusual, reason for jumping into politics. An ordeal four months earlier during which he was held at gunpoint for 12 hours in his lavish home in Edmonton had focused the 40-year-old's attention, perhaps for the first time, on his mortality.

Pocklington spent the fall and $300,000 jetting to packed rooms in Halifax and North Bay to sell his steely Ayn Rand brand of economic policy, while innocent political writers filled pages with descriptions of the buccaneer millionaire, nourished by caviar, fine wine and standing ovations. By Christmas Pocklington needed a break; he took his wife Eva to their condo in Hawaii.

---

* In late 1982 a $10 million mortgage held by Crown Trust on the Peel-Elder apartments came up for renewal after a year's term. However, new Crown owner Rosenberg demanded 5% for the roll-over, instead of the more usual 0.5% to 1%. "Leonard called the loan," a Crown Trust executive recalls. "He was mad at Peter Pocklington at the time because they were negotiating about whether Rosenberg was interested in taking over Fidelity and then Peter Pocklington decided he shouldn't deal with Rosenberg because of the publicity."

Events were closing in. Already that summer Pocklington's soccer team, the Drillers, had folded, leaving him with a loss of $13 million after four years of ownership. Later in the fall Westown Ford dealership, Pocklington's former money machine that had once moved more than 4,000 cars in a year, changed hands, with the general manager essentially purchasing it from creditors. At about the same time, Pocklington launched a plan to sell 49% interest in his wholly owned and much-beloved Oilers but he abandoned the plan just as buyers came forward. Nonetheless, when Pocklington negotiated a $20 million line of credit with Canadian Commercial Bank soon after, he was asked to hand over the shares of his hockey club (to be held in trust) and the contracts with the team's players, including Wayne Gretzky, as collateral.

No sooner was this done than Pocklington quietly renegotiated the local and national television rights to the Oiler games for a one-time, up-front payment, in return giving up the rights for a number of years. Other hockey clubs received payments for these lucrative rights annually.

Undeterred, the man who believed anyone could do anything if he thought positively enough formally declared his candidacy for the now-official Conservative leadership race. In a superb account of the Pocklington campaign in *Alberta Report,* Link Byfield described the launch: "The hall in Edmonton's Terrace Inn was impressively jammed when Mr Pocklington strode in behind bag-pipers and campaign workers. At every step in the Pocklington program, a crowd of 800 cheered, and an electric organ issued a staccato, hockey-style flourish." The centre-piece of Pocklington's feast of free enterprise beliefs was a proposal for a universal 20% flat tax rate that would benefit individuals and deprive big business of its tax shelters. Pocklington became a right-wing champion, aided in large part by strong links to Amway Corp., an evangelistic-style home selling organization that was fined $25 million in 1983 for defrauding Canadian customers.

The façade of Pocklington's campaign was as real as a Hollywood set. "Everything is on the block except the Oilers hockey club and the baseball team. This is because of the political situation,'' Pocklington declared to a reporter during an interview in his lush, 25th-floor Edmonton office. In truth, federal regulators were insisting Pocklington put up $20.6 million in new capital for Fidelity in order to correct its overborrowing, or sell to someone who could. To drive the point home, Bob Hammond, the superintendent of insurance in Ottawa, slapped a red flag on the company on March 31 — an unheard-of two-week licence.

So frequent had Calder's calls to Dick Page and Bob Hammond at the department become that he had their office and home numbers added to the speed call list installed on his telephone. It was now public knowledge that Fidelity had lost almost $7 million in the first nine months of 1982 and Patrician was bleeding badly. Calder was allocating the accounts payable and consulting with Page on who should be paid and who forgotten. Pocklington could no longer make deals or spend money on behalf of the drained Patrician, and his schemes for rescuing the company fell on deaf ears in Ottawa. The Fidelity motto on Calder's office wall — "Get a lot done and still have fun" — was a reminder of more optimistic times.

Pocklington's empire suffered further blows: his drilling company dropped into voluntary receivership by early April 1983, owing the Continental Bank $13.4 million; Patrician's real estate holdings faced an ever-increasing battery of loans and lawsuits; the Elgin car dealership went into receivership as Pocklington was accused by the former owner of failing to make payments on a 1979 purchase agreement. The Eastern division of Gainers was sold to an employee group.

Pocklington was so strapped for cash that in March he arranged an extraordinary loan for $715,000 with Winnipeg-based Genevieve Holdings Ltd., owned by Arnold Portigal, with a rate of interest set at the Toronto Dominion Bank prime rate plus 6% for the first month, TD prime plus 11% thereafter, compounded monthly. (He had paid it off in two instalments by early July.)

Amidst the chaos, Pocklington campaigned. In early May he

announced with great fanfare at a Montreal press conference that he had a buyer for Fidelity: Triple Five Corp., owned by the eccentric Ghermezian family of Edmonton. The announcement bewildered Calder and Hammond. There had never been a buyer willing to invest the $20 million that Ottawa wanted for Fidelity.

Nagging questions about the leadership candidate's fraying finances began to surface. Pocklington met them with a mixture of paranoia and bravado. His business failures became a political statement. "A lot of my problems increased the deeper I got into politics. Pressure was put on," Pocklington darkly told fellow Tory right-winger *Toronto Sun* columnist Peter Worthington. "NEP [National Energy Policy] has destroyed the West. . . . The real estate market is wrecked. It's hurt me along with others."

When the Conservative party finally met to elect a new leader in a sweltering Ottawa hockey arena in mid-June, Pocklington fell fast in the first round of balloting, the most lasting impression a newspaper photo of the diminutive Pocklington siding with a towering Brian Mulroney.

By the end of June Fidelity was gone. Ten days after the leadership convention concluded, Calder announced that Fidelity's board had agreed to hand over the company to First City Trust, owned by the Belzberg family of Vancouver. (Calder ceased running the operations of the company in July 1983 but didn't formally resign until August 1984, when he was installed as president of Toronto-based Counsel Trust.)

First City's new president, Ed Daughney, six days into his new job, had read in the newspapers that Fidelity was for sale and had taken a group to see Calder about a deal. But during the day-long meeting Daughney had realized that a normal business transaction was not possible and had left. A week later Daughney encountered CDIC chairman Robert De Coster at a reception in Vancouver. De Coster mentioned the interest First City had shown and invited Daughney to bid for Fidelity on an agency basis.

Following a precedent set with Crown Trust a year earlier in

Ontario, the federal government had been quietly soliciting the trust industry for proposals to take over the branches and business of Fidelity under a five-year management contract. Aside from First City, Victoria and Grey, Guaranty, Montreal, Standard and Pocklington's choice, North West, had all jumped at the chance to take management fees while gaining access to Fidelity's $700 million in good assets. And good assets they were, because the troublesome Patrician assets were stripped out, and a month later the government named Toronto management consultants Laventhol & Horwath to dispose of them. Patrician's book value was set at $350 million, but collapsing land values in Alberta made realizing on them (accounting jargon for getting someone to pay what you think they're worth) extremely unlikely, even over the five-year term of the contract. Collecting quickly proved an impossible task. Laventhol & Horwath sent feelers out into the real estate market and determined that Patrician's liabilities probably exceeded assets by $100 million. By March 1984 Patrician was in receivership.

For Pocklington's part, the summer of 1983 was marked by a steady stream of large and small claims. The Royal Bank grew nervous about $4.6 million in loans to him; and of the $800,000 spent on his campaign, he still owed about $150,000 in small debts to campaign workers and suppliers who had had a difficult time collecting.*

By August Pocklington claimed to have paid off more than $50 million in outstanding debts in the previous three months. Part of this Herculean fiscal feat was achieved by selling some of his legendary collection of Emily Carrs, Renoirs, Kreighoffs and Group of Seven works.

A year and a half later he had surrendered the last of his great assets — the lucrative 21-year personal services contract

---

* His speech-writer from the fall campaign protested that he hadn't been paid by Pocklington according to an oral agreement. Eventually the writer was paid — later and less than he expected — but the experience prompted him to relate the story of a phone call from Pocklington asking him what the word *peccadillo* meant. The peeved writer told him to find it in the dictionary, to which Pocklington replied, "I haven't got a goddamn dictionary. I'm at home."

between himself and Wayne Gretzky — to a bank, as collateral in exchange for help in rearranging his debts. Armed with five companies — what remains of Gainers in the West, the Oilers and the baseball Trappers, a new real estate company and a small drilling company — Pocklington claimed to be better off for cash than he was in 1982.

"When you are worth between $60 million and $100 million, you are not dead yet," he told yet another interviewer. That news would be of interest to the more than 700 Fidelity preferred shareholders, many of them elderly, left in the lurch by the trust company's collapse. And to the federal insurance body that advanced $175 million to protect Fidelity depositors.

8

Licence
to Steal

"Astra Trust Company. Trust Company??? No, no, no. Right name for them will be Bloodsuckers Company because they are worse than any leech-infested place smothered with slime . . .

"Most of these leeches do need quite truly solid and proper investigation right now. I mean right now, not a year from, but now, now, now. If you do not do it now, then it will be too late as their methods and style are swindle, loan-sharking, organized crime, mafia — use any of these names and it will apply."
— One investor's written warnings to trust regulators, 1975

William Davis strolled to the media room of the Ontario legislature shortly after lunch on Monday, February 2, 1981, surrounded by a crowd of reporters who knew he was to announce a provincial election. The procession passed by the doorway of the legislature's justice committee hearing room; inside, a dozen legislators and a smattering of scribes were watching a very different kind of history in the making. John Clement, a former Ontario cabinet minister who had lost his Niagara Falls seat in the 1975 election, was squirming under hostile questioning. Opposition MPPs were convinced he had abused his position by pressing civil servants in his former ministry, Consumer and Commercial Relations, to allow a man about whom they had doubts to operate a trust company in Ontario. That man, Carlo Montemurro, had proven to be a liar and a thief.

It was the committee's final hurrah. The Opposition was bested in the 1981 election. When Davis returned with a majority, the committee was forced to abandon its scrutiny of the regulatory process that had allowed Astra Trust and the other strands of Carlo Montemurro's empire to flourish.

There will always be carnies out to bilk suckers. Montemurro's motivations and the power he exerted over others may be worthy of a psychological treatise,* but the crimes committed are clear-cut and well documented. In contrast, the role of government officials who allowed him to operate in regulated segments of the financial industry for eight years — the last three of those with a trust charter — has never been satisfactorily labelled. When Montemurro stood in the dock in early 1984 and pleaded guilty to six counts of fraud and theft, he stood alone. Although civil servants had to testify at the trial of six Montemurro associates charged with the same crimes, their own contribution to the financial debacle was not questioned. Yet outdated regulation, political influence and, sadly, incompetence all figured in the loss of depositors' money before Astra was placed in receivership in April 1980. What emerges from the incredibly elaborate web of events and actions surrounding Astra Trust is a serious indictment of our regulatory system.

John Clement, when Ontario's Consumer and Commercial Relations Minister in the early seventies, held court in his ninth-floor ministerial chamber at 555 Yonge Street in Toronto. He

---

* Supreme Court of Ontario Justice Patrick Hartt, in his decision on the charges against Montemurro's associates, said of Montemurro, ''Even in absentia, he was a dominating presence during the entire trial. He was clearly the central figure behind the activities of the five companies — the guiding force behind the whole operation. His activities . . . revealed the picture of a man of wealth, influence and charm who displayed a puzzling ability to influence the behaviour of others — decision makers, regulators, professionals, associates and employees.

had the standard team of aides skilled in screening out unwanted visitors, but the door was open for constituents or social acquaintances. When he heard, one nameless day in late 1973 or early 1974, that Pat Luciani had dropped by, Clement said, "Fine, bring him in." He had known Luciani, who practised law a stone's throw from Clement's riding, for 20 years.

Luciani introduced Carlo Montemurro, a Niagara Falls mortgage broker and key man in an application for a federal trust company charter. Luciani and Montemurro believed the Ontario Securities Commission, the province's brokerage industry regulator and an arm of Clement's ministry, was feeding false information about Montemurro to the RCMP. The mortgage broker had been a salesman for Investors Overseas Service (IOS),* and the OSC was spreading this information around; Montemurro felt discriminated against because he was of Italian descent. Clement told him he doubted the OSC would act on prejudice but that Montemurro would have to take his complaints to chairman Ed Royce. Clement said he didn't interfere with the OSC. But if there was ever anything else he could do, they should just call.

Clement did casually ask Royce about the matter a week later. Anyone with an IOS connection, Royce replied, would have a hard time getting a trust licence. Clement let the matter drop. If he had checked further — if he had asked for a written report on past investigations or looked at public records lodged in his own ministry — he would have found a record of run-ins between the regulators and the mortgage broker.

In 1972 Montemurro opened C&M Financial Consultants and a related real estate development company, First C&M Financial Realty Corp. Ltd. C&M was registered as a mortgage broker, able to invest public funds in mortgages.

---

* IOS Ltd., a multi-billion-dollar mutual fund investment organization that had three of its largest companies incorporated in Canada but operated mainly in Europe, had collapsed in the early seventies, leaving Canadian officials embarrassed at the lack of regulation the group had received, and liquidators scrambling to collect money siphoned off by an executive who disappeared. Officials are still working on the file.

A year later OSC investigator David Mitchell received a complaint about the way Montemurro was trying to raise money for a trust charter. He was selling "expressions of interest" in a future issue of common stock of First Canada Trust Company Limited. In essence, Montemurro was trying to raise the $1 million in capital he needed to set up a trust company by selling pieces of paper promising stock when he received a charter. Montemurro was quite open about his intentions in his tête-à-tête with the OSC official: "Montemurro told me he was trying to get the charter with the influence of the late Real Caouette." Montemurro's family ran a healthy grocery business based in Rouyn, Quebec; this tie to respectability was his most frequently played card. "He claimed Real Caouette had introduced him to someone at the federal level." Mitchell was led to believe by Montemurro that he already had the charter, although that wasn't the case. The OSC told Montemurro he had to give back any money he'd raised through his unorthodox methods.

Clement did not have close contact with the approval of trust companies. They weren't one of the "trouble spots" in his lumbering ministry. He couldn't keep track of all 3,000 employees, after all. "These people did not run in and say, 'We have got an application for a trust company,'" he later explained. "I would say, 'Why the hell are you telling me about it? Go and process it.'"

The provincial department did "process" one by Montemurro in 1973. He was sent away after an investigation by Walter Kowtun, the department's one investigator and a new addition at that. Montemurro had no criminal record; he told Kowtun he was not employed but was devoting his time to gaining a provincial trust charter and had applied to the federal government as well. Kowtun sat in when Montemurro explained to the OSC how he was raising the money for the charter, and he knew Montemurro had been an IOS employee. Ontario's trust legislation has a provision for refusing an applicant on the basis of a lack of public confidence in the new venture. That was the reason given when Montemurro was informally told he had no hope. Murray Thompson, who was soon to be promoted to the position of registrar of loan and trust companies, believed from that point on that Montemurro wasn't the kind of man to be trusted with other people's savings.

After Montemurro's refusal by Ontario, his C&M was named in an OSC decision against Western Ontario Credit Corp., a mortgage broker with an interest in recently formed Income Trust. The 1974 decision criticized Western Ontario's mortgage syndications or group investments; C&M was acting as a salesman.

C&M's own loans during that time were later shown to be fraudulent. They didn't live up to promises to invest money safely in residential or Ontario commercial properties for a maximum of 80% of the properties' value. The most flagrant example was the million dollars that went to a Spanish condominium development in which Montemurro and Luciani both had a stake. Of $4 million raised from the public for mortgage investments, only $1 million was invested in mortgages. Two-thirds of the million went to mortgages on properties owned by companies related to Montemurro, Luciani or a C&M employee. There were no property appraisals; there were no credit checks. The rest of the money went to loans to Montemurro and associates.*

First C&M, Montemurro's real estate development company, also was riddled with fraud. In its eight years of operation more than $800,000 was collected from 140 investors, who were sold an interest in properties but not told about sales commissions. Only $137,000 was used to buy land. The rest of the money was paid in commissions or in loans to related companies. First C&M claimed it kept 20% equity in each property, but actually it often syndicated the properties for more than their total value. At one point some investors were paid off

---

* These associates include two related Montemurro companies, Canadian Recycling Laboratories and First Canadian Metal Laboratories. Later, C&M funds would be used to pay Astra officers. One interesting $100,000 loan was to associate Florindo Volpi's construction company. Volpi also had dealings with Steve Axton of Dominion Trust in 1982.

with other investors' funds. Montemurro received properties from the company as a gift.

Despite his boasts of influence, by 1974 Montemurro still wasn't having much luck federally with his quest for a trust company charter. The regulators wanted more information about his business prowess; that was the last thing he'd want to give them. Montemurro and his associates decided a change of lawyers might help their case. They dumped their Montreal counsel and started again, choosing their lawyer more carefully this time.

Richard (Dick) Stanbury was a young senator. A graduate of the first postwar law class, he was appointed to the Senate in 1968, coincidental with the beginning of his five-year term as president of the Liberal party of Canada. But Stanbury wasn't partisan in his contacts. In April 1974 he received a telephone call from George Bagnato, a man known for his fund-raising activities for the Conservative party and his power base in the Toronto Italian community. He was also a man who associated with organized-crime figures, one who liked to brag about his political pull and of whom Ontario politicians were warned to steer clear.*

Stanbury didn't know those things at the time. They had never met, but Stanbury gave Bagnato his ear. Bagnato was incensed that some Italian businessmen were being given a raw deal in their application for a federal trust company charter. Would Stanbury meet the key man, Montemurro? Montemur-

---

* An excellent article by *Globe and Mail* reporters Peter Moon and Jack Willoughby outlined Bagnato's links to organized crime and to politicians. He was an active Ontario election campaign worker. In 1978 then-Solicitor General George Kerr warned Larry Grossman about associating with former campaign worker Bagnato. Bagnato also donated time to former Attorney General Allan Lawrence and other Conservatives and made a campaign donation to future Metro chairman Paul Godfrey when he ran as a controller in North York. Godfrey was a childhood friend. Bagnato's influence in the Conservative party was so great that he managed to spring a temporary release from prison for another childhood friend, an organized-crime figure, during the 1971 election. The criminal did volunteer work for the Tories during the campaign. "I do whatever I can for people in the Italian community," Bagnato told *The Globe* in 1978. He died of cancer in November 1980.

ro repeated the allegations of discrimination, and Stanbury
decided it was within the bounds of propriety to ask the
Department of Insurance what the matter was. He also agreed
that Cassels, Brock, the Toronto law firm in which he was a
partner, would do the legal work for the charter. (The firm
would eventually bill about $100,000 for its services.)

On May 23, 1974, Stanbury met with Dick Page, federal
director of loan and trust companies. The federal Department
of Insurance was awaiting statements of the applicants' net
worth and letters of reference. Stanbury told Montemurro to
hand over the material and let Cassels, Brock put a professional gloss on it.

In mid-June Stanbury let his partner, David Anderson,
know that much of the Montemurro material was ready. It
would look better, he thought, if Anderson approached Dick
Page this time. The Senate does not have a formal code of conduct for business dealings, but Stanbury had set his own limit.

Anderson, though not a senator, was certainly no political
neophyte. He had been part of the tight-knit Liberal group that
rebuilt the party in the late fifties and early sixties; he had been
defeated in a 1955 bid for office but had helped many successful candidates and counted cabinet minister Donald Macdonald among his friends. (He later was appointed a county
court judge.)

Anderson learned that federal and Ontario trust regulations
differed in one important respect. The need for a company to
serve the ethnic community was a factor provincially but not
federally. Financial viability was the main federal concern, and
new entrants were looked at closely. They must show that these
investors had money and the type of financial history that
would make them responsible trust operators.

Since people are measured by the company they keep, one
way to show themselves worthy was to have solid recommendations. It didn't take Montemurro long to think of John Clement. The mayors of Rouyn-Noranda and Niagara Falls and
the Niagara Falls Chamber of Commerce had supplied testi-
monials, but what could be better than a recommendation

from the man in charge of the provincial ministry that registers trust companies?

Montemurro had no trouble at all in securing the recommendation. Clement was happy at the thought of a new trust company in his riding. He knew about Montemurro's IOS involvement; he also knew that many of the worries about people that beset civil servants were unproven. "I do not care whether Mr Montemurro was associated with IOS or not. He obviously was not associated with it to an extent that any charges were ever laid against him, or that he was involved in matters of that serious magnitude," Clement later explained. He didn't ask his own trust company people about Montemurro — his own department, which had turned Montemurro away as not able to open a company that could gain public confidence — or check again with the OSC.

"My God, I have written hundreds of letters of endorsement for all kinds of people." That included many letters on ministry letterhead for matters that would eventually fall under the overseeing eye of his ministry; he saw no conflict of interest. In mid-October 1974 he wrote to Senator Stanbury, recommending lawyers Luciani and Philip Lococo of Niagara Falls; John Buscarino, a real estate agent and former mayor of Port Colborne (who later parted company with this group and eventually founded Seaway Trust); and Montemurro.

There were other matters to settle. The federal department wanted to ensure tight control over who could own the company. It suggested that all the major shareholders set up a trust with a few people voting the shares, if and when they got the licence. This "voting trust," which gave Montemurro and Luciani effective control of the company, was to be used by Montemurro and his associates to their own financial advantage as soon as they received their charter.

David Anderson was also smoothing the way on the IOS matter.* He and Stanbury weren't concerned about Montemurro's former employers. As Stanbury later explained it:

* Montemurro was entangled in a legal suit arising from IOS's liquidation.

"You cannot judge people simply by one index. As far as I am concerned, what you have to do is depend on what people say about them, and from everything we found out people were saying they were fine fellows."

By April 1975 the application had been completed and Anderson was polishing Montemurro's approach for an upcoming "hearing" in Ottawa. It would not be a mere formality; the department let Anderson know there were many applicants without adequate financial clout or expertise who weren't actually turned down but, well, simply faded away, discouraged by endless delays. Montemurro was being checked on his business judgment. No one thought to look closely at his operation of C&M or asked Ontario's mortgage broker regulators to do so. But as he didn't have any background in the trust business, the federal people wanted to check out who he was hiring to run the company. Anderson emphasized in a letter to Montemurro that it would be style over substance. "It is very important that we are able to answer all questions that might be directed towards us in a way that will favourably impress them. It is important to realize that the accuracies of our statements are not the governing criteria, but rather the effect that they are going to have on the civil servants with whom we are meeting."

Montemurro and friends had clearly passed the initial scrutiny: in mid-March 1975 they were allowed to advertise the company's slated incorporation, one of the official steps preceding a charter. The public had its first notice of the new financial institution, but there were some readers whose eyes lit up at some of the names in the notice. Mr and Mrs Zenon Bril had invested and lost money through IOS. They were in the midst of a battle over a mortgage investment with lawyer and potential Astra director Philip Lococo. They wrote to warn the Ontario government about the bloodsuckers who were gaining a trust company charter.

The letter was forwarded to Ottawa; suddenly there seemed to be reason for a police investigation before things went any further. At this point no police check of the applicants had been done; the federal department obviously hadn't talked with its Ontario counterpart or checked C&M's books closely.

Montemurro was keen to know what was holding up the works. If it was only one person, they could remove that person's name from the application and add him later on, after he'd been cleared. Who were they investigating? By late May he was told the investigation was centring on three people — and Montemurro and Luciani were not among them.

But it was about Montemurro that Dick Humphrys, federal superintendent of insurance, asked when meeting with Murray Thompson, the new Ontario registrar of loan and trust companies. Thompson pulled out the three-year-old OPP report his department had run during Montemurro's informal provincial application and handed it over. Later he phoned Humphrys and said, "I think I have some more information that you want." As far as Thompson was concerned, this particular piece of information would put the lid on the application. Even if there wasn't proof of criminal involvement, it would still mean no charter, he reasoned.*

Dick Page, Humphrys's assistant responsible for federally licensed loan and trust companies, told Anderson in June that the RCMP had decided the matter was worth a full-blown study. A woman had complained about something that did not involve any charges. It must be Mrs Bril after Lococo, Anderson concluded. He wrote himself a note to have Lococo's full name at hand when Jack MacDonald called. MacDonald was executive secretary to Solicitor General Warren Allmand. Anderson had already contacted MacDonald to explain their side of the Bril complaint: a "trouble-maker with . . . a long history of making unfair and unjustified complaints" was upset about a lawyer's foreclosing on a long-overdue mortgage. Anderson wasn't looking for any special favours, of course, but could the investigation be speeded up? MacDonald

---

* What scuttle-butt was passed on has never been revealed. A written report on it was never handed in to the justice committee. But Thompson later said that on a scale of one to ten, this gave Montemurro a reputation rating of negative one. He would fail the test of public confidence. "To me, it was a valid good reason for refusing."

agreed to look into the matter. In the meantime, Anderson told Montemurro not to stir things up.

But it didn't take Montemurro long to confirm that it was Mrs Bril who was causing trouble. He told Anderson she had been bragging about writing the letter and had sent a copy to the attorney general of Ontario — John Clement in his new cabinet role. Anderson suggested that they might short-circuit the matter right there by getting Clement to send the federal solicitor general's office a copy of the letter with a note saying he'd already checked into the matter and found there was nothing in it. But Clement had never received a copy. Anderson decided it wasn't worth pressing him for help; Anderson was making his own inroads in Ottawa.

He was feeling the pressure. It was hot gossip in the Niagara area that his clients were being held up in their licence application. Lococo was particularly emotional about the delay, says Anderson: "He was saying, 'I am here and I have a thousand descendants in this area. . . . I have told everybody that I am going to set up a business. And now you are saying you will not give it to me.'"

Things weren't looking good. When Anderson talked to Page on August 1, 1975, Dick Humphrys had left for his vacation without having made up his mind what he should recommend to Finance Minister John Turner. There was a real possibility he would decide against the licence on his return; the police report, which dealt with rumour as well as fact, had not been favourable.

Senator Stanbury was still very aware of the negotiations. One of Anderson's ideas had been to beef up the trust company's board. He interested another lawyer, former Niagara area Liberal MP Don Tolmie. Tolmie called John Swift, Finance Minister Turner's executive assistant, and was told all was fine. But when Stanbury rechecked the situation, Swift, who was an old family friend, explained that on this one the inspector had asked for the minister's personal scrutiny; this would not be a rubber-stamp situation. But it didn't mean it was necessarily a problem. And the fact that the RCMP was concerned didn't necessarily mean a refusal either; it could be a minor matter.

The resignation of Turner that September threw the federal Finance Department into disarray. Stanbury kept track of the movement on the political chess-board. "My own guess is that we are going to get nowhere until the new appointment has been made and the new minister has had a little time to get settled."

Anderson began rechecking the principals with his own contacts in the area. John Matthews of legal firm Matthews and Matthews, one of the senior Liberals in the area, called the Lococo clan "probably the best-thought-of family in the area." Luciani was also well thought-of; Montemurro not known as well, but there was nothing against him. Meanwhile Montemurro was doing his own brand of lobbying. He contacted MP Roger Young; Young would be pleased to talk with Anderson, whom he had heard of through Matthews.

Donald Macdonald won the finance portfolio, and on October 16 Anderson had a long telephone conversation with his old friend Ethel Teitelbaum, Macdonald's assistant. Like Swift, she pooh-poohed the reliability of RCMP reports. She thought the department wouldn't be "overly awed" by the police information. But Montemurro was dialling Anderson three and four times daily, at times with upsetting news about the investigation. The department had been going over a list of people and suggesting that Montemurro was strong-arming people over collections, a charge he denied.

As month followed month the industry began to talk. Industry lobbyist Bill Potter of the Trust Companies Association of Canada contacted Stanbury quietly in December to tell him just what was going around about his involvement with the Astra charter. It was a friendly nudge from a Bay Street contact. His name was being used in an undesirable way; naturally his friends were concerned. At a meeting requested by Montemurro, Potter was appalled to hear Luciani say that they had Senator Stanbury working for them, and "don't you worry, he can deliver for us." Jack Russell and Potter had heard about the RCMP investigation and knew the province was against the charter. At the federal level, Dick Humphrys, they said, was stalling out of obvious concern.

Stanbury was stout-hearted enough in his reply: there was always a police investigation when there was a complaint. An arson allegation* had been looked into. But inwardly he was shaken. Luciani denied making the comment, but Stanbury decided to distance himself from the charter application.

After Clement's September 1975 electoral defeat and subsequent return to a private legal practice, Montemurro had retained him to do some work for his C&M mortgage brokerage company. Anderson called Clement, who assured him that the provincial government had no aversion to a federal charter. Clement also pointed out the vagueness of RCMP reports: they once gave him a list of 12 "off-limits" Niagara hangouts when he was solicitor general, and one of them was an unlicensed lunch bar! Well, the owners did also own a drinking spot next door, but it was perfectly harmless. After all, he said, 35% of the population in the Niagara area is Italian. Clement couldn't see a reason for refusing the licence. Murray Thompson, Ontario's trust registrar, is an old friend, Clement added.

In January 1976 Clement and his old law school classmate Thompson had an eyeball-to-eyeball discussion about the Astra licence. Clement asked if Ontario was the sticking point for the application and came away satisfied it wasn't.

Montemurro was itchy to do business. His relationship with Anderson took on an adversarial tone when Anderson said he shouldn't pull stunts like telling investors using C&M mortgages for RRSPs that Astra would soon be able to take over the trust role now provided by Lincoln Trust, which operated in the Niagara area — a move that Lincoln had complained about to Thompson's Ontario trust group.

Anderson kept on stirring the waters. The lawyer was worried about the weight that lobbyist Bill Potter's views would carry in Ottawa; he felt Montemurro needed more political

---

* An insurance company had taken Montemurro to court over a fire in a building he had owned, but lost its case. Anderson had checked with Quebec Superior Court Justice Beauregard, who had acted for Montemurro, and had come away satisfied that there had been nothing to the claim.

support as a counterbalance. The problems were not at an end. On March 19 Anderson had to inform Page that one of the passive investors in Astra had been convicted of tax evasion and was pulling out. Anderson also detailed his recent searches into the pasts of all the directors. Then he touched upon the sensitive topic of the Brils. He said Clement — pointedly referred to as the former attorney general of Ontario — had received complaints about the couple during his tenure as Ontario's chief law officer. "In his opinion and with the information that he had, there was no reason why this application should not be proceeded with." He mentioned the addition to the board of Don Tolmie, a two-term MP and former chairman of the federal justice committee. Then back to Clement, his Ontario ace in the hole, for the clincher: "I have spoken to the Ontario Provincial Police authorities and, as I have told you, to Mr John Clement, former attorney general for the province of Ontario. I have visited and looked personally, as I have stated, into the grocery business of the Montemurro family in the Rouyn-Noranda area. As a result of these investigations, I personally believe that the applicants are fit and proper people to be granted a trust company charter." At the bottom of the page a notation showed that a copy would be forwarded to John Mc-Nicholas, Finance Minister Macdonald's executive secretary.

The jockeying, the negotiating, the frequent telephone conversations continued. Sometime in March the department took another look at Montemurro's businesses, visiting C&M's offices. They didn't spot anything amiss, despite C&M's outrageous lending policies. Dick Humphrys had begun to lean in the direction of acceptance. He knew that the applicants' reputations were on the line; he was being heavily pressured by Anderson; he had to decide whether he had adequate grounds to turn him down.

After hearing which way the wind was blowing, Anderson again called his best contact in Don Macdonald's office, Ethel Teitelbaum. She asked for background information — just in case the minister inquired. Anderson was candid in his "Personal and Confidential" letter; he didn't have to weigh his words with an old friend. He outlined how they came close to getting the charter in 1975, and he took pains to let Teitelbaum know that he had personally checked out all the applicants. He couldn't find any reason why they shouldn't have a licence. (And, of course, she knew he was a man of good judgment.) Despite what the trust industry representatives were saying, he saw the applicants as keenly interested in developing trust operations.

The department dithered all summer. By July Dick Page had decided he was uncomfortable with John Bentz, Montemurro's old IOS sales buddy and a C&M manager. Page was worried that Astra managers would take in money at a trust company and tell the depositor the investment was insured when in fact it wasn't. Page was demanding a letter stating that Bentz would be only a shareholder, not an officer or director of Astra, since Bentz was with C&M; he wanted Montemurro's promise that Bentz would not be involved with any other companies raising money from the public. Much of the negotiating was about the future of C&M. Montemurro was following a time-honoured tradition in working his way up from a mortgage company to a trust company. But with deposit insurance, the department was trying to be careful that these operations didn't exist side by side. It didn't want mortgage company investors to think they were insured for their high-rate, high-risk investments.

Humphrys was still hesitating in late October. He told Anderson he needed something concrete in order to tell Don Macdonald he had changed his mind. Anderson pointed to Tolmie's active involvement as having produced a stronger board. On November 12, 1976 — after four years and interminable delays — Humphrys gave them the go-ahead. It was no dice on the information Ontario's Murray Thompson had passed along; without a criminal conviction it was nothing more than rumour. The federal regulator couldn't deny them a licence. On January 31, 1977, Donald Stovel Macdonald, minister of finance, signed both the Department of Insurance certificate to do business and the licence for Astra Trust.

Clement had been laying the groundwork for Ontario registration since September, filing material in dribs and drabs ahead of the formal application, advertising in the *Ontario Gazette* in December 1976. But the official application for registration — a prerequisite for doing business in the province — was made February 15, 1977; the licence was handed over two days later.*

The documents were supplied to Clement by Cassels, Brock and Montemurro's Niagara Falls lawyers. Indeed, Clement only skimmed over documents submitted under his signature. The forms were strikingly slipshod; there were five technical errors in the information sheet. But Clement was active enough. He spent his $150-per-hour time delivering documents to his old employees at the ministry. "I might give it to the receptionist and say, 'Here.' I might see somebody walking through and say, 'Will you give that to your boss when he is clear?' and turn around and walk out. I knew a number of the staff by sight." He made his presence felt.

Clement's messenger duties extended to picking up the charter — at one of his old haunts. "I personally went up to Queen's Park and picked up that certificate and brought it down. We held it until a courier from Astra Trust in Niagara Falls picked it up to take it down, so they could open the following day." John Clement had brought Astra across the final barrier and into the trust business.

He didn't know that on the very first day of Astra's operation, a Saturday, a director's meeting was held. One of the matters agreed to was Clement's fee (he was paid $5,000). Another was a five-to-one share split, never reported to the regulators. The trust company was in direct violation of its charter on its first day in operation.

The Astra share split is stunning in its wild disregard for regulations. The shares were originally sold at $5.75 each, with a value of $5 — the extra 75 cents was for preincorporation ex-

---

* The two-day turnover was amazing, since it takes a day for any mail to pass through the byzantine delivery system from the mail room to its destination within the ministry.

penses. But the value of those shares didn't stay at $5 for long. The directors voted to split the shares five times — to make each share worth five shares and sell partial interests in each. These were sold as voting trust certificates, with each one-fifth of a share priced at $4-$6 — on the basis that when the voting trust ran out in 1991 that's what these partial shares would be worth! Aside from the sheer avarice of this move, it flagrantly broke the rules of sale of securities. No legal document detailing the value of the company, or prospectus, was issued. No notice was given to the securities commission that a sale or redistribution of shares was taking place. Astra's managers didn't tell anyone what they were doing or check which rules they were breaking — they just did it.

Anderson, who had worked on the licence since 1974, didn't attend the company's first meeting either. He didn't know about the stock split; the arrangements were made locally. Montemurro very quickly shed the Toronto corporate trappings that had led to a trust company charter. Lococo was squeezed out of his board seat within six months; Tolmie remained, but his presence on the board didn't influence operations.

With the slogan "More than just a bank," Astra quickly set up operations. Investors walking in the door expected that because it was a trust company, all the savings and investment products sold were protected by deposit insurance. But that wasn't the case: higher-interest-rate investments were actually investments in C&M and other Montemurro companies and weren't insured.

"There is no question but that Astra operated in part as a legitimate trust company," said Supreme Court of Ontario Justice Patrick Hartt in his 1984 judgment of Luciani and associates. "Without the façade of legitimacy to support them, the questionable transactions simply could not have been executed."

A customer could choose a chequing account. Insured. Or a GIC. Insured. Or, for a higher rate of interest, an investment in an Agency Investment Certificate (AIC), which had trustee

Astra investing the funds in the customer's best interest. Insured, the folks at Astra said — but it wasn't. Or an RRSP that specialized in mortgage investments. Insured, if it followed the rules — which it didn't. At an even higher interest rate, a syndicated mortgage was sold, with a certificate guaranteeing the money would be invested in a mortgage — with one of the mortgage companies owned by Montemurro. Not an Astra product, not insured, although these features weren't always made clear. If the customer had some capital and was interested in a long-term investment, he or she could buy a voting trust certificate, redeemable many years down the road for stock of Astra — and sold at five times its value, without OSC approval or a prospectus. Not insured. It was company policy to steer clients with money to the branch manager, so one of the riskier products could be flogged. Sales commissions were higher on these products, and Montemurro pushed staff to promote them.

The rates were higher on the riskier products. But the belief that the trust company employee must be selling a trust company product — therefore an insured product — underlay the sales. As Thompson said later, "If you go to a bank and talk to the manager you expect that man to be an employee of that bank. You are dealing with him on a banker-client relationship. You do not expect him to be selling securities for other institutions, whether related or not."

There were constant overdrafts by companies owned by Montemurro or associates. In one instance, RRSP funds were invested in a fourth mortgage on one of Luciani's properties. There was scant documentation for AIC investments, no evidence of security, credit approval or set terms of repayment. AIC money went to Montemurro's other companies as unsecured loans, and sales commissions were high.

Of course, with the high-powered Toronto lawyers out of the picture, no one outside Astra knew the unusual features of the company's set-up. The federal regulators were concerned from the start about poor documentation and lack of administration, and they checked the company quarterly. But though they stumbled across the AICs in December 1977, they didn't ferret out the sinister reasons behind the company's mismanagement or try to stop it. They didn't uncover the blatant fraud.

Clement didn't hear from the folks at Astra until January 1978. Montemurro called to ask when Clement would next be in the Falls to visit his relatives — nothing urgent, but he had something he'd like to run by him. They met at Astra's office a couple of Saturdays later. Montemurro explained that Astra wanted to offer innovative, imaginative "investment vehicles" — the AIC — and wanted Clement's firm to check out how such an offering would comply with regulations. Clement said it would probably have to clear the OSC. When Clement called to check a couple of months later, he was told Astra wasn't ready. In April Montemurro travelled to Toronto, and Clement introduced him to his partner John Judson, who specialized in securities law. They told him he'd need OSC approval to sell what was essentially a mutual fund.

There was a retirement party at Consumer and Commercial Relations the third week in April. All the provincial civil servants were there, including Thompson and Jim Da Costa, then deputy director of enforcement for the OSC. Clement bumped into Da Costa and managed to mention that he would be telephoning about a business matter, an agency fund being set up by Astra Trust. But it was Da Costa who placed a call to Clement a short time later. He asked if Astra was already accumulating money through the AIC; he had heard it might be. Da Costa didn't tell Clement his source was the provincial Department of Insurance, which had been tipped off by the federal regulators. Clement assured him it wasn't true.

On May 3 Ontario registrar Thompson's second, Harry Terhune, received an anonymous letter succinctly summarizing what Astra was up to. Terhune walked it down to Hal Roach, the chief examiner, who sent it on to an employee with a note to record it as a complaint. "Keep a photostat and return the orange to me. I have already talked to [federal trust inspector] Slavic [Kvetoslav] Janda on this."

Coincidentally, the very same day Janda had phoned Roach

to tell him the federal trust people had found problems with the AIC fund during a routine field examination of the company. Page called the next day and said he'd send down photocopies of what the feds were getting. The agency certificate problem had begun.

After hearing from the OSC, Clement called Montemurro, just to make sure everything was all right. On Monday Montemurro called back. Everything was not. "He said, well, yes, they were raising some money, had in fact raised some and were pooling it. I asked him how much, and he told me he thought approximately $6 million." Clement was stunned. They couldn't do this — the OSC would have to be told. Montemurro reluctantly agreed to have Clement handle a call to Da Costa. For the next six months the former minister would constantly be reaching for the phone to dial provincial authorities.

Trust officer Al Elliott was at his desk in Toronto analysing Astra's first annual results. His report, filed July 10, 1978, poked holes in the entire operation. The provincial regulator had unconditionally renewed Astra's registration to do business in Ontario at the end of June; by July it felt it had a case to hold a hearing and either severely restrict or revoke that registration. But it didn't; it relied on the federal government regulators to look after limiting a company that they had, after all, been the ones to license. It also relied on the OSC, which was to freeze the agency fund so it could do no new business.

The federal regulators could have simply shut Astra's doors. Ontario could have refused to let it do business in the province, which would have had the same effect. "If I can call it the agony of the regulator," said Murray Thompson later. "To shut it down today and take away that licence, who is going to deal with the hundreds of people who come tomorrow?"

Instead of shutting Astra down, Dick Page wrote Montemurro detailing why the federal department had ample reason to do so. Janda's examination had shown there were too many consumer loans; three loans were far too large; records were a mess; and already two branch offices had been opened and two more were slated, while Montemurro had agreed to limit branches to one in the first year and two more in the second. Page said baldly that the department wouldn't have granted the licence if it had known he planned to expand so quickly; branches cost a lot of money, and if they were successful they'd push the company above its borrowing limit. (He didn't know, of course, that the staff was very busy pushing items besides the normal Astra deposit.)* The government felt it was playing hardball in sending the letter to Astra's directors.

In mid-July the OSC brass were briefed. Trust regulators had found an unlawful mutual fund. The money had gone many ways, including to a condominium development in Spain. No prospectus had been filed. There were other questionable loans in the agency fund, which, OSC investigator Dennis Bigham reported, totalled about $700 million, money raised from 400 investors. But the smaller problems were eclipsed by the major one. OSC vice-chairman Harry Bray was particularly concerned about the structure of the Spanish loan: the money was taking a very indirect route to Spain. Already more than $2 million had been advanced to one Sam Carpenter, a contact of Luciani's described by Bray as "some nebulous figure who is allegedly down in New York City."

The OSC never located Carpenter. The most it ever extracted from the Astra crew was that Carpenter was to forward the funds to Spain, but there was no documentation of the transactions after Carpenter received the money. "Nobody is sure that the money got past New York," Bray said later. "To this day I am not sure anybody really knows . . . all the links in the chain."

The federal government restricted Astra's licence so that it could not sell any more agency investment certificates. On July 24 Bray and the OSC staff met again with Ontario's Thompson

---

* Page described the department as "shocked and dismayed" at Astra's mortgage loans, which included a $698,000 loan secured by a motel, one for $350,000 backed by a golf and country club and a $210,000 loan to a manufacturing plant. Anderson had said in 1974 that the company wanted to concentrate on residential loans.

and Terhune to chart a course of action. And on July 25 the OSC placed a temporary freeze order on the agency fund. A formal investigation order was issued, allowing OSC staff to place the agency fund under a microscope. Dennis Bigham and two others were named to the team.

Any payments from the fund had to be requested by the trust company to the federal government, passed through Thompson and approved by the OSC; they wanted satisfaction that that was where the money came from. But the chain of command meant that the OSC's approval was virtually automatic: Humphrys had okayed the payments, Thompson's office had seen them and Bray understood that the federal government was backing the depositors anyway. And, in practice, Clement also had a role to play: when investors' interest cheques were due, for example, Clement would contact Thompson with a request that the OSC approve the cheques. Clement would quickly hear from Montemurro or Astra comptroller Andrew Ferri whenever there was a delay in getting approval.

The OSC reluctantly allowed a $100,00 payment to Spain from the agency account in late July, although it seriously questioned whether Astra even had title to the property. It was a federally monitored trust company, and the feds were crawling all over it on a daily basis. And Dick Humphrys was implying that if there were any loss to the fund, the investors would be covered by CDIC — even though they perhaps technically shouldn't be. As a director of CDIC, as well as the chief regulator, he should know the ins and outs of insurance coverage, OSC's Bray reasoned.

Ontario's Thompson thought matters were serious enough to have his minister, Clement's replacement Larry Grossman, sign an order freezing Astra's operations in late July. But he never used it. Thompson was worried about being caught in the middle. If he went ahead with the freeze, it was tantamount to openly admitting that the agency fund was a pooled or mutual fund, technically not covered by deposit insurance. They would have to have a hearing and air the issue with the company. Some of the certificates were stamped "Canada Deposit Insurance Corp." If the CDIC wanted to display its fire-power,

Ontario was providing it with ammunition. Although they were working so closely together, Bray had the idea CDIC had agreed to cover the fund, but Thompson knew better. It could be a point of contention, he decided, so the best thing to do was not to deal with it. He didn't actually ask the CDIC what its position would be. "We wanted to leave that alone." Without an answer, Ontario could go along assuming that the fund was insured. Thompson told Humphrys and Page he thought any action on the province's part would be redundant.

While the federal government was making its attempts to crack a whip and Ontario was agonizing over whether it should ask the federal insurer whether the agency fund was covered and the OSC was dissecting the agency fund, the boys at Astra were busy. As soon as the OSC froze the agency fund, they set up another. This one was called the Personal Investment Account (PIA). Same idea, different name. They raised almost $1 million in eight months. Money went in many directions. There were no books for the PIA excepting a single spreadsheet. The regulators were unaware of its existence. The only way they could ever have stopped these characters would have been by shutting them down.

Thompson's second, Harry Terhune, working closely on the case, thought Astra would be better in receivership. Interest income would not cover expenses; many of the investments weren't paying. About $390,000 was due to investors by the end of 1978. It was a ridiculous situation, he told Thompson in a prescient memo. "As I see it, we are acting beyond our authority, have no way of enforcing any directive, certainly no way of ensuring that a directive is carried out, and could be laying ourselves open for legal action. I strongly recommend that a receiver be appointed by the OSC."

Thompson's relations with Clement continued to be cordial. He obviously didn't hold it against Clement that the former minister had pushed for quick provincial registration of Astra. The regulator and the lawyer met for a friendly lunch on August 9, with a client of Clement's from the Ontario Dental Association. Clement had offered to set up the meeting when he heard Murray complaining about a regulatory problem with some prepaid dental insurance plans. But Clement also managed to work the conversation around to Astra and assure Thompson that his clients were going to get a handle on the agency fund themselves. They would guarantee that the investors wouldn't lose a cent. It was only one of many proposals. OSC investigator Dennis Bigham talked with Clement at least weekly that summer, and Clement began to learn how the trust company really operated. Once the OSC investigators began to look at Astra's agency fund trading activity, they couldn't miss the voting trust units.

The OSC also became concerned about C&M when investigators found it hadn't been wound up as Montemurro had promised it would be when he was granted the Astra licence. There was good reason to be worried. Since June, C&M had been paying old clients with money from new clients. By September the OSC unwittingly had three parallel investigations into the Montemurro empire: a formal investigation into the agency fund and two informal fishing expeditions on the Astra voting trust units and the state of C&M. On October 17 Bigham and OSC investigative accountant Jim Widdowson drove down to Niagara Falls and spoke with Montemurro and his assistant Sandra (Sally) Barmstone. They also made sure they photocopied some of Astra's records, which showed Astra syndicating mortgages — like the ones Montemurro had sold for Western Ontario Credit back in 1973. To Bray these were "funny pieces of paper." The OSC continued a series of in-camera, under-oath questionings of Montemurro, branch managers and helpmates such as Barmstone.

On October 23 Thompson hosted a meeting to discuss the state of Astra. His alter ego Terhune was there; Humphrys and Janda for the federal government; and Clement and his partner John Judson with clients Montemurro and Luciani. Baillie, Bray and Bigham represented the OSC. It was, in civil service parlance, "a senior meeting." The mortgage brokers' registrar, who had regulatory responsibility for C&M, wasn't invited because the main concern was Astra, and government types like to deal with these things in neat compartments. The topic of the day was the Spanish condominium: how Montemurro and friends proposed to pay back the agency fund, how much money had been advanced, what personal interest they had in the project, the security for Astra's loan, the difficulties there might be in bringing funds out of Spain. And, first and foremost, what documentation of ownership was there? Luciani said he had some sort of certificate of title from a Spanish lawyer somewhere in his files. He had with him a guarantee and a declaration of trust that he was holding shares in the company constructing the condo on behalf of Astra. OSC chairman Jim Baillie and vice-chairman Harry Bray weren't buying it. No more money would be winging to Spain — or wherever it was landing — until someone showed title to the Spanish property. It was the OSC, not the trust regulators, who laid down the law.

Montemurro and Luciani unrolled a set of architect's drawings and suggested that one of the officials fly over to check out progress. No one jumped at the offer. But Judson, at Montemurro's request, flew over with Astra comptroller Andrew Ferri in mid-November, staying almost a week.

A couple of days after Thompson's meeting, the OSC's Bigham went over to the mortgage brokers' section of the ministry to look at its files on C&M. He told Norm Baird, the assistant registrar of mortgage brokers, about the OSC investigation. It was the mortgage broker overseer's first notice that anything was amiss, although Montemurro had been asked by the federal authorities to wind down C&M two years before.

In fact, C&M had taken $1.7 million from the public since the promise that it would shut its doors; $1.2 million of it went straight to Montemurro and associates, to cover their debts and fund their ventures. No regulator knew this.

Bigham began to sniff around C&M and called Clement in early November to see about taking an informal look at the books. They agreed on a November 16 visit.

In mid-November David Anderson became active in the company's affairs again. With the company's licence on the line, Montemurro called in the Toronto law firm responsible for guiding him through the labyrinth of federal negotiating in the first place. Anderson was aghast at what he found at Astra, but they were properly contrite, he says, so he again took on the case, telling the directors they had to settle the Spanish loan problem or they would never get their licence restored. Of course, other lawyers were still dealing with the nutmeat of the business, the new mortgage loans. Anderson and Clement had been brought back only to nurse the problems.

When the OSC investigators arrived at C&M's offices for their informal look at the books, they expected Montemurro to co-operate. They had, after all, checked with Clement. But there were no books and no C&M employees on the premises, only Astra's Andrew Ferri. Bigham and Ferri had been on bad terms for months. This time, after verbal explosives, Ferri hustled to phone Clement, incoherently claiming Bigham had grabbed his throat, a report that differed from Bigham's account of the meeting.

Bigham told a full gathering of OSC commissioners the next day that C&M was not winding down its business as promised. The OSC began to slam shut the doors of Montemurro's empire. It obtained a search warrant for C&M, ordered C&M and associated First C&M Realty to stop selling mortgage syndication contracts and added First C&M to the list of companies under formal investigation.

Clement contacted the OSC about the Ferri run-in; it wasn't the first time he had complained. The OSC had agreed back in July that any investigations of Astra would be discreet, he reminded them. Since then there had been incidents: in one case investigators had taken an investor in Thorold, Ontario to the local police station to photocopy his investment certificate! That was bound to get people talking. He also asked Bigham to back off a bit. His client was trying to settle everything, Clement claimed, but there were a lot of loose threads. Montemurro arrived for another examination on November 20; his explanations just didn't justify the types of loans Astra had been making.

Still, the OSC delayed a week before using its search warrant for C&M. It had called the Investigations and Enforcement Branch of the ministry's Business Practices Division and requested someone to tag along as an observer since C&M was, after all, a mortgage broker licensed by the ministry. For a week Tom Johnston, the token observer invited for the ride, cooled his heels. OSC chairman Jim Baillie decreed that his investigators wait until Judson returned from Spain. The OSC was walking on tiptoe.

"Behind all this was the concern of the federal suprintendent as to the integrity of the financial system that he administered, that there should not have been a run caused on this depository," Bray said later. "Perhaps he did not conclude that Montemurro was honest but he did behave as though he believed he was honest. . . . Baillie said, 'Let us give them a chance to prove it.'"

Judson had promised to call Bray at home when he returned on Sunday, November 26. There was no call Sunday. No call Monday morning. More than once Bray picked up the phone and called Judson at Shibley, Righton and McCutcheon. Finally Judson called back. Bray didn't need to mince words with Judson, who was a regular face around OSC meeting rooms. "I said to him, 'John, what's the report?' His reply to me was, 'I have no instructions from my client.' I said, 'You have no instructions from your client? You went over there to get certification title and you have no instructions from your client?' He said, 'I'm sorry, but I have no instructions from my client.' I said, 'I guess I know what the report is.'" The next morning Bigham's team again arrived at C&M. Again the records had been removed from the building.

Bray knew a problem when he smelled it. "When a lawyer says to me, 'I have no instructions,' that is bad news." Bray, who died in 1983, was the heart and soul of the OSC, having joined the investigation staff on July 2, 1951, and, except during a brief stint in the attorney general's office in the early sixties, dominated the commission for three decades. Chairmen, plucked from the private sector to head the OSC, came and went; Harry Bray endured. Vice-chairman since 1968, he had handled a slew of financial collapses. He realized he was now handling another one. His management diary usually served as a mere appointment book, but on November 26 and 27, 1978, Bray made copious notes about his actions. He contacted

Thompson, Humphrys and the federal people and let them know exactly what he thought of Montemurro's agency fund. Bray and Thompson arranged to see Robert Butler, deputy minister at Ontario's Consumer and Commercial Relations, at 9:30 the next morning. In the morse code of the civil service this was definitely an S.O.S.

Bray also mentioned C&M to Butler. It was licensed by the ministry, and his own people had come back empty-handed from their search. But he concentrated on Astra, which should not have been an unfamiliar name to Butler. Each month Murray Thompson filed a terse three-page report outlining the operations of the Financial Institutions Division. Astra and its "problems" had often featured in the report since January 1977, when Clement was busily lobbying for registration. The reports were sent to the executive offices on the ninth floor. Thompson had to assume someone read them.

Bray next dropped in on Bob Simpson, the man at Ontario's Consumer ministry to whom the provincial registrar of mortgage brokers, I.B. (Gus) Weinstein, reported. Bray told Simpson that both the OSC and the trust people were very worried about Montemurro's integrity. He explained that the agency fund problems at Astra were the immediate concern, but he thought Simpson should know about the C&M raid.

While Bray was pressing the alert button, the federal authorities were curiously untouched by the lack of a report from Judson. They continued to negotiate with the principals of Astra and again accepted their promise to clean up the mess. On November 30 Clement and Anderson helped the department draft an agreement for Montemurro, Luciani and associate Frank Vasco to buy back the Spanish loan from Astra for $2.4 million, to be paid in stages. This agreement was made with the expectation that Astra would live to see another day.*

* Federal regulators assumed Montemurro's grocery holdings were worth at least $1.5 million. He did sell them eventually at that price, but they were already pledged against other borrowings. Montemurro, Luciani and associate Frank Vasco agreed to pay back the Spanish loan to Astra with 10% interest. The first payment of $250,000 was due December 15; another $250,000 was due in mid-January and $500,000 was due, beginning in mid-March, on a quarterly basis until March 1980, when the balance was to be paid.

Yet another lawyer from Montemurro's stable, Gerry Kluwak of Bastedo Cooper, called Bigham to negotiate the turnover of C&M's books. OSC accountant Jim Widdowson began poring over them December 4. Bray called a meeting for December 6 at 10 A.M. This time Montemurro and friends weren't invited. The plan was to alert everyone to the facts, the fears and the suspicions that had been building about Montemurro's business finagling, to ensure that each piece of the puzzle was in place. Thompson was there, of course, with Terhune and another official flanking him. The OSC's own people were on hand. Simpson was invited from the Ontario Consumer Ministry, as was Dave Mitchell, who had dealt with Montemurro in 1973 for the OSC but was now heading Consumer's investigative branch. He brought his assistant, A.A. Coleclough. Coleclough briefly thumbed through the mortgage brokerage files on C&M and its subsidiary Cana Management before rushing off; since this was a special deal, Norm Baird from mortgage brokerage delivered them to save him time. But Baird was not invited, nor was his boss Weinstein. They were registration functionaries, in Bray's eyes. The others could fill them in. Besides, their boss knew the situation. Bray didn't know Weinstein or Baird; they weren't at his level in rank.

When a strong personality takes charge of a situation, others involved begin to feel relieved detachment. The OSC has always been the investigative presence in the Ministry of Consumer and Commercial Relations. Bray tried to communicate his sense of urgency and alarm, to make sure everyone was on alert and would do their utmost to stop any further damage being done by Montemurro. The meeting itself, he felt, should have set the stage for action: the heads of three divisions were there. "I have never had a meeting like that before." But those listening to Bray that day felt like a crowd at an accident. Coleclough spent his time scribbling notes to get up to date on the situation, not questioning the OSC about its actions or its expectations of him. "I really didn't understand what the issue was and the talk went fast and furious." When Coleclough and Mitchell left the meeting they didn't feel they had to do anything about C&M; the OSC was handling it. Theirs was a "watching brief." The information about C&M was based on the OSC's analysis, and the OSC would let them know when it had hard evidence.

Early the next morning Coleclough spoke to Gus Weinstein, outlining the situation as he understood it in case Weinstein needed to deal with the OSC eventually about revoking C&M and Cana's registrations. Weinstein didn't take notes. If Weinstein wanted him to do anything more, he should let him know, Coleclough said. But Weinstein, although usually a worrier, never did get back to him on this one.

Mitchell agreed that it wasn't the ministry's show. After all, the OSC, the OPP and the Niagara police were all investigating. It looked like mortgage fraud; that was outside the scope of their work. They had about 200 other cases to deal with and no experience in the mortgage brokerage area.

The Spanish loan pay-back agreement with the federal government was signed on December 15; from that point on Astra had only a monthly licence.

The OSC decided in December to place C&M in receivership. But its court application received a major setback when the judge decided there would be a better chance for investors to recover their money if Montemurro remained involved in cleaning up the dubious loans. Lawyers for both sides ironed out an agreement in the judge's chambers in mid-February: accountants Touche Ross would watch Montemurro's every move, and C&M's owner would produce $500,000 as security — in case he couldn't pull the company out of the fire. Touche Ross was a receiver without the title or the rights. Bray wanted Montemurro out, but the OSC didn't force the show because a financial institution — Astra — was at stake.

In early January the full board of Astra met in the Cassels, Brock office to discuss the exact terms of the agency buy-back agreement made with the federal government. One of the board members had the courage to ask Clement whether, in his opinion, anyone connected with Astra had broken the law. Clement said yes, he thought that by selling the voting trust shares people had crossed the legal line. Montemurro held his tongue in front of the other directors. But later he let Clement know that he didn't appreciate that kind of behaviour from Astra's corporate counsel. That was the last time Clement and Montemurro met on Astra business, although Clement continued to sweep up the pieces.

With Touche Ross in at C&M and a freeze on Astra's agency fund, the matter was moved to a back burner at the OSC. After all, the operation was being closed down; the federal authorities had people in the Astra offices every week checking out affairs.

Bray did ask his investigator, Bigham, a very relevant question. Where was Montemurro getting the money for this $500,000 commitment at C&M and his pay-back of his share of the Spanish loan? Bigham dug around. Ostensibly it was being supplied by a Rouyn bank loan backed by grocery company shares, and by Montemurro's brother Santo. There was always that "golden carrot," the 25% ownership of the grocery business, which was mentioned whenever hard cash was needed. But in reality there was a more disturbing answer, which no one guessed, not even Harry Bray with his suspicions about Montemurro's integrity. It was an answer that was to expose an incredible degree of regulatory incompetence. The money was coming from the public.*

---

* Of the $500,000 pledged by Montemurro to C&M under the court agreement, $325,000 was obtained from Astra and his mortgage company, Re-Mor. The $225,000 that came from Astra was lifted from the Personal Investment Account, about which the regulators knew nothing at that time. Much of the money to pay back the Spanish loan under the federal agreement came from the trust and mortgage companies as well. Five instalments of the $2.4 million owing were eventually paid, totalling $1.8 million. Of that, $235,000 was supplied by Montemurro associates who were also having loans made to them by the financial institutions; $200,000 came from Re-Mor and $810,000 from the illegal "Re-Mor division," which was set up temporarily while the Re-Mor Investment Management Corp. charter was pending; $100,000 arrived indirectly from an Astra Trust RRSP account loan on an already-overmortgaged property of Luciani's; and Montemurro paid $210,000 by misappropriating funds from an account he set up at Astra for a "Mr Sidney Lanier."

It was while preparing for the C&M receivership application, one morning in mid-January 1979, that OSC investigator Bigham learned how much gall Montemurro possessed. Bigham telephoned Norm Baird in the mortgage brokers' office to check when C&M's licence ordinarily would run out. All licences expire in June, Baird replied. And by the way, Montemurro had submitted an application for a new mortgage brokerage licence. The application had been hand delivered January 4. Baird hadn't thought to inform the OSC, but with Bigham on the line he mentioned this interesting bit of information.

Bigham. was incredulous. They couldn't give Montemurro another licence with the OSC trying to close down his current operation. The two men agreed to meet and hash out the problem later that day.

The next jarring note was a telephone conversation with Gerry Kluwak, Montemurro's lawyer that season. Kluwak was checking on a rumour that the OSC was interfering with Montemurro's application for a mortgage broker's licence. In reply to this questioning, which was rather aggressive considering C&M's shape, Bigham was non-committal. He could hardly believe the question since he had heard about the application only that morning and had discussed it with only one person.

Baird arrived at Bigham's office around 3 P.M. with a copy of an application for Re-Mor Investment Management Corp. Bigham gave Baird five good reasons why Re-Mor shouldn't be licensed. Astra's federal charter had been issued on the basis that Montemurro's mortgage brokerage activities be wound down. The Ontario trust people had uncovered highly questionable investment practices at Astra. The OSC was trying to put a receiver in C&M because of the same type of problems with its portfolio. Montemurro's application — a sworn document — denied that there were any writs of execution against him, but Bigham believed there was one. And Bigham couldn't understand the Re-Mor shareholdings; they didn't tie in with any information he had on Montemurro's holdings.

Bigham also pointed out that the Mortgage Brokers Act allows denial of a licence if officers and directors are not deemed financially competent or responsible. Surely that would apply here. They'd need a hearing to deny the application; in fact, Bigham would be willing to handle it for them.

Baird came back early on January 26 with Weinstein in tow, and they went over the same ground again for the registrar, who seemed, to Bigham's mind, somewhat uneasy about the hard line being pushed. C&M's court application for a receivership was due on February 2, so Bigham suggested they stall until then. He fully expected a judge's decision that Montemurro shouldn't be entrusted with other people's money. That would make a refusal much more straightforward and everyone more comfortable. He again offered to act as counsel at the hearing. When the pair of mortgage men left, the OSC investigator was sure there would be no licence for Montemurro.*

They did take Bigham's advice; they did stall. On the 29th they sent a letter saying they were unwilling to consider an application further at that time. It was a "please go away" letter. But Montemurro hadn't been deterred by three years of such messages from the federal government, and he wasn't going to give up now. He needed money — badly — to pay his way out of his problems. He would huff and puff and blow down this house of straw.

The C&M hearing, of course, was settled without a real receivership. Bigham believes he told Baird or Weinstein of the judge's decision. He didn't hear again about a licence for Re-Mor, and he never asked; as far as he was concerned it was a dead issue.

But it wasn't.

Weinstein and Baird turned the matter over to their legal counsel, one P.J. Wiley. Baird walked the file over and left it on Wiley's desk with a note mentioning the OSC investigation

---

*   Weinstein testified that when he left the meeting he was puzzled about its purpose. "I can only remember crossing Wellesley Street with Mr Baird and asking him, 'What did we really learn at the meeting?' . . . I had learned effectively nothing." Bigham replied after hearing this, "The premise for the meeting on the 26th was to advise them of reasons why they should not grant a new licence. I had the impression that both were in agreement that the new licence would be refused."

and Bigham's offer of help, complete with phone number. Wiley spent a quarter of an hour glancing at the file; five days later he returned it to Baird, with a note asking for more information. He felt the mortgage brokerage people should provide him with the details; he shouldn't have to telephone Bigham. He needed further documentation before deciding even if a hearing could be held to defend a refusal. After holding the file for five days he noted that he'd like the information ASAP. Wiley picked up his daybook and recorded the file returned. He never heard of the matter again, and eventually the orange-hued duplicate of his return memo ended up in the miscellaneous file. That was the end of the first and only suggestion from the mortgage brokerage registrar that a hearing be held to refuse a licence.*

Despite the collapse of the trust company he had brought to Ontario for provincial registration, John Clement wasn't shy about doing business with his former ministry, nor it of hiring him. In February 1979 his firm, Shibley, Righton and McCutcheon, surfaced as a recommendation by the attorney general's department — one of his former ministries — for the job of winding down a pyramid sales firm. The operation would be supervised by mortgage broker regulator Weinstein as part of his duties as director of commercial registrations. Weinstein, A.A. Coleclough, Bob Simpson and a government lawyer met with Clement to discuss the firm's potential appointment, although it was eventually another partner who shouldered the work-load. The meeting took place while Weinstein was deciding the fate of Re-Mor, but no mention was made of the Montemurro case.

Weinstein, buffeted by Montemurro's demands and faced with his lawyer's return of the Re-Mor file, approved the licence. He had doubts about Montemurro's integrity. He knew about C&M. He simply didn't know how to turn it down.

---

* When the Liberals were poring over the civil servants' documents two years later they found a curious alteration in this file: the phrase "the OSC will back us up" appeared with a question mark. In a copy of the same document submitted as part of another pile there was no question mark.

Later, facing a number of civil suits for his action and promised legal protection by the government, a very distraught Weinstein described himself to a reporter as "an innocent player, trying to exercise total wisdom."

For months, while Re-Mor operated, with Astra officials selling risky Re-Mor certificates, the regulators and lawyers crawling over Montemurro's business dealings knew nothing of it. They didn't know that Astra's invisible Personal Investment Accounts were shifted to Re-Mor. They didn't know that before its registration, a temporary, illegal division was set up using the Re-Mor name but run through a company of Luciani's, Via Mare, managed to collect $2 million and broke every promise it made to the public. Those accounts were also assigned to the new legally licensed Re-Mor. In short order it too collected more than $2 million, its green brochure boasting that it was "Taking the Risk Out of Mortgage Investment." It promised guaranteed investments in Ontario mortgages to a maximum of 85% of the property's value. Each promise was repeatedly broken as Montemurro raised cash to bail himself out of past mistakes. Most of the mortgages were shams.

By April 1979 Dick Humphrys was demanding that Montemurro find new investors to shore up Astra with additional capital. At the end of the month Clement and Anderson met with the OSC's Baillie, Bray and Bigham to discuss a possible prospectus that would allot real shares to the voting trust unit holders and issue additional equity to outside investors. But no business solution solved the deep problems in the company. In May the OSC laid Securities Act charges against four Astra officers, including Luciani, for selling the voting trust units. (The charges were, however, laid secretly, and no record was kept at the courthouse so that no one would stumble across the charges and begin to worry about the trust company. They were never proceeded with.)

Ontario Consumer Minister Frank Drea, the latest to warm the seat, signed the consent to prosecute. He immediately called Murray Thompson. Was this Astra Trust a provincially chartered company? Thompson assured him it wasn't. He didn't bother to ask whether Drea had ever heard of Astra, so often featured in his monthly reports to the ninth floor.

In July 1979 an angry investor wrote to the provincial trust officials when he found that his investment in Astra had been funneled into something called Re-Mor. He later wrote to say that his money had been returned. No one followed up this lead. Re-Mor's licence was renewed in early September 1979. Margaret Kerrigan, who had been a clerk in the mortgage brokers' area for quite a while, had been the one to cover the C&M, Cana and Re-Mor files with new, red jackets in February, on instructions from Norm Baird. His short, handwritten note said simply: "Re Re-Mor Investment Management Limited. Okay to issue registration to above, but red flag it and its two sister companies, C&M Financial Consultants Ltd., Cana Management Corp. Ltd." Kerrigan asked another clerk what red flagging meant; she was told to place a red file around the plain manila one. Kerrigan was on holidays in August when the C&M and Cana files went up to Baird for special licence renewal approval. But when she returned after Labour Day to deal with the pile awaiting her, she didn't connect the red Re-Mor file with the note of the previous winter or with the two other files that crossed her desk September 5 on their way back from Mr Baird. "It didn't strike me at the time," she said later. She issued the new registration September 9 without checking with her superiors. Perhaps it didn't matter that the licence was renewed; Re-Mor had already been operating for two months without a licence, waiting for the renewal to work its way through the system.

By autumn of 1979 Montemurro had stopped making his payments under the federal Spanish loan buy-back agreement. Harry Terhune, Murray Thompson's second, began to suspect the worst — that the interest in the grocery business was an empty shell, already pledged elsewhere. He was proved right. By February 1980, with Astra on a bi-weekly licence, Humphrys still had not received an assignment of the grocery company shares from Montemurro. And Dennis Bigham was again in court, this time trying to get a decision on whether or not the OSC had the power to seize Re-Mor's records. Re-Mor, as far as he was concerned, was an illegal offshoot of the Montemurro empire, an unlicensed but operating company taking money from the public.

He learned it held a legal licence when the OSC again contacted the registrar of mortgage brokers' office. Another investigator was drafting an affidavit to back up a Re-Mor search warrant request. A promotional brochure claimed the company was a registered mortgage broker. Bigham told him he could include that as an example of a false claim; it couldn't be true. But the investigator felt he had to go through the motions of checking, so he called Baird. When he found out that Re-Mor *was* actually licensed, he hurriedly told Bigham. The pieces of the puzzle began to make an ominous picture.

"It would appear that there is a definite possibility that the funds that have been going into the Astra Trust agency fund, presumably from Carlo [Montemurro], have, in fact, been siphoned off Re-Mor," ran a Terhune memo to Thompson that month.

By this point $1.6 million of the Spanish loan had been paid to Astra, however nefarious the means by which the money had been raised. But that only cleared the way for the regulators to deal with Astra's more basic problems — the branch expansion, the other poor loans, the desperate need for capital. Humphrys was still scrambling to find new shareholders to rejuvenate the company, driven to what were in 1980 unheard-of lengths in an attempt to prevent a disaster. No one was interested.

In late March Montemurro backed out of his commitment to C&M, and on April 2 a receiver was put in. That month Astra auditors Coopers & Lybrand blew the whistle: they couldn't sign the company's statements. They didn't want to make the report public while Humphrys was looking for capital, so they were holding off. The Spanish loan was short $800,000 in their estimates; the rest of the properties mortgaged were worth about the value of the mortgage instead of the 75% of value stipulated by law. There wasn't any money; there was certainly no money for the $25,000 audit fee. On April 24 Re-Mor was placed in bankruptcy (Deloitte, Haskens and Sells were named as receivers), and Clarkson Co. was appointed to liquidate Astra.

Harry Bray was incensed about Re-Mor's licence, and he made waves. Bob Simpson, executive director of the Consumer Ministry's Business Practices Division, was awake to the trouble at last and wanted to know what had gone on with Montemurro's mortgage companies. He asked Dave Mitchell in the Investigations and Enforcement Branch; Mitchell asked his assistant, A.A. Coleclough; Coleclough assigned one John McWatt to the file. McWatt was still gathering information in late April 1980 when OPP inspector Ralph Smith complained to Coleclough about overlapping jurisdictions. Smith was in charge of a five-man criminal investigation of Re-Mor, and he didn't appreciate another government investigator wearing down the grass. McWatt was called off.

In May 1980 Gus Weinstein finally dropped into Coleclough's office to talk about Montemurro. He was worried about the criticism from Bray and others; did Coleclough think Gus had done everything he should in the Re-Mor case? "When I had completed looking at the files, Gus asked me what I thought," said Coleclough later. "I said, 'Gus, through January, 1979, your actions were super. On February 8 [when Weinstein sent the "please go away" letter] your actions were great. I have one question: Before the registration, why did you not either telephone the Ontario Securities Commission or come to us?'" Weinstein answered, "I don't know."

Throughout the case Weinstein seemed not to know, not to remember, to have a mental block about anything to do with Carlo Montemurro. Incredibly, Coleclough had to remind him on two separate occasions later that year about the Montemurro case. Perhaps the best version of department meetings comes from Dave Mitchell: "There is a lot of ad hockery. . . . In the washroom, quite frankly, a lot of things were discussed."

The enforcement group took a hard look at the mortgage brokerage area as a result of Re-Mor. The investigation group had little experience in that business and was, Coleclough says, "abysmally unprepared to handle a critical problem."* They discovered that although under the act mortgage brokers must submit extensive financial statements, that regulation hadn't been enforced. The department began to catch up to the changes in the industry, such as the emergence of mortgage banking and syndicated loans, which Coleclough says "just skirts in between" mortgage brokerage and trust legislation.

Bigham says it didn't matter that Re-Mor was granted a licence: it had already collected $1 million of the $6 million it took from the public before the licensing, under the umbrella of Luciani's licensed mortgage company. Still, that was only a stopgap measure. The Re-Mor licence gave Montemurro another way to raise money from the public.

And Astra gave Re-Mor an aura of respectability, the same aura it had earlier given C&M and the agency fund and voting trust certificates. "The privilege granted by the government was that he could solicit and obtain funds from the general public and reinvest them," said Ontario Supreme Court Justice Gregory Evans during his sentencing of Montemurro in 1984. "The granting of such a charter and licence by the government created the impression with the public that they could have confidence in dealing with this man and the institutions which he controlled and represented."†

Liberal party researcher Tom Zizys was sitting in the Ontario justice committee hearings in mid-May 1980, a primed reporter at his side, waiting for a question on problems with a home-

* It brought in two "reputable" brokers to train a few of its people on the finer points of mortgage brokering in February and March 1980. Next the group looked at cross-directorships between mortgage brokers and trust companies, and whether this was a "safe practice." After that came a computerized "supplementary registration file," or a checklist of names. Sometimes the names are added because of "bad vibes," sometimes because of something more.

† Montemurro was sentenced in January 1984 to six years in prison. Six of his associates were charged with fraud and theft: Patrick Luciani, John Bentz, Frank Vasco, Andrew Ferri, Gunnar Doerwald and Sandra Barmstone. In September 1984 Luciani was sentenced to five years; Bentz to two years less a day; and Ferri to six months. The others were found not guilty. Luciani is appealing his sentence; Ferri and Bentz are appealing their convictions.

builders' warranty program. Wentworth North MPP Eric Cunningham began questioning the licensing of a mortgage brokerage firm called Re-Mor. "I remember thinking, 'Oh Jesus, Eric's going to eat up time'" with some technical financial industry problem, recalls Zizys with a grin.

Re-Mor's problems were public knowledge but hardly common currency. Jack Willoughby, a *Globe and Mail* business writer with a sharp eye and good OSC connections, had published a piece in Feburary linking Astra to C&M because of Montemurro's position in both. There was a small run on Astra as a result of the story. Willoughby wrote another story in May, about the confusion surrounding Re-Mor's licensing, and Cunningham picked up the scent.

With both Astra and the Argosy Financial collapse* to make sense of, researchers in Ontario's Opposition Liberal party began sorting out these technical and seemingly politically unprofitable regulatory muck-ups. Zizys landed Re-Mor with the toss of a coin. One corporate search led to fifty and to an index file of names that appeared again and again. A few of those names had rumoured association with organized crime. By July 31 the Liberals had compiled enough information to issue a press release saying that within the present regulatory system it was impossible that Re-Mor should have received a licence. Consumer and Commercial Relations Ministry critic Jim Breithaupt, a director of Bernie Walman's Income Trust in Hamilton, began asking questions about Re-Mor in the legislature. Other MPPs were receiving telephone calls and mail from burned constituents.

By November, their pressuring began to pay dividends. Drea promised he'd release the Re-Mor files, then reversed his position because of the police investigation. But the Opposition

---

* Argosy Financial Group of Canada Ltd. collapsed in 1980, leaving 1,940 investors in the lurch. Argosy syndicated mortgages on properties, as did C&M. But Argosy principals diverted much of the $24.5 million invested in mortgages to their own pockets. Fraud and theft charges are now working their way through the courts.

was determined to thrash out the Re-Mor matter, and the Liberals and NDP agreed on a many-legged approach that would bring the Re-Mor licensing before the justice committee.

They succeeded, in large part because neither the Conservatives nor the press was paying attention at first. On November 18 the required 20 members petitioned the legislature to send the Consumer Ministry's annual report to the justice committee for scrutiny. When the committee met the next day, no Tories attended to hear a tame presentation by the Insurance Brokers of Ontario. Representing the brokers was John Clement, the former minister himself. The insurance matter — regulated by the same department that registered Astra Trust in Ontario — was pushed aside as Re-Mor and Astra's operations were debated. The committee drafted a list of bureaucrats to appear and explain the licensing procedure; Bray and Thompson were on the list for the next day. Clement sat and listened as his present client's business was held up by a call for a close look at a former client's very questionable activities. One story has him storming out of the room, accosting a Conservative member and asking him why in hell there weren't any Tories around. In the committee room a motion to ask Frank Drea to deliver the papers for committee scrutiny passed easily.

Drea arrived on scene at the tag end of the discussion. He and Clement, his former boss and sometime mentor, had chatted briefly outside the committee room.*

There were two very tough fights in the house before the committee won the right to receive all the government's documents and dissect the registry of Astra, the licensing of Re-Mor and the OSC's involvement with Montemurro's companies. It was the first time in the four-year minority Tory government that the two Opposition parties had openly worked together to force public acquiescence from the government;

---

* Clement would later be asked to leave his law firm as a result of the widespread publicity over his role in Astra's licensing.

any deals had been made by party bosses, not on the floor of the legislature.* Attorney General Roy McMurtry also exerted behind-the-scenes pressure on Opposition members who were lawyers and would worry about interfering with anything in police hands.

Eventually a speakers' warrant was issued and the government's files handed over. An agreement was struck: a special subcommittee would comb the documents and agree on what could be made public. (Only half a file drawer was classified as secret, although two police officers had to guard the files constantly. They passed the time watching TV programs, one of their favourites being "Barney Miller.") The Opposition-dominated committee tackled Re-Mor first as the most readily understandable case of lax regulation. Astra's licensing was not expected to be as politically potent. But David Anderson's memos and letters outlined Senator Stanbury's and Clement's involvement in obtaining the federal and provincial charters with odd, titillating references to federal political luminaries such as Donald Macdonald, John Turner and John Munro.† The focus on federal Liberal cabinet ministers had not been expected by the provincial Liberals when they took on the onerous job of dragging the Astra/Re-Mor affair into the light.

The committee, particularly the NDP members, did not hesitate to heap abuse on the politicians and bureaucrats involved from the safety of their protected positions as sitting members of the legislature. A typical blunt summation of events came from MPP Mitro (Mac) Makarchuk: "It is the federal people who license . . . the vultures; give them a licence to steal, and then let them loose in the province of Ontario."

---

* The Tories threatened a snap election to try to bring the NDP, low in the polls, into line. *The Toronto Star*'s five-star edition headlined a potential election call caused by the Re-Mor documents during the second house debate.

† Humphrys and Page didn't appear before the committee. The federal government stood firm on its right not to have federal actions examined by a provincial committee. At this point there was also a battle going on over which level of government should pay Re-Mor investors.

The Opposition, stopped in midflight by Davis's election call, hoped Astra/Re-Mor would be an election issue. Re-Mor investors, who weren't covered by deposit insurance, did organize and picket the premier. But it was merely an unpleasant aspect of a very pleasant campaign that swept Davis into office again, this time with a majority. And Davis succeeded in burying it when the legislature convened. After all, criminal charges had been laid during the election. And eventually almost everyone would be repaid at least part of their investment funds.*

Again there was a new political boss in the ministry. In mid-1981 minister Gordon Walker unveiled a series of improvements in internal communications, better lines to the police, more information on licence applicants. There was no need to continue the committee's review, no need for a royal commission to look at the regulatory process. He made everything sound just dandy. And he made a promise: a regulatory blunder like Astra/Re-Mor would never happen again.

---

 * Astra depositors were insured for up to $20,000 each; those with agency fund investments have received about 45 cents for each dollar invested, with a partial payoff by the federal government. Re-Mor's depositors were reimbursed for $5.2 of the $6.6 million lost in 1983 by an Ontario government chastened by an ombudsman's report that suggested payment. C&M and First C&M investors, however, are still awaiting pay-backs, which might be anywhere from 10 cents to 25 cents for each dollar invested.

9

Asleep at
the Switch

It happened again.

Ontario's Gordon Walker didn't know it, but as he spoke reassuringly about the new-found strength of the regulatory system, the stage was being set for Greymac, the largest financial disaster in Canadian history. Neither the federal nor the provincial regulators realized that their methods of keeping track of companies simply didn't work any longer.

Astra, rather than serving as an example of a failure in the regulatory system, was dismissed as a single, isolated example of a crook's slamming his way into the business. Ontario bureaucrats concentrated on tightening operations in the mortgage brokers' department, the most obvious area of incompetence. They did not look at trust company regulation.

A government audit manual drafted during the late seventies was basically untouched by Astra. Instead, the audit crew was reminded in its "charging brief" from the chief examiner "to be more aware of that type of a scam." Because Astra "went wrong in the early birthing period," new trust companies were asked to voluntarily submit monthly statements to the regulators, who thought this meant they were nursing companies through their early stages. They didn't seem to realize that this request wouldn't have stopped an Astra, since Montemurro would have submitted false statements without flinching — and it wouldn't stop anyone else who wanted to play fast and loose.

The Ontario politicians took a different tack. They weren't interested in examining the entire industry either; their motivation was fear that there could be another Astra lurking somewhere. A telephone book of important revisions to the provincial Trust Companies Act, which a middle-level team at the Consumer Ministry was polishing after five years of tossing around ideas and grinding out potential regulatory changes, was put on ice. For the last couple of years the group had met each Friday to concoct a new act based on a 1975 select committee report on loan and trust regulation, and it had finally forwarded the results to Walker. But without a section marked "Astra Solved," there was no hope of changing the rules. And the legislation had a few big holes that desperately needed filling.

One of those holes was a lack of screening of new company owners. Carlo Montemurro had spent four years running after a brand new charter for a trust company; his life would have been much easier had he simply bought an existing one, as the celebrated Steve Axton, Lenny Rosenberg and Andy Markle did in 1981 and 1982. It was assumed — by the financial community and certainly the financial press — that the seller had a moral obligation to approve the ethics of the buyer. The sellers, however, saw that kind of screening as the government's role. And the governments, both federal and provincial, had no provision for refusing a charter transfer on the basis of the owner's suitability. Ontario didn't even know about Axton's purchase of Dominion Trust until he filed a standard change-of-ownership form a month after the fact.

Staff had to be pulled away from the regular duties they already couldn't keep up with when crises arose. Murray Thompson's office received a panicky call in late 1981 from District Trust, a London, Ontario, company in deep financial trouble. The company had a number of bad mortgages; it

hadn't been paying attention to matching its assets and liabilities and now was caught in an interest rate squeeze. But the
death blow for the company was a $16 million fraud. Between
1979 and 1981 Ronald Bobbie, a District vice-president, made
loans to two small business development corporations (SBDCs)
through a friendly lawyer and investment manager, without the
trust company's knowledge.

The money moved back and forth between the two companies, but they didn't have the assets to back the loans, and
when District finally discovered Bobbie's actions and called
one $2.8 million loan in the spring of 1981, the companies
couldn't pay back the money. Investors ended up selling their
SBDC shares to the company for 35 cents on the dollar, pushing District even further into financial oblivion. The London
police were called in early 1982, and a three-year investigation
ended in 1985 with 680 fraud and theft charges against the
loans officer, the banker and the solicitor involved. These included a charge against Bobbie for attempting to defraud the
Continental Bank of Canada after he had left District and was
trying to raise money to invest in a condominium project on
Paradise Island in the Bahamas. That time he didn't get hold of
the cash.

The District matter was not caught by Opposition politicians
or alert journalists, as the Astra affair was. The regulators
looked on it as a time-consuming bother; the general feeling
was that any company could be caught by one bad actor. Queries about why management wasn't more vigilant and why the
regulators didn't catch and question the size of the loans and
the concentration of investment didn't arise. There was still no
early-warning system.

Ontario's registrar of loan and trust companies, Murray
Thompson, tried, in a half-hearted way, to set up an early-
warning system in early 1982; during February and March his
chief examiner, Howard (Hal) Roach, requested specific
reports from companies he feared had troubles. But with the
annual push for routine reviews of all companies in March,
he was pulled off this special duty. Walker, while displaying

parliamentary umbrage over Astra, didn't think the department needed stepped-up regulation forces. Indeed, he wasn't willing to support the department when a freeze on hiring left it short-staffed. The trust examinations staff lost two of its nine examiners in 1981. There were fewer bodies to examine an industry whose assets were growing at an unprecedented rate. Those who were there were not at all organized; the word *system* could not be applied to this group. Examiners were only routinely scanning company filings, not even writing down their recommendations or conclusions, at times not even signing their review forms. Examiners would make visits to companies, then never tell the companies' management the results of their inspections. The files were a mess. Even the basic examination reports were not being completed.

The provincial enforcers needed help badly. That was amply evident when they didn't catch Steve Axton before he had looted Dominion to the tune of $2 million and didn't catch Lenny Rosenberg and Andy Markle until they reached for a deal so politically loaded it turned the minister's attention to their business practices.

Rosenberg's Greymac Trust and Markle's Seaway Trust, both relatively new, provincially licensed trust companies with burgeoning assets, and their subsidiaries, Greymac Mortgage and Seaway Mortgage, both federally licensed, had the same basic problems: overmortgaging, on the basis of poor or no appraisals, in order to feed money to related parties; loans that were too large; other loans and transactions arranged with friends or associates of the owners that did not conform to proper business practices. At both the trust companies, the books were kept in a style that echoed Montemurro's: the energies of the owners were obviously elsewhere.* Real estate appraisals were slapdash and at times non-existent; justification for loans was often no more than a belief in the predictions of wealth made by real estate syndicator Billy Player, Markle and

---

* It might have been hard for regulators to tell this from quarterly filings; in 1982, 44 of 59 trust companies filed late and 11 more didn't file at all. This mass delay wasn't unusual, and penalties weren't enforced.

Rosenberg's constant companion and a regular corporate borrower.

With Astra, the province initially thought that Carlo Montemurro shouldn't have a licence but couldn't convince the federal regulators; with Greymac, the federal government was cracking down on Greymac's loan company licence through restrictions on the borrowing base and liquidity of Greymac Mortgage, and it was the provincial regulators who let things get out of hand.

Ontario told Lenny Rosenberg in March 1982 that his companies were unprofitable, and loans were in arrears. Unless things changed, it said in a letter to Rosenberg only three months after approving the change of the name of the company he had bought from Macdonald-Cartier Trust to Greymac, depositors' funds could be at risk. Federal inspectors were sitting in the Greymac Mortgage operation all that spring, enduring Rosenberg's paper airplanes and verbal abuse.* They must have been tripping over Hal Roach's team of inspectors from Ontario, who set up camp at Greymac Trust from April 27 to June 10, 1982. By that time, the regulators at both levels knew about the links to Billy Player, the overborrowing from the public, the mortgage arrears, the lack of trained personnel and the incredibly poor management.†

Ontario showed the same naïve belief in people that the federal government had in its earlier negotiations with Montemurro. It placed Greymac Trust on a monthly licence on June 30, in tandem with federal restrictions on the mortgage company. But trust registrar Murray Thompson allowed Rosenberg's purchase of old-line dowager Crown Trust in early

---

* Rosenberg sold federally restricted Greymac Mortgage to Billy Player in September, and the restrictions on its activities continued until the January 1983 seizure of its assets and its eventual wind-down.

† A November 1983 department report that attempted to explain away regulatory responsibility by documenting this early knowledge spoke of an "absence of meaningful budgets and absence of ledger and bank account reconciliations" and called Greymac a lender of last resort. It begged the question: if they knew all this, why didn't they act?

October. As obnoxious as Rosenberg had been to them, the authorities were mesmerized by the spectre of Crown's falling into the hands of controversial real estate and produce magnate Joe Burnett. The OSC had launched an unusual hearing about Burnett's suitability for a trust licence, based mainly on an outstanding criminal income tax *charge,* not a conviction, but really fuelled by stories that had trailed Burnett for years. The details of the stories included loan sharking, squeezing out small contractors in shopping centre developments, not being overly careful about who he lent money to or acted for in at least one legal matter and a friendship with John Pullman, in turn a friend of former U.S. Mafia kingpin Meyer Lansky. Burnett bitterly sold the shares he had accumulated — for a $6.5 million profit on stock held for six weeks — before the hearing even started, only to be tangled in technicalities with the OSC for another year. He also made Rosenberg an $11 million short-term loan to help him close the deal, only one of several transactions they had helped each other out with that year.

Burnett was not acceptable; his former mortgage brokerage employee Rosenberg was. That simple fact had the development community chuckling and the trust industry buzzing in October 1982. Industry Cassandra William Somerville, president of Victoria and Grey Trust, warned the province that it should think carefully about this decision. But Rosenberg's purchase of Crown suddenly made Rosenberg acceptable to Thompson, who lifted the restriction on Greymac Trust's licence in late October when Greymac's chief financial officer Lyon Wexler signed an agreement that the company would clean up its act — including questionable valuations on mortgages. Wexler's name should have sounded an alarm, as he had recently been fired from Hamilton-based Income Trust for arranging questionable mortgage loans. And since owner Rosenberg had been thumbing his nose at authorities for years, there seemed no real reason he would stop now. It was a clear case of the regulators being steamrollered by Rosenberg's purchase of Crown Trust.

The lack of control of unctuous Andy Markle's affairs is equally inexcusable. His small-town newspaper chain, BayWeb Printing, bankrolled the Midland, Ontario, native's purchase of Seaway Trust in September 1980. He'd been dabbling in real estate deals since 1972 with Player, who hailed from nearby Elmvale, Ontario, and bought Seaway at Player's suggestion. Ontario knew his loans to Player had valuations based on tax benefits rather than properties' resale value and that Player was a shareholder in Seaway's parent holding company — which made his status as a borrower at least questionable.

Thompson's regulators had been seeing Player's signature for years, first at troubled London Loan and then at Seaway. He bought properties and resold them in small chunks to investors. He made money on the resales — they were always at a higher price — and on the management fees he charged. Player charged a very high price for his often-second-rate properties but guaranteed an annual return. He arranged mortgage loans from Seaway on the basis of appraisals predicated on what buildings should be worth in a decade. Seaway received very high rates for the loans and a tidy up-front fee for agreeing to make them, which could be used immediately to balloon the trust company's capital base.

Markle was making too much money to worry about regulatory matters, and Seaway was placed on a quarterly licence in June 1981. That became a monthly licence in April 1982. But in the meantime Markle was allowed to add a mortgage company subsidiary — purchased from the Eaton-Bay Financial group — to his already badly mismanaged trust firm. Federal officials clearly fell down in allowing the sale to go through. They now say they were worried about Markle's reputation, but they would argue that, after all, the man had a trust company. Ontario again picked through Seaway Trust's business dealings, and a departmental report in July stated that depositors' funds were at risk because of the self-serving, greedy and unwise investment policy followed by Markle. It is unforgivable that the department let itself be stalled by Markle's bafflegab and empty promises. In October they launched into yet another study, the fourth major dissection of the company in 18 months. And in November Seaway made the famous apartment loans that would, finally, force bureaucrats to do something.

Buying the largest single collection of apartments for sale in the country and flipping them at double the original sale price is bound to call attention to exactly how many other times the same deal has been made in miniature form. Thompson's office was already aware of the deal; not even he could miss something this politically volatile: all those upset tenants, with a municipal election on the horizon.

Everyone knew that Rosenberg's Greymac Credit Corp.* was buying the 26 Toronto apartment buildings from giant public developer Cadillac Fairview Corp.; the news was in the daily papers as early as August. *The Toronto Star* particularly enjoyed painting a picture of terrified tenants awaiting the arrival of slips of paper in their high-rise mailboxes with "50% rent rise" written by the new landlord in a soulless script. Rosenberg sealed his doom November 2 when he lied to the new consumer minister, Robert Elgie, a pack-and-a-half-a-day man who uses arrogance as a mask to hide his sensitivity to criticism. Elgie fancies himself a patriarch, sent to lead the nation to redemption by legislating a better way, and he has all the credentials: a law degree, a medical degree and a father who had also been in the business of dispensing good government in Tory Ontario.

After contracting to buy the apartments from Cadillac Fairview for $270 million, Rosenberg told Elgie he planned to keep the apartments and would be a good landlord; he even discussed the possibility of laying new carpets. Then he pulled the rug out from under Elgie — whom Rosenberg took to calling The Good Doctor — three days later when he flipped them from his Greymac Credit to Billy Player's Kilderkin Investments Ltd. for $312 million, using the profit to help pay for

---

* Ownership of Greymac Credit was actually split between Rosenberg and mysterious Zurich financier Branco Weiss, usually a silent partner.

Crown Trust without ever paying a cent or actually owning the buildings for more than a moment. Player also instantaneously resold the apartments and trotted out one Adeeb Hassan Qutub, a Saudi Arabian who looked as if he came from central casting, as the representative of the foreign investors who would own the buildings through a series of carefully anonymous numbered Ontario companies. The $500 million final price-tag was even more impressive than the story-line.

But the most amazing fact was that Rosenberg's brand new acquisition, Crown Trust, his Greymac Trust and Markle's Seaway Trust lent the final buyers, whoever they were, $152 million in mortgage funding. These were *third* mortgages, which ranked behind a number of long-time first mortgages and a special set of second mortgages provided for Rosenberg's purchase by Cadillac Fairview. Crown, Greymac and Seaway put depositors' funds at risk on the basis of the $500 million sale. They placed their faith in Player.

Despite the doubling of the sale price, if the apartment flip had been arranged with finesse it would have withstood regulators' scrutiny. Everyone knows foreigners are willing to pay higher prices for property and take a lower return on their investment, in return for a safe haven for their cash. With proper planning, no one would have ever figured out that the investment money to back the appraisal valuations didn't exist.

The sloppiness was Player's fault. It was to be a standard Player deal with the numbers magnified: he'd take care of everything for ten years and make the buildings pay, and then he'd receive a whopping management fee. The $500 million price-tag actually represented what he figured the buildings would be worth in ten years if everything worked out. But this time he hadn't arranged all the details about those final buyers yet. Whoever *had* committed didn't place any money up front; they didn't want to take any risks until Player proved the buildings' rents could be increased enough to make the huge new mortgage payments. So Player set up a number of accounts at a friendly bank in the Grand Cayman Islands and arranged 26 back-to-back loans, which all added up to $109 million borrowed and $109 million deposited. The paper shuffling made it look as if the down payment had been made, but once the regulators began scrutinizing the deal it would easily unravel before their eyes.

Rosenberg wasn't paying close attention; the apartment sale wasn't as big as everything else he was piecing together. Crown was the linchpin in a financial structure that he dreamed could include Fidelity Trust and even First City Trust of Vancouver. Rosenberg's business life was like a jigsaw puzzle of his own construction, each piece carefully carved to fit, each deal piggybacking on the profits of the last and finally depending on the profits of the next. He sought notoriety, but he didn't realize how closely Bay Street began watching him in mid-1982. He didn't stop to consider how it would react when the old guard had seen enough pieces of the puzzle to recognize the picture.

His passion for the perfect deal had become intertwined with his vision of a mega-bank. He told *Maclean's* magazine in mid-1983, "Cadillac Fairview was just a drop in the bucket. The bank was the thing." This perpetual reach for a bank of his own is not a rational decision on Rosenberg's part. He hates the smug world of bankers, the men who can turn up their noses and turn him away. "One of my pet peeves in life is banking," he once said. "I hate bankers."

Among Rosenberg's dealings with Joe Burnett in 1982 were two deals that involved Canadian Commercial Bank, of which Rosenberg was a new director and part-owner. Rosenberg had big plans for CCB. Earlier that year he had tried to combine his holdings with his sometime partner Howard Eaton, CCB's chief executive officer, to create a financial-resource conglomerate.

The fat kid from Hamilton (Rosenberg has been known to wear a T-shirt that says, "That's not fat, I'm pregnant") couldn't be ignored by the Western bank; he had, in the space of months, become its largest shareholder. He bought 10% in early 1982 and arranged for Player and Markle to buy as well, for a total of 27% among the trio. He and Player even signed a voting pact that gave Rosenberg sole voting power of 17% for a few years, a violation of the federal Bank Act.

CCB was only one of two banks of which he tried to capture control in 1981 and 1982. The other, Dixie National Bank of Florida, was a small-time ($55 million in assets), two-branch Miami money shop for which Rosenberg offered $11 million in late 1981. But Florida regulators stalled and finally — with help from Ontario in 1983 — blocked him at the door. (In 1984 he tried again, unsuccessfully, this time for an interest in tiny Orange State Bank of Miami.)

Rosenberg had crossed the unseen line drawn by those in the corridors of power. He and his associates could get away with any number of small finaglings; regulators were too lethargic to keep up and too irresolute to force him to stop when they did uncover his tick-tack-toe games. But he wouldn't get away with financing the apartment sale partially through old-line Crown Trust, or with holding effective control of Canadian Commercial Bank. It was inconceivable. So were some of the stories about the trio that made the rounds in the weeks following the apartment sale. Rumours filled the air, unsubstantiated hints of international laundering and sinister connections. "When all else fails," says Rosenberg, "accuse someone of being involved in organized crime, because there is no defence."

Suddenly it was important to Dr Elgie — and naturally enough, to those working in his ministry — to find out everything possible about the operating habits of these fast-buck speculators, who weren't playing by gentlemen's rules. Elgie must have realized that his staff should have been on the backs of these people months or even years before. Besides, he wanted to be personally involved, and he needed advice. A doctor doesn't take advice from nurses: Elgie hired two specialists for a consultation. In walked accountant Jack Biddell, newly retired chairman and CEO of Clarkson Co., and lawyer Bill Macdonald, a senior partner at McMillan, Binch — Elgie's equals in the social sphere and men at the pinnacle of their own professions, fit men to provide a minister of the Crown with advice on such a sensitive subject.

The government had already appointed Touche Ross accountant Jim Morrison — a genial jelly-bean addict whose softshoe approach belied the skills that had served him in the wrap-up of Atlantic Acceptance in the sixties — to examine the books of the trust companies. The supremely confident tactical thrusts of his suspendered lawyer, Fraser Beatty partner John Lorn McDougall, added counterpoint to Morrison's mild-mannered ways. But while Morrison was off on his own track, asking the kinds of questions bureaucrats should have known the answers to after their many forays into the books at Greymac and Seaway, Macdonald and then Biddell arrived to change the attitude of Elgie's ministry from cautious to righteous.

The first step in that transition had already been taken with the Morrison inquiry and the simultaneous appointment of septuagenarian Stuart Thom to head a group taking a multi-faceted look at Ontario's rent controls; these moves safely pushed the tenant issue past the next election. The next step was the December 21, 1980, passage of legislation apportioning clear powers to the registrar of loan and trust companies to stop a transfer of trust company shares.* The third step, engineered by Bill Macdonald, a man used to designing corporate action plans with only his client's best interests in mind, and justified by Jack Biddell, a lifelong corporate undertaker, was the January 7, 1983, seizure of Crown Trust, Greymac Trust, Seaway Trust, Greymac Mortgage and Seaway Mortgage.

It was Ontario's show. Flanked by its high-paid, strong-willed corporate surgeons, the province took the lead, and the federal regulators, ever conscious of the power structure, fell in line. The province had learned one lesson from Astra: it isn't worth letting someone else make the decisions if you are going to take the blame. The federal government was about to learn the same lesson.

---

* Amazingly, Premier Davis used the excuse of Steve Axton's attempted transfer of Dominion to a 20-year-old Lanzino complete with hot rod to gain the Opposition's acceptance of the measures, blinding them to the ramifications of provisions that allowed unprecedented seizure of trust companies without the usual hearing process.

The decision to pay off depositors had two components. The one that captured the public imagination was the pay-off of all depositors, including those not covered by deposit insurance — that is, those with deposits of more than $60,000. This was a policy decision with political roots. There was a potential for legal action by large depositors against the Ontario government for, at the very least, negligence in renewing Greymac Trust's licence and allowing Rosenberg to take over Crown Trust. The Canada Deposit Insurance Corp., as the insurer, could be tied up in court for years fighting such claims. Neglect of large depositors would also bring other political problems. Some of the large depositors were pension funds, so to ignore their claims would be counted a personal injury both by the companies involved and by the individual voters who looked on the pensions as their personal safety nets. Other depositors included municipalities and school boards funded by the province.

The second component of the decision was the five-year agreements allowing companies to act as agents for the Ontario government and slowly work through the wind-down of the three trust companies. The agents were hired on a fee basis — paid from the seized companies' coffers — to caretake and, they hoped, absorb depositor and ordinary lending business. The problem loans were not their concern. They would slowly wind down the businesses with the least possible disruption for the public. They would sell any properties in the "ordinary" portfolios, but the problems were in the governments' hands. Once the CDIC said it would pay off all the depositors, it was necessary to get as much money as possible for the properties held by the companies. The regulators weighed the odds that carrying the properties would cost more than simply selling them off at fire-sale prices, and decided it was worth the risk to hold them.

Ontario's hand moulded these decisions. It was receivership expert Biddell who came up with the idea of separating the questionable assets and having agent companies slowly absorb or dispose of the rest. All this made perfect sense from Ontario's vantage point. With the depositors paid off, the political bomb was defused. With the "soft," or risky, over-valued assets peeled off for direct dealing by the government, the provincial government continued to control the future of what were for it crucial pieces of evidence. Their value must remain low to justify Ontario's walking into the companies. Lenny Rosenberg and his associates would be battling them in court for years over the seizure of private assets, and the value of the soft assets would be a keystone of their defence of their actions.

CDIC was letting Ontario off the hook. Although it agreed easily to Ontario's proposals, its interests were in fact quite different. CDIC, stuck with paying the interest on mortgages that ranked prior to its claim as creditor on a number of the properties, needed to sell everything at top price to recover the money it spent paying depositors and holding the problem properties.

The Greymac Affair was in the main Ontario's fault; the province had happily handed Crown Trust to Rosenberg three months earlier.* Yet Ontario walked away from its unconscionable seizure of private property without having to explain why the regulators didn't know what was going on in the companies. Voters accepted that if the government felt it necessary to trample over individual rights to catch crooks, it was because there was no way to regulate chicanery. It was a more comfortable explanation than the abdication of duty clearly proven by the political opposition, which backed up Liberal leader David Peterson's vocal assertion that the regulators had been asleep at the switch for the past two years.

---

* Greymac also echoed the political pandering of Astra. John Clement, unbelievably, had been a director of Greymac Mortgage for six years and was on the Rosenberg-appointed board of Crown. So was former cabinet minister Stanley Randall. Greymac's nominal head, the corpulent David Cowper, was a Toronto insurance salesman who was a model for fat cat Tory fund raisers. The former campaign manager for Attorney-General Roy McMurtry had made the Park Plaza's Prince Arthur room *the* place for blue-suited Toronto politicos to breakfast. He recruited Randall and tried to bring famed author and former John Robarts advisor Richard Rohmer onto the Crown board. Cowper already had a blotted copy book: he had been an outside director of mortgage brokerage operation Argosy Financial, whose principals were later convicted of fraud.

The federal regulators' share of the blame came from not properly regulating the two federally licensed companies in the group, from not forcing Greymac Mortgage into receivership when it knew of its problems, and from not catching these problems at Seaway Mortgage. It was chastized, not for these real faults, but for the unforeseen results of its weak-kneed, thoughtless acceptance of Ontario's solution to the mess both governments were in. Because CDIC supplied the money to pay off depositors, CDIC was to be stuck with the remnants of the Rosenberg-Markle empires. It would not be able to push the scandal behind it as the Ontario Tories successfully did. It would learn that it did no good to do others favours. During the next two years, the docile insurer would undergo a metamorphosis and emerge much tougher. But other events would add to the bill from the Greymac debacle, leaving CDIC bloodied and the entire system of deposit insurance in question.

The Canada Deposit Insurance Company was a sleepy organization. It had been created by Ottawa in 1967 to insure deposits for the man and woman in the street, the ordinary citizen upset by the collapse of British Mortgage, although the idea had been kicking around since the Porter commission report in 1964.

A Crown corporation founded to protect the ordinary depositor, CDIC is funded by two major groups of financial institutions that accept deposits, banks and trust companies, which pay an annual fee of one-thirtieth of 1% of their domestic deposits for the privilege of wearing the grey CDIC sticker on their doors. It was designed to be a safety valve, building up funds in case a company ever again failed and it had to pay back depositors up to a maximum — originally $20,000, increased to $60,000 when Crown, Greymac and Seaway were seized. For years it had a tidy surplus of funds in the vaults, and it ran very quietly, collecting premiums and laying low. Between 1972 and 1982, it even handed out rebates totalling $109 million to members.

The need for CDIC was amply demonstrated, however, at

the very time its incorporating bill was working its way through the federal Parliament. Ontario, worried about the fate of a small company, York Trust, quickly introduced a modified version of the draft federal insurance bill in its own provincial legislature and passed it just in case. York, which had severe problems with a mismatch of its assets and liabilities — short-term deposits and long-term mortgages — was bundled off to merge with Metro Trust. With that particular scare past, Ontario's act was shelved, with an agreement that it would come under the federal umbrella. (Quebec has its own deposit insurance plan for provincial companies' deposits in Quebec, but CDIC insures Quebec-based federal companies.)

With this *raison d'être* and immediate history, it would make sense that the CDIC would be a vigilant insurer with its own small army checking for problems in companies. But that wasn't the set-up. Instead, the act enshrined a part-time chairman, and the office had only four employees, clerks equipped to collect premiums from the banks and trust companies. It seemed to the public that for 15 years the CDIC ran problem-free, that it was only Greymac that caused its crisis of confidence. That wasn't the case. During the seventies there were isolated loans and pay-outs. In 1970 the CDIC paid back depositors at Vancouver-based Commonwealth Trust, to the $20,000 limit. In 1972 a small company called Security Trust folded because of mismatch problems.* One bank required a $50 million loan in 1980.

There had been companies with serious problems that didn't end up in the CDIC's lap but could have, companies such as United, Metro and London Loan. The 1979 collapse of the Abacus real estate pyramid could have pushed Fort Garry Trust on CDIC if Fidelity Trust hadn't picked it up.

Then came the small failures of the eighties, starting with Astra but followed by District in early 1982. AMIC Mortgage, a small Alberta loan company, was being watched by CDIC long before it folded in July 1983. It was time for the CDIC to

* This is not the Ontario-based Security Trust now in operation.

wake up and think about the monitoring aspect of its insurance business.

But it didn't wake up; it was bound not to. The CDIC is controlled by the groups it insures. The federal superintendent of insurance is not its chairman, but an influential board member along with the inspector general of banks and the governor of the Bank of Canada. Together with the part-time nominal head of the corporation and the deputy minister of finance — or a substitute — they set policy for the insurance company. They tended to follow the path of least resistance.

That tendency changed very dramatically after the Crown Trust collapse. The changes centred on the pay-back decision forced on the CDIC in a polite sort of way by Ontario in early January 1983. The forces that supplied the CDIC with its money and those responsible for its life grew very worried about the corporation's ability to cope with life as a major creditor.

It was clear from the start that the CDIC couldn't handle the task. Its people were clerks who knew nothing about real estate. Even the chairmanship was in flux. Jack Close, former Royal Trust executive and a bon vivant who in his seventies still follows a rousing game of squash with martinis at Montreal's University Club, was stepping down from this sinecure for retired minds. He officially left as of November 1982; he stayed on another three months as a favour to the new appointee, Quebec City executive Robert De Coster, an accountant who had spent his career in a revolving door of public and private appointments in Quebec. The new man couldn't possibly report for service until February 1983. He had to clean his business slate and had made plans to spend January — the most crucial month in CDIC's history — in Florida. This attitude was to set the tone for De Coster's term in office.

When De Coster finally reported for duty, he was only one of many new faces around CDIC. A dozen-odd consultants began operating out of a brand-new Toronto branch after the trust company seizures, and during 1983 they dealt with the bulk of the technical problems tied to winding down sizeable companies. A couple of them were Ontario's recruits who latched onto the CDIC's continuing need for hired hands after the province stepped back from the corporate carcasses.

These paid-by-the-job men helped CDIC flex its muscles in legal dealings with Rosenberg, Markle and Player. The trusts' assets had to be sorted through, and the "hit list" of depositors not paid their money because of known or believed associations with the companies' owners had to be dealt with. As the companies were all placed in long-term agency arrangements — Crown with Central, Greymac Trust with Standard Trust, Seaway Trust and Mortgage with major Markle creditor Midland Bank Canada — CDIC gained its sea legs and began to wade through a wave of new responsibilities. Its treatment of Player's Greymac Mortgage showed its new, stiffer backbone. In August 1983 it forced the company into Standard's hands. Technically it had control only of the assets, not of the ongoing business of the federally licensed mortgage company; that was all the control the regulations allowed. But with $55 million forwarded to depositors by June, CDIC had a claim that allowed it to force the company into receivership over Player's court protests. "I feel that's the only way to go," chief operating officer Jean Pierre Sabourin said at the time.

Sabourin's star was in the ascendant. J.P., as he is not very affectionately known, enjoyed the rough-and-tumble of jousting with the trust company owners; he liked the sense of power that came from control of so many assets. Although he didn't possess the skills necessary to handle CDIC's new-found real estate portfolio, J.P. had one attribute: he could push opponents into a corner with sheer bravado.

Ontario was also experiencing a change in personnel. Murray Thompson was finally on his way out as registrar of loan and trust companies. As registrar, the responsibility for the regulatory somnolence that spawned the Greymac Affair rested squarely on his shoulders. Elgie shielded Thompson effectively by shifting the focus to Rosenberg's misdeeds, but shipped him out of the trust regulator's office as soon as it was decently possible, and shifted Chief Investigator Don Reid in. Greymac had cost Thompson his reputation as a strong regulator, and its aftermath established the prowess of Reid, who played up an image of the super-sleuth from Scotland Yard to admiring reporters.

Reid had been brought on board in 1981 — one of the few post-Astra changes in the department — to head up the investigations side of the Financial Institutions Division. He had a mandate to expand the operation. But he wasn't responsible just for trust and loan companies; indeed, for eight years Wally Kowtun, the investigator who checked out Montemurro's original provincial application for a trust licence, had been handling both trust and loan and insurance companies on his own. (He had one helpmate, briefly, who moved on shortly before Reid joined.) Kowtun, a former RCMP officer who moved to the softer government job after 25 years with the force, had spent 85% of his time on insurance cases, and Reid would find they occupied much his time as well. The investigation side did police reports when applicants applied for a new licence, but other than that officialdom felt there was no need for them to be involved on the loan and trust side. Until Reid arrived, they had to be invited to work on a trust company, and they didn't regularly receive any copies of examiners' reports. In fact, one old-timer says he can't remember Kowtun's ever being sent a copy of a field examination.

Greymac — and Reid — changed Ontario's practices dramatically. Reid made sure in his cool, quiet way that he knew about every problem. When the examiner found falsified appraisals in Dominion's drawers in March 1983, Reid naturally took charge of the seize-and-rescue operation that saw the company recapitalized under new ownership and Axton leave the country. This time every wheel was well oiled; Reid finessed the company into government hands rather than brutally storming the doors in the Macdonald and Biddell style. Reid liked to talk of using a "smell test" on company operations, but he didn't want a whiff to emanate from any operation he headed. A man who measured corporate performance from such subtle, telling criteria as whether the receptionist spent time polishing her nails was careful always to strike the right note. He was involved in the department's restructuring, which took place during much of 1983 and 1984 and included a painful internal review. When it was finished, he naturally assumed the job of chief trust and loan watchdog — the type of step up the bureaucratic ladder he'd been manoeuvring for down the line but wouldn't have managed so soon had the department not been such an organizational disaster.*

While Ontario was uncovering Axton's finagling at Dominion, CDIC and the federal bureaucrats were winding up operations at Pocklington's Fidelity and its Patrician Land subsidiary. They chose First City Trust to handle the trust company's business. Toronto accountancy firm Laventhol & Horwath and Eddie Cogan, real estate broker extraordinaire, were given a contract to dispose of Patrician Land's holdings. Cogan and Laventhol's head, Harvey Hecker, had already done the same deed for Cadillac Fairview Corp. when it decided to shed its residential holdings — including the fated apartment buildings that Cogan sold to Rosenberg. Two such different and yet eminently compatible men as Hecker and Cogan could hardly be found. Hecker has a well-clipped beard, an old-world fustiness, careful diction and superb manners; he looks out of place at Cogan's luxurious annual yuletide soirées at Rooney's disco in midtown Toronto. Cogan is a man of beige suits and perpetual tan, flashy smiles and a measuring mind. He massages buyers with his eyes and lassoes them with his technique. He has the audacity to cancel a luncheon at Winston's and then stroll in and eat at another table, should he so decide, leaving Hecker to deal with the affronted.†

---

* Jim Wilbee, a career civil servant, was brought in from Treasury as registrar; a new position was created for Reid as the man responsible for loan and trust companies, reporting to Wilbee.

† Patrician ended up not being worth the bother of an agency agreement: too many creditors were wrangling about their rights, so in early 1984 it was placed in receivership under the stewardship of Lloyd Lavine, the Laventhol partner who had handled Argosy.

By late 1983 all the receivers and agents were beginning to put properties on the market. And they were being closely watched by real estate agents eager for deals, by financial companies and auditors jealous of the contracts and by institutions ready to point a finger if the trust properties weren't sold at the highest price possible — since as CDIC members they would have to pick up any shortfall. The critics began to claim that in at least one instance a property had been sold by a government agent, then flipped by the buyer for a hefty profit the same day.

De Coster was in a quandary. He was worried about CDIC's getting the best deal for its properties, now that they had started to sell. If it didn't, there were sure to be phone calls, perhaps even open criticism, from the banks about paying fees to paper over the regulators' and insurers' mistakes. In spring 1984 he flew to Toronto to talk to the bankers and find out what they would do were they in his shoes. It was Bill Poole, senior vice-president, real estate, at Toronto Dominion, who laid it out: what the CDIC needed was a good real estate guy, a guy who could sort through and finger the good and the bad. This was a different type of expertise from that of the columns of lawyers and accountants the CDIC already had on the payroll. Poole gave him a list of possibilities, and De Coster began to make the rounds.

Bill Grenier was one of the names on the list. A former Air Canada pilot who was known to quote Wordsworth while airborne, Grenier had built a profitable real estate syndication business in his spare time. He was always looking for new ways to do business, negotiating with the Italian government about the possibilities of taking over a group of partially constructed buildings in 1981, hosting a crew from the People's Republic of China to discuss building tourist accommodation in 1982. Grenier had earned $400 an hour for his work as chief executive-cum-corporate umpire in the complicated settlement of Mississauga, Ontario, real estate developer Bruce McLaughlin's failed Mascan Development Corp. in late 1983.

De Coster was despondent. He was openly admitting his ignorance. Grenier suggested that the government treat all the real estate as if it were one giant portfolio. It didn't matter if the property came from Crown, Greymac, Seaway, Fidelity or others. The trick was to package the good with the bad properties so that losses were mitigated by at least some gains. What was needed was a team of deal makers. Naturally, that team would be led by Grenier.

But there was the political side to consider. Everything had to be viewed by the public as the cheapest, best way to deal with the properties. De Coster didn't want any more talk on Bay Street about properties being sold for less than their worth — particularly since the crack sales team would be earning their pay when properties were sold.

Grenier solved that problem by suggesting a second group, a volunteer group stacked with prestige, which would vet the deals packaged by the real estate agents and make sure the properties were peddled at defensible prices. Defensible to the banks, since they were the ones bellyaching about the CDIC premiums' being increased from the normal annual stipend to pay for the agency's pay-backs and bad loan write-downs. What better defence than to put a few of them on a board and have them approve the deals?

De Coster thought it was a terrific idea. He took the plan back to his board in Ottawa, with Grenier and TD's Bill Poole along to explain the structure. Grenier and Poole were chosen to head the CDIC's new Action Group and Advisory Committee, respectively. Grenier drafted a document outlining their respective roles; then they flew back to Toronto and chose their boards.

Grenier telephoned super-broker Eddie Cogan and his associate, former Cadillac Fairview Corp. president Neil Wood, who were already involved in the receivership of Patrician. Cogan, best known for the Cadillac apartment sale, also had a pivotal role in the Mascan negotiations. Grenier also lined up Joe Barnicke, who had built the largest independent commercial real estate brokerage operation in Toronto, Lou Orzech, from stockbroker Nesbitt Thomson's realty arm, and Clive

Millar, a smooth, smart South African native who made a mark at top office leasing specialist A.E. LePage before crossing the street to the huge U.S.-based Coldwell Banker.

Poole — dubbed "Mr Real Estate" by a rapt De Coster — turned to John McCool, his counterpart at the Bank of Montreal; David Howard, head of Citicom, the firm that knows more than anyone else about Toronto parking lots; Joe Berman, one of the original nice-guy developers who still has millions invested in his old firm, Cadillac Fairview Corp.; Ken Rotenberg of Rostland Corp.; and Herb Stricker, an apartment landlord who spends his spare time writing virulent letters to MPPs about the deathly effects of rent controls.

Grenier was to be the liaison between the two committees. They patted each other on the back. De Coster was particularly relieved; this "strategic marketing" approach would "add credibility" to CDIC's portfolio. "The message is loud and clear," he commented happily. "No one should be looking for a bonanza." He also painted a picture of everyone working happily together: "The receivers are accountable to the courts but everyone [keeps] in mind the CDIC is a very, very dominant creditor."

Then they tried to put the idea into practice. The obstacles thrown up were partially raised by self-interested Ontario receivers and bureaucrats, but there were also some very ticklish matters to square away.

It was fine for CDIC to decide that it would package the good properties with the bad, in order to shed problem holdings. But if the two were being managed by different receivers, the one with the saleable property could run into troubles in the courts. If a good commercial property in Greymac Trust were coupled with a parcel of Alberta land from the Fidelity portfolio, the Greymac Trust receiver could be asked by the court why it sold its property for a price lower than it would have received had it marketed and sold the building on its own. The receiver's duty was to get the most for his particular company's assets, not to minister to the CDIC's headaches. A cynical observer could also argue that receivers like to take the slow but sure approach to property disposition because their fees are paid on a quarterly basis.

Ontario's priorities certainly didn't reflect CDIC's. The insurer was making monthly interest payments to Cadillac Fairview Corp. to keep the Toronto apartment building loans that ranked ahead of the seized trust companies' third-ranking mortgage loans in good standing and wanted to see the buildings sold and its money recovered. Ontario, faced by lawsuits in which the value of the apartments was a key element, and by a tenant population watching the apartments' fate with an eye for any move on the government's side to boost rents, wanted to leave things in limbo. Rosenberg, after all, wanted to see the apartments sold at a good price so he could say I told you so. The province wanted to avoid that at all costs — it was not Ontario that was paying the bills.

Of course, every real estate expert not invited to the committees questioned the government's choices. It was a festering ground for rumours about who was and who wasn't doing the job properly. Everyone was on edge, sensitive to any little darts flying out of the woodwork. One bureaucrat whose name was always mentioned was Sabourin, who was not about to be ousted from his new-found position as undertaker of the largest property portfolio in the country. The committees agreed that any property sale that was being negotiated could proceed but that there should be no more listings until they had looked at all the properties and begun to package them. Then they, not the receivers, would be in charge. David Richardson, Clarkson Co.'s hard-as-nails successor to Jack Biddell as head of its receivership arm and Ontario's custodian of the soft assets, understood the concept but didn't agree. Lawyers on all sides became embroiled in heated debate about powers and responsibilities. "We have to make sure we're not compromised by CDIC, it's not a partnership," George McIntyre, Ontario's assistant deputy minister responsible for financial institutions, was to say soon afterward.

With one of the few practical solutions to its huge credit obligations not panning out, CDIC had a lot of explaining to

do to the groups that funded it. From mid-1983, when it became aware of how much money it could end up paying for
the pay-off of the Crown, Greymac and Seaway depositors, the
banking community began to exert pressure on Ottawa to do
something about the CDIC. It was relatively quiet at first, but
before many months were over it would publicly erupt over the
amount of money being spent.

Charles de Lery joined CDIC in April 1984, agreeing to take
early retirement at 60 from the pressures of new management
at Royal Trust after 35 years with the company. He made a commitment to the government: no matter how bad things were,
he'd stick around for a number of years. It was the government's solution to the mistake, embedded in the outdated act,
of placing a part-time businessman in the position of chairman.
With 12 companies being wound down through agency agreements or through straight liquidation proceedings, CDIC
needed a chief executive.

Like De Coster, de Lery didn't move house to Ottawa. The
white-capped de Lery's work schedule was to belie his retirement status from Royal Trust. Like his part-time boss, de Lery
had spent much of his life in Quebec City. His father had been
the trust company's manager there before him. But he had
shifted to head office by the time of Royal's mid-seventies ex-
odus to Toronto, and that was now home. He designed his
schedule at the Crown corporation around Friday and Monday
meetings in Toronto so he could squeeze in weekends with his
wife there. They were usually working weekends, although he
also worked through many of his "bachelor" evenings. The
problems that ate into de Lery's waking hours were the old
ones, the companies that had already gone bust; he didn't have
much time to worry about those that still might. Every property that wasn't working out required an accountant to say why
and a lawyer to explain the answer to the court. They huddled
with the contract consultants to plan the strategy of each fore-
closure. For de Lery, it was "one bad story after another."

Another company almost arrived on the doorstep scant days
before de Lery joined. Ontario was playing nursemaid to

Termguard Savings & Loan. Its owner, Saskatchewan pharmacy chain owner Ben Mah, had, according to his bankers, taken too much money from the company in management fees and loans to other companies he controlled. This time CDIC made it clear it wasn't going to be a softie. In the months to come tempers would fray on both sides as the province found it couldn't kick CDIC around anymore.

Ontario had also changed its tactics. The province's new quiet, ruthless approach to companies with regulatory problems, first demonstrated by its last-ditch handling of Dominion's sale, was brought into play again in March 1984 with the take-over of Termguard. The company's capital base was eroded by pay-outs to Mah and his associates and the shares pledged against loans to creditors — such as the Royal Bank of Canada, the biggest loser with an $18 million loan to Mah. For months fix-it man Don Reid and Royal's Calgary commercial lending man Doug Robertson, well known and not universally liked for his role on Royal's cardiac team, chatted about the company's capital problems and potential resale. CDIC baldly stated that it would pull its insurance if the problem wasn't solved. On March 31 Mah placed a call from Robertson's meeting room and handed effective control over to Reid.

Reid pulled out the chairs around the Termguard directorate and set government-picked nominees in place. At the head of the table he sat Ainslie St Clair Shuve, whose second career after his departure from Crown Trust had been launched when Ontario rushed him in to oversee the dissection of Crown Trust — followed by a stint at Dominion — and who still ran his part-time business affairs from an office in the old Crown Trust head office, part of Central's booty. (Shuve would remain a government consultant, a semi-permanent fixture with an office at the ministry and a role as Reid's aide-de-camp whenever a company was in trouble.)

Reid spent months trying to find a buyer for Termguard. It could have been an easy matter. There were a number of trust companies interested in the company's run-of-the-mill mortgage loans. They'd seen the deals the receiver-managers of

Crown and Greymac had been given: no bad loans, the choice of which mortgages they wanted to pick up and a tidy management fee. They were aggressive in their demands for Termguard.

But CDIC was not co-operating this time. Sabourin and de Lery met with Reid and Robertson in Calgary and said flatly that they were not going to end up with any of the company's bad loans. "Why should we allow a shareholder to make money with member institutions' funds?" asks de Lery. Every decision is haunted by the Crown deal, where Rosenberg, the common shareholder, and a large contingent of small preferred shareholders lost their investments when Ontario seized the company and sold it to Central. "I think it would be a very dangerous precedent if we said let the shareholders get some money. I think we'd just be saying to the shareholders of Crown Trust, 'Sue us.' And they'd have some reason to sue us." So proposals by Standard Trust, Financial Trust and Guardian Trust went by the boards, and for a year after Ontario moved to solve Termguard's problems the company operated without an adequate capital base. There was no love lost between CDIC and Ontario regulators on this one.

CDIC had reason to be on edge; by April 1984, a year after it arranged to dismantle Seaway under an agency agreement with creditor Midland Bank Canada, it had already poured $150 million into Seaway Trust. It reviewed the decision and decided the agency idea hadn't been such a good one after all. It despaired at being able to collect, from sale of properties over-mortgaged by Seaway, enough to pay the interest on the loans that stood ahead of its claims. Instead, it would simply pay back all depositors immediately — to the tune of $152 million — and liquidate. Seaway was the worst of the lot.*

---

* By mid-1984 CDIC had advanced more than $1 billion to eight companies: Seaway Trust, Seaway Mortgage, Greymac Trust, Greymac Mortgage, Crown, Fidelity, AMIC and District. Of that total, $750 million went to the Crown-Seaway-Greymac companies. The portfolio was valued at about $2 billion when seized; CDIC had written that down by half and believed the billion was gone forever. At year-end it had upped the figure to $1.25 billion advanced.

Bruce Robertson, a former Clarkson Co. man, was brought in as liquidator. "Most of the assets are soft; basically there is no revenue coming in," Sabourin admitted at the time. "It's losing money unbelievably on a month to month basis." Saskatchewan's Hill family, who owned most of downtown Regina through companies called MaCallum-Hill and Harvard Developments, had tried months earlier to buy Seaway for its huge tax write-offs. But CDIC wasn't selling anything. "I would hope the liquidator wouldn't go and peddle the stuff right now," Sabourin said, envisaging prickly lawsuits. In typical bureaucratese, he added that he hoped the corporation could "maximize our opportunities for recovery."

That's what Bruce Robertson planned. He saw his role in the straight and narrow traditional sense; he was the liquidator, and this company was his sole responsibility. The appointment of Robertson would further hurt the portfolio strategy espoused by De Coster and the special Advisory Committee; some sources say CDIC's lawyers, Tory, Tory, DesLauriers & Binnington (Torys), made a plain mistake in their zeal to sell properties. By advising CDIC to appoint the receiver they were presenting further legal tangles for the action committee's portfolio sales. Another interpretation is that Torys wasn't enamoured with the heralded "portfolio" approach to the asset sale in any case. The approach certainly didn't thrill McMillan Binch, Ontario's lawyers and Torys' floormates in the aptly gold-plated Royal Bank of Canada tower opposite Toronto's Union Station; it could only cause trouble for Ontario in the province's lawsuits with the trust company shareholders.

Robert Elgie lay low in the Consumer portfolio all the while as Ontario coasted through the summer of 1984 waiting for William Davis to make up his mind about the next provincial election. There had been talk for a while that Elgie would hang out the banner of the Red Tory wing of the party at a leadership convention should Davis decide to retire. If he had, he could have expected opposition from the angry group that still held Crown Trust preference shares. They had been left out of the equation when Crown was assigned to Central Trust in

February 1983 and for a year and a half had been negotiating with the Ontario government for compensation — a property or two, shares in a Crown corporation, anything. They had been organized — the big institutional shareholders such as Canadian Imperial Bank of Commerce noticeable by their absence — by Wallis King, former Royal Trust employee now a dapper investment adviser with silver-spoon connections who was volunteering his time and tactical expertise. He never dreamed the job would soak up both for years to come.

In mid-1984 King found out that a year and a half had been wasted in negotiating with the wrong government. Elgie was negligent about answering his letters, and finally in late May De Coster wrote to tell him the CDIC had first claim on all assets and there wouldn't be anything left for the shareholders. King was incredulous that the political party he and most of the shareholders had supported for years would treat them like this. They had staged a letter-writing campaign to Premier Davis and had all received polite replies. At their June monthly meeting in the cosy Hughes, King boardroom in the new National Bank building, the six senior citizens, homemakers and fund managers who made up the motley group's executive decided to show the public their outraged sense of injustice.

They carefully staged a meeting with Elgie, placing a few calls to media types always happy to see an embarrassed cabinet minister. Roger Chittenden, at 75 the executive's oldest member, believed Ontario had seized Crown from a "sense of desperation" caused by lax regulation. Chosen as emissary because his snow-white beard and wooden cane would make good television, Chittenden approached the consumer minister at about 9 A.M. on July 30 at Toronto's Harbour Castle convention centre as the minister was about to step on a podium and open an international securities regulation conference. Elgie, happily assuming that it was his address that had attracted the cameras, was content to shake hands with the vaguely familiar Chittenden, whom he didn't quite remember from their past meetings on the Crown matter. But he wasn't prepared for what came next: Chittenden handed him a Supreme Court of Ontario writ.

The writ cited both negligent supervision of the company before the seizure, and actions contrary to the search-and-seizure sections of the federal Charter of Rights, and asked for damages. King asked Davis to fund the suit, but instead Ontario passed an order-in-council protecting Elgie and regulators from damages.

Rosenberg had served government officials with a similar writ in early July. Ontario was still more worried about him than about a group of irate voters. Rosenberg's lawyer Ronald Carr went to court August 24 to ask the apartments' receiver to tell everyone when and how the 26 buildings would be sold. The receiver successfully stalled by saying he needed to "consult" with the CDIC and others; eight months later Carr would still be awaiting an answer. The buildings were finally put up for sale in July 1985. This pressured legal manoeuvring made the uneasy truce between CDIC's Action Group and Ontario's receivers more fragile than ever.

As August melted into September, bureaucrats in Ottawa floated in suspended animation awaiting the coming change in government. A retiring Marc Lalonde had been left to keep a lackadaisical eye on the problems of the CDIC and trust industry when the Ministry of State for Finance was disbanded by a John Turner more interested in public platforms than public policy. Brian Mulroney, who became prime minister on September 4, had promised the moon during the campaign, but no one expected him to deliver.

When rookie Minister of State for Finance Barbara McDougall arrived in Ottawa, she wore a naïve belief that she and her party would make things happen — quickly. Legislation for financial institutions had been far too long on the drawing board. She would have it through in a few months.

She'd been involved on the periphery of the trust companies issue for some time and drafted a response to the federal 1982 trust companies White Paper while executive director of the

Canadian Council of Financial Analysts. She quickly found herself in the middle of a financial shake-out that had a number of companies in deep trouble — including her old employer, North West Trust.*

McDougall had a lot of people coming to her West Block office in the Parliament buildings: Western companies, singly and in a group; representatives of the larger, Eastern-based companies; bankers, insurance companies, investment dealers. Many of them she knew from her stint with investment house Odlum Brown in Vancouver or her five years with A.E. Ames on Bay Street — McDougall has impeccable business connections. They usually had particular problems on their minds, but they all let her know they were running out of patience.

It required patience even to get through McDougall's door during the autumn of 1984. Delays and rearrangements were blamed on the newness of the minister and her staff, but by spring the situation was still every bit as crazy. McDougall proudly related that she had more responsibility than any other minister of state had ever carried. Certainly her predecessor, Roy MacLaren, had been able to set aside more time for quiet, thoughtful conversations on issues such as the need to restructure the financial services sector. MacLaren could be found in the same West Block Parliament Hill political office a year earlier, calmly munching an apple, no assistants in sight. McDougall sips herbal tea in exhaustion with senior bureaucrats lined up in the outer hall.

Not just Finance Minister Michael Wilson but the Tory caucus was enchanted with McDougall; this female with business experience, cornflower blue eyes, a wardrobe that must be colour analysed and a laugh that rolls up from her belly was a very hot political prospect in the eyes of the Tories, although she did manage to alienate certain members of the press. In a well-

* When she arrived to work for Dr Charles Allard at North West in 1975, McDougall found out firsthand how thin the walls are between an entrepreneur's various enterprises. There wasn't enough to do running the tiny company's investment portfolio, so McDougall also hosted a weekly business show on Allard's Edmonton television station.

written, bitchy March 1985 *Toronto Life* article, Elaine Dewar proposed the thesis that McDougall had been given her job as a salve to loyal Tory business supporters. McDougall's handlers were furious at the story, which dragged out items such as McDougall's marital break-up (she's now a widow) and the smidgen that she hennas her hair. They said Dewar's attitude was set on arrival but festered when Dewar failed to get access to the minister. The reporter was left sitting in the entranceway chatting with the French teacher, one aide explained, while the notoriously late McDougall went about the business of the nation.

Minister of state is an anomalous role in any department, but Wilson put McDougall to work as a member of his inner circle. She was part of the budget strategy team and helped with the very high profile first public signal of Tory strategy for the dollar and the deficit, the November 1984 economic statement. She sits on many of Wilson's cabinet committees as well as her own, easily fitting into the role of Wilson's second. "If he's got something he really feels strongly about then we'll talk about it first. Once in a while he'll come in to heavy up the argument. But it's never in place of, it's in addition to."

But all this running hither and yon meant McDougall's schedule was constantly in flux. Her arm, injured by two years of gladhanding potential voters in one of the longest individual campaigns preceding her party's sweep into office, still ached in April, but she held off painkillers until the final meetings of each day were over. McDougall found it hard to adjust to the disorderliness of parliamentary life; the routine of the business world was hundreds of miles away. That distance was evident when business came calling, and she didn't try to bridge the gap the way her boss the prime minister invariably did. At an Ottawa meeting with Andy Kniewasser, president of the Investment Dealers Association of Canada and a big man on Bay Street, the roles were clearly marked: she called him Andy, he called her Minister McDougall. Heady stuff for a woman who had waited years for vice-president stripes at a stock brokerage firm that was on its last legs.

There was much more to contend with than the daily schedule. MacLaren had found time to pull together an advisory committee with a smattering of representation from each segment of the financial community, headed by loyal Liberal William Dimma. The group met monthly during the spring and summer of 1984, and at first it looked as if it would be authoring a report on changing directions in the financial system. (Directions were changing so quickly that Dimma switched from heading A.E. LePage Ltd. to be one of the well-paid courtiers of Edward and Peter Bronfman's Trilon Financial Corp. when LePage merged with Royal Trust's realty operations in mid-1984.) But it was really meant as a think-tank with then-Deputy Minister of Finance Marshall (Mickey) Cohen, a man who thinks in 15-minute time slots, picking and choosing from the ideas proffered. Those ideas were usually prompted by papers drafted by his staff, and tossed around by the group over dinner. (One member reports that the menu was a major point of discussion.) McDougall studied the transcripts and decided to let the group have its final meeting, slated for early December. She attended but left early for a vote in the House. The policy making didn't involve much of her time yet. There were too many practical problems.

Two months after McDougall's appointment, the bankers were bellyaching in public about the amount of money CDIC was spending. The Canadian Bankers' Association (CBA) took the insurer to task for the Crown depositors' bail-out in a brief to McDougall and, more important, a briefing for the press. After all, while the Crown investors had lost all their money, the depositors had been bailed out for large amounts well over the set $60,000 limit. The CBA wanted only partial coverage of deposits of more than $20,000; they wanted a seat on the CDIC board. They didn't intend to pick up the tab for Crown Trust, and they made it clear that if they paid, their depositors would pay.* The basic complaint was with the way CDIC

---

* The CBA brief stated that CDIC would lose at least 69 cents for each dollar advanced during the recent wind-downs, compared to 11 cents per dollar in the early, pre-Greymac wind-downs.

had handled the Greymac case. The bankers saw money pouring down the drain and didn't think the insurer had thought the matter through. They didn't know just how muddled the situation still was.

The CDIC and the provinces had signed agreements drafted by the CDIC's Advisory Committee, placing it in charge of evaluating and marketing the properties sitting idle as a result of the agency agreements. But there was no way to enforce the committee's mandate. Month followed month with CDIC guaranteeing interest payments on properties that didn't deserve them. These were payments on loans made on already-mortgaged properties by the trust company principals, Rosenberg, Pocklington and the by-now various and sundry others. They were often bad loans, but the CDIC officials were afraid to stop paying the loans and thereby let the properties fall into the laps of the other mortgage holders; they would then lose any claim to the property. They preferred to let good money follow bad while they dithered. "Bureaucrats," sighed an observer, "have no time clocks."

Receivers continued to sell property piecemeal without committee approval. One deal the action group was negotiating almost fell through because one group started accusing another of leaking information; to the slightly paranoid it looked like sabotage. In December 1984 the Advisory Committee sent CDIC a blunt ultimatum: if things don't change, we'll walk.

The Advisory Committee had its day at the CDIC board meeting on January 8, 1985; they spelled out the troubles they were having and pointed out that so far, no property sales had been approved. Place the properties in our hands and give us real control, they said. Let's take over the Cadillac Fairview buildings; then we can sell them. And let's start walking away from the unsolvable problems instead of paying interest on them — a position the government had already decided was the sensible one.

Ontario had created this situation; CDIC would give it no quarter. The province was negotiating with an interested buyer in early 1985 when CDIC leaned on Termguard. It felt antsy about the company's undercapitalized position. It didn't matter to the federal bureaucrats that they were making it hard for the province to put a deal together; they weren't going to stand for a company's going month after month without enough capital. With a marked changed in approach to provincial problems from its "whatever you think is best" attitude of early 1983, CDIC informally stated that if things weren't soon solved it would withdraw its insurance. It wasn't going to be caught with a badly handled failure on its hands again. "If you don't get more capital in, eventually CDIC is going to have to put up the insurance. And why should we put up with that?" said chief exec Charles de Lery.

But in its eagerness to assert itself, CDIC neglected to give the formal notice needed before it could withdraw the insurance. Ontario scrambled, and in late March the sale of Termguard to Brendan Calder's Counsel Trust was announced. CDIC didn't seem to realize that Termguard's assets were by then in good shape, thanks to Ontario's mop-up job. It would have preferred to push it into liquidation. Said one participant: "This is one trust company that CDIC didn't get to kill."

By mid-March the advisory group had lost patience, and the lauded "portfolio approach" had disintegrated. The final straw was when the CDIC board rejected a proposal to replace the several receivers with only one, Patrician Land receiver Laventhol & Horwath, acting for CDIC. That proposal was blown to bits in a board meeting when Tory, Tory lawyers differed with the legal opinion collected by the committee from Toronto commercial law hotshots Goodman & Carr. Tory, Tory, known for caution, didn't think CDIC could pull all the strings required to make the massive receivership fall together.

As a face-saving move, CDIC requested that the Advisory Committee, still headed by Bill Poole, remain nominally involved to "advise" the insurer on property sales. But the individual receivers were asked to draw up their own plans for disposition of the assets. Grenier's paid-on-sale action group disbanded. De Lery said after the decision had been made that the plan wasn't feasible because "the province of Ontario wanted to make sure that in all cases where there were assets to be sold the courts were giving their blessing.'' The shadow of Leonard Rosenberg's claim that his property had been unlawfully seized hung over the properties more than two years later.

Before it was disbanded the coterie of real estate agents making up the Action Group managed to negotiate only a few sales. One dropped in their laps in late 1984 when Bell Canada Enterprises called to see about buying Crown's 50% interest in a downtown Vancouver office tower recently completed by Daon Development Corp. Bell ended up taking a close look at Daon's books as a result of negotiations, which stretched through the Christmas season, and decided to buy Daon, management and all, in January; the government sold its half of the Vancouver building in mid-April. It was the Action Group's last hurrah.

It was Barbara McDougall's baby, but Michael Wilson couldn't avoid hearing about CDIC. He was getting his ear talked off at business dinners where he came into contact with the financial community. He was warned by one member of the committee that the problems with the CDIC wouldn't just go away. ''This thing is like a canker in the mouth, it's just getting bigger and bigger.''

The unsolved problems at CDIC had proved the federal government unable to cope with the aftermath of the trust company collapses of 1983. But the Western Canadian economy had ensured that federal regulators would have to cope with new crises of confidence.

A favourite story making the rounds among Alberta lenders during the winter of 1985 was the one about the banker who said he'd just taken over a 500-acre ranch in Calgary, and the only problem was that it was full of houses. It was a reflection of the bleak state of Western Canada in the eighties.

The oil and gas boom of the seventies had ricocheted through the Western Canadian economy. Industrial parks sprang up, opulent office towers crowded downtown avenues and residential developments ballooned in suburbs. Excess was a place to start for the entrepreneurs and their bankers. But the heady pace was not sustained, and in 1982, after a couple of short years, jobless Albertans were walking away from mortgaged homes, and tottering corporations were cancelling office and plant leases. The boom's bankers, in offices filled with the most ostentatious furniture and art money could buy, pondered for the first time non-performing loans and valueless collateral.

The appraisals made in the go-go years of the Alberta oil boom were based on bouyant assumptions that the bubble would never burst. It was the mentality of the times. The infection spread from Alberta on into Saskatchewan and B.C. Big-time lenders now made deals in the booming U.S. sun belt, catching flights to sunny Phoenix in February to sign loan agreements, and in the oil patches of Texas and Colorado. The fact that many of them did not know the U.S. market did not hamper their confidence.

It seemed like magic: even those who knew little about real estate development made money in spite of themselves when values sky-rocketed. It worked for years and hundreds of millions of dollars. Analysis of properties was replaced by raw demand. "When you had cities like Calgary and Edmonton growing as quickly as they did, you didn't have to be a genius to make money," says one expert. Entrepreneurs grabbed up huge tracts of land that wouldn't be touched for a decade, and often resold them for big profits. They projected office rents on an upward spiral and climbed their own staircases to higher and higher construction and land costs. "And they said, 'If the thing didn't quite fit, it'll work out in the end because office space is at a premium and so we'll get more.'"

It was this attitude that took them to new markets without proper preparation and led them to expect more — always more — success, never failure. The trust company owners had a vision of Western real estate as a panorama of profits stretching out to eternity.

The fall of Abacus Cities in 1979 should have been seen as the harbinger of doom. It wasn't. Abacus Cities, hero of the oil patch in 1978 and father of one of Western Canada's worst financial disasters, was run by two brothers, William and Ken Rogers. Abacus was the focus of a wide-ranging financial empire with assets on the books of $500 million, built on the shifting ground of the then-popular federal tax shelter, the MURB. Abacus developed townhouses, duplexes and condos and sold the projects at a hefty premium to 3,300 individual investors lured by the prospect of immediate tax deductions and eventual steady returns from the property. But original construction estimates proved way off base, and the Rogers brothers turned to non-arm's-length lenders, controlled directly and indirectly through an elaborate system of numbered companies and allied boards of directors, for the funds. They included Winnipeg-based Fort Garry Trust, the Paramount Life Insurance Co. and Calgary-based AMIC Mortgage Corp., which together advanced Abacus almost $30 million.

Finally the house of cards broke down, under the strain of financing costs that exceeded the value of the properties. In early May of 1979, regulators in Alberta ordered an investigation of Abacus and 43 other companies. The intricate corporate web caused investors to lose as much as $43 million after the collapse, and left the non-arm's-length lenders devastated.

Abacus was a scandal that stood on its own, a black mark on the pure religion of Alberta real estate. It would be three years before other houses of cards also would scatter with the first cold wind of reality.

The downside was, inevitably, as brutal as the upside had been exhilarating. The effects of bust first felt in 1982 would be suffered for years, and many financial institutions hung on by their fingernails until they finally dropped in 1985.

Even then, many Western trust owners and managers would not acknowledge that the wounded Western financial industry was a victim of plain bad management as much as of a bad economy.

By early 1985 the federal government was swamped with bad news from the West. In December 1984 tiny Winnipeg-based Northguard Mortgage Corp. was quietly placed in the hands of liquidator Touche Ross & Co. Northguard had collected about $30 million in long-term deposits and specialized in making second mortgage loans on Alberta homes during the boom. The company had followed the rules: when it provided a second mortgage, the two loans didn't add up to more than 75% of the property's value. But a second mortgage loan ranks behind a first when a home-owner walks, and as Alberta home values sank the second mortgages became meaningless. "All of a sudden the value of their assets just melted away," says Robert Hammond, Dick Humphrys's 1982 replacement as federal superintendent of insurance. The owner didn't have money to prop up the company, so the liquidator was sent for.

The public missed this quiet corporate mop-up, but the heat was turned up the next month when a January 4, 1985, Canadian Press story splashed across the front page of *The Globe and Mail* claimed that CDIC could soon be responsible for another $1.5 billion in assets if four endangered Western trust companies collapsed. The story had an innocuous beginning: in mid-September Lou Howard, a government appraiser working for Public Works, toted a sheaf of sample properties with him to an Appraisal Institute of Canada national council meeting in Montreal. He was worried after reviewing large sections of Western companies' portfolios for the CDIC: a number of appraisers were valuing futures, he told an executive committee still jumpy because of the similar method used to boost the value of the Rosenberg-Player apartments.

In the next few months Howard let other appraisers know that there was about $1.5 billion in overappraised property out West, much of the overappraisal due to the same unorthodox methods used in flipping the Cadillac Fairview buildings. It made the $500 million Toronto apartment sale "look like a children's tea party," says one appraiser. The word spread through the Toronto mortgage brokers' community and was reported in an association publication. Wily CP business writer Gord McIntosh recognized the potential fireworks and exploded the story.

It's not just that the Western companies' appraisers had used the future-value appraisal, or discounted cash flow method, says one observer; it's that they had "the same sort of optimism" as Player's appraisers in assuming cash flow would rise much more quickly than "might reasonably be anticipated." For a few commercial properties, the format was very similar to Player's myriad deals with Markle: forget about what the property is actually worth, Mr Lender, and the fact that it won't be making money for years; I'll sign a long-term lease that says I can deliver to the investor down the road. The developer promised to pay inflated prices for unleased space as part of his earnings projections. One cluster of shopping centres was given mortgages on the basis of this type of lease — and the person providing the guarantee had ties to the lender. The deal was not at arm's length, and the lease was questionable, according to the Howard reports.

Some of the appraisals had so many back-door clauses they were virtually useless. The appraiser cloaked almost every statement he made with an "I'm not responsible if" condition. They leaped out from the paper like red flags on a slate tarmac: if the underwriter didn't see them as danger signals, he didn't know his business — or didn't care.

The federal government started to check company appraisals only in autumn 1982; Greymac Mortgage was its first case, and the result was a cut in its borrowing ratio and limitations on borrowing and investment of funds. Robert Hammond rues the result: "We just wish we'd been a little bit faster." This is a sample of the classic understatement that emanates from the soft-spoken, circumspect bureaucrat with a secret sense of humour.

Although Greymac signalled troubles with valuations, the department didn't immediately launch a full-scale hunt for bad loans. It checked only appraisals on loans already in trouble, in case they were dumped on the insurer. No one has ever bothered to ensure that trust companies are following the rules when making mortgage loans.

Regulators developed a rhythm when checking appraisals. Federal examiners, admittedly not real estate experts, felt the pulse of a company's mortgage loans while doing their annual check-up; if it was uneven they asked for copies of loan documents, carried them back to Ottawa and shuffled them over to the Department of Public Works. Appraisers there, including Lou Howard, reviewed the work, and if they too thought something askew they had the regional office draw up a list of independent appraisers back in the company's home town who could take another look. The company might have been asked to volunteer names for the list, or even make the final choice. But Public Works then spelled out, appraiser-to-appraiser, exactly what the trust regulators were looking for: the property's worth if it were sold at that moment. "Not," says Hammond, "what you can sell it for 20 years from now at low cost financing."

No appraiser would risk being too optimistic when working for a regulator. "Of course the story floating around is that the minute Public Works gets involved . . . the outside appraiser is going to be very cautious and underestimate the value of the property," says a defensive Hammond. There was plenty of griping among regional trust companies about the knuckleheads in Ottawa who didn't know anything about real estate values. In at least one case there was a major disagreement, and pressure from the government of Alberta led to a reappraisal of a trust company's assets that reset the valuation at a higher level than the federal regulators initially wanted; but in the end Ottawa usually decided what was acceptable. "There can be some to and froing," says Hammond, "but then push has to come to shove and we have to make up our minds. We say, 'We believe it's this and we're going to insist you set up a reserve of this amount.'" Trust company managers began paying the price of having fed a suggestable appraisal industry — an industry that for years allowed them to take risks. "In this part of the world," says Al Bray, superintendent of Alberta Treasury Branches, a quasi-bank operated by the province, "everything has to be written down to below replacement value."

Annual inspections by the department's 60 examiners begin each spring. The trust company operator who arrives back from his Florida March break with the family to find the department on his doorstep knows he has trouble. Examiners will already have sifted through the books at their desks in Ottawa. In the worst cases they arrive in spring with questions and return a few months later to make sure the questions have been answered. A number of Western companies became familiar with their Ottawa babysitters as real estate prices and their capital bases eroded in unison.

The Western push began in spring 1983, when the feds were picking over the skeleton of Fidelity Trust and its Patrician Land subsidiary. The regulators had their eyes opened by Pocklington's conjuring tricks. "They had, I suggest, a sobering experience about the value of real estate," John Cormie, president of Edmonton-based Principal Savings & Trust, laughs humourlessly.

They also realized that the auditors' viewpoint and their own could be very different. Auditors allow a property's value to stand as long as they think there's any chance real estate values could bounce back in the foreseeable future. "Auditors in the past I don't think have been too concerned about real estate values," says Hammond. "People tend to forget that in Fidelity we had an audited statement done by a national firm just three months before we were taking action."

Regulators began setting thumbnail rules of how property must appear on the books. Land held for redevelopment and agricultural land was cut to half its old valuation across the board. The new reserves that companies had to hold against losses ate at companies' capital bases. Hammond began placing investment and borrowing restrictions on licences of federally chartered companies, and CDIC was sending letters to the boards of provincial companies demanding the same limitations on business. Western-based federal trust companies booked flights to Ottawa to hear the bad news about their futures. Principal Trust, an Edmonton company, was refinanced by its owners, the Cormie family; Vancouver's Yorkshire Trust sold a $5 million preferred share issue, but the still-profitable company was piling up loan losses, and its owners put up a

large For Sale sign. (It was sold in 1985 to Quebec's Lauren-
tienne Group.)

North West Trust is perhaps the quintessential example of what
went wrong in the West. Its current owners actually bought the
company in 1982, when doom for Alberta real estate was a
well-documented fact, and "diversified" its assets by investing
in strictly regional banks, creatures of the same outlook and
naturally enough, prone to the same problems. The incestuous
Western business world, in which board directors and senior
managers jumped from company to company, land company
presidents became trust company presidents literally overnight
and financial institutions swapped crummy properties had
produced a half-dozen failures in the West in the space of 18
months. North West existed as of mid-1985 only because the
Alberta government could not endure another large collapse
and, willing the trust not to die, had fortified it with a hefty
subsidy.

Housed in splendour — despite its impoverished state —
North West has offices in the whimsical pointy-shaped Inter-
provincial Pipelines Tower on Jasper Avenue in Edmonton. In
1984 the trust company lost money for the first time in its
history and did it in a big way. North West had only $760
million in assets, but it lost $21 million in 1984 on revenue
of $90 million. It had fallen victim to the double whammy of
holding real estate and mortgages in Alberta that had to be
written down by almost $10 million, and holding large 8%
shareholdings in two problem-plagued Western banks, Canadian Commercial and Bank of British Columbia, which had to
be written down on the books by nearly $12 million.

North West was clearly in bad shape. It had grown rapidly,
but its capital base in 1984 was dangerously low on equity. In
the previous four years the company had had three sets of
owners and four chief executives. Its current owners, two beefy
real estate developers, Irving Kipnes and Larry Rollingher, had
been put on notice by provincial and federal regulators that
they would have to find more capital at the start of the year,
but the only willing source was the provincial quasi-bank,

Alberta Treasury Branches (ATB), which forked over $10 million in subordinated notes (debentures that rank after some securities but before other loans). Only a year later, ATB was bailing North West out once more. During a four-week period at the beginning of 1985, ATB guaranteed $85 million in preferred shares for North West's parent, enabling it to immediately transfuse the trust company with $25 million in capital. It was an astounding amount, given that the trust's existing pool of equity consisted of capital stock of only $4 million and retained earnings of $27 million.

North West's main problem was its dependence on commercial properties in its mortgage portfolio. The company was known in the industry for lending on residential land that was slated for commercial redevelopment, basing the loan not on the current market value but on the anticipated value to a developer. This was the type of loan abhorred by the government. The potential for profit was equally potent as a loss if the market turned, which it did, sending values to 25% of their 1980-81 appraisals. At the time the justification for the valuation was the dictate of the market: plenty of real estate was being sold in the West — enough to give appraisers an accurate fix on price. But the value of these properties was assessed on what they believed the real estate would be worth after redevelopment rather than its current market value. This formula had been working at North West for decades.

Charles Allard, known universally as the legendary Dr Allard although he made his mark largely in business, not in medicine, was the prototype Western developer with a desire to meld a financing vehicle with real estate in the 1950s. In 1958 he bought dormant North West Trust, which had $200,000 in assets under its control by the end of that first year.

Although the sixties were hard on trust companies in Alberta, North West continued to grow as Allard's burgeoning real estate empire extended into a wide range of other businesses. The company always made money. But in July of 1980, in a surprise move that observers later interpreted as indicating that he knew when to get out, the 60-year-old Allard sold North

West, which by then had $460 million in assets, and the rest of his 50%-owned real estate, energy and financial conglomerate called Allarco Developments Ltd., to Calgary's Carma Developments for $130 million in cash. The tide was already turning in Alberta. Carma had been after the Allard empire as a way of diversifying out of real estate. When North West changed hands, it began the most unsettled period of its history. Under Allard, the trust company had been ruled in an autocratic but unfocused manner. Carma inherited from Allard several white elephant loans, particularly a $12 million loan on a luxury ski condominium development called Moguls on Big White in Kelowna, B.C. The project hit the market in the spring of 1982 "just when the market turned south," a former North West executive recalls — and he isn't talking geographically.

Two years after purchasing North West, a financially desperate Carma sold the still-profitable trust company to developers Kipnes and Rollingher. The two had roamed Western Canada and the U.S. making deals. Rollingher had built apartment buildings around Edmonton; Kipnes, a variety of commercial and residential projects, some with Sam Belzberg. Kipnes and Rollingher had been partners since 1968 in Chateau Group, a merger of their two companies.

Trouble erupted first over the manner in which the two acquired the trust company. Pocklington had perfected this method and Rollingher and Kipnes were the last to get away with it. It was the old "using the trust to buy itself" trick.

On November 1, 1982, the pair's Chateau Developments paid Carma $40 million in cash in return for 95% of North West. But one day before, the trust company's real estate subsidiary had spent $43.5 million acquiring property and mortgages from Chateau. In short, Kipnes and Rollingher hadn't spent a cent to take over the trust company and now had control of $535 million in assets. The loans and real estate, which should have been written down before the sale, were devalued once they were in the trust company, which was the only loser. All of this had been speedily and willingly approved by Alberta's director of trust companies.

From the time of the sale to the time of the spring 1982 annual meeting, North West's assets jumped 18% to $655 million as Albertans flocked in for RRSPs. But earnings failed to keep pace with the heady growth. They had fallen 98% from 1981, and mortgage loan losses were running at more than $8 million. Shareholders were not anticipating a dividend payment.

"Would these properties have been bought if the company hadn't been bought by Chateau?" asked Robert Kallir, former corporate secretary and legal counsel, who had made a point of attending the meeting. "The shareholders are entitled to know what return on investment these properties acquired by North West Trust are bringing the company."

Then he pointed out a $13 million bank loan appearing on the books for the first time. "That's rather a lot of money and should be dealt with now," he demanded and asked the accountants, Touche Ross, what they thought about the property appraisals. "We are not appraisers," replied Touche, who were slated to be replaced by Clarkson Gordon at the meeting anyway.

Then Kallir launched into a diatribe about the hefty management fees and lousy mortgage portfolio performance, but he was cut off. Douglas Matheson, a prominent Edmonton lawyer, jumped to his feet. "I've been a director of this company for 25 years and seen people come and go," he said. "But I take objection to a person no longer in our employ coming to a meeting and disturbing our business." The meeting ended, the Carma regime gave way to the incoming Kipnes-Rollingher contingent and North West's course was set.* By 1984 North

* Kallir and his boss, Don Lyons, Carma's president at North West who had arrived from a post at Canada Permanent, later scouted out another small trust company, North Canadian Trust. They sold to giant insurance/health-care congolmerate Crownx Inc. of Toronto the idea of rejuvenating North Canadian Trust and renaming it Coronet. First they had to clean up bad loans that were typical of 1984, but since any losses from the old loans came off the price paid to the old owners of the company, it was no skin off their noses. Lyons and Kallir had managed to be among the very few to collect scavengers' profits from the carcass of the oil patch.

West stood to be one of the pickings around which vultures gather.

Many of Kallir's unanswered questions have come back to haunt Kipnes and Rollingher as their bad loans have ballooned and their capital base has disappeared. One of the elements that has damaged North West the most, however, is something Kallir didn't mention. The company's investments in Canadian Commercial Bank and Bank of British Columbia have proven perhaps the worst buys of all. The bankers' judgment in investing heavily in energy and real estate loans had been no better than that of the trust managers who placed their faith in cross-investment with their age-old allies.

Kipnes and Rollingher had compounded their mistake of buying North West at exactly the wrong time by having North West buy shares of CCB at exactly the wrong time. Later the Alberta government would help bail the federal bank out with at least one eye on the trust company.

In one way North West is an exception: in the ease with which it has commanded government help. Rumours persist about Kipnes and Rollingher's excellent political connections at the provincial level. Certainly the help they received from the Alberta Treasury Branches was highly unusual.

Saskatchewan's Pioneer Trust, as big a presence in that province as North West is in Alberta, was not as fortunate.

Management of the Regina-based company made a trip East in May 1984 after Ottawa regulators had reported to the Liberals' MacLaren that Pioneer had too much real estate on the books — much of it from foreclosures — at too-optimistic values. Mortgages weren't being paid, it needed a higher percentage of liquid assets and it had too much money invested in the U.S. It was the same old story of lust for empire, this time featuring controlling shareholder Will Klein, a former executive director of the Regina Chamber of Commerce, and a group of his cronies involved in Pioneer and other companies in the Canadian Pioneer Management Ltd. trust/insurance/ oil and gas/real estate business. They had sold shares to small investors throughout the province, as well as to some of Saskatchewan's elite and even former governor general Ed Schreyer, a Winnipeg native. But while some of their ventures made them money, the trust company suffered from non-arm's-length deals and poor decision-making. Federal regulators decided it needed $27 million in capital once loans were revalued.

The regulators wanted to cut Pioneer's borrowing ratio and make sure it invested new deposits only in cash or short-term, easily converted investments. They also proposed an upper limit on the interest rate Pioneer could offer for deposits. The aim was to limit growth and bring the company's deposit base down to its reduced borrowing capacity. It was a formula they had tried with Greymac Mortgage and with Fidelity; it hadn't worked either time.

It was the toughest they could get without closing the company's doors. There was a series of hearings, the company arguing that it was salvageable with a bit of time. In June, MacLaren was made revenue minister by John Turner; he wasn't replaced. Lame-duck Lalonde decided in July to give Pioneer until December to bring the company's business in line with the reduced borrowing ratio.

The list of abandoned properties, unpaid mortgages and sinking real estate values mounted, and the capital base shrank. Pioneer even tried swapping properties with other institutions and developers, a common but, in this case, fruitless tactic to nurse balance sheets in Western Canada. By November Pioneer didn't have a hope of bringing deposits in line with its borrowing base without someone's putting a lot of money into the company. "We said, 'Look, you'd better get down here. It seems to us that you're not going to meet the objective and there's got to be a plan to deal with the situation,'" says Hammond. But president Will Klein asked for two weeks' grace to negotiate. "They arrived down here with a letter saying the Government of Saskatchewan was going to guarantee a preferred share issue." Klein certainly had healthy connections to the provincial Conservative government; both he and his wife had received government board appointments in return for their long-time labours for the party. A rash of Pioneer Management executives had just joined the Grant Devine government as senior civil servants — including former Pioneer Trust president Doug Price, who became president of the Saskatchewan Economic Development Corp. — and Klein was a fund raiser for Mulroney in the 1984 election campaign.

One less problem, the Ottawa regulators thought in relief. It came as a complete surprise when at the end of January 1985, buffeted by a political storm over the obvious motivation for the Pioneer bail-out, Saskatchewan changed its mind.

Pioneer management had been shopping the company around. At first, Eastern companies were keen, but the longer they looked at the books the less interested they were. "A few people told us they might be interested in helping us under an agency agreement" à la District-Crown-Greymac, CDIC's de Lery admits. But the insurer wasn't going to fall into that trap again. For both Pioneer and Northguard, "we did our arithmetic and we decided it was best to go through liquidation." Fidelity was the case that changed the department's mind: "I wasn't involved in that," de Lery says, "but Fidelity is a company that is going to cost CDIC a lot of money." In its drive to wind up the Pioneer matter quickly, Ottawa wasn't interested in anything the least bit complicated. Bank of British Columbia had to push hard even to get CDIC to agree to let it take over the Pioneer branches instead of simply shutting them down.

There is, of course, the usual tap dancing about who pushed the button. De Lery says it was McDougall's decision; McDougall says she took her advice from the CDIC, but it was really management's choice when it didn't find more money. McDougall doesn't enjoy the role of corporate hangman. "It landed on my desk, yeah, and it's not fun, no," she sighs. "I didn't spend two years of my life trying to get into public office so I could put under financial institutions. It's not the most creative part of the job."

Touche Ross was appointed liquidator as it had been for Northguard the month before, but when Pioneer was being wound up, CDIC's J.P. Sabourin was Johnny-on-the-spot. He co-ordinated the two-week effort by a private company aided by consultants — all Toronto imports — to computerize Pioneer's 11-branch operation. The government felt it needed the records on computer before it could tell just how bad things were.

But the moment Pioneer fell under the wheels of the federal government, there was one painful problem regulators knew they'd have to face. A lot of Saskatchewan farmers had invested their money in Income Averaging Annuity Contracts (IAACs), a tax product devised by Ottawa in the early seventies — and discontinued in 1982 — that allowed them to spread the tax on money made on a bumper crop or the sale of their farm. IAACs were dreamed up in the federal Finance Department; so was deposit insurance. But IAACs have a term that stretches longer than five years, the maximum time length for CDIC deposit coverage, so they weren't covered by CDIC, and farmers with money in Pioneer were going to be very unhappy.

CDIC also doesn't insure U.S. dollar deposits. It was set up to insure the savings of the "ordinary depositor," and at first this policy covered only savings and chequing accounts, but pressure was successfully applied to have it cover Guaranteed Investment Certificates. This coverage aided trust companies particularly, since in the late sixties most of their deposits were higher-rate, longer-term GICs. Of course, corporations, municipalities, pension funds and very wealthy depositors also use GICs. The clout of these big-dollar depositors was the reason everyone was paid all their money at Crown — everyone, whether under the insurance umbrella or not. The same treatment wouldn't be given at first to the farmers and the savers who had deposited a total of $1 million in the now-common U.S. dollar accounts at Pioneer.

As in Astra, people who weren't insured thought they were. As in Astra, they had good reason to think so. Whenever a company folds, people scream about their lost money. In Pioneer, any trace of wrongdoing centres on what customers were told — and weren't told — about deposit insurance coverage of the IAACs.

Consumers naturally assume, when an institution's doors

sport the little grey sticker that reads "Member of the Canada Deposit Insurance Corp." that anything they invest in the institution is insured. CDIC's by-laws stipulate that any products not insured must have that important fact marked on the paperwork. Pioneer opened its doors — complete with grey sticker — in 1974. A year later federal regulators pointed out to Pioneer management that it had made a mistake. It wasn't stating on its IAAC certificates that they weren't insured. Management obligingly included the caveat — on its IAAC application form, not the certificate. "There's a lot of talk that nobody knew," says Robert Hammond. But it was on the application form. "Now it wasn't in great big red bold letters, but it was there."

The next year the examiners discovered the mistake. (They were lucky they caught it that early; checking that forms include this disclaimer isn't a priority on the busy examiners' checklist of responsibilities.) Management promised to fix the matter, but it hadn't been altered when regulators returned in 1977: the notice was still on the application form, not the certificate. "Finally we insisted, and they did change it," says Hammond. But the management took the regulators literally: having the notice in the application form didn't constitute compliance, so they took it out. For a time it wasn't stated anywhere that the IAACs weren't insured. In early 1979 — five years after Pioneer began selling IAACs, and four years after the examiners first caught the problem, the caveat appeared on the IAAC certificate.

Even when the disclaimer was on one form or the other, there's a possibility that the information was being cancelled out by assurances from uninformed tellers that the investment had CDIC coverage. Hammond defends what he believes was an honest mistake. "If they told people it was insured, I think they honestly believed that it was. You're dealing with employees who aren't being paid that well, who were trying to do the best jobs they could. I certainly have no indication that they were deliberately trying to mislead people." Whatever the employees' intentions, it wasn't Ottawa's plan to compensate the farmers who had invested in IAACs, even after de Lery received a rash of telephone complaints from people who had lost their money. In May another arbitrary bail-out — this time of a Western bank, Canadian Commercial Bank (CCB) — increased the pressure on the Saskatchewan government to gain satisfaction for the IAAC holders. Only then, and only after stoutly proclaiming for four months that they wouldn't, did Ottawa and the province announce a $39 million joint payback package.

While the problems weren't going away, the CDIC chairman was. De Coster flew to South America for a five-week holiday at the beginning of January 1985; he touched down briefly, then was off to Florida for the month of March. McDougall insists that during her tenure he reported in regularly. "He's put in a lot more than his two days a week." Still, any consultations with the chairman — including a few board meetings — had to be managed by conference call. He left officially in mid-1985.

Western trust company operators made sure Minister Mc Dougall saw the bruises they had developed from Ottawa's tough treatment. "I know they feel injured," she grimaces. She may be echoing the opinions voiced in a closed-door meeting by her Alberta counterpart, the earthy Alberta farmwife Consumer Minister Connie Osterman, whose language is somewhat stronger: "We feel victimized by this." The compact, strong Osterman thought she had valid complaints about federal — and Ontario — regulators' treatment of Alberta-incorporated companies. Her trust industry people were protecting homegrown companies against Ottawa's aggressive advances through 1985, and she was keeping close tabs. Provincial regulators all knew the score. Their Ottawa counterparts didn't like having the provinces in the business of regulating financial institutions. Ottawa had a "secret mandate" to get them out. It couldn't do anything concrete about it — it's as old a conundrum as the section of the BNA Act spelling out the provinces' responsibility for property and civil rights. But one slightly paranoid provincial official opined in early 1985 that the reason more small trust companies would be allowed to go under was that Ottawa was not displeased when the provinces looked foolish. This long-time feeling in Ottawa that the provinces shouldn't be in the business was only exacerbated when Ottawa was burned by CDIC's playing yes-man to Elgie's ministry during the Crown Trust clean-up. The theory of a sub-aqueous shift in the currents of federal-provincial regulation was unspoken but understood. If it is accepted, some startling inconsistencies in regulatory attitudes fall into place.

During 1984 de Lery kept close track of federal reviews of the trust and loan companies' books. Federal companies' licences were restricted. Provincial companies were informed by letter that they were being closely watched by the insurer. By law the directors had to acknowledge the letters. But de Lery didn't bother with the banks. He had not heard directly of any treks west by bank examiners by March 1985, although he was sure there had been some. He simply hadn't been told whether William (Bill) Kennett, the inspector general of banks, was doing anything about checking the loan portfolios of Western banks. And he hadn't asked. Still, he was comfortably sure the inspector general was "doing his job." This was de Lery's view March 19, the very day Kennett was flying in from his Venezuelan sailing vacation to deal with the imminent collapse of Edmonton-based Canadian Commercial Bank.

The rescue of CCB confirmed the relative positions of the CDIC and the bank regulators on the Bureaucrat's Chain of Being. Kennett and Governor of the Bank of Canada Gerald Bouey outrank De Coster, de Lery and Hammond by a long shot. Bouey master-minded the CCB negotiations, with Kennett and Mickey Cohen on his team; CDIC provided the funds but wasn't an important voice in the decisions. It's a home truth among business people that the reason CCB didn't fail is that Bouey had hastily contacted *The Globe and Mail* two years earlier when a connection between president Howard Eaton and Lenny Rosenberg soiled the bank's reputation and shareholders' roster. In a bizarre conversation that let everyone know how worried he was about CCB, Bouey told *The Globe* that no Canadian bank would be allowed to fail. Rosenberg, Markle and Player owned 27% of CCB at that point, as part of Rosenberg and Eaton's plan to set up an international real estate, oil and gas and financial services empire.*

CCB subsequently arranged new management and shareholder support. But real estate and energy loans — many of them U.S. investments fathered by Eaton — were too much for the bank. Management preferred to take a very optimistic view of loan values and the chances that bad loans could be nursed along. In March 1985, only 19 days after the bank promised to pay $600,000 in dividends to preferred shareholders, the company was forced to go begging for a federal bail-out.†

CCB became the first financial institution to receive a big government bail-out and remain in business. Depositors had been bailed out at Crown, Seaway and Greymac, but the companies hadn't survived. Bank of British Columbia, which, like the Western trust companies, eroded its capital base with write-downs of non-performing loans, had been allowed to bend the rules of good business practice the previous fall, but it hadn't been handed a cash advance.

CCB was given $135 million by Ottawa without a public flinch. Of course, the impact of the federal largesse was diluted by donations of $60 million each by Alberta and the country's six largest banks — with the banks to be paid back from 50% of CCB's annual earnings whenever they begin to appear. The banks also agreed to buy $225 million of CCB's $544 million in bad loans.

---

* Eaton, who resigned from CCB following the revelations of non-arm's-length transactions with Rosenberg, has been waiting since late 1983 to hear whether his Commercial Capital Savings & Loan, a California company with plans to specialize in real estate, will be given federal insurance approval.

† The bail-out loans could take up to 15 years to pay back; there will be no dividends on common and preferred stock until then. The preferred shareholders were once again simply forgotten by government and financial industry negotiators. The $30 million convertible preferred share stock issue had been backed by four major securities investment houses 14 months earlier. The $25 stock, which never traded at that level, was at $19.63 before the bail-out. It dropped to $3.50 as some investors sold for whatever they could get.

When McDougall announced the bail-out in the House of Commons March 25, she said in dry tones that a failure of CCB would have damaged the Canadian banking system. "We will support confidence in our financial institutions."

Three large Eastern trust companies didn't have much confidence that the rescue plan would protect their investment in the bank. Canada Trust, Montreal Trust and National Victoria and Grey Trust had purchased CCB bonds totalling $39 million. They were called up to Ottawa for a Sunday meeting — the day the negotiations spawned the rescue package — and asked to sacrifice principal and interest payments on their money for 12 years. It was the bankers' idea: why should trust companies be paid when the bankers were each forking over $60 million with a very slow pay-back? Perhaps when Merv Lahn, Robert Gratton and Bill Somerville flatly refused to agree to the idea, they were mindful of the different treatment always afforded banks. The stand-off stretched through the night: CCB was the closest it had ever been to liquidation. At dawn the trust operators found they had won the Mexican stand-off: Ottawa, Alberta and British Columbia each bought $13 million of the debentures. Alberta and B.C. agencies already held CCB's remaining $10 million in outstanding debentures.

As in the pay-offs at Crown, it was the large depositors who were being protected. CCB is, as its name states, a commercial bank. It doesn't have small walk-in consumer traffic. Yet while they criticized the CCB bail-out as the latest example of Ottawa's preferential treatment of the banks, Alberta trust companies had to secretly sigh in relief that Peter Lougheed added his considerable weight to those pressuring Ottawa for an aid package. In keeping with their regional pride, a number of them used CCB as one of their major bankers. The weekend the bank could have gone down the drain, there was about $100 million on deposit at CCB that belonged to the already-strapped Western trust companies. A failure at CCB could have been the first domino in a series of Western collapses. As it was, Edmonton's North West Trust, fresh from its Alberta

Treasury Branches hand-out, had to hold back its financial statements for two weeks to arrange a $12 million write-down of its shareholdings in both CCB and Bank of British Columbia before it could announce its stunning 1984 loss in early April.

Again the regulators didn't keep a close watch on the bank — and when they did watch it, didn't force it to clean up accounting practices frowned on but allowed by its own auditors. Inspector General of Banks William Kennett trusted management. "The history of CCB has been marked by a series of imprudent lending practices, questionable accounting policies, inadequate information disclosure and lack of supervisory enforcement," a House of Commons finance committee stated in mid-1985, when analysing the company's collapse.

The public had heard that four was the magic number of small Western trust companies that needed watching. With Pioneer and Northguard already gone, de Lery was still worried about nine trusts. Even without the threat of a CCB dragging trust companies under, in mid March de Lery was fully expecting another couple of small trust companies to fail. "I'd like to say 'No' but I can't say that," he shrugged. "Is Canada big enough, is the West populated enough to be able to carry all these institutions?" De Lery provided his own answer, one reflecting his years at an institution that believed smaller trust companies existed at its pleasure. "Maybe they should be looking at mergers out there, rather than trying to compete."

De Lery knew Ottawa was about to abandon another company to the Three Fates. In early January Hammond's department had given Vancouver-based Western Capital Trust, a four-branch construction lending and second-mortgage operation with $200 million in assets, until March 31 to pump enough money in to cover its devalued mortgages. Federal regulators must have known the demand was impossible, because Western Capital had been beating the bushes for money since October 1984. Western's owner, Douglas Day, wrote directly to McDougall appealing for help while Bouey and Co. were "tripping over themselves" arranging the CCB deal. Day detailed loans to his Western Capital Investment from Royal Bank and Bank of British Columbia, which were backed by trust company shares. "Should the trust company be placed into liquidation," he wrote the minister, the banks "would almost certainly lose every penny of their $5 million in loans."

He was looking for $7-$10 million in capital, but it was no go. The letter was never answered. Day pulled the plug himself March 29 rather than have CDIC force him into liquidation. The insurer would end up paying depositors almost $77 million because the government wouldn't lend the company one-tenth that much cash. "They have their own depositors and shareholders to answer to," Day told one reporter. Hammond, when asked why a bail-out was arranged for CCB but not for Western Capital, replied: "That's not a question for a regulator." It emerged in conversation that Inspector General of Banks William Kennett had been instrumental in the CCB deal. Hammond admitted that Kennett is, indeed, a regulator.

It was one more drain on CDIC's resources, and it wouldn't make anyone feel any more kindly towards the bankrupt insurer, which had a deficit of $871.4 million at the end of 1984. The bankers weren't happy, the private sector consultants weren't happy, the provinces weren't happy with CDIC's performance. Solving the problem of the CDIC had become a more immediate political problem than sorting out the future reach of financial institutions. The new government had chosen the traditional response to a pressing problem. In January it appointed a three-man committee to study the theoretical problems of a deposit insurance system, rather than changing the structure of CDIC's daily operations with new management and a new mandate. Part of MacDougall's formula for "recognizing the regional realities" of the financial system was to have a Vancouver stockbroker, W. Robert Wyman, chairman of Pemberton Houston Willoughby, head the CDIC study team. He would understand the complaints of the West — and what's more, "he will be *seen* to give it a good hearing."

Joining Wyman were representatives of the two factions funding the insurer, National Bank senior vice-president Andre Bedard for the bankers, and the recently retired National Trust head Les Colhoun for the trust companies. The team initially planned a year-long look at the reasons behind deposit insurance, its use and abuse in other countries and alternative systems that could work in Canada. It was to be a sober second look at the decision made 18 year earlier to create CDIC. But that wasn't what Ottawa had in mind: it wanted a quick fix, an initial report at the end of March and a final one at the end of April. They compromised on a May report that would set down the alternatives, such as higher premiums for companies that offered above-average rates on deposits or a co-insurance scheme with the private sector providing additional insurance on a user-pays basis, an idea that had been running through Michael Wilson's mind for a couple of years.

The report appeared in June, held up by the rush to translate and print federal budget papers the month before. It recommended that CDIC take a more active role in regulation as well as insurance of companies and be given the power to put companies on a short leash itself, so that it would gain respect from regulators at all levels and so that company heads would begin to supply it with the information it requested. CDIC had, it stated, been feeling "a great deal of frustration" with its role of offering bail-outs at the last minute. It proposed a new level of management for CDIC, vice-presidents who would be skilled in these regulatory areas. CDIC should be taken seriously; CDIC should have its own data on companies, its own early-warning system, should be able to wind down companies on its own intiative and step in if regulators aren't doing the job when they should; CDIC should not be second-guessed. The committee also recommended that private-industry premiums be upped from one-thirtieth of 1% of deposits to 1%, to eliminate the insurers' deficit, and suggested private sector board members, a more flexible system of insurance premiums and terms to punish and reward member institutions and a scheme of co-insurance so that 10% of depositors' funds would always be at risk and depositors would be more careful in choosing a bank or trust company. But it emphasized that CDIC should be involved in revamping accounting and supervisory procedures and that the regulatory changes far outweighed the structural changes in importance. The regulatory changes should be implemented immediately. By advocating yet another level of bureaucratic policing of banks and trust companies, the report was, in essence, condemning the present regulatory system.

It was a blunt warning that things had to change. Still, it was only another discussion paper, a document that could salve but not heal the sore. And almost immediately, Barbara McDougall rejected the more politically unpalatable recommendations. CDIC still sat overloaded with next-to-worthless properties, making interest payments it would never recover. And while the Wyman group — "a committee to study the committee to study the committee that didn't commit" — pondered the future, major players in the market-place were drastically changing the rules for themselves. By the time the federal government had roused itself to action, it was following, not leading.

10

The More Things Change . . .

"The choice is, do you want all of the authority in these enormous institutions all focused in one man or do you want it more broadly based than that?"

This is Trevor Eyton talking. You might think he is arguing for wide ownership of the country's financial institutions or, more particularly, of those institutions now controlled by an individual shareholder or a cosy group of associates. You might think he is putting forward the case that someone like, say, Peter Bronfman should not be in the position of calling the shots in not one, not two, not three, but four institutions. You might, but you'd be wrong. Trevor Eyton is talking about the threat posed by a Big Five bank chairman with no one to account to but a passle of uninformed little shareholders at tame annual meetings.

Eyton presides over a happy little ship called Brascan Ltd., a lean coterie of two dozen executives installed in fine Bay Street gloss high up in the Commerce Court West Tower at the centre of the financial vortex of downtown Toronto. It is from here that Eyton directs with a free hand the affairs of his masters, brothers Peter and Edward Bronfman.

His title is chief executive officer of Brascan, but titles don't mean anything. Eyton's most important role is as the eyes, ears and brains of the Bronfmans. He sits on the boards of 20 companies, including all those in which the Bronfmans have an interest. He and Jack Cockwell, executive vice-president of Brascan, are trustees of the personal family trusts of Peter and Edward. Eyton and Cockwell hold millions of dollars in stock in their employers' companies.

Eyton is also the last line of defence before the Bronfmans are faced with the repugnant glare of public scrutiny. The brothers are part of that fabled circle of reclusive multi-millionaires in whose hands the power of corporate Canada is increasingly concentrated. They do not talk to press or public. They meet with business associates and government behind closed doors. They play equity and debt shuffleboard with the co-operation of similar-minded market handmaidens such as Jimmy Connacher's Gordon Capital Corp. They employ full-time tax rule artistes like Jack Cockwell, who spend their time figuring out how to buy a company without spending a nickel in cash, how to pay senior executives with as little as $50,000 salaries (with a share purchase plan), how to pay dividends but as few corporate taxes as possible. Theirs is the new Family Compact.

Edper Investments Ltd., the brothers' personal holding company (the name is a contraction of Edward and Peter), really doesn't like unfavourable publicity. (*Empire,* for one thing, is not a word they like, Brascan's vice-president of corporate affairs Wendy Cecil-Stuart makes clear.) And the group has long memories when uppity reporters make trouble. In the September 30, 1984, edition of *The Toronto Star,* Diane Francis introduced the brothers to *Star* readers as "Charter members of what some see as a 20th Century reincarnation of Upper Canada's Family Compact." That, along with the rest of the full-page article, was nothing but inaccurate sensationalism according to Cecil-Stuart, and the direct cause of a complete ban on press interviews in the following months.

What makes the Edper empire so endlessly fascinating not

only to nosy reporters but also to inquisitive stock analysts and Bay Street gossips is not simply the vision of its swallowing companies in an attempt to construct a financial organism that may some day rival the Big Five banks, but also the method of the avaricious empire-builders.*

"We do think financial institutions should be publicly owned," Eyton says in a rapid-fire mumble, "but with a large share-holder who has enough of a stake so that he can look over the shoulder of the managers. I'm paid to think that," he adds with a twinkle.

The wish to look over the shoulders of the hired help isn't the only reason the Bronfmans uphold the principle of controlling public companies. They also like the leverage afforded by other people's money. They are masters in the art of holding just enough for control but not so much to bear the full burden of financing.

The technique has brought them the rich rewards and satisfaction of sitting at the top of the most powerful *personal* financial empire in Canada. Through Edper, the two control or influence a dozen major Canadian companies with assets calculated at $95 billion. Their influence is felt everywhere.

The empire is roughly divided into three arenas, but there is much cross-over in shareholdings, business activities and board directors. The original sphere, Carena Bancorp Holdings Inc., was formed when the brothers still lived in Montreal in the early 1970s, struggling under the shadow of their richer cousins Edgar and Charles, who had inherited the bulk of the Seagram fortune from their father, Sam Bronfman. Through direct and indirect holdings — nothing is ever straightforward — Bronfman interests own 80% of the public company. Its most important holdings are a 19% chunk of Canada's seventh largest

---

* In the space of six months in 1984, branches of the empire took over no fewer than six companies, but the Edper forces were reluctant to fan the publicity because of security risks, not just for the Bronfmans but for Eyton and even the little-known Cockwell. When friends observed Edward Bronfman jogging alone on Bloor Street using the same route every day, they approached an Edper retainer at a Christmas party to send a warning to him about the risk of abduction.

bank, Continental Bank of Canada, with assets of $5 billion, and 65% control of huge real estate concern Trizec Corp., whose assets almost hit $3 billion.

In their second sphere, within Hees International Corp.,* the Bronfmans run a merchant banking operation that has built quite a nice little business out of investing in struggling companies, turning them around and making a pile of profit on the results. Hees has grown to $720 million in assets from $128 million in 1979. It has acquired large stakes in North Canadian Oils Ltd., Bankeno Mines Ltd., Merland Explorations Ltd. and builder Bramalea Ltd. It also holds a half-interest in a company that owns major Canadian movie producer Astral Bellevue, which in turn owns pay-TV company First Choice-Superchannel. And Hees also traffics in preferred shares, virtually creating the market in the past three years, during which it did $2 billion worth of business.

The third sphere of influence is the focus of much of the Bronfmans' money and energies these days because it stands to give them what they want most: a giant presence in Canadian finance.

Brascan Ltd. became the property of the Edper Bronfmans in 1979 after one of Canada's bloodiest take-over battles. Engineered by Eyton, who at the time was a lawyer with blue-chip Toronto firm Tory, Tory, DesLauriers & Binnington, it was the first public show of strength by the two Bronfman brothers.†

At the time of the take-over, Brascan was largely a cash-rich Brazilian power utility, so rich that its acquisition immediately made available to the Bronfmans $500 million. In the years since, Brascan has shed many of its foreign assets, with the proceeds funding the rapid purchase of a wide range of major

---

* When the Bronfman forces acquired it in 1970, its chief value was a listing on the Toronto Stock Exchange, but in the old days National Hees Industries Ltd., which once belonged to former Conservative cabinet minister George Hees, was Canada's most prominent venetian blind manufacturer.

† The huge, prosperous and influential firm of Torys has furnished the Bronfman stable with several financial thoroughbreds aside from Eyton, including Hees senior vice-president Williard (Bill) L'Heureux and Trilon chief operating officer Gord Cunningham. James (Jim) Tory sits on Royal's board.

Canadian companies. But the Brazilian government likes its
corporate citizens to withdraw from the scene gracefully, so
Brascan still owns sizeable investments in Brazil, from cattle
ranches to a Rio luxury hotel. The Edper flair has, however,
usually been successful in pulling dividends out of the
currency-restricted country by doing third-party financing: for
example, Brascan Brazil would lend Bank of Montreal funds
for the bank's Brazilian operations, but the bank would pay
Brascan back in Canada.

In Canada, Brascan has large stakes in some of the largest
resource companies in the land through 70%-owned Brascade
Resources, which in turns holds Westmin Resources Ltd.,
Lacana Mining Corp. and Noranda Inc. Among Brascade's
assets of $6 billion are chunks of forestry giant Macmillan
Bloedel, Kerr Addison Mines and the nation's biggest gold find
in years, the Hemlo Golden Giant Mine. Up to now, however,
Brascade has been hobbling Brascan's progress with substantial losses, the victim of commodities vagaries, labour strikes
and vicious competition on the world market. One analyst who
follows the Bronfmans and Brascan closely, Joseph Leinwand
of Capital Group Securities Ltd., studied the severe effect that
resource losses during 1983 and 1984 had on Brascan. Its profit
over that period came in large part from non-operating earnings: the disposal of assets in Brazil and an accounting ma-
noeuver that allows the holding company to record as income
the dilution that results when a subsidiary issues equity. As a
result, Brascan may soon be forced to raise hundreds of millions of dollars — some of it uncharacteristically by selling
common shares in the company.

Nevertheless this crack in the Bronfman earnings magic is
papered over by strong performances in Brascan's other holdings: a lucrative 25% of U.S.-based Scott Paper Co. and 37%
of consumer product giant John Labatt Ltd., which in turn
owns food companies Catelli, Sealtest and Dominion Dairies,
Chateau-Gai Wines and U.S.-based Chef Francisco, as well as
the Labatt beer operation and the Toronto Blue Jays baseball
team.

These are all nice shops to own, but toilet paper and chick

peas do not hold the promise of the future. The part of the empire causing the greatest controversy because of its interrelated dealings and spectacular growth is the financial sector, where Edper has a grip on securities trading through Great Lakes Group, a dominance in near-banking with Royal Trust, a growing presence in insurance of all kinds and a corner on real estate brokerage.

When George Mann took his run at Union Gas in the winter of 1985, he had a hidden ally that proved its worth in the final days. It was Great Lakes Group, a spin-off by Brascan designed to do huge private underwritings and equity placements outside the regulated securities industry. The shell used was a Brascan subsidiary called Great Lakes Power, a utility that delivered electricity to Northern Ontario. But in July 1984 Trevor Eyton created out of it a financial institution to inhabit a world of secret deals and friendly alliances among the players in the stock-market who do not seek the protection and interference of securities commissions. It is known as the "exempt" market — as in exempt from many securities regulations. Great Lakes's strength derives not only from a capital pool of $400 million and assets of $750 million, but also from its two major partners, Canadian Imperial Bank of Commerce and Merrill Lynch. Brascan owns 49%.*

Just how Great Lakes and the rest of the companies within the Edper orbit worked could be seen in the Union Gas-Unicorp tussle. Edper held about 16% of Union Gas through Great Lakes. Jack Cockwell and Brascan senior vice-president Bob Dunford, who sat on the Union Gas board, had spent 1984 steaming about the way former Ontario treasurer Darcy McKeough was running Union. What they deemed bad management and a misguided reorganization of the company finally pushed the Edper guys past the point of tolerance. They wanted

---

* "What makes Great Lakes so intriguing for its owners," wrote *The Globe and Mail*'s Martin Mittelstaedt in August 1984, "is that it has the potential of causing further crumbling of regulations in the financial industry." He went on to point out that unlike banks, investment dealers, trust companies and insurance companies, all obligated to follow strict regulations, Great Lakes would fall through the cracks.

out at a profit, but it transpired that that was going to happen only if they sold the block to Mann, an entrepreneur who makes the Edper boys look as sober as undertakers. When Mann hit the scene with his bid for Union, Great Lakes tendered its block to Mann early on, taking the preferred shares in Unicorp that Mann was offering to everyone. But in the open market-place there was little faith in the intrinsic value of Unicorp's stock, and after weeks of mud slinging and manoeuvres more familiar in American take-over battles, Mann finally wrested control of the southwestern Ontario gas utility only after four Edper companies and Jimmy Kay, who had indentured himself to Hees when his companies were bailed out in late 1984, stepped in with their cash. It was the operating principle of "We do you a favour, you do us a favour."

When institutional holders of Union stock began selling for cash into the market, the Edper forces began picking it up, eventually acquiring and turning over to Mann 10 million of the 15 million shares he acquired. Only after weeks of uncomfortable public Ontario Energy Board hearings did the pivotal role of the Edper clan become clear. In addition to the original Great Lakes stake, Continental Bank and Kay's holding company had sold Union shares to Mann in return for Unicorp preferred stock. Royal Trust (which is Unicorp's transfer agent) and North Canadian Oils found themselves with Unicorp shares which they had bought for cash from other institutional investors who had tendered their Union shares to Mann on the understanding that they would not be left for very long with the Unicorp stock. Between the two manoeuvres, the Edper group of companies wound up with 71% of the preferred stock that Mann had tried to flog to Union Gas shareholders in lieu of cash.* At the hearings

---

* The rest were accumulated for Mann by his banker, National Bank, and the ubiquitous Gordon Capital. Its chairman, Jimmy Connacher, is notorious for his secrecy and reclusiveness. But he was forced to appear at the hearings and was horrified to find a gang of photographers waiting to take his picture, the first in many, many years. Agitated and angry, Connacher took on the appearance of a hostile trial witness as he covered his face with his hands while his lawyers stepped in front to push the financial paparazzi away.

Cockwell told an incredulous Energy Board that despite the fact that the Unicorp shares had received the lowest rating possible from bond rating companies, the "completely autonomous managements" of Royal Trust, Continental Bank and Great Lakes Group, plus Jimmy Kay personally, had independently decided to make the investment. While he admitted that Mann had tried to sell the deal to Hees, Cockwell adamantly maintained that Hees employed no control over the other companies. That was news to Edper watchers and an interesting departure from Hees's own public declaration in a securities document that Hees "exercises significant direct or indirect influence over the affairs of [its affiliated] companies."

Edper companies rarely use cash for their growth drive. They prefer using "paper," preferred share issues, sometimes sugar-coated with warrants (rights to buy additional stock at a certain price at a specific time) and conversion rights (rights to exchange the preferred shares for common stock) to raise capital and acquire operations rather than using retained earnings, which tend to go in dividends to shareholders. For example, when a financial services subsidiary, Trilon, acquired a property and casualty insurance company in the fall of 1984, it paid $130 million — all of it paper. When Carena Bancorp, Trizec's parent, bought 43% of Costain Ltd., it paid the $39 million in shares and warrants.

Complex financings are routine for Bronfman companies. Non-voting preferred share issues, debentures at fixed interest rates or floating with the prime rate, and revolving lines of credit take the empire constantly to market, and "family member" companies often buy parts of each other's issue.

"We're good at financing, strategy, tactics. We're good at acquisitions, and we're pretty good negotiators in corporate transactions," says Eyton, running down the Edper litany. "We have lots of relationships with people and governments and we can help make things happen."

Edper's influence does indeed extend into the public arena when its enterprises can benefit from associating with government.

When the federal government's Green Paper on the Regulation of Canadian Financial Institutions was released in April 1985, one newspaper report called it Hal Jackman's legislation. But that simplistic analysis overlooked the effective pervasiveness of Edper. An organizational chart in the Green Paper showing possible corporate set-ups was striking in its resemblance to Trilon.

When the Mulroney government made seven appointments to the Canada Development Investment Corp.'s board to spearhead divestiture of its Crown corporations, four were directors of companies in the Edper empire, including the pivotal Eyton. But the appointment that drew criticism because of possible conflicts of interest was that of Canada Development investment Corp. president Paul Marshall, who bears an unfortunate resemblance to Maurice Strong. He was named to replace Joel Bell, but he held onto his post as president of Westmin Resources. (Unlike Bell, Marshall is not paid for his Canada Development Investment Corp. work.)

As important as those early 1985 appointments were, at the same time the busy Eyton was immersed in a grand plan to organize, under the aegis of Brascan, a private sector group to back Toronto's domed sports stadium. Two Edper companies, Trilon and Labatt (the latter owns the Toronto Blue Jays), were members of the 12-company group that successfully excluded competitors from getting in on the action. At the time there were objections to a "closely knit, hugely wealthy" group's commandeering the project with the blessing of the provincial Conservative government, then led by William Davis.* The Edper grip on the pulse of the business and political communities was as sure and as strong as any modern-day family compact could want.

* A few months after the dome stadium agreement, one of Davis's closest advisors, lawyer Edwin Goodman, moved from the Labatt board to the Brascan board. At the time he was playing a helpful role by representing George Mann at hearings into Mann's bid for Union Gas.

In late summer 1983 Trevor Eyton launched Trilon Financial Corp. as a 39%-owned umbrella subsidiary of Brascan, and shuffled in Brascan's 98% holding in London Life Insurance Co. and 51% in Royal Trustco to provide a vehicle for financing growth and acquisitions. In effect, the action gave the Bronfmans a running start in the race to create financial conglomerates in Canada.

Never mind the rest of the Edper empire, Trilon is enormous: corporate assets of more than $12 billion, assets under its administration of more than $55 billion, its total earnings of $75 million in 1984 up 97% from the previous year. According to its 1984 annual report, its chief components are powerhouses in their own right: Royal Trust with $11 billion in corporate assets and another $49 billion in its care; London Life with $5 billion of its own assets and another $49 billion worth of life insurance in force. Then there's Trilon's own direct financial activity — bond trading, interest rate swaps and commercial lending — in which it raises "commercial paper" against its corporate worth and lends it out for a handsome fee. (Commercial paper is analogous to a demand loan secured against a person's worth rather than a collateral loan secured against a particular asset.) A measure of its success and place in the financial conglomerate is its earning record: $2 million one year, $10 million the next.

In 1984 the Brascan folks pulled out the stops in a race to put Trilon in front as a new-wave financial institution. It acquired three companies in rapid succession, starting in October, when it bought half of the country's largest real estate broker, A.E. LePage, and merged it with Royal Trustco's real estate brokerage operations, creating an industry giant with 9,000 agents and 321 offices earning $350 million selling property. That move was followed *a week later* by the acquisition of 100% of property and casualty insurance company Fireman's Fund Insurance Co. of Canada, quickly renamed Wellington Insurance, from the American Express group in the U.S. Two months later Trilon closed a deal to acquire 51% of Canadian Vehicle Leasing, a major car leasing company, as a first step into other leasing activities.

It was a shopping frenzy that grabbed the attention of competitors and regulators. Trilon represented a new version of the old way of doing things in the financial world — that is, using the three Cs: control, connections and clique. That spectre stirred the Big Banks to action.

Marshalling the acid tongue and combative temperament of their lobbyist, Canadian Bankers' Association president Robert MacIntosh, the banks took over the front pages of the nation's newspapers in late March of 1985 with the revelation that Trilon's holdings were bigger even than those of the country's largest bank, the Royal. Brandishing a freshly minted report on concentration of power in the financial services industry, McIntosh offered the proof: using 1983 figures, Trilon's assets were calculated at $48.8 billion, while the Royal Bank weighed in at $46.2 billion — an astounding piece of news. But the bankers had added together Trilon's corporate assets and assets under administration at Royal Trust and London Life.* Then the wily bankers had lopped off all of the Royal Bank's foreign currency assets, which, when counted, bring the bank's total assets up to a more familiar number $88 billion. The bankers' report featured a chart that compared the "popular view" (held by everyone) with the "realistic view" (held by the banks).

When the Bronfman strike force finally wrested control of Brascan, they got 30% of London Life as part of the bargain. It was, to hear Eyton tell it, a "company in transition," which is corporate diplomatese for a drowsy company that needs some waking up. The Jeffrey family of London, Ontario, had owned and run London Life for generations, but by the late 1970s even they realized something had to be done, and there was no apparent heir within the family to take on the task.

Even before Eyton turned his attention to the venerable old insurance company, board members like former Brascan chief

---

* Where the bankers got their numbers is anybody's guess since, according to its annual report, Trilon's corporate assets of $10.2 billion and administered assets of $47.4 billion add up to $57.6 billion.

executive Jake Moore, Allen Lambert and J. Allyn Taylor from nearby Canada Trust had taken a stab at revitalization. They had hired a consultant named Earl Orser who arrived on the scene steps ahead of the Edper boys. "Like so many consultants," Eyton says with winning candour, "he was in the process of writing a report that said, 'The one thing you've got to do is appoint me as chief executive.' And he was writing his own contract to boot!"

Eyton soon realized his company needed a good deal more than a 30% shareholding to effect the changes he felt were necessary, so he began working on the Jeffreys, winning their confidence and finally securing their agreement to sell control to Brascan. Orser survived his impertinent start and was charged with the corporate make-over: Eyton wanted a shake-up in attitude, he wanted the company's managers to be more demanding of themselves, he wanted a clear-eyed evaluation of what the company was doing.

Meanwhile, the brouhaha over Royal Trust had writhed its way to a conclusion, with control of the dowager trust company landing in the hands of the Bronfmans and the Reichmanns — truly one of the most savoury ironies in Canada's corporate history.

Over the course of 1982, during a slow dance for supremacy in the executive suite and in the boardroom, Eyton gradually moved in. An Edper executive in good standing went on the Royal board first. Machiel Adriaan Cornelissen, called Michael in print and Mike in person, was parachuted into Royal from a turnaround posting at Trizec, where he had made a name for himself reining in the development company's financial problems by matching the company's assets against borrowings, using market studies and detailed planning. He had no time for starry-eyed developers dreaming of buildings, and Trizec was soon judged the best-managed company in the business.

When Royal's old-guard president John Scholes left for health reasons, Cornelissen took the spot. Eyton had never thought of him as a candidate for the job; rather, the suggestion came from Royal board incumbent Fraser Fell. Surprising, considering Cornelissen's yeoman service for Edper companies. The South African accountant had spent a year in Montreal in 1967 for his firm, Touche Ross. While there he became friendly with Touche colleague Jack Cockwell. Back in South Africa, Cornelissen determined he would return to Canada and contacted his friend, who had moved to the Bronfmans' Hees operation. In 1976 Cornelissen joined him, moving into Trizec when the Bronfmans took control.

Cornelissen is a professional manager. As Royal's president, he is tough and hard-driving, a methods and process man and a tireless workaholic who puts in a 75-hour week and calls it fun. In short, he is as different from the genteel old Royal managers as anyone could be.

One Royal manager who lived through the company's evolution from 1973 to 1984 recalls that Ken White ran the place like a boot camp, assessing his managers according to his personal prejudices. Under Cornelissen, performance is the only criterion, and the few survivors among the upper ranks at Royal have watched a lot of colleagues fall in action. Where White's motivation was preservation of the monarchy, Cornelissen is spurred on by a mission to turn Royal into gold dust for the Edper group.

White in his time was well known for his skill at dispensing with the company's annual meeting in record time, with no questions asked and therefore no "unnecessary" information imparted.

The March 1984 annual meeting, where Cornelissen had his first real chance to shine, astounded observers with a flashy video show, with music to get the adrenalin running, and a dozen questions from the audience, answered by managers taking turns at expounding fully.

But the questions had been planted in the audience, and the responses well rehearsed. The show had been conceived and orchestrated by Cornelissen, perhaps as a result of a private meeting earlier that year at which Bay Street's stock analysts had roundly criticized the company for being abnormally secretive about its affairs and for producing some of the most unhelpful financial statements in the industry.

In the years under White and Scholes, the company took not months but years to come out with a new product. The competition, particularly Canada Trust, was furlongs ahead. But by the middle of 1985 Royal was meeting Canada Trust on its own turf — mortgage lending — and consistently beating it on rates and payment gimmicks.

All of this was the fruit of a thorough house-cleaning executed cold-bloodedly by Cornelissen after he assumed the presidency in August of 1983. He had been observing the company from his board seat since the previous April, but little was accomplished until White retired as chairman in late 1983 and Trevor Eyton slipped in to replace him.

Cornelissen's first job was to get rid of the Florida banks. The old Royal had bought them as a step towards becoming more international. But the state-chartered banks in a largely retail sun belt market were virtually useless as a vehicle to the international corporate lending world, the only internationalism of which Eyton could conceive.

Cornelissen presents the problem in his highly analytical way: the choices were to do nothing, to go very big very fast or to sell. He chose the last option, and in a genuine coup bypassed expensive merger and acquisition middlemen and flogged the thing himself to a U.S. bank for a $19 million profit. The move won him kudos at the Brascan level, but when asked if he celebrated the signing of the Florida deal, he replies in cool fashion, "I don't celebrate, I just get the job done."

Getting the job done meant an overhaul of the management and operation of Royal. He tightened up the upper ranks, turfing out two dozen managers and eliminating an average of three, but as many as five, levels of managers. He "encouraged" close and continual communications among people. Operating decisions were made at a much higher level than in the past. Information about operations was routinely sent higher up the ladder, and reassessment of lower-level decisions was regularly done by senior managers. There was tighter control of every part of the trust company.

Cornelissen began rooting out every hidden value in the

enormous company. He was captivated by the growth potential of Royal's languishing British bank operation and unearthed an undervalued office building in downtown Montreal, where the old regime had rented 70% of the space for $3 a square foot while the market rate was $15.

In their minds, Eyton and Cornelissen had a clear vision of Royal as a new financial institution: lean, tough-minded, aggressive and efficient enough to compete with the banks for corporate and individual customers. The slow-moving, backwater image of trust companies was not only anathema to high-octane Edper; it was suicide in the rapidly changing environment where trust companies were in direct competition with other financial institutions.

The word went out to Royal's employees that the slogans that sprinkled Cornelissen's speech — heightened expectations, superior performance, work ethic and commitment to quality — were warnings.

"We can't be an institution or a bureaucracy any more," he says in the tight cadence of South Africans. "We can't survive. Instead we must ask, 'What are you interested in a company providing?'"

A five-year business plan carved out by Cornelissen and Eyton put a top priority on developing a product focus as a key to the future direction of the company, and during 1984 managers sweated out details on the kinds of products to offer, pricing, packaging and distribution through the branches. It was mortgages and RRSPs as Big Macs.

One vice-president from the previous regime, Phillip Armstrong, worked day and night during the spring of 1984 to develop a "Double-Up Mortgage" in which mortgage payments could be doubled any time without penalty. Easily understood, simple and eminently marketable, it was the kind of thing the public had come to expect of Canada Trust, not Royal.*

---

* Aside from marketing, Royal also faced a huge gap between itself and its competitors in computerization. At the time of the take-over, the company was losing important pension fund management accounts because of its archaic systems. Over a five-year period Royal will spend $80 million on computer development alone.

Royal can plug into Edper's ability to engineer large, sophisticated corporate financings; it can also engineer them itself. In 1984 the trust company raised $150 million in preferred shares and 30 million British pounds on the Euromarket — far more capital than its regulated deposit-taking ratio of 25:1 required, providing enough room to almost double business without raising another dollar. Part of this expensive excess capital will leverage a drive for as much as $2 billion of commercial and corporate lending during the next two years. That means this crucial component of Royal's five-year plan can be accomplished without diluting the interest of common shares.

By the end of 1984, Royal had become the trust industry's most profitable financial institution as measured by return on assets and return on equity. Its earnings had hit a record $85 million, sky-rocketing from the $44 million the company earned in 1982, the year Brascan took over. The sacred right enshrined in Royal's financial statements — the right of shareholders to an above-average return on their investment — was becoming reality as the rate of return climbed from 10% to 15%.

As swift and remarkable as Royal's turnaround was, it was only a part of Edper's bigger creation: the emerging giant, Trilon.

"Our goal," says Trilon president Melvin Hawkrigg, "is to become Canada's leading diversified financial services corporation. And the opportunity to offer a unique blend of financial services on a cost effective basis to Canadians from all walks of life is very clearly at hand." Mel Hawkrigg is a hell of a nice guy. He smiles almost all the time, he likes to use the soothing platitudes he learned as a Fuller Brush executive and he has the team attitude of a professional football player, which he used to be.

They think big at Trilon. Allen Lambert, former chairman of the Toronto Dominion Bank, on his second career as its chairman as well as that of London Life, says it has "long been" the policy of the two-and-a-half-year-old holding company to diversify into "world class companies, which while leaders in their respective businesses, do not dominate any particular market." The pussyfooting in Lambert's statement betrays a chronic worry at Brascan that a groundswell of opposition to concentration of corporate power might result in government action to restrict their activities.*

All of the Brascan and Trilon executives regularly stress the group's set of corporate principles: that Edper-owned businesses operate through public companies, that their ownership in these public companies is usually limited to 51%, that affiliated companies have "independent" boards and directors and that the role of a holding company such as Trilon is to "help affiliates to be low cost producers."

But when push comes to shove, they don't pull their punches. "I have one comment on this," Hawkrigg begins genially, "and I use this with my regulatory friends when I talk to them and they start saying you guys are getting too big and too powerful. The dilemma that I have and that I pass on to them is this: 'We've got the money to invest and we're not going to put it in the mattress. Would you have us take that money, and because you say we're too big, invest it in the U.S.?'"

The other clear message from the "family," as Hawkrigg calls the group of senior executives from Brascan and Trilon, is that senior management in the affiliate companies is autonomous and works for minority shareholders as much as for the controlling one. Minority shareholders, however, are along for the ride; they don't take a turn at the wheel.

Brascan "partners" Eyton and Cockwell — that's how they refer to themselves — have recruited and placed senior management in the companies they have acquired and these man-

---

* When the 1984 LePage-Royal Trust merger was announced, the federal Combines Department investigated the corporate links between the Bronfmans and the Reichmanns, who own 12% of Trilon, and whose family company, mammoth real estate developer Olympia & York Holdings Corp., owns major Western real estate broker Block Bros. The deal was subsequently approved, but Trilon remains a lightning rod in the stormy debate on whether financial companies should be owned by dominant shareholders and have links to companies in the "real" economy — that is, to industrial companies that could benefit from self-dealing.

agers clearly identify with Edper. This identification is rein-
forced with large stock purchase plans that senior officers are
"encouraged" to participate in because it gives them a financial stake in the company they are running.

"The amount of assets I've got tied up in the companies I'm
involved in is très significant. I'm very interested in what's happening to shareholder values," says Hawkrigg, who has borrowed more than a million dollars on the stock plan. "I don't
want to sound like it's straight profit-motivated, and I guess
it is to a degree, but when everybody on your team is a shareholder, the commitment and dedication to your planning process and the results you want, it's a very nice way to go through
life."*

It was the potentially fortune-making share ownership plan
and the dynamics of this close-knit team that attracted some of
the best WASP talent in the financial industry, imparting to
Trilon and its subsidiaries a blue-chip image it sorely needs as
an antidote to its buccaneer press. Aside from Lambert, the
biggest coup was Eyton's luring of 53-year-old Hartland Molson McDougall from his position as vice-chairman of the Bank
of Montreal to that of chairman of Royal Trust. MacDougall
was courted ardently, but the promise of eventually succeeding
Lambert as head of Trilon wasn't as persuasive as changes in
the ranks at BMO under its dictatorial chairman, William Mulholland. Several disenchanted bank executives followed Mac-
Dougall to Royal.

Eyton, a tennis buddy and neighbour of MacDougall's in
both Rosedale and the Caledon countryside, was the recruiting
officer. "His blood," says Eyton, "is a special colour blue. His
connections across Canada are superb. We're going to use that
asset."

---

* At Trilon's 1985 annual meeting the biggest stir was caused by the generous
policy of providing senior officers with interest-free loans so they could buy company shares at discount prices. As one disgruntled shareholder, a London Life
agent, said in the only question from the floor, "The smiling picture of Mr Hawkrigg, Mr Orser [London Life president] and Mr Lambert are because of the money
they made on the share plan," well over $1 million.

The fiction of an autonomous Trilon and an equally autonomous Royal is maintained more in word than in deed. Trilon itself actually consists of four executives (Lambert, Hawkrigg, chief operating officer Gord Cunningham and chief financial officer Frank Lochan) and a secretary; it shares with Brascan its offices, a receptionist and the same brass front door that whips open and shut on the unsuspecting like a guillotine.

Similarly, the boards of the affiliate companies are dominated by Edper associates. It is a new version of the old family-compact-style interlocking directorships. On London Life's board, for example, Trilon, Brascan and Trizec executives control the audit, executive, investment and management development committees. The more they control, the less likely the voices of minority shareholders are to be heard. At the 1984 annual meeting, Trilon asked Royal Trustco shareholders to change a company regulation that restricted voting blocks to 10% no matter how much stock was owned. That was entirely acceptable. What wasn't was a statement a week before the meeting by the "autonomous" Cornelissen, subsequently refuted by Eyton, that the controlling shareholders had been ignoring the rule since Brascan and then Trilon took control of the company "because they didn't consider it valid." It was difficult to imagine Canada Trustco president Merv Lahn saying the same thing.

For three days in early April 1984, the top people from Trilon, Royal and London Life held a pow-wow in the sleepy theatre town of Stratford. Here the curtain came down on the old way of doing business. The new act would feature financial conglomerates of the future.

Earl Orser, who looks the part of a hotel dining room maitre d', was there from London Life, as was Bob Lackey, who as vice-president, corporate development, spends much of his time combing the U.S. for take-over targets. Cornelissen was there for Royal. Hawkrigg was there. Going into the meeting, underlings had already identified 75 projects as possible joint ventures. The CEOs were treated to a presentation on them;

four ideas were immediately recognized as not worth imple-
menting, another half-dozen failed as priorities. Others require
further investigation, and the underlings were told to get on
with it. Two really got the blood pumping.

First, the April meeting produced an immediate plan to sell
Royal home-ownership savings plans through London Life
agents as a pilot project in London. The cannibalization that
would result from selling competing products like RRSPs was
anticipated, so there would be no cross-selling of those.

In a potentially far more profitable move, Royal and London Life decided to examine sharing the enormously costly
computer systems they both needed.

There would be more cross-fertilization to come and it would
be touted as pioneering stuff, although the true pioneer is
Alberta-based Principal Group, whose supermarket set-up has
been selling trust services, mutual funds and savings and lending — all of it integrated by computer — under the same roof
for years.

For strong-minded, long-established agents in the London
Life stable, having to bother with some trust company's GICs
goes against their self-image as independent businessmen. And
they said so. "It's got to be worth me going out in the morning and starting my car," complained one. But they would be
asked to do so anyway. Part of the problem facing Trilon, at
any rate, is that London Life is the last remaining insurance
company whose agents sell only its product, and do so by selling explicitly against other companies' products.

"Those are attitudes," says Eyton dismissively. "People
have got to change and undoubtedly over time will. Or we're
wrong. That's the other possibility."

Since that April meeting there have been others, and the
group has expanded to accommodate executives from Trilon's
1984 acquisitions, LePage and Wellington. Three "synergy"
committees sift through ways of using each other's resources
and customers. In July 1985, Royal LePage Real Estate, as it
was named after the merger, burst onto the hot mortgage market with a scheme not even George Mann would have at-

tempted: the company announced it would begin offering mortgages to home buyers through its 300 real estate offices. The mortgages would be processed and pre-approved by Royal LePage even before a property sale. Royal Trust would fund the loans.

For the most part, referral between Royal, LePage, Wellington and London Life people is a far more workable idea than actual sales of each other's products. And the synergetic minded will reap the benefits. In mid-May 1985, one London Life agent walked into Royal's main branch with a client of his who had $1.4 million in unencumbered assets and was looking for an investment manager. Royal signed up the account and the London Life agent was awarded a "small consideration" in Trilon shares.

The game plan for Trilon, says Hawkrigg, who never seems to run out of clichés, calls for visible results by the end of 1985 or early 1986. Trilon still very much wants to acquire a mutual fund, an investment counselling firm and a U.S. insurance company and plans to fund the next shopping spree with the proceeds of its sale of up to 4% of London Life. And as soon as Trilon has Wellington Insurance humming to the family's tune, that 100% stake will be reduced, too.*

By 1986 Cornelissen will have Royal Trust structured just the way he wants it, and he will turn his howitzer attention to "Vision 1990," the ultrasecret project Royal Trust has devised for its version of the future.

Vision 1990 has both Royal Trust and London Life branches selling all the products from the two companies. Slick packaging will be paramount.

In 1986 the first pilot branch will hit Toronto, confronting the unsuspecting customer with a bank of automatic teller machines in the lobby. The "service group" out front will feature

---

* Once again taking the unexpected route, Trilon chose to take an obscure subsidiary, Lonvest Corp., which actually holds the investment in London Life, public. In June 1985 Lonvest announced it would be raising at least $200 million through the issue of common shares and warrants. This would effectively reduce Trilon's stake in the insurance company to between 57% and 66%.

one teller to do the things the machines can't do — open new accounts, sell RRSPs and GICs. In the back, the financial planner will marshal the forces of Trilon to provide the customer with the more complicated services. London Life agents will still beat the bushes for prospects, but the administration manager located in the branch will answer questions and pass clients along to the agents. Marketing studies will refine the plan, which continues to evolve, likely including LePage and Wellington in the set-up. And expected changes in federal legislation governing financial institutions could open the door even wider for Trilon's plans.

The ultimate plan involves hamburgers. Financial products will be sold, and branches will be run, like a McDonald's franchise. Branch managers will get base salaries and a cut of the action.

One synergy committee, headed by Bank of Montreal emigré Bill Harker, is studying means of meshing the computer systems of all the Trilon companies not only to reduce costs but also to make the system more effective.

More effective? "The group is big enough," says Eyton brightly, "that in time we should literally have most of the households in the country on a machine somewhere. So we should know when a family's oldest boy turns 21."

It is Robert Jellett's yellow cards on a Rolodex gone high tech.

11

Gentlemen's Rules: The Future of the Financial System

On a late Saturday afternoon in mid-March 1985, Donald (Don) Blenkarn, QC and Member of Parliament for Mississauga South, was sprawled in his untidy constituency office in a khaki-coloured converted house next to a gas station. It had been, as always, a hectic two days back in the riding, and Blenkarn, a man whose girth reflects an expansive approach to life, was a bit woozy. But the chairman of the House of Commons Committee on Banking and Finance happily peered out from behind thick lenses at the political horizon, outlining how he would cope with the bundle of financial institutions legislation that was about to land on his desk.

Blenkarn was planning a series of "summit" hearings across the country, a travelling road show to bring this rather weighty subject to the unwary constituents of the nation — to Vancouver, Calgary, Winnipeg, Halifax, Montreal and, of course, Toronto. Three weeks of hearings should wrap up the public input into the future shape of the financial system. He ticked off the months on a mental timetable. They would advertise the "consultations" by May and be on the road by June.

As always with any plan dependent on the process of government, the timetable had to be rearranged. Barbara McDougall's Green Paper on the regulation of Canadian financial institutions — the blueprint for the industry — arrived in April 1985. She wanted responses from the industry by the end of July, and legislation by the end of the year. Her CDIC group's report was handed in on April 25 but didn't make it out the other end of the translating/printing monster's clutches until the very end of May. The Green Paper's technical appendix was caught in the same bottle-neck, so Blenkarn asked for an extension of his deadline to October 31. His committee grabbed headlines throughout May and June without budging from Ottawa, however, by questioning regulators about the surprising suddenness of the Canadian Commercial Bank collapse, then moving on to the regulatory neglect that had fostered 14 trust company collapses in the past half-decade.

Political scrutiny can bring to the mystical, rigid, myth-ridden world of banking and finance the sanity of the common touch. What really matters to politicians is not how much power any particular company has but whether the whole kit and caboodle is being properly regulated in the first place. Blenkarn's committee is concerned that the government inspectors know how to read the books.

"Up until now — and even right now — the federal government has abandoned its jurisdiction by delegating its [role] to the Ontario inspection system, and frankly that's why we got in trouble in the Greymac, Seaway, Crown Trust episode." Blenkarn's voice rises to a squeaky pitch when he begins to laugh about the *unbelievable* negligence of Ontario in allowing Rosenberg to have Crown, in advising school boards and municipalities that Seaway and Greymac were acceptable companies for their deposits. But the same can be said of the federal regulators who didn't pull the insurance, he says, his voice again hitting the ceiling. "Federally, we were insuring these agencies, and *knew* — and *knew* — back in March of 1982 or earlier that the two of them were in deep trouble." The laughter is mocking. "Knowing they're in trouble and continuing to do nothing is pretty serious. They led the investors down the garden path and I think it hurt."

It did hurt investors. It hurt at Pioneer and it hurt at Fidelity Trust. And the pocket-books of the public matter more to the politician than "overall legislation to guide the course of the industry to the turn of the century." Legislation may be heady stuff, but the government has higher priorities. "People aren't being put out of work in trust companies and insurance companies because there's no new four pillars legislation today."

The politicians are more interested in extending their own circle of authority than in worrying about whether banks or trust companies will want to do the same thing. Salt-of-the-earth Blenkarn is no different from the rest: "In my view we would say, 'Lookit, provinces, you shouldn't have been in this business in the first place, and if we're going to use the credit of Canada [CDIC] to cover you, we're going to supervise you too. If you fellows don't want to be supervised by us — don't! And we won't insure you. We're taking that funny little sticker off your door.'"

Thoughts like this sound a warning for the now-retired but never retiring regulator Dick Humphrys. "The industry must think how far it wants to go in [deposit] insurance," he warns, "because if the government has to pick up the tab and guarantee the company, it will regulate them so tightly it will be de facto nationalization."

But it was not the regulatory crack-downs that excited the minds of the business community when the Green Paper came out. They ignored the distinct warnings of over-the-shoulder regulation to ogle the future shape of the financial system. Trust companies had so mutated in 25 years that Ottawa was proposing they could be split in half. The original "trust" business would be the basis of one kind of company in a new financial conglomerate. But the second kind would be a carbon copy of the companies that had originally created the trust industry, the companies the trusts had admired, served, lusted for and finally succeeded in imitating. Banks.

Underpinning the federal government's new direction was the conviction that free enterprise should be allowed to reign. Honourable gentlemen would be rewarded with profitable companies in the banking, insurance and trust business. But dishonourable gentlemen would be, in Barbara McDougall's elegant terminology, "hammered." The rules of play are still, most definitely, gentlemen's rules.

Essentially, the ground was laid for the future by the federal Green Paper in two areas: the new forms financial companies might take, and a proposed increase in the policing power of regulators. Both areas of change were reflections of the two pressures for change on the government: the rise of the Trilons and the fall of the Fidelitys. By far most important, the Green Paper accepted the concept of financial holding companies with fingers in several pots. And in fact added a pot, commercial lending, by creating a new classification of holding company that would solve the problem of separating fiduciary business from commercial lending by throwing up distinct corporate walls between a trust company and a newly minted deposit-taking and lending institution.

The paper also shifted the basis of investment restrictions for non-aligned trust and insurance companies from the quality of the investments to the amount invested in any particular area. It promised a regular review of trust and insurance laws, similar to those for the banks; it increased the regulators' surveillance and enforcement powers; it banned self-dealing between a financial institution and its holding company or any other related company; and it decided to deal with the inevitable conflicts of interest this system would engender by creating a government office that would help complainants such as small investors or depositors, and by having companies police their own internal barriers between conflicting types of business. Finally, it called for ministerial approval of share transfers. The new direction was a mixture of obvious wisdom and patent naïvety. Some proposals — like rules for the diversification of investment portfolios — were old hat and had been in the works since they were first suggested by the former Liberal government.

The most lasting contribution no doubt will be the addition of a new letter to the lexicon of legislative debate. In the 1980 Bank Act revision, foreign-owned or "suitcase" banks gained legitimacy when they were allowed to register as full-fledged Canadian banks even though they were wholly owned subsidiaries of foreign banks. They were called Schedule B banks under the law; chartered banks were Schedule A. In mid-1985, with the proposal to allow commercial lending through federally licensed banks 100%-owned by domestic financial conglomerates, the Schedule C bank was born.

The subtext is that the federal government should take charge of these multi-tiered financial empires — even though they might own provincially incorporated trust or insurance arms as well as a federal C bank. For some incomprehensible reason, Ottawa believes its regulatory record outshines those of the provinces. Federal regulators who speak of Greymac are neatly forgetting that they handed Astra a licence to do business.

Aside from possible territorial gains by Ottawa, there were clear winners and losers in the capital's Lego world of corporate layering. But the holding-company-with-subsidiaries proposal inspired Edper's Trevor Eyton and Jack Cockwell to volunteer a private promise to McDougall that they wouldn't gobble up Continental Bank; that friendly gesture demonstrated their approval of events as nothing else could. McDougall's Green Paper invited, nay *insisted*, on empire building through holding companies. Then it neatly tied the tentacles of over-reachers in knots: no self-dealing, no conflicts of interest. Deregulation and re-regulation in the same package. All the regulatory measures were outlined in the final section of the paper, leading one wag to wager that only the first pages would survive long enough to become law.

The surprising proposal for an end of the dualistic trust business is the result of decades of political neglect. Trust companies have waited fifty years for a legislative overhaul. If it had come even a few years earlier, it would certainly have taken a different route.

The federal government promised trust company legislation after a Bank Act revision was finally pushed through Parliament in December 1980. In 1982 the Trudeau government released a White Paper. Trust companies would be allowed to do more commercial lending; they would have more latitude in investment. But the two main planks mapped out the business's future. First, those who wanted to would be able to sell off their trust business and become savings banks. Second — after the take-overs of Royal Trust and Canada Permanent had been ignored by Ottawa power brokers unwilling to end up on what could be the losing side of a corporate battle — the government audaciously proposed that there would be ownership limitations on trust companies. There was even talk of making the limitations retroactive. Whoa there, Genstar; hold on, Brascan; look out, E-L Financial; your investments could be subject to retroactive legislation. The industry went berserk. With Canada Trust's Merv Lahn smiling, others spewed bile over newspaper reports that this was all the idea of Bill Kennett, chief bank policeman and outspoken critic of concentrated ownership of financial institutions. But Dick Humphrys was every bit as much in favour of wide ownership, which cut entrepreneurs out of the business, as was his fellow CDIC board member, Kennett. The White Paper was Humphrys's last major act before retirement.

The industry's divided loyalties effectively shelved that paper and delayed passage of legislation until nothing could be done about the ownership situation. Political Ottawa simply didn't care enough to push it. There were too many other issues; it was hard enough pushing bank legislation through even though the banks' strong lobbyists always presented a united front. The trust industry's weak-kneed industry association, on the other hand, is starved for cash at the best of times. It is a lobbying group without an official press list, and it rarely sends out releases. The Canadian Bankers' Association set up a lavish suite at the Chateau Laurier to help along the banking legislation; the Trust Companies Association of Canada's fussbudget executive director, Bill Potter, takes himself up to Ottawa every once in a while to visit with officials. The Minotaur is safe from Potter's advances through the labyrinthine complexities involved in lobbying for legislative change. In any case, the lobby can never be effective as long as the membership is split. Merv Lahn pulled Canada Trust out of the group in early 1984, instantly reducing its budget by a third.

The trust industry couldn't be clear about what it wanted because it didn't know what it wanted. Aside from the internecine war on ownership, the owners and executives of trust companies couldn't even agree on how to implement increased commercial lending powers. But they were growing desperate for new legislation. The ownership restriction proposal had never officially died, and the banks, eager to shackle the growing trusts, began linking financial deregulation and the need for shareholding limits. While the trust companies struggled to find a united voice, individuals set out to get what they wanted.

The quietest, most effective kind of lobbying is done from within the political structure. When Robert Elgie called in William Atwood Macdonald, QC, to contain the political damage wrought by the Greymac affair, he crossed party lines and went for a masterful behind-the-scenes Liberal. Macdonald did so well during the crisis that Elgie continued to rely on him to shepherd the November 1983 version of Ontario's White Paper on proposed loan and trust legislation. It did not seem to matter to Elgie that Macdonald was deciding the fate of a regulatory environment in which the biggest player was Henry Newton Rowell Jackman's provincially chartered Victoria and Grey Trust — a company whose fate Macdonald's family had figured in for three generations.

Most of the proposed changes in the Paper would have little effect on law-abiding Victoria and Grey; they were aimed at preventing another Greymac-style trust scandal. But one decision crucial to Victoria and Grey was tucked into the sheaf of papers: the notion already espoused by the federal government of placing limits on trust company ownership was abandoned. Macdonald, a significant shareholder and board member at Victoria and Grey for 18 years, says he had nothing to do with the decision — it was a political one. Indeed, there would have been no need for Macdonald to do any politicking. Hal Jackman and his alter-ego Victoria and Grey president Bill Somerville were doing that, each in his own inimitable style.

Jackman is everybody's idea of a trust owner. Ask the man

on the street about trust companies and he readily offers
Jackman's name. He is perceived as the last of the old guard,
because of his Tory-Rosedale-Establishment roots, his frater-
nizing with the likes of Conrad Black, his Wasp wealth. This
astute, cigar-chomping and quintessentially patrician man controls a financial and railroad empire estimated to be worth $10
billion. It includes Algoma Central Railway, two insurance
companies — one life and one property and casualty insurance
— and the third largest trust company in the country, with $27
billion in assets under administration. His financial companies
are proper, profitable and very comfortable with their status.
No financial supermarkets for them; they want to see the proof
that there are benefits from networking before they take any
plunges.

Everyone has an opinion about Jackman. One embittered
mortgage financier was moved to say, "He epitomizes what a
lot of people hate about the Establishment." Establishment
though he may be, at Victoria and Grey he has been something
of a new boy, having purchased a controlling interest in the company with a portion of the family fortune less than two decades
ago. The board is still dotted with the names of many decades-
long shareholders from the 16 companies that over the years
were larded together to form Victoria and Grey. President
Somerville has been with the company since its take-over of
British Mortgage. Although Jackman owns about 42% of the
trust company, he has not filled the board with allies. He is
a rare financial company owner who allows his companies
to stand free of each other with no management or board
integration.

But his stature as evolutionary throwback in the corporate
world goes further. Jackman meshes business with politics in
an overt way, while the Bronfmans, the Desmaraises and the
Blacks of this world do their politicking behind closed doors.
Jackman also has an effective backstage role but has chosen to
play his part up front, promoting his policies in an onslaught of
public speeches, motivated equally by self-interest and A Sense
of Personal Responsibility, as he once described it from a table
at Winston's.

Jackman was not always the ubiquitous trust company owner. For years he hugged to himself the fact that he was also controlling shareholder in National Trust. It is in the past few years that he has engaged in a joust with public opinion as the prize, mounted on his trusty steed *noblesse oblige.* Challenged by bankers, especially Canadian Bankers' Association president Bob MacIntosh, a former director on one of Jackman's insurance company boards, Jackman set out to prove there is a difference between his ownership and that of Lenny Rosenberg. Along the way he and MacIntosh have managed to spear each other handily to spectators' cheers and jeers.

Just as his battle to vanquish the forces advocating ownership limits was a solitary crusade, Jackman himself is a unique figure in Canadian business, his intellect, his eccentricities and his obliviousness to the rigours of conformity facilitated by an inherited fortune. Among the relics of a life of acquisition, annual meetings and anecdotes lies the campaign literature of a doomed politician. It is 1964 and the tall, immaculately topcoated Jackman looms over a black woman outside her home in inner-city Toronto's Regent park, his face composed in tight neutrality. It is a posed photograph for Jackman's campaign to win the Rosedale riding for the federal Progressive Conservatives. Another photo, another attempt at appearing appropriate for the general viewer: Jackman is seated at the breakfast table with his wife and young daughter, mismatched coffee mugs, two large cases of beer behind them and a heavy silver candelabrum on the table. It is perhaps not surprising that he was a three-time loser. In contrast to this failure at outreach to the man in the street, Jackman's successful crusade for the right to retain control of Victoria and Grey had him playing himself, to a business community who could relate to his roots and his view of life.

A position in party politics brings with it many links. Jackman worked in tandem with Barbara McDougall when she managed David Crombie's election campaigns in 1979 and 1980; he was one of her early supporters for her own nomination, hosting a coffee party before the Minister of State for Finance had party backing. And not long after Ontario declared its support for single controlling-shareholder institutions, Consumer minister Bob Elgie's wife Nancy also ran for a federal riding nomination in anticipation of the 1984 federal election. She lost her bid, but not before Jackman and Somerville had unexpectedly arrived at a public meeting in a show of support.

Bill Somerville is a Liberal, but although party politics is the very breath of life and he too has lost in a bid for election, he crosses the barriers easily. At the trust company's 1984 annual meeting, Jackman joked about the lilac boutonieres provided to directors. In past years directors had chosen between red and blue flowers, but this was Jackman's year of political triumph, and they were Royal Mulronian Imperial Purple. Somerville laughed with ease; he was gloating over the business triumph of a merger with National Trust. National's former chairman, Les Colhoun, spent much of the meeting at the head table with his head held in his hands, while Somerville went on about how lucky Colhoun was to be retiring. Somerville, of course, wouldn't be caught dead retiring. There is an ongoing discussion in the business community about whether Somerville is Jackman's creature or his equal; the majority opinion is the latter. Certainly consummate tactician Jackman, honed by diligent study of history and literature, provides a counterpoint to Somerville's aptitude for gossiping and squeezing nickels. Not only does Somerville run his own show, he likes to tell others how to run theirs. A famous gossip, he was warning reporters and the Liberal Opposition in Ontario of impending doom in the trust industry — not just at Greymac, but at Fidelity and other small companies — in 1982. He was, of course, right.

Somerville is a hands-on manager, a parsimonious small businessman running a huge company. In the early eighties when high interest rates and then the recession drove mortgage defaults up, Somerville headed his own SWAT team and travelled to cities such as Windsor to renegotiate terms and conditions and work problems out with clients. When he shakes up a company, executives often find out if they still have a job by checking the latest staff list. After the September 1984 merger with

National — arranged by Jackman's quiet negotiations to persuade Canada Life Assurance and the Canadian Imperial Bank
of Commerce to finally sell the shares they had owned for nine
decades — Somerville cut off paid overtime, extended the work
week for staff and withdrew National's full medical benefits
for retired employees. The last were reinstated after bad press
coverage, but he found himself suddenly dealing with a union
when unhappy branch staff revolted. In Victoria and Grey's
long history of taking over troubled companies, starting with
British Mortgage, through Metro Trust to National, Somerville
has shown a knack of making big writedowns for dubious
assets. Many are "recouped" later, enhancing his reputation
for managerial expertise as well as the bottom line. After the
merger with National, the name was changed to National Victoria and Grey for a few months, but the intention was always
to end up with National. A small-town rural Ontario company
— Somerville still operates during part of the week from the
old British Mortgage Taj Mahal in Stratford — had hit the big-
time. One of the reasons to adopt the National moniker was
typical of a company that has often had the best earnings
record in the business and whose nickname is Vicious &
Greedy: there was a lot of perfectly good stationery around
bearing the National logo.

In spring 1985 Somerville sat gazing out the window of his
corner office at the old National Trust headquarters in Toronto, quietly stating the shape of the world to an anonymous
telephone companion. Tantalizing tidbits mouthed in his quiet,
parched tones floated through the air: "Trevor Eyton; Continental; Kennett; Ontario Cabinet; his personal assurance."
One thing was certain; Bill Somerville was not happy with the
federal Green Paper. He and Jackman had planned to turn
their Premier Trust, a federally-incorporated company picked
up by Victoria and Grey but still operating separately, into a
bank. They wanted to do it over a 10-year period. But the
federal government's proposals could force them to move with
the tide of the Trilons and others structuring financial empires.
Somerville and Jackman had succeeded in their main goal.

Ontario-licensed trust companies would not be forced to implement ownership restrictions. But Ottawa was now presenting a new version of the future.

The clamouring was finally too much. The provinces were moving ahead, the institution failures continued, the marketplace was taking the lead. As the team from federal Finance* began to immerse itself in the questions of change and rejuvenation facing both the trust and insurance businesses, a broadbrush approach to financial institutions legislation gained political and corporate support.

Until mid-1983 the cadre of glorified clerks had been worrying about gut issues like 20% interest rates; now it could sit back and play pleasing mind games with the structure of companies that had been whipped by the lash of those rates. It wasn't an entirely new process; different people in the same chairs had begun dissecting the banks back in 1976.

When Minister of State for Finance Roy MacLaren announced his discussion group on the future of the four pillars in January 1984, its work was already six months along.† The

* They were originally from the Capital Markets Division, an offshoot under the bone-dry leadership of Gordon King. It co-ordinates debt management with the Bank of Canada, looks at the government's monetary policy and caretakes financial institutions. In the inexorable fashion of the ever-burgeoning federal civil service, it grew into "branch" status in the Ottawa forest and was renamed in mid-1984 the Financial Institutions Policy Branch.

† The 14 original committee members were: Don Bean, president of Wood Gundy; Michel Belanger, chief executive at National Bank; Raymond Blais, president of the Confédération des caisses populaires et d'économie Desjardins du Québec; Norm Bromberger, chief executive of the Saskatchewan Central Credit Union; Larry Clarke, chairman of Spar Aerospace; Ed Crawford, president of Canada Life Assurance; Dimma; economist Marie-Josee Drouin; Frank Lamont, president of Richardson-Greenshields; broadcaster Betty Kennedy; Earl Orser, president of London Life; Daniel Pekarsky, president of First City Financial; Grant Rueber, president of the Bank of Montreal; and Somerville. With seemingly incredible naïvety, one member of government later said, "They were quite explicitly not *industry* representatives. They were there as knowledgeable people. But of course each of them had different industry backgrounds. But the bankers were not there to represent the banks, the trust company people not there to represent the trust companies explicitly."

public and the press for months misunderstood the position of the advisory committee. They assumed it would actually have a hand in devising the strategy for the future shape of the business. In reality the MacLaren committee was simply a supper club. The financial institutions team, under slight, bespectacled and wryly humorous Allan Popoff, a recent returnee from the International Monetary Fund and the Bank of Canada, was the real "advisory" group. The committee merely commented on the range of options mapped out by Finance in a series of nine background papers that looked at issues such as industry efficiency; solvency; self-dealing and conflict of interest; and competition.

Although the committee never made a formal report, certain members thought they knew exactly how they had swayed the government's opinion. At National Victoria and Grey's annual meeting in downtown Toronto's economical Holiday Inn in March 1985, Bill Somerville publicly chortled with pleasure over the government's soon-to-be-released report. Observers were certain he had beaten Bill Kennett on the ownership issue. Indeed he had; or at any rate, the government had chosen the same tack to which Somerville subscribed. But somewhere between the last meeting of the committee on December 20, graced by the presence of Minister Barbara McDougall herself, and the report's April release, a new solution to the shifting problem of industry structure was planted in the political mind of McDougall. Her Green Paper proposal to split the trust and banking roles of trust companies undermined the 18 years Merv Lahn had spent fashioning Canada Trust into a savings bank. (The paper stated: "There are now no longer any trust companies that are clearly widely held." Canada Trust had been captured, in Ottawa's opinion.) For rival chief executive Bill Somerville, his plan to turn federally chartered Premier Trust into a savings bank while keeping Ontario-chartered National a traditonal trust company, slowly building a new institution, has been pre-empted.

Minister McDougall had made sure that Bill Kennett visited the Big Bankers the week before the report's release to explain the government's stand: no review of the Bank Act until 1990, thus giving a running start to the new set of banks that could be owned by their old banks' closely held competitors. The banks were for the first time to be left on the outside looking in at new legislation and expanded powers. The air was blue with muttered oaths quickly picked up by all Bay Street. When McDougall appeared at the Sheraton Centre in mid-May 1985 for the second stop on her self-promotion-cum-Green-Paper-introduction tour, the most common joke was about the Canadian Bankers' Association's Bob MacIntosh's exclusion from the head table at the crowded luncheon. "Have you seen Bob MacIntosh?" trust company execs chuckled. "He's standing at the end of the line."

The more astute ones modified the jest slightly: "But he's still hoping to get a ticket." MacIntosh's ticket was already printed and waiting for him, tucked away inside the Green Paper in a single phrase. "The government is prepared to begin consultations on the 1990 Bank Act review." With a line like that, there is bound to be plenty of talking with Ottawa by the ever-persuasive bankers. There will have to be concessions.

In any case, banks and other financial institutions are going to be able to do what they want most: "network." The word means make money. Ottawa says it sees the potential benefits to the consumer of allied or independent companies selling one another's product to the public and plans to remove restrictions that prevent it.

That action will make the banks' street-corner branches, emptier each day as customers line up at banking machines, once again the best real estate plays in the country. Royal Bank chairman Rowland Frazee likes to compare it to the rejuvenation of schools, where new uses are found for those lying dormant: "Our networks are valuable assets that can be utilized for the distribution of financial services."

There are three potential approaches to the so-called "blurring of distinction" in the financial market-place: one institution that can do everything; a series of interlocked institutions under a financial holding company; or networking, which allows one institution to create a product and another to market it. This range could include a marketer offering more than one company's version of the same financial product. That is, after all, what a supermarket does. Institutions that offer only one choice will not be supermarkets; they'll be company stores. An automatic teller machine (ATM) system shared by several institutions is the ultimate example of networking — a machine that allows the customer to decide which banking account to access. These machines will also provide on-screen information about rates at various institutions. With customers able to move funds from one financial institution to another with the press of a button, competition among those institutions will be tougher.

It is likely that the industry will choose one of the last two approaches, which in real if not institutional terms mirror option number one. There is little difference between a bank's selling an insurance company's product and the insurance company's doing it. And the banks certainly don't want to have to create insurance products; they just want to sell them.

When a consumer walks into a trust company branch today he can deposit his money in a number of different chequing and savings accounts, often with better bells and whistles than are available at a bank — cheques back free, lower service charges, higher interest rates. He can make a longer-term investment in a GIC. At a side desk he can invest money in a tax plan for his retirement, buy travellers' cheques or foreign currency, apply for a credit card. He can inquire about a car loan or another sort of personal loan, although the specialty is still a home loan, that is, a mortgage. He can invest in a mutual fund that in turn invests in stocks, bonds, mortgages and precious metals. He can arrange an appointment with a trust officer and find out about planning his financial future, perhaps even placing it in the hands of a personal financial planning expert; start a family trust to reroute money for a child's education; make a will; and plan for his estate. He can inquire about buying or selling a house. In Quebec, he can place an order to buy or sell stock. Soon he will be able to buy an insurance policy.

This is all contained in the new personal branch systems that have been set up by the major trust companies, which have divided their businesses into personal and corporate markets and are trying to field the largest possible list of products in each. And all of it must be firmly in place before the banks are given the ability to network on every conceivable product — investments, insurance, advice, the works.

In the U.S., which has been "deregulating" since the seventies, banks were first allowed to engage in brokerage business in 1983. Many began with discount brokerage operations and lobbied for access to the full line of activities. Banks are both federally and state chartered south of the border, as are insurance companies and savings and loans. Some states have acted on the principle of giving the local boys a break. South Dakota, for instance, allowed its banks to underwrite insurance outside the state. In late 1984 a group of state banks gained the right to underwrite corporate securities. (There is an all-too-familiar power struggle among U.S. federal regulators over these changes, and outright fights between federal and state levels. One wrangle has had more than 200 new California savings and loans waiting to go into business because the federal deposit insurance agency doesn't approve of the loose California state legislation on the types of business these savings and loans will be able to operate — including real estate development.)

The best-known networking and linked distribution system is indubitably that run by Sears, Roebuck. It sells insurance, houses and stocks right in department stores; this is the simplest and most-used as an example of one-stop financial shopping. No Canadian companies are comparable, but they sure are trying. Trilon is by no means alone.

Montreal Trust grabbed the headlines only when its parent companies announced ownership restructurings in early 1984, but the fundamental change at the company had begun much earlier. Controlling shareholder Paul Desmarais finally grew tired of mediocre earnings and shrinking market share, so the company brought in Robert Gratton, who grew up at Crédit Foncier and thought of the retail deposit side of the business as the only side. That was what Desmarais and the Montreal board wanted: someone who could bring the company into the banking business in a meaningful way. It had officially been in the intermediary business since the early sixties but had never succeeded at it.

Gratton drafted a list of general principles for running the trust company and organized a series of board meetings at which he presented his conclusions: the company needed a complete restructuring, based on a new corporate philosophy. He saw a breakdown into two companies, one selling to the consumer, one to the corporate client. That meant a shake-down that reorganized the branch system and made each manager responsible for a more specialized range of products. It also meant a shake-up, with senior executives "retiring" or leaving and replacements arriving from rival companies, particularly the banks. The banks had been making the same decisions about their branches and had long been structured at the senior levels along product rather than geographic divisions.

It took Gratton a year and a half; by the time he had finished analysing and moulding Montreal, the rest of the industry was talking about consumer and corporate markets as if it were the most natural thing in the world. It helped that Trilon had made the same decision. By late 1984 Guaranty Trust was drafting similar plans, as was Canada Permanent.

In July 1985 Genstar Corp. went two steps further. It spent $15 million on 10% of stock brokerage firm Gordon Capital Corp., then announced within a week a $434 million bid for control of an industry leader, Canada Trust. A merger of Canada Trust with the less profitable Permanent was in the wind. If successful, the merger promised to give Genstar the best retail financial network next to the Big Five banks.*

Gratton is in the anomalous role of a principal player trying to both improvise and harmonize with a score being orchestrated off-stage. His hiring was only part of Paul Desmarais's long-awaited reshaping of his financial companies, which corresponded to the rise at Power Corp. of his son, Paul Jr. The Power Financial Corp. subsidiary was created in 1983, with Montreal, Great West Life Assurance and mutual fund com-

---

* Among the Permanent's investments is a small holding in Edper-dominated Great Lakes Group, which has close informal ties to Gordon Capital.

pany Investors Group Ltd. hived off for a definite purpose. It was time to see whether the long-pondered "networking" of the three product lines would work.

Robert (Bob) Bandeen at Crownx Inc., hates the word *networking.* But this bull-necked alumnus of CN certainly likes the idea. Bandeen is, like Gratton and Hilliker, one of the new managers without preconceived notions about what will work. At Crownx, he too separated the financial arm — at that time really only venerable Crown Life Assurance — and agreed to build tiny Coronet Trust from the ground after abortive attempts by his predecessors to take over a major trust company. He sees Crownx, which also owns a real-estate-rich and profitable nursing home operation, as an international rather than a Canadian company. It bought a U.S. stockbroker that also sells term insurance, and purchased 40% of Canadian investment advisor Beutel Goodman in less than a year.

Chairman Michael Burns (whose family is a long-time major shareholder and also founded and still runs Toronto investment house Burns, Fry) was able to declare proudly by May 1985 that within a year Crownx's head office would house a trust company, an investment company and a bank branch as well as its insurance company. He bumbled — he meant that a TD bank branch would be opening on the ground floor of the head office, not that Crownx had plans to start a bank — but one analyst in the audience was already speculating on the possibility of a bank's growing from a potential merger of a Crownx with, say, a Canada Permanent.

The whole financial industry had caught Trilon fever, a strain developed during the past three years and seemingly incurable. As much as Bob Bandeen objects to the word *networking,* he is going to have to get used to hearing it. It has begun popping out of the most unlikely mouths.

At 9 P.M. on a rainy night in late November 1984, dinner at the Canadian Tax Foundation's meeting at the Toronto Harbour Castle Hilton convention centre had still not been eaten. The roomful of accountants had become positively raucous, pressing one another's flesh whenever possible. Rowland Frazee, chairman of the country's largest bank, the Royal, would not find the ready audience his handlers had planned. But the weary conventioneers settled into their seats, ever-respectful of the country's most powerful banker and mindful that this was the last bit of serious business before a series of meetings at the hospitality suites. Still, they couldn't possibly have grasped the importance of this speech to the Royal Bank of Canada. Its management had been preparing for this declaration of independence, this move beyond the official stance of the Canadian Bankers' Association — whose chairman at the time was the Royal's president, Alan Taylor — for a year. Strategy sessions, studies, more strategy sessions and finally a report on where the Royal should be positioned for future income had led to this carefully chosen dinner forum and the bank's major policy statement of the decade. The elephant had arrived at the dance.

There had already been some evidence of the bank's stance. The Royal and the Bank of Nova Scotia each held 2.5% of Power Financial, at Desmarais's invitation, a match to the TD's 9% interest in Trilon. But Frazee's speech would raise hopes and fears across the country. He wanted his English merchant bank, Orion, to be able to operate in Canada. That would give the Edper boys a run for their money. Frazee wanted the ability to engage in any kind of financial business, and he didn't care who else did banking as long as the door swung both ways. The Royal was willing to talk to anyone about marketing and distributing their products. The gauntlet had been dropped. "Every time I talk to someone in another [financial] industry, we talk all around the subject and we joke and kid a bit, but we all know that changes are in the air, pretty dramatic changes."

With the competition — and potential partnerships — from the likes of the Royal Bank, there was clear evidence that restructuring had gone beyond the point where Ottawa could rewind the tape. There were those who thought that, as usual, Canadians were simply following an American lead, for no logical reason. But it no longer matters where the idea originated.

It *was* a U.S. model, but it had long had the support in one

Canadian province known for its independence. Quebec's 1969 Report of the Study Committee on Financial Institutions, immediately and forever dubbed the Parizeau report after economist Jacques Parizeau, then a civil servant and later long-time Parti Quebecois finance minister, set the tone for the next 15 years. Parizeau, who headed the committee, wanted regulation by function rather than by institution, with the doors open for provincial institutions to compete with the federally favoured banks.* He gained his chance to do something on becoming René Levesque's finance minister, and the idea became a legal reality for insurance companies in June 1984, the same year the aggressive, independent Quebec Securities Commission ordered the Montreal Stock Exchange to allow financial institutions to register as brokers. (The commission also said brokers could invest in other financial institutions, but still restricts mergers between the two.) Royal Trust was among those that immediately did.

"A very simple deal was proposed to financial corporations," Parizeau explains. "Their powers of investment of gathering funds or operating in other fields than their original one would be considerably broadened. But, at the same time, they would accept stringent controls exercised by the newly appointed inspector of financial institutions." Trust companies were next, and a draft allowing commercial lending and anything else they pleased was in the making in autumn 1984 when Parizeau abandoned his post to defend his virtue as a separatist. By August 1985 the trust companies were still waiting, the promised legislation still on hold and its content basically the Parizeau draft. Without strong backing, it could still fall under the wheel of federal/Quebec politicking.

Ontario, transfixed by the regulatory debacle of Greymac, had concentrated its efforts on more and tougher rules and requirements for trust companies as they exist now. It set about to draft trust legislation, not financial institution legislation. But the province finally acknowledged the tide of structural change when it appointed in mid-1984 a three-man commission

---

* This approach has been recently chosen by Australia.

headed by J. Stefan Dupré, a University of Toronto professor of political science to — yet again — study the four pillars.

It's interesting to note that the draft trust legislation released in Ontario a year later, proposing the first overhaul since 1912, subscribes to the traditional view of the "deposit in trust" relationship between the consumer and the trust companies. Quebec's version, revolutionary in so many ways, will also subscribe to that tradition. The debate about deregulating financial institutions isn't just about companies fighting for turf; it's also about governments scrapping for territory. Any move to a debtor-creditor relationship would take jurisdictional rights away from the provinces and put them into federal hands because of the British North America Act's divisions of power. The manoeuvres began in June 1985 when Quebec threatened a court battle if Ottawa moved into its jurisdiction.

Ontario utterly failed to recognize the radical proposals to split pure trust functions from banking ones contained in the already-released federal paper. Instead it gave the largest Ontario-chartered trust company, Somerville's National, exactly what it wanted: increased commercial lending power in the same corporate structure.

What happens to the draft, which was buffeted about in the political turmoil of Ontario politics in early 1985, is anybody's guess. With a new, minority Liberal government taking power in June 1985, new legislation could be put on the back burner, dumped entirely or lost in another election.

But if it does go ahead in a form resembling the released draft paper, the issues of self-dealing and conflicts of interest that have dogged trust regulators since British Mortgage will be dominant strains in the new law: more public disclosure, clearly spelled out responsibility to depositors as well as shareholders by directors, one-third of whom would have to be outsiders — all the things British Mortgage's caretaker president Harold Lawson called for in 1965.

There will be ways to deny an extra-provincially chartered trust company the right to do business in Ontario on the basis of competence or character of management and other things. Real estate, of course, is of particular concern. Companies would have to prove to regulators the market value of properties, and that value would be the basis of companies' ability to make loans. Officials would have the power to lower valuations and note them in financial reports. Most real estate deals between company insiders or shareholders and the trust companies themselves would be banned.

Ontario's proposals also raise the minimum capital requirement to $10 million for trust companies, hoping to weed out the underfinanced fast buck artists who have plagued the province for so long.

Yet barring small players would be a dangerous thing too. Not everyone wants to be a Power or a Trilon, and not all consumers seek that omnipresence.* The niches in the industry will have to be filled by the smaller guys as long as the present trust company set-up remains in existence — and perhaps these niches will be only at the provincial level.

In the West, for instance, an Indian band has set up Peace Hills Trust, doing business from a brass-and-marble palace in downtown Edmonton, although its board of directors does not appear to have much in the way of financial experience.

Donald Cormie, who had made a reputation on successful mutual fund management, broke new ground during the seventies with his financial supermarket. Using branches of his Edmonton-based Principal Trust as a base, he sold Albertans on GICs, RRSPs, mutual funds and loans under the same branch roof and mixed the variable risks of these businesses under the same corporate umbrella. (No one else was doing that, and even today, although the concept of the financial supermarket is rapidly gaining acceptance, Cormie's trust company has repeatedly been barred from entering Ontario.)

When Gerald Pencer, who bears a remarkable if unfortunate physical resemblance to Leonard Rosenberg, bought Financial Trust from George Mann in 1981, he moved the company's base to Calgary and rolled in not just more real estate but com-

---

* A Dupré commission survey by leading Tory pollster Allan Gregg's Decima Research found 7% strongly favoured financial deregulation, 45% favoured it, 8% didn't care and 41% opposed it.

pletely unconnected businesses such as car dealerships and energy companies and began to advertise the company as a "merchant banker." High-roller Pencer, who has no experience in the financial industry, is betting on a big future for Financial. Maybe a take-over or two, he hints, and with that in mind the trust's parent holding company raised $50 million in early 1985 through very expensive "junk" bonds (bonds with high interest yields but low credit ratings) that it floated through new York investment house Drexel, Lambert at 16% interest, payable in U.S. currency.*

In the eighties, now that federal and provincial regulators have started allowing take-overs and issuing licences after their post-Greymac moratorium, applications from small and revamped trust companies are swarming in — just as they did in the sixties and seventies.

Montreal's Guardian Trust, which was partially owned by an investment advisory firm and is now controlled by an insurance company, derives about 40% of its income from buying and selling in the precious metals and foreign currency markets. It also has a large fee income from advising other funds' managers in precious metals. Fee income has kept earnings healthy: it has had returns on equity of between 22% and 50% in recent years.

In 1978 the Sobey family of Stellarton, Nova Scotia, picked up a licence and named their company Merchant Trust; they initially planned to use it for family trust business but set up an active operation in 1985. It has potential for the family's large food chain business.

Household Trust Co. was first incorporated in P.E.I. in 1980 and then received federal incorporation in 1984. It is taking a very aggressive approach with billboard and subway marketing in Toronto, equating doing business at the company's branches with a teddy bear's picnic and offering free teddy bears with $50 deposits in new accounts. It ran into trouble, however, for

* The Drexel connection — unusual for a company the size of Financial — comes courtesy of former CanWest executive Gerald Schwartz, whose wife, Heather Reisman, is a recent appointment to the financial board.

one policy: mailing $1,500 "cheques" to potential customers to solicit loan business with a 21.96% interest rate. The business was sought by the trust company on behalf of the parent finance company since the trust company had already hit the ceiling on allowable personal loan business. It is an innovative way to use a dead-in-the-water finance company, and Household Trust's potential has already attracted James Pitblado, chairman of brokerage firm Dominion Securities Pitfield Ltd., to its board of directors.

In Toronto, Counsel Trust, a dormant company reactivated in 1981 by a group of real estate entrepreneurs, is making waves on Bay Street with its totally property-oriented operation, its 300% growth rate and its higher-than-average interest rates. Its president is Brendan Calder, late of Fidelity Trust, who has won the approval of Ontario regulators — Counsel was given the contract to take over Termguard's operations in 1985 — but not of the feds, who have steadfastly refused to approve the company's take-over of London-based District Trust. Counsel packages real estate investment funds, manages properties for clients, lends mortgages and does mortgage banking. The company's controlling shareholder, Alan Silber, is well known in the real estate and mortgage broker world, and minority shareholders include the Reichmann family. Counsel is also representative of a new breed of financial institution enamoured with "disintermediation". That jargon, picked up from the U.S., means making money from fees and deals that are not included in the company's assets and liabilities on the balance sheet. One example is Counsel's Guaranteed Mortgage Certificates: Counsel's customers buy a certificate and the money is pooled by a Counsel subsidiary and lent out as mortgages. They are not Counsel mortgages, but Counsel takes a fee for the administrative work and for underwriting, or guaranteeing, the loans. In the U.S., banks are doing this with car loans as well as mortgages. What disintermediation means is that a trust company is not obligated to increase its capital base, because the obligations involved do not appear on the company's books as liabilities — even though they are.

Nothing will ever be totally satisfactory when it comes to regulating financial institutions. When the companies are small, they are vulnerable not only because of their size but also because of their need to grow. When they're big, the problem is their invulnerability, their "infallibility" — that is, the government's refusal to let them fail — because of their crucial place in the financial system.

Ontario is tightening the screws of its creaky department. The federal government is suggesting an early-warning system, and the CDIC is advocating increasing powers for both insurers and regulators so that they can step in and run a company before it folds — something that Bob Hammond lamented in the Pioneer case. "The way it goes now," he says, "you can't really stop [a company] until it becomes insolvent and by then it's too late." But that doesn't take into account the extant right to revoke and restrict a licence — a right Liberal Finance Minister Lalonde chose not to exercise. In all of this there is the bureaucratic approach at its most refined level of self-service. The regulators fell down on the job? Blame the regulations. Make them tougher, spell it out, increase authority to compensate for a lack of regulatory will.

The key in the end is the people doing the policing. A proposal in Ottawa is the creation of an official "curator" who could move in and run a troubled trust company *before* the interminable liquidation proceedings. This would answer Hammond's dilemma over when to pull the plug. But it ignores the reality of regulation. This curatorial power is already in the Bank Act, and it was not used in the case of the Canadian Commercial Bank. In mid-1985 Hammond had an opportunity to push Continental Trust into the hands of a carefully picked board, as Ontario's Don Reid had done with Termguard Savings & Loan a year earlier. Hammond hesitated, and the opportunity was lost. He ended up in court fighting to wind down the company.

The structure is not as important as the people. The Edper/Trilon model of corporate ownership being proposed as the industry standard is also the Greymac and the Pioneer model. With split jurisdiction over financial institutions, federal and provincial regulators will still be responsible for various companies, and the same human errors that stopped Ottawa in early 1982 from strongly stating to Ontario the obvious — that there was a big problem in Lenny Rosenberg's empire — will still be possible.

It took flagrant, flamboyant rule-breaking to bring to the politician's attention the carefully crafted and endemic self-dealing that has always existed in trust companies. Royal Trust's Trojan battle to stay out of the clutches of a single owner illustrates the worst of conflicts of interest and loyalties to friends rather than shareholders. And then there are the cases of banks using their own pension funds to buy trust company stock during a take-over bid, definitely not only for its investment value and definitely a risk for the bank employees depending on those pension funds, but a way to ensure that continued business would flow from the trust company to the bank. When Canada Life and the Commerce Bank agreed to sell their shares in National Trust to Victoria and Grey for a bargain price, thus dictating the price for minority shareholders, they still retained a portion of the merged trust company's insurance and banking business. An insurance executive assured his counterpart at Royal, Ken White, that he would check to see what his company's segregated accounts — accounts sold to investors on the basis that they would be managed in those individual's best interest — were planning to do about the bid. Trust company management tipped large shareholders to hang on when small investors didn't have the same information with which to make their decisions. None of this emerges readily into the public arena. Without a vigilant OSC — a quality that depends far too much on the predilections of its stewards — such breaches of fiduciary responsibility have not been revealed.

The suggestion by Ottawa that a Financial Conflicts of Interest Office be established to deal with potential conflicts and even launch court battles is so inane when measured against past management peccadilloes that it can have been thought up only by the out-of-touch minds that have previously inflicted on the public film tax credits, the National Energy Policy and other ridiculous, ineffective and damaging forms of social engineering. In such company, the new corporate censor board is relatively benign: it will merely cost a pile of money and give consumers a false sense of comfort about the regulatory system. Yes, it might take up the cudgel and knock heads when a lender tries to force a borrower to use a particular insurance policy. But the big abuses — the use of trust funds to buoy up a commercial customer's financial situation through stock purchases, or the reverse, the purchase and sale of stock in trust accounts because of inside information on commercial clients — will never be caught that way.

There is a pecking order among Ottawa's regulators that will not be displaced by new rules. Gerald Bouey, the central banker who is nominally responsible only for the operations of the Bank of Canada, in reality wields an inordinate amount of influence over financial institutions. He is a voluble member of CDIC's board; he was an active adviser on the Green Paper. One maddened trust company executive went as far as calling the paper's proposals Bouey's creations, but Bouey disproved that by telling Blenkarn's committee that, like Kennett, he favours a 10% ownership limitation.

The justification for Bouey's omnipresence is that these institutions are integral parts of the system whose levers he pushes and pulls to make the interest rate and the dollar dance. But his interference in the affairs of CCB in 1983 should never have happened. Had any bureaucrat seen fit to call a newspaper to say that contrary to insidious rumour, CCB was *not* on the brink and he would not let it tumble anyway, it should surely have been the regulator responsible for the banks, Bill Kennett.

Kennett was not happy with the developments that led to the release of the Green Paper. In a move unusual for Ottawa's faceless ciphers, he had been making statements since 1982 about the ownership issue. He wanted widespread ownership in the trust industry, and he thought it should be retroactive. This public stance made him public enemies, but heightened his profile in Ottawa. Kennett made it clear he would protect his banks — and his turf. They truly are his banks. (One Western banker who formerly ran a trust company attests to the difference in the relationship between Kennett and the banks on the one hand, and the superintendent of insurance and the trusts on the other.) On the flip side, he is their creature, his office paid for by the institutions he regulates. Yet while his prejudices are known, his position is such that CDIC's Charles de Lery wouldn't approach him to find out exactly what he *was* doing about the Western banks although CDIC had to take part in Bouey's bail-out of CCB.

The government from Barbara McDougall on down argued that CCB was bailed out to minimize the impact of a failure on the financial system. It looks suspiciously like the kind of costly, arbitrary action Ontario took with Crown Trust, bending over backwards to compensate for regulatory breakdown. There was bad management: CCB's portfolio wasn't diversified and executives were too optimistic about bad loans. There was bad regulation: the basic problem, let alone its implications, was never caught. The fact that de Lery was crawling all over the trust companies says much about the Ottawa power structure. Trust regulator Bob Hammond doesn't protect or play favourites. And he openly admits the difference in style and power between himself and Kennett. If the idea of one regulatory structure for all federal financial institutions goes ahead, its tone will be set when a choice is made for the top job.

The deference built into the pecking order does not augur well for a system that must pinion offending companies. Regulators cannot afford to be gentlemen or to treat trust company heads as if they were. That doesn't mean, however, that entrepreneurial spirit should be trampled, only that it should be tempered. The "smell test" advocated by Don Reid, Ontario's director of loan and trust companies, for the Ontario companies he patrols is fine only so long as he does not base his actions on smell alone. There is a fine line between astute policing and systemic discrimination. Reid is a new type of regulator who pushes companies to write down or transfer risky assets out of trust companies or turns down companies seeking to enter the lucrative Ontario market. A strong mind can use moral suasion, can force board changes as in Termguard's case. The peril at Pioneer should have been subject to the same force.

A key is that the regulator should not be "of" the industry, He or she must have a critical eye, not be susceptible to the charms of an empire. But even a strong mind and a critical eye are useful only in an energetic official. Old trust hands would say Dick Humphrys had both, but he allowed Astra's licensing, and after stalling for years, he still didn't have his people monitoring the company closely. He didn't even check to see whether the conditions for licensing had been met. What is called for is an automatic nursing period for all new companies.

Western Capital Trust, a small Vancouver-based company that succumbed in early 1985, is a perfect example. Founded in 1979, it operated for only five years; Hammond says he began watching it closely in 1983. But that year it spent $204,000 on legal fees; only much larger Royal Trust, Canada Trust, Central Trust and Canada Permanent spent more. Continental Trust, with its obvious capital problems and legal wrangle with Dominion, spent $145,000. This sort of detailed information has always been available to the regulators. A year after the data were collected, Western Capital failed. An early-warning system will give regulators more information sooner, but will they use it? Greater powers to intervene will allow them in sooner, but will they go?

Innovation in the financial industry should not be inhibited; it can benefit the consumer as well as the shareholder. But discipline in the market-place should be the price of these benefits. Co-insurance is a good idea. Consumers will have to take on some responsibility for their financial actions, and a higher interest rate on their deposits should entail a higher risk. But it should be understood that in political terms, giving the federal insurer, CDIC, the rights of a regulator is essentially a back-door way of allowing Ottawa to achieve regulatory supremacy over the provinces.

The regulator will always look like an ox playing tag with a gazelle. Still, some tenets of the legislative attempt to catch up with reality are sound. There is a need for risk in a dynamic, effective financial system. There is no proof that the holding company structure of the future will bring with it greater risk of instability and eventual insolvency. Links between institutions are not an automatic precursor to chicanery, contrary to the age-old whispers at the National Club. But the more concentrated the business and the larger the holding company "empires" are, the more they move towards the infallibility of the banks. If government won't let banks fail, large financial holding companies won't be able to fail, either.

This conclusion leads to a series of interesting questions. The federal government bailed out Dome Petroleum to protect the company's creditors — the banks. Would it bail out a Noranda to protect a large financial holding company, because of a potential run on the bank when consumers realize the two have the same owner? Could Edper's Trilon gain the mantle of infallibility if its financial connections were so large and interlinked that Ottawa was forced to protect them if something went wrong?

With ownership ties between the financial and industrial sectors, the artificial dividing line between the two is like a chalk mark on the street after a hopscotch game. It fades.

Why is the financial institution sacrosanct in Canada? Ottawa believes the unique position of the financial institution in providing funds and directing their flow makes the economy run. It also uses the argument that if one institution goes, the rest will all topple. That's not a valid argument. Nobody should be assured of safety. Our system can withstand failure.

It is fallacious to say the public won't distinguish between a poorly run or fraudulent operation and a fault in the system. After Crown, Seaway and Greymac collapsed, deposits at large trust companies such as Royal rose. People didn't mind leaving their accounts in Central Trust when it took over Crown's operations. They continued to invest in uninsured products such as U.S. dollar accounts at Western trust and loan companies even after the collapse of five Western trust companies in three years, the near-collapse of CCB and the papering over of problems at North West and Bank of B.C. Millions of dollars were withdrawn from CCB after its bail-out, but that was a judgment of the company's future potential rather than a judgment of all banks. The behaviour of the public — the small, insured depositor — doesn't justify the concerns the government has so piously expressed about the domino nature of the system.

Are trust companies safe? The big ones, currently enjoying very high profitability, are as safe as banks precisely because the government feels the economic system depends on them. And that attitude is not likely to change.

Minister McDougall says that the "policy stamp" of the Green Paper, the creation of Schedule C banks, was her idea, that she pushed bureaucrats into all-night sessions to answer her questions before the early 1985 decision-making was done. But most everyone believes it is a long-tended regulator's paper, a Mickey Cohen-headed effort.

A few months after the paper's release there was a rising tide of feeling that its proposed regulatory restrictions for related companies are too inflexible and will be unenforceable. A ban on self-dealing, observers began to say, could tie corporate hands up in knots in efforts to ensure each button is always fastened. Blenkarn and other politicians added their voices to those of lobbyists, and air began to seep from McDougall's trial balloon. But if it is deflated as quickly and completely as other Conservative policy papers and even if the government reverts to a safer, more traditional approach to the business's shifting structure, the issues will have to be dealt with. There have been too many problems for the industry to escape political scrutiny. Hammond told Blenkarn's finance committee in June that he knew the argument: "There is a concern on the part of the industry that you cannot give the regulator arbitrary powers; the shareholders have to have some rights. The problem is finding that delicate balance between the rights of the public to be protected and the rights of the shareholder to carry on business."

Of course, it is not public debate that is shaping the government's thought, it is lobbying by vested interests. Concerned observers can't help but worry that once again change will be delayed in a regulatory machine that was developed for the old boys and has never functioned in a consistent, rigorous fashion.

Whatever changes *are* pushed through, there is reason to believe that the lobbying of entrenched interests by the new guard will dictate the shape of the system. When Marc Lalonde was still finance minister, a group of worthies organized by Hal Jackman, including Trevor Eyton, Allen Lambert, Sam Belzberg, Paul Desmarais, Albert Reichmann and John Craig Eaton, flew to Ottawa to make their case against proposed ownership restrictions on the trusts. TD's Lambert, now chairman of Trilon, stuck out as the only turncoat banker in sight.

Lalonde started the meeting by turning to Lambert. "Well, Allen, I'm surprised in a way to see you here now speaking about the 10% limitation on ownership. Can you explain that?"

"Oh yes," said Lambert, "I can, easily. The 10% rule is not necessarily bad for banks, only bankers."

The structure changes, the faces change, but the rules of conduct live on. At the luncheon where McDougall unveiled the Green Paper to Bay Street, she was challenged on how the government makes such momentous choices as the rescue of Canadian Commercial Bank while smaller financial institutions are allowed to drop by the wayside. She reached for the quick, cheap laugh. "It depends on how I feel when I wake up in the morning."

Appendix

CANADA'S TOP TEN TRUST COMPANIES AS OF 1984

Company and year end	Assets ($000)	Return on capital 1 yr.	Return on capital 5 yr.	Operating revenue ($000)	% change over prev. year	Profit ($000)	Asset Mix mtgs. (%)	Asset Mix loans (%)	Interest rate spread	Provision for investment losses ($000)
Canada Trustco Mortgage (De84)	11,749,993	19.25	14.47	1,340,033	13	74,340	45	19	2.25	na
Royal Trustco (De84)	11,157,000	16.38	15.22	1,467,000	11	85,000	51	15	2.10	16,000
National Victoria & Grey Trust (Oc84)	8,223,562	17.25	16.89	639,575	26	40,286	63	7	1.96	5,262
Cda. Perm. Mortgage (De84)	7,638,823	11.24	6.53	1,032,897	9	51,145	56	16	na	13,539
Guaranty Trust Co. of Canada (De84)	3,174,458	11.38	7.96	406,267	9	10,615	48	30	1.72	na
First City Trust (De84)	3,059,699	13.26	10.01	612,057	1	40,947	42	13	na	27,146
Central Trust (De84)	2,627,299	13.05	5.89	313,088	12	10,005	64	20	2.12	7,650
Trust Général du Canada (De84)	2,550,520	14.45	12.26	324,626	16	14,481	56	3	1.72	na
Montreal Trustco (De84)	2,529,217	11.44	14.14	347,137	16	15,633	54	5	na	1,241
Standard Trustco (De84)	1,035,905	1.99	5.66	144,686	25	4,621	48	29	na	5,307

na = not available. mtgs. = mortgages. Asset mix indicates percentage of assets invested in mortgages and loans. Interest rate spreads (the difference between interest rate earned and interest rate paid) are shown as percentages and are on a taxable equivalent basis.

Reprinted by permission of *The Globe and Mail Report on Business Magazine.*

Index